THE

PHOENIX

GAMBIT

DOUGLAS McDONOUGH

www.dmcdonoughauthor.com

An Alternative History of the Confederacy

Book One..... The Phoenix Gambit
Book Two..... A Manifest Destiny (2012)

This is a work of fiction. All actions, statements and
thoughts by any character are completely creations of the
author.

Copyright Registration Number
TXu 1-654-472 | May 12, 2008

ISBN-10: 1466248068
ISBN-13: 9781466248069

Authors Acknowledgements

To George Entwistle, for employing his consummate command of prose on behalf of this book; to Diane Bruscela, JoAnn Canino, Gerard and Susan Frevola, Lilly McDonough, and Robert Stock for their many valuable suggestions and comments; and to Michael McDonough, for his art work

Major Characters

Confederate

Arnold, Sam ..... Confederate Agent
Booth, Edwin ..... Brother to John W Booth,
Confederate Agent
Booth, John, W ..... Confederate Agent, Actor
Breckenridge, James ..... General, CSA,
Creator of the Phoenix Gambit
Brown, Thomas ..... Sergeant, CSA
Campbell, John ..... Director, CSA Intelligence Service
Chester, Harry ..... Confederate agent, KKK Grand Dragon
Davis, Jefferson ..... President, Confederate States of
America
Forrest, Bedford ..... General, CSA
Hill, A. P ..... General, CSA
Johnston, Joseph ..... General, CSA
Lee, Robert, E ..... General, CSA
Longstreet, James ..... General, CSA
Scruggs, Jethro ..... Confederate Immigrant to Mexico

Semmes, Raphael ..... Captain, CSN Commerce
Raider, *Alabama*
Venable, Charles ..... Colonel, CSA, Robert E. Lee's Aide

Union

Conklin, Rebecca ..... Ezekiel Sinclair's girlfriend
Custer, George Armstrong ..... General, USA
Farragut, Daniel ..... Admiral, USN
Garrison, John ..... OSS Regional Director,
Texas Zone of Reconstruction
O'Reilly, Patrick ..... Union Congressman, New York City
Johnson, Andrew ..... President, USA
Lincoln, Abraham ..... President, USA
Mead, Gordon ..... General, USA
Patrick, Jason ..... Captain, USN frigate Potomac
Pinkerton, Alan ..... Director, Office of Strategic Service
Sanchez, Emillio ..... OSS Ranger Officer
Sheridan, Phillip ..... General, USA
Sherman, William ..... General, USA
Sinclair, Ezekiel, "Easy" ..... Union soldier, OSS Operative
Strong, Arthur ..... Staff Lieutenant, USN
Thomas, Abel ..... Captain, USA
Ukimbe ..... Freed slave, Sergeant, USA

Mexico

Emmanuel, Orto ..... Soldier, Juarista Army, OSS Ranger
Garcia, Miguel ..... General, Revolutionary Army
Juarez, Benito ..... Mexican Revolutionary

Moreno, Jesus ..... Captain, Juarista Army
Santa Anna, Antonio ..... Ex Dictator of Mexico, Politician
Zaragoza ..... General, Commander, Juarista Army
Maximilion ..... Emperor of Mexico

Foreign Legion

Du Pont, Henri ..... General
Fromage, Alan ..... Private
Laurency, Jean ..... General, Commander,
Foreign Legion, Mexico
Petain, Phillip ..... Captain

German Empire

Baron von Steuben ..... German Industrialist
Kaiser Wilhelm I ..... German Emperor
Von Hindenburg, Paul ..... Liaison officer to CSM

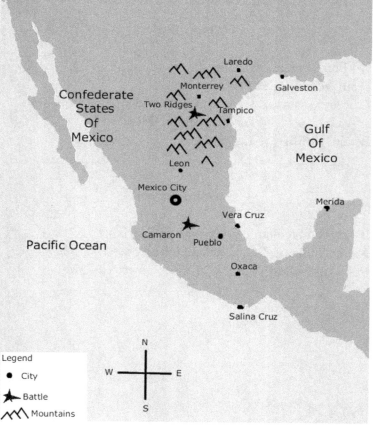

United States Of America

Laredo

Monterrey

Galveston

Confederate
States
Of
Mexico

Two Ridges

Tampico

Gulf
Of
Mexico

Leon

Mexico City

Merida

Vera Cruz

Pacific Ocean

Camaron

Pueblo

Oxaca

Salina Cruz

Legend

• City

★ Battle

⋀⋀⋀ Mountains

N

W —— E

S

CHAPTER ONE

July, 1863

Confederate Lines, Gettysburg, Pennsylvania

The two forces had met on this Pennsylvania battlefield as much by chance as by design. Amazingly enough, each Army held good ground; well positioned on parallel, grass-covered ridges, separated by a shallow, hook-shaped valley. Occasional granite outcrops and copses of foliage, heavy with July green, dotted the landscape.

It was almost two o'clock on the stifling hot summer afternoon. The merciless midday sun beat down on the verdant Gettysburg countryside. On top of Seminary Ridge, General Robert E. Lee, sat his horse. Lee was Commander of the Army of Northern Virginia, the Confederacy's premier field force. Both man and beast were only partly protected from the cruel heat by the heavily-leafed branches splaying from a stand of large oak and elm trees.

More than three hundred Union and Confederate cannons faced each other on a two mile front. Continuous fire from the massed artillery batteries had reached mind numbing proportions. The hot, humid air was continually rent by the screech of shells. The ground trembled from explosions. Earth and flesh spewed into the air and the detonations could be heard five miles away.

With his telescope, Lee viewed the opposing heights, noting the entrenched infantry and artillery. He withdrew the telescope from his eye and looked down to the base of the ridge he was on. Directly below him he could see gray clad infantry forming, two proud, veteran Divisions, Pettigrew's and Pickett's commands. Just inside the tree line the men slowly coalesced into tightly-spaced and neatly-ranked units. Battle flags and officers moved to the front ranks. Drums began their insistent beat. With a magnificent precision and absolute bravery they left concealment and advanced into the open. They paused a moment to dress ranks then swept across the valley and up the hill. Their goal was a low stone fence and a group of trees on the ridge top just over a mile away.

He lifted his telescope back to his eye and swept the heights opposite him again. A battle flag, flying in the center of the blue formations, caught his attention. My God, he thought, it's Hancock, the best they've got.

The Confederate attack advanced across the field and up the incline. Bayonet- tipped muskets held at high port, state and unit flags leading the way. On the opposing heights, the Union defenders opened fire. Explosive shells, grapeshot, and Minnie balls shredded and tore at the advancing ranks. Despite tremendous losses the assault continued. Some of the lead units reached the defender's line, and the fighting became fierce, hand-to-hand.

He watched the combat swirl about the crest. One more effort, he thought, just one more. Tension wracked him, and his horse, ever sensitive to his emotions, stirred uneasily. His eyes glued to the battle, he leaned forward, unclenched his fist and patted Traveler's heavily-muscled neck.

From behind the blue ranks he caught sight of more battle flags and masses of troops advancing over the crest and into the fray. Reinforcements! Hancock, he thought, of course. The merciless slaughter on the ridge top intensified. Shots, screams, curses and shouted orders drifted down to him, and for a few precious moments the issue was in doubt and he believed he would snatch victory from the brink of defeat.

It started on the left flank, a platoon, a company, and then suddenly an entire regiment of grey clad soldiers. Some walking slowly, stopping to return fire, others running, some helping their wounded brethren; all of them retreating back down across the blood-drenched, body-carpeted, incline. Musket and artillery fire ripped into the retreating men, scything them down like wheat. The blue uniformed troops stood and began chanting, "Fredericksburg, Fredericksburg." He felt his emotion rise, his blood boil, and he had to grasp his horse's reins tightly to restrain both the horse and himself.

Despite his internal turmoil, Lee sat in stoic silence as the remnants of his proud divisions streamed back, passing him, moving up and over the ridge top. Off to his right, General Longstreet, the only senior officer to disagree with today's assault, was surrounded by aides and moving towards the rear. He saw General Picket striding through the retreating men, one of the last officers to leave the field; his wide-eyed, tear- stained face glaring about, and thought, now is not the time. I must give them time, time to heal and regain control of their emotions. Without a word, Lee turned, and with a gentle flick of the reins made his way through the troops and back to his headquarters.

It was evening when he reached the sturdy-brick farm-house that housed his small headquarters staff. A corporal's guard and Colonel Charles Venable, his aide, awaited him. Lee dismounted, handed the reins to a waiting sentry, stepped onto the porch and entered the parlor. As per standing orders the clerks continued about their tasks, only Venable looking directly at him. He continued walking and went into the kitchen, waiting until he heard Venable follow him into the small room before turning to face the Colonel.

Robert E. Lee was a study in contrast. By birth a member of southern gentility, urbane, cultured and sophisticated. He was a military engineer, graduate of West Point, polite and considerate to subordinates and vanquished foes alike. He had served with distinction on General Winfield Scott's staff during the American invasion of Mexico. On a field of battle however, Lee was an extremely aggressive and ruthless commander.

Lee said, "Colonel, I wish you to prepare marching orders for the Army." Looking directly at Venable he continued, "1st and 2nd Corps are to begin movement no later than morning of the sixth. Our goal is the Virginia border." Lee gave a slight sigh, sat down, and in a low voice continued, "Have those orders issued tonight."

He waited first for Venable's, "Yes, sir," then for the sound of footsteps as his aide left the room. His physical and emotional exhaustion complete, he sat and cradled his head in his hands, closing his eyes. The room was immersed in silence as he asked himself, now what? What alternatives remained, or was his cause truly lost?

Almost seventy two hours later Lee received the most incredible yet welcome news from Brigadier General J.E.B. Stuart, his Commander of Calvary. Stuart reported that Lee's Army had completely disengaged from the Union Army of the Potomac. Moreover, Stuart advised Lee that there was no Union pursuit and the columns of battered Confederate troops were escaping without any interference. Lee ordered his senior commanders to join him on the following morning.

The campaign which had recently ended in disaster on the body-strewn fields of Gettysburg had cost the Army of Northern Virginia dearly. The battle had been the result of Lee's overly-ambitious strategy; a strategy based on taking the fight to a better supplied, numerically superior enemy in the hope that one savage thrust would end the conflict. For three days he had hurtled his men against an entrenched foe. The result had been a severe mauling with a catastrophic loss of manpower. Many units were down to half-strength and there was a critical shortage of field grade officers. His strategy had been a mistake, and in his heart of hearts, he knew it.

As the badly-bloodied Army of Northern Virginia, slowly and painfully made its way home, General Robert E. Lee sat awaiting the arrival of Lieutenant General James Longstreet, who commanded his 1st Corps. Longstreet was a West Pointer and proven veteran. He had also served as a field officer under General Scott in the Mexican-American War. He was a quiet, intense man, strategically a more prudent officer then Lee. Most comfortable in a defensive strategy, Longstreet preferred to rely on firepower and fortifications. He had protested strongly against Lee's battle plan at Gettysburg, especially the charge by General's Pickett and Pettigrew. A good officer, he had, in the end, followed orders.

The command tent was well worn, heavily patched, but clean. It, along with the tents of attendant staff and security personnel, sat just south of one of the few remaining 10 lb. Parrot gun artillery batteries. The guns and tents were situated on a small field just below the "military" crest of a hill. The five remaining cannon, along with their caissons, horses and crews were situated on an east-west line, each gun facing north. The warm, moist, morning air smelled equally of horse sweat, horse manure, burning wood and breakfast.

Longstreet was escorted into the tent by Colonel Venable. Lee rose from his seat to greet him, reaching out to grasp his hand, thinking, this man is my most capable officer, but how much more can he give? How much more can I ask?

Lee gestured towards the other assembled officers, his other two Corps. Commanders, Generals Ewell and A. P. Hill, and Stuart, who had all arrived earlier. Lee regarded them with a somber expression and, said, "Gentlemen, as you know, despite our best efforts we have suffered a serious setback at Gettysburg. We are here to consider our future most carefully. I would like your thoughts on this."

"General," replied Longstreet, waving away an orderly offering a cup of coffee, "our combat capability has been seriously degraded and it will take some time before this command will be capable of assuming anything but defensive operations. We require substantial reinforcements and resupply of just about everything." He stopped for a moment, rubbing his brow in a vain attempt to assuage the headache which had dogged him for several days, before continuing. "I have companies commanded by Lieutenants and regiments by Majors. My recommendation is to continue south, find a good position, then assume and maintain a defensive posture as soon as it becomes practicable." He looked at Lee, saw his pain, and thought, does he know what he's done? Can he repair the damage, or are we lost?

Lee sat quietly for a moment, observing that the other Generals held their silence. He realized they had left it to General Longstreet, the most senior officer, to voice what were obviously their joint concerns.

"Very well, then," responded Lee, "I am of a similar mind. This Army has recently fought a major battle and a brutal campaign." He faltered slightly, remembering that horrible hill, tattered remnants of proud regiments, Pickett's face, and a nameless private holding Traveler's leg and pleading for a second attack. Glancing at the other officers he asked, "Gentlemen, have any of you anything to add?" Lee paused for a moment, but there was only silence. He looked down, regained control and continued in a strong, firm voice. "General Longstreet, I concur with your assessment. We shall implement your advice. Thank you all. Please return to your commands. I shall inform Richmond."

The road south into Virginia wound its way around and through a series of forested foothills, and as Colonel Venable ushered the officers out, Lee got up, left the tent and began walking down the gentle slope. Halfway down he suddenly stiffened at a glimpse of furtive movement in the bushes off to his left. This was Maryland, and a lone Union soldier or even a disgruntled local farmer with a shotgun was possible. The movement became a man, the man a soldier, one of the omnipresent cavalry troopers assigned to security duty from one of Stuart's Brigades. The soldier saluted and stepped back into cover. Lee continued down the slope until he reached a point where he could see the road and watch his troops pass by, while remaining unseen himself.

He had listened to the staff discussions and read the after-action reports but that was not seeing and this he needed to do. In the rear of the column were the hospital ambulances and ambulatory wounded, slowly making their way through the hot, dry summer afternoon. Lee stood quietly, watching and listening as the medical units rolled by below him. Low cries and moans provided a horrid counterpoint to the clatter of squeaks and groans emanating from the ambulances themselves. Scattered amongst the vehicles were the walking wounded and their helpers, most of whom were wounded themselves, the lame serving the shattered.

A wagon, dripping human blood from its rear platform, awash in the unmistakable stink of human intestines rolled by; the shriek of its ungreased axles mimicking the cries of its wretched cargo. The driver, himself injured, waved weakly at the clouds of flies that swarmed about his vehicle and its occupants.

After several ambulances had passed, more of the walking wounded appeared. Lee observed a group of three soldiers walking abreast. The man in the middle had lost a leg below the knee and was supported on one side by a man whose entire head was wrapped in bandages and on the other side by a man whose left arm ended in a stump. All of the wounds and bandages were heavily stained with body fluids.

After the last wounded soldier and blood-stained vehicle passed he stood for a while, head down, hands clasped behind his back. Turning, he retraced his steps upward. He thought, such suffering, such heroism, must not, can not be in vain. I pray you God! Show me a way to victory with honor for my people! I beg you!

Later that day Lee sat in his tent writing a dispatch. "I have the disagreeable duty to

inform you that as a result of our recent campaign the Army of Northern Virginia has suffered grievous losses in men and material. This command will require substantial refit and re-supply. It is my opinion that this force will be incapable of offensive action for a substantial period of time."

With a sigh, Lee rose and left the tent, calling to Venable to attend him. Shortly thereafter, a dispatch rider left Army headquarters, on his way to Richmond and President Davis with the unpleasant news.

Confederate Capitol, Richmond, Virginia

James Breckenridge read Lee's communication. Breckenridge was a Renaissance man, adept at law, business and military matters. He had served as Vice President of the United States under President Buchanan, then had run for President in 1860 on the Dixie/Democratic ticket on a pro-slavery and states-rights platform. He was a cultured world traveler; a successful business man and politician, naturally intelligent, very well educated, and an internationally ranked chess master. At the outbreak of war, he was commissioned first a Brigadier then Major General in the Confederate Army. He had served with distinction in several battles on the western front. Because of his political, business and military competence, he was currently serving as the military liaison to the President of the Confederate Government. Regardless of where or whom he served, his was a voice to be listened to.

His office was small, cramped, with only a single window and, on this summer day, uncomfortably hot. The building had been a hotel, taken over by the fledgling Confederate government, and was now a maze of similar rooms, filled with similar occupants.

He leaned back in his chair, drew and exhaled a cloud of cigar smoke and sighed. As the senior military advisor to the President of the Confederate States of America, the communication had been routed to him. He read and then reread it, frowning as its import struck home.

A mistake, he thought, from the very beginning, a mistake. He had considered it a bad idea and had said so, but his opinion could not stand against Lee's. Now what? Desperate times call for desperate measures, he thought. It's late, but perhaps not too late. We still have a few alternatives, some choices. He picked up his quill, wrote a note and called for his adjutant and directed that both communications be delivered to his immediate superior, the Confederate Assistant Secretary of War, John Campbell.

Campbell also served as the Director of the Confederate Intelligence Service. He was a capable, career bureaucrat and competent spymaster. Under his leadership the CIS had developed into a small but effective service, fielding a few teams in the Washington D. C. area.

Breckenridge left his tiny office and made his way upstairs to the building's top floor. Climbing the topmost stair he turned left and made for the double doors guarded by two soldiers that ended the corridor. Known by sight he passed both sentries and entered the office.

"Is he in? I've something quite important to discuss and time is a factor."

The man at the desk stood up and opening the door behind him passed through leaving Breckenridge alone. He returned almost immediately, held open the door, said, "He will see you now, sir."

Breckenridge entered and Jefferson Davis, President of the Confederate States of America gazed at him. Davis was in a most difficult situation. He was head of a government whose entire legislative body was wholly supportive of the concept of states rights and a limited federal government. Embattled on the political front, he was simultaneously prosecuting a war against a much more powerful foe, one with substantially greater industrial and manpower resources, while simultaneously trying to achieve international recognition from wary foreign powers. Despite these many issues he was a firm believer in his country's cause and labored mightily on its behalf. The toll this had taken showed in his haggard face, gaunt features, and quick, birdlike gestures.

"Yes, what's so urgent it just can't wait?" He asked, asperity plain in his tone.

"It's Lee, he's been defeated in a battle in some place in Pennsylvania."

"Beaten, my God! How badly? Is he injured? Where in Pennsylvania?" The questions came fast and hard, leaving no room for individual answers.

Breckenridge waited a moment, let the silence stretch out until he was sure of Davis's complete attention, said, "I've given some consideration to this possibility, sir. I've some ideas for your consideration." As he spoke he closed the office door and went to a chair next to the presidential desk. The two remained in conference for almost two hours.

Campbell was in his Richmond office, and as usual, awash in paperwork, when his secretary announced the arrival of dispatches from General Breckenridge. Rising from his desk he took them directly from the secretary. Dismissing the man with a wave, he read them, left his office, and walked down the hall towards the office of the Secretary of War, James Seddon.

Late that night a meeting was convened. The capitol office room, located on the building's third and top floor, was poorly served by the open windows due to the hot and humid night. In attendance were: President Jefferson Davis, Secretary of War James Seddon, Assistant Secretary of War John Campbell, and Major General James C. Breckenridge.

President Davis brought the small group to order with the statement, "I have received a dispatch from General Lee. We are in serious straights. Our foray into the north has not met with our hoped-for success. In fact, the opposite has occurred. Our Army fought a major battle and has been forced to withdraw into Virginia after suffering major losses. The General has requested instructions. I want your input regarding our response. What shall we tell him?"

"Gentleman," said Breckenridge, "despite the valiant efforts of our Armies our cause is in great jeopardy. It is apparent to me that we must look to other means. As we have discussed, Mr. President, I have been working on a solution, but I want our senior officers, Generals Lee and Johnston, to be present when we discuss it."

John Campbell asked, "Are you referring to your...?"

"John, please! Not another word until we are all together," interjected Breckenridge.

Davis nodded his assent and said, "General, I agree. I will arrange for a meeting as soon as possible. I'll order all necessary parties to the capitol."

Seddon and Campbell rose and left the room, leaving just Davis and Breckenridge together at the table.

"I've received additional communications from the Army of Northern Virginia. It is as you said it would be," said Davis, his voice tight with fear.

"Mr. President, we knew it was a gamble, and so did Lee. It seemed to be the best of several bad choices."

"Do you really think we can carry off your plan?" asked Davis, a hint of desperation in his tone. "It is so intricate, so complex."

"Desperate situations call for desperate measures. If not this, then I truly believe we are lost, Sir."

"I will not accept that our nation and its ideals shall vanish from the earth," said Davis, who had staked his fortune, future and possibly his life on Secession. He looked at Breckenridge and ordered, "We shall proceed as you suggest."

"As you wish, Sir," was the reply. Though the words were a mere formality, the reality was they were going to risk everything.

Naugatuck, Connecticut

While the Confederacy struggled to deal with its defeat, news of the great victory at the battle at Gettysburg spread like wildfire throughout the Union. The news was flashed by telegraph and trumpeted by newspapers from Maine to Maryland.

A few miles outside the quiet hamlet of Naugatuck, Ezekiel Sinclair, on his second day home on leave from West Point, woke, washed the sleep from his eyes and dressed. Before the sun's morning rays tinged the horizon he was in the kitchen, lighting the stove in order that his mother could prepare breakfast for the family. Although he'd been attending the U. S. Military Academy at West Point for the past year he had quickly resumed his daily routine within days of his return home for the summer recess.

Ezekiel "Easy" Sinclair was tall and slim, well muscled, with unruly dark hair and pale-blue eyes. A serious, quiet and intense young man, he was the oldest of four children, having one sister and two brothers. Growing up on a well-tended, prosperous Connecticut farm, he had learned the virtues of hard work and proper planning from his parents. One of his proudest days was the day he had been assigned his very own, personal, farm chores.

Easy had been a diligent student and at his request his father had petitioned his congressman for an appointment to the U.S. Military Academy. He had completed his first year and was eager to join the fray and reinstate the Union. He worked hard at his military studies. His nickname had been bestowed on him by his West Point classmates, in recognition of his personality as well as his calm and relaxed response to dangerous, high pressure situations.

Having prepared the stove for use he stepped outside to savor the morning air from the front porch. From this vantage point he could see the acres of tilled fields and tended orchards along with herds of livestock that composed the Sinclair holdings.

He stood quietly, admiring the well-tended farm and the soft silence of the morning. At the sound of a door closing he turned to face his father.

"Morning, Pa."

"Morning, son," returned his father, joining him on the porch to share in silent reflection. For a few moments the two stood gazing out.

As though reading his son's mind he said, "It's good land, Easy, rich, well-watered."

"I know it, Pa. I love it too. It's a part of me."

"You know, as the oldest, it'll be yours if you wish it, son."

Easy turned to look at his father, said, "Dad, I truly love this farm, but I don't think my future is here."

"I know that, I knew from that look in your eyes, your mother calls it your faraway look." He smiled ruefully, said, "She says you got it from me and I expect that's true."

Easy smiled.

Sounds of preparation emanated from behind them and his father said, "Breakfast will be ready soon, let's not keep mother waiting." Suiting his actions to his words he turned and re-entered the kitchen. Easy took a last deep breath of fresh air, and then followed his father.

Seated at the kitchen table were his siblings, Jacob, Benjamin, and Sarah. All three regarded their older brother with adoring eyes. As the Sinclair brood had grown, Easy had always willingly assumed responsibility for his brothers and sister. He had taken his role as protector to heart. As his parents pursued their daily farm duties he often cared for all three, willingly and well. At school he was always there for them. They, in return, had responded to his selfless care with love and regard.

The two, father and son, had scarcely taken their seats when his mother put a plate in front of him, saying, "Three eggs, sunny-side over, bacon well done, my love. Just as you like it."

"Thanks, Ma."

"Son, as soon as we're done with breakfast I want you to hitch up the horses. I'd like you to go to town for supplies."

Easy's face lit up with anticipation, and he said, "Sounds like a plan to me, Dad."

Shortly, breakfast was done and he was on his way. Arriving in town, he left the horse and wagon at the hitching rail and entered Conklin's Dry Goods store. Easy began walking up and down the isles, matching the store's inventory to the list his father had given him. As he filled his order he kept one eye on the stores proprietress, Rebecca Conklin, and one eye on his purchases.

Rebecca, "Becca" to her friends, Conklin, had been born nineteen years ago. She was bright, willful and determined; with auburn hair, hazel eyes and a tall, slim figure. Her brother William, the oldest child, had been born with serious brain damage and would remain intellectually five years old forever. Her parents, Harold and Diane, had begun Conklin's Dry Goods some thirty years earlier. Harold had died four years ago and from that time, Rebecca had shared the responsibility of running the business with her mother. When she finished school she had eventually taken on most of the duties of running the business. Now she spent almost all her time working in the store.

Attending the town's one-room school she and Easy had become more than friends. Growing up together, they shared secrets and goals. Quietly confident in their future, comfortable with their relationship, they saw Easy's military commitment as not much more then an interlude to be dealt with. Conklin's Dry Goods had been Easy's first stop when he had returned from West Point. The relationship had rekindled immediately and since, the two found as many reasons as possible to spend time together.

As Easy neared the counter he saw the town newspaper and its headlines "Great Victory" along side it was a second article titled, "Lee Routed, Mead Victorious." Picking up the paper, Easy quickly became totally absorbed in the articles and added the paper to his purchases.

From her place behind the counter Rebecca saw Easy's response to the paper. She totaled the bill. As Easy handed her the money their hands touched and their eyes met. She saw the turmoil in his face, her soft look acknowledged his distress. Relinquishing the hoped-for conversation, Rebecca watched as he quickly loaded his purchases on the wagon and made for home.

The moment the farm supplies were off the wagon and in their proper place, he brought the papers to his father's attention.

"Looks like it could be over pretty soon, Dad."

"It does seem Robert Lee finally got the worst of it. 'Bout time, too."

"I don't think it'll last much longer."

"God willing, son, God willing."

Easy's voice hardened, became resolute. He said, "I'm not going to miss it, Dad. I've thought it over. I'm going to resign from the Point. I'm going to enlist."

His father said nothing for a few moments, then spoke. "Easy, it's your life and you know I'll support your decision. But it might not be a bad idea to take some time to rethink. There's a world of difference between a soldier and an officer, son. Good officers are worth their weight in gold. I think you've got what it takes to be good, *very* good."

The two stood next to each other in silence for a moment more.

"Dad, I appreciate everything you've said. But according to the papers things are changing fast. After the beating he just took I don't think even Robert E. Lee himself can keep the Confederacy going. The Point's graduating classes after three years, but that's still another two years for me." He paused for a moment to gather his thoughts, continued, "It's important to me, Dad. I feel a need to be part of it. The war, I mean. I've thought it through and I've decided to enlist."

His father quietly regarded his oldest son, then with a sigh said, "I see your mind is set. Fact is I enlisted with Scott for pretty much the same reasons." He shrugged his shoulders and with a rueful grin said, "Tell your mother before you go."

The next evening found him back at the store, waiting for Rebecca to finish for the day. As she bustled about, locking and closing, she became aware of him, waiting quietly on the store's porch. Chores done, she walked resolutely to the door and stepped outside. He faced her squarely, his face sober and she knew a moment's dread.

"Becca, there's been a great battle. It looks like the Confederacy's just about done."

Looking into his eyes, she responded, "Isn't that a good thing?"

"I want...I *need* to be part of it."

He paused, reached out and caught her in his arms, " Becca, I'm going to resign from the Point and enlist."

She paled, stepped back, looking up and into his demanding eyes, saying nothing.

Returning her gaze he said, "I don't know how long I'll be gone."

After a moment's hesitation, with a soft smile on her lips, she responded, "I see. I'll make no promises, Easy. Life goes on. We both must do as we must. I expect you'll return when you think the job's done."

"I will."

He held her gaze for a moment and then pulled her body close. They kissed, lips hard and demanding, and then he turned away, mounted his horse and rode away. She stood on the porch watching his figure fade into the distance, absently brushing away an errant tear as it trickled down her cheek. Two days later, his resignation from West Point in the mail, Easy enlisted in the United States Army as a private.

CHAPTER TWO

August, 1863

Richmond, Virginia

In response to the summons from Jefferson Davis, Generals Lee and Johnston had arrived in Richmond two days apart. They had traveled by direct routes, hiding in plain sight, doing nothing to arouse undue attention. As soon as all were present the meeting was called to order.

Carafes of water and open windows fought a losing battle against the summer heat and humidity. In attendance were: Jefferson Davis, John C Breckenridge, James Seddon, John Campbell, and Generals Robert E. Lee and Joseph E. Johnston.

General Johnston had commanded the Army of Northern Virginia until he was wounded in 1862 and replaced by Lee. While Johnston was generally well liked and considered a good officer, Lee had proved to be a superior tactician and better leader. After his recovery Johnston was offered command of Confederate formations in the western theater. First and always a soldier, he neither like nor disliked Lee, but considered him given to rash, needlessly-dangerous actions. Lee, on the other hand, considered Johnston to be stodgy and lacking in imagination.

"Gentlemen," said Davis, standing and gesturing for quiet, "We are assembled here to discuss the future of our country, to determine where we go and how we will get there. I know that our brave soldiers and officers have given their utmost, but we have not met with the success we had hoped for. The enemy has both numerical and manufacturing superiority. Our major ports are closed to us. Our European friends have informed our State Department that they are in the process of re-evaluating their position regarding the possibility of diplomatic recognition. In light of our recent military reverses they will not provide us with the kind of support we must have if we are to retain our independence." Davis, a fiery and passionate believer in the southern cause, paused and looked around the table, glancing in turn at each participant, finally resting upon Lee, who acknowledged him with a nod.

"I believe you are correct in every aspect, Sir. At this point we are militarily incapable of offensive action without major increases of our forces," said Lee, rising and looking at each man in turn. "Our troops have displayed unparalleled heroism in the face of overwhelming odds. They have triumphed despite inadequate rations, inferior fire power and a numerically superior enemy. They have in truth, done all that their country has asked of them, many times over." He stopped for a moment, cleared his throat and then continued on. "I have come to the conclusion that we can not achieve victory on the battlefield and without that hope I can no longer order them to continue the fight."

"General Lee, I do not concur with your views at all," said Johnston, heatedly. "I propose that we conserve our forces and defend the territory we still hold. We also have the option of breaking our larger commands into smaller, fast moving units. We can...."

"Good God! Sir!" responded Lee, his voice harsh with emotion, "have you heard nothing I've said here. Can you not understand? If we have no hope then what point is the suffering of our soldiers? How can we justify more death and destruction?" Slamming the table with the flat of his hand he stared hard at Johnston. Lee, a man who prized restraint and decorum, flushed slightly at his own outburst.

Johnston stared at Lee for a moment, his face gray, without expression, then in a subdued voice said, "So, then. All has been for naught?"

"I see no viable military option, General," replied Lee in a soft voice, "and our diplomatic efforts for foreign assistance and recognition have failed."

"Gentlemen," said Breckenridge, as he rose from his chair, "as it happens there may be another option available to us. I am sure every man at this table is aware that the situation is grave and our choices few. Our country and our way of life lie in the balance. We can continue our defensive strategy and slowly be bled dry. We can disband our Armies and emulate Quantrill's use of hit-and-run tactics. I believe that each of these choices merely serves to delay what will be the inevitable defeat of our Confederacy."

Breckenridge paused and regarded his audience for a moment, then continued, "I believe I have an alternative for us. For the past few weeks John and I have been considering a daring but possible alternative. I believe we have more than

23

the bare bones of an idea that may allow our Confederacy to live again. Every man present must appreciate that all aspects of this plan must be held in absolute and total secrecy. Each of us has an important part to play. Success will require stealth, fortitude, and the ability to plan intricate moves and counter-moves, ours and our foes, with great precision and accuracy. For all of us to succeed, each one of us must succeed."

He stopped and looked at each man in turn for a moment, and then continued. "Gentlemen, I give you the Phoenix Gambit."

Breckenridge started with a brief review of the current situation then, after a moment or two, began to present the components of his plan. He stood up, gesturing with his hands, his face and voice animated. As Lee listened to the diplomat/general officer speak, he was, at first dismissive, but as Breckenridge continued he found himself drawn into the scheme. Lee, a man given to audacity, found himself caught up in the intricacies and daring of the winner-take-all proposal. Giving no outward sign, he kept his council to himself. Thinking, as piece by piece the Phoenix Gambit was exposed, by God, yes, this can be done! In the last analysis it was the sheer, unbelievable audacity of the plan that brought him over. Looking around, at the others at the table, Lee made his decision. He would declare for the plan!

Completing his presentation Breckenridge sat down and looked to Davis, who rose from his seat and said, "As you can see, this plan is bold, one might even say audacious. If God wills it so and we are successful, the result will be our country reborn. What say you, gentlemen?"

One man at a time Davis fixed each with a stare, holding it until he was acknowledged with a yah or a nay. Man by man each responded in the affirmative and the plan was accepted.

The Command Team of the Confederate States of America filed from the room until only Generals Johnston and Lee remained. The two men were contemporaries. Both were graduates from West Point and senior officers in the Confederate Army. Both Lee and Johnston had seen war first hand and both commanded an army in the field. Each was thoroughly aware of the difficulties inherent in the military components of Breckenridge's "Phoenix Gambit."

Almost simultaneously, they stood and turned to face each other. Johnston, reaching out almost hesitantly to touch Lee's arm, spoke. "General, if it comes down to it, we shall give our very best effort, and if it must be, our lives."

Lee looked directly at Johnston, placed his left hand on Johnston's shoulder and replied, "Joseph, we will both be taxed to our limits. Success will require all our abilities." Reaching out with his right hand, Lee concluded with, "I offer you my hand in friendship and support."

Johnston grasped the offered hand and answered, "May God be with us."

That night, alone in his room, Lee sat, awake and deep in thought. He continually reviewed the afternoon's meeting. True, he thought, we cannot meet the Union's economic and manpower strengths. Now we cannot hope for any help from Europe. We will, if we keep to this course, eventually be defeated. But does Breckenridge's plan really show us the way? Can a plan so complex, so daring be consummated?

He looked back in anguish at the battle he had instigated in hopes of a great victory. In his mind's eye he saw again that horrible, heroic charge, the indomitable yet ultimately

25

ineffective courage of his soldiers. His anger and frustration flared. By God, he would lead his army to ultimate victory! He would not allow such men to taste the bitter dregs of surrender and defeat!

Several days later a group of senior officers of the Army of Northern Virginia were summoned to Lee's headquarters. None were given an explanation. Venable had chosen a two-story brick house for Lee's headquarters. The home was sturdily built with a covered verandah around the front and sides. A well-appointed living room was to be the setting.

The skies were heavy with angry, tumultuous clouds. A rain-soaked wind accompanied General Stuart into the home. Slamming the door behind him he turned to the waiting officer and handed him his heavy cavalry cloak.

"Well, Venable, here I am. Where is he?" he asked.

Venable replied, "Awaiting your arrival in the living room, Sir, along with Generals Longstreet, Hill, and Forrest." Stuart walked from the small vestibule into a room furnished with several chairs and couches.

"Welcome, General Stuart," said Lee, his voice warm.

"Thank you, sir," responded Stuart, looking at the other officers in the room, "a good-day to you all."

"Gentlemen," said Lee, "I have asked you here for a most vital reason. There was a conference in Richmond earlier this month regarding the war and its conclusion. A plan was conceived and it is my duty to explain to you your parts in this plan. I pray you make yourselves comfortable because there is a great deal to cover." Lee then gestured to Venable to roll a chalkboard on wheels into the center of the room.

As Venable completed his task Lee regarded his senior commanders with some apprehension. When Venable finished placing the table, Lee placed his hand atop the chalkboard and, in a firm voice said, "I present to you our hope for the future of the Confederacy, the Phoenix Gambit." For the next several hours he introduced the four Generals to the military components of the plan for the future of the Confederacy.

CHAPTER THREE

December, 1863

Dafuskie Island, South Carolina

The navy of the Confederate States of America had been formed by an act of the Confederate Congress in 1861. Having neither ships nor funds or time to build them it was decided to attempt to buy them, made to order, from naval construction yards in England or France. England agreed to build six ships. Each ship was to be fast, capable of long distance travel, and powered by both steam and sail. The vessels were to be armed with one Armstrong eight inch, breech-loading, swivel-mounted, rifled cannon and four thirty-two pound cannons, arranged as two broadsides.

In 1862 the first of these commerce raiders, the *Alabama*, was completed, launched and delivered to its Confederate crew. It was commanded by Captain Raphael Semmes, CSN. Semmes, born in 1809, had served with distinction in the United States Navy from 1837 to 1860. He was considered to be a brilliant naval tactician by his peers and senior naval officers. The captain and his ship had since accounted for the sinking of dozens of American merchantmen and one United States Navy sloop-of-war.

In early September the *Alabama* had returned to the Confederate Navy base on Dafuskie Island, one of a chain off the coast of South Carolina. Captain Semmes had found a set of sealed orders marked *"Urgent and Secret"* awaiting him. He had been ordered to remove his thirty- two pound guns and most of his ammunition. Semmes was then to use the space to add cabins and rooms for unidentified passengers. The changes to his ship had taken several months to implement as the Confederacy suffered from dire shortages of trained naval carpenters as well as raw materials. The Captain, however, had labored ceaselessly to successfully acquire the men and supplies, and since completing the renovations both he and his ship had sat idly, as ordered, awaiting further events.

A subsequent communication from Naval Command had advised him that he would receive his final mission tasking from General James C. Breckenridge immediately upon Breckenridge's' arrival at Port Daufeskie. This message had also been marked as *"Urgent and Secret."* Several days after he received this message, a group of men, led by Breckenridge, arrived on the island.

The two men, Breckenridge and Semmes, met. Breckenridge had been briefed on Semmes, and based on that knowledge had developed a positive feeling regarding the naval officer. As Breckenridge began to relate his plan and the part the *Alabama* was to play, Semmes was at first dubious, then as the scope and importance of the mission became apparent, determined and exhilarated.

At the meeting's end Semmes had received orders from Breckenridge to have the *Alabama* remain docked until the weather gave them the best chance to run the Union Navy blockade undiscovered. Several days later the opportunity presented itself.

The early winter storm, fuelled by the chill Atlantic waters, had descended with a vengeance. Roaring out of the east and driven by almost hurricane-force winds, the sleet and snow was pounding the tiny port.

The Captain awoke immediately upon hearing the knock on his door. "Enter and report," he ordered, sitting up and running his hands across his face. His cabin door opened to admit the *Alabama's* Officer of the Watch, Lieutenant. Robert J. Bragg, who saluted and said, "Wind gusting to twenty-five knots, visibility less than one mile and it appears to be decreasing fast, sir."

"Thank you, Mr. Bragg," replied Semmes, standing up and donning his sea coat. He quickly left his cabin and ascended the steps leading to the quarterdeck. Walking to the port rail, he surveyed the turbulent, grey sky and white-topped, choppy sea. "Lieutenant, I believe you are correct. It does seem that the storm is freshening. I want General Breckenridge and his party notified immediately. Tell him that, in my opinion, we can sail as soon as they are aboard."

"Very good, sir," answered Bragg, who immediately turned and began issuing the orders that would send the ship's small boats ashore, to return forthwith with General John C. Breckenridge and his staff of experts and diplomats.

Within hours the boats returned laden with Breckenridge's team. Climbing up the *Alabama's* gangway at the rear of his party Breckenridge saluted the waiting Semmes and said, "I'm the last man, Captain; it's your party now."

Semmes replied, "Well, then, General, let's get under-way." With that he turned and barked a flurry of orders, "Cast off all lines! All hands to sailing stations! Lookouts aloft! Engine room full power!"

Under steam power the *Alabama* slipped her moorings and quickly disappeared from the sight of those on shore. For hour after hour Breckenridge stood next to Semmes on the snow and ice-slick bridge. Both men were swaddled in oilcloth, soaked to the skin, chilled to the bone, and taut with tension. In anticipation of the worst, all hands were at battle stations, the crew and ship ready to fight or fly at a second's notice. Time seemed to stand still as the *Alabama* cautiously made her way through treacherous waters, the blockading Union warships and dense, rolling fog banks that were often punctuated by fierce, sudden downpours of frozen precipitation, before finally emerging into the open Atlantic.

A few tense hours later, Semmes turned to Breckenridge, who had mirrored his position on the quarterdeck the entire time, and said, "General, it is my pleasure to report that we have successfully run the blockade. The *Alabama* is in the open Atlantic and proceeding on course to our first port of call."

Breckenridge smiled and responded, "Captain, if everything goes this well we shall be more successful then I had dared to hope."

"The *Alabama* will do everything in her power to make it so, General," answered Semmes.

After a second he called out, "Oh, sir!"

Breckenridge, turning to leave the bridge, halted and turned to face Semmes responded. "Yes, captain."

"Merry Christmas."

Having cleared the blockade, the sleek warship turned to a south-easterly course and steamed into the bleak, storm-tossed Atlantic.

San Marcos, Mexico

The small, coastal, fishing village, situated on the Yucatan Peninsula, the east coast of Mexico, was filled to overflowing. The Mexican and Confederate contingents had arrived within a few days of each other and had almost doubled the local population. Several large tents had been erected to provide additional meeting rooms and living accommodations. A few miles off shore twin funnels of smoke marked the *Alabama's* position, as she awaited shore-side events.

The teams of representatives had been meeting constantly. They had conferred and negotiated vigorously for several days and had eventually hammered out a plan acceptable to all sides. This meeting was more of a social event, a formality to allow the leadership to officially accept the terms and conditions of the agreement. Breckenridge sat at a small table near the cantina's only fireplace. Across from him was the Mexican representative, Antonio Santa Anna. His short, slightly overweight and balding figure occupied the only other chair at the table.

Santa Anna had been a fixture of Mexican politics since he had first assumed, and then lost, the title of Dictator. He had commanded the Mexican Army and at first had been extremely successful in putting down the revolts that wracked his country. Later, leading Mexico's incursion into Texas and at the Battle of the Alamo, in the War of Texan Independence, he had been defeated and captured by Texans under the command of Sam Houston. He had returned in disgrace to Mexico but had subsequently regained power, only to lose it again because of his military failures against the American General Winfield Scott, in the Mexican-American War.

He was, at heart, a gambler. His career was often based on successful risk taking, doing the unexpected. Breckenridge's plan appealed very much to his nature. During the negotiations each man had taken the others measure and neither had found the other wanting. The two had worked together closely and each had gained the others respect and, more importantly, trust. Both men felt that each had an ally upon whom they could depend.

"So," said Breckenridge, "We are agreed."

"Yes, we find your proposals acceptable. For our part, we will begin implementation and await further word from your government. We hope that the remainder of your mission is as successful, Mr. Breckenridge. We wish you Godspeed and good luck." Lifting a glass of wine to his lips, Santa Anna said, "A toast, Sir, to our mutual success."

Breckenridge, locked eyes with Santa Anna, lifted his own glass and replied, "To our mutual success."

CHAPTER FOUR

March, 1864

London, England

Henry Temple, Viscount of Palmerston, Prime Minister of the United Kingdom, and loyal servant of Her Majesty Queen Victoria, sat in his London, England office overlooking the Thames River. He finished reading the report. Frowning, he sat back in his chair and thought. After some time, he rang the bell on his desk. A few moments later his personal secretary, Robert James-Attwood entered, and after closing the door behind him, approached Temple's desk.

"Yes, my lord?"

"This proposal, from these Confederates, have you read it?"

"Yes, my lord, I have."

"And?"

"I consider it to be as ingenious as it is dangerous."

"Quite. It is, of course, impossible for Her Majesty's government to deal with rebels.

You will, therefore, exercise the utmost caution in all negotiations with them. You will keep me apprised at all times, nothing in writing, and, needless to say, you will make no binding commitments on our behalf without my express authorization." Temple picked up the next report, glanced at James-Attwood and said, "That will be all, Robert, Thank you."

The *Alabama* had been docked for several weeks at the cold, gray Thames River docks while Breckenridge and his team had tried, without any success, to meet with a senior government official or well-connected businessman. To all appearances the plan was doomed to failure, as they had been rebuffed at every turn. Every government, business, political or social contact had been deaf to their proposal.

Breckenridge and Semmes were in the captain's cabin, grimly trying to think of yet another means of access to any government official, when their desperate contemplations were interrupted by a knock on the cabin door.

"Enter," ordered Semmes.

"Watch officer's complements, sir. There's a gentlemen on the dock who says he would like to speak with Mr. Breckenridge about a matter of some importance."

Semmes looked at Breckenridge as he ordered, "Bring him aboard and send him to my cabin."

A short while late James-Attwood entered the cramped cabin, offered his hand to Semmes and then Breckenridge, said, "It has come my attention that you gentlemen are attempting to contact His Majesty's government. I believe you have been unsuccessful and are in need of some assistance. I am here as a private agent in regard to your recent proposal. It has been reviewed and deemed to be, shall we say, of interest. It may be possible for us to unofficially accommodate each other's needs, to some extent. Would you gentlemen be amenable to further discussion?"

CHAPTER FIVE

May, 1864

Baltic Sea, Five miles off the coast of Germany

The sleek, sharp bow of the CSN *Alabama* drove through the choppy, white- crowned, Baltic waters, hastening on her way. The midday sun was barely shining through the heavy, scudding cloud cover. Breckenridge and Semmes conferred on her wind-whipped bridge.

"In all my business and political experience that was by far the most frustrating negotiations I have ever been involved in," said Breckenridge. "Around and around, not one single straightforward statement, week after week of maybe and might. My God!"

"Well, it's done with. We've gotten all that we're going to. It may not be as much as we hoped, but they are willing to provide some help. I can understand their being hesitant and their need for deniability," responded Semmes.

"I hope that the Prussians prove to be more responsive and direct."

"At our current speed we'll find out in a few days."

Several days later found the *Alabama*, having weathered the turbulent Baltic, safely docked in the Prussian port of Keil. The day the ship docked Breckenridge and his team began a sustained and coordinated attempt to make contact with political and business contacts. The Confederates were polite but determined and their efforts slowly began to be bear fruit.

In one of the many small offices just off the King's royal throne room a meeting was held. It was attended by three men, the King of Prussia, his Privy Secretary and his Chancellor.

"My Lord, I have read these proposals quite carefully. I think that they align themselves with your stated aspirations regarding the territorial expansion of our

Empire. I must point out that there does exist some danger regarding the United States of America. However, I believe that these issues are substantially mitigated by the economic and military possibilities inherent in this proposal."

Frederick turned to the third man in the room and bluntly asked, "Your appraisal?"

"As Your Majesty has frequently stated, the Empire deserves its rightful place among the great nations of Europe. I believe expansion into the America's is appropriate for a world power. This plan could provide us with a very solid foothold as well as a strategically-positioned ally. I think we should proceed." responded Otto von Bismarck.

Frederick turned to the Privy Secretary and ordered, "Advise the Minister of State to begin negotiations immediately."

"Yes, you're Majesty."

CHAPTER SIX

June, 1864

Atlantic Ocean

General Winfield Scott's original strategy for defeating the Confederacy was called the "Anaconda Plan." Designed to isolate the south from any European assistance, it mandated the United States Navy implement a massive blockade of the entire Confederate coast while the Army cut the south in two.

Union war-ships patrolled outside Confederate ports from Charleston to New Orleans. Their mission was to interdict merchant vessels attempting to run the blockade and enter ports with contraband cargo, as well as destroying the occasional commerce raider or confederate naval vessel seeking re-supply.

Fifty miles east of Georgia the azure blue, cloud-filled summer sky merged almost imperceptibly with the wind-swept sea on the horizon. The sun had just begun to brighten the morning sky as the USN steam sloop *Kearsage* reached the southern-most point of her patrol station. The sloop began a leisurely one hundred and eighty degree turn to port, a prelude to retracing her course northward yet again.

High in the mainmast seaman first class Robert James squatted in the crow's-nest. The sailor held on tightly as the ship rolled and pitched wildly in response to the long Atlantic rollers. James waited until the ship had been settled on her new course for several minutes before standing up and searching the southern horizon. After a few minutes observation, his telescope came to rest on a distant smudge of smoke. Confirming his sighting, he called down the estimated course and speed of the unknown vessel.

The captain ordered the crew to general-quarters, in response to the lookout's shouted hail to the deck. The sloop immediately began to turn to the south and come to full speed, pursuing the ship that was attempting to run the blockade. Although it took only a few minutes for the *Kearsage* to complete her turn and the crew to reach battle stations, it soon became apparent that despite her best efforts the unknown ship was simply too fast to overhaul.

Several miles south of the Union warship the *Alabama's* lookout shouted, "Ahoy, deck, Ship to starboard bearing south by south east!"

"By God, we're gaining on them, Sir," shouted Lieutenant Bragg, as the *Alabama*, columns of dead black smoke spewing from her dual smokestacks, emptied the last of her coal bunkers. The whole ship was vibrating as she made a furious bid to outrace the last Union patrol ship between her and the safety of home.

Raphael Semmes squinted into the sea spray that occasionally swept the open bridge to gauge for himself his executive officer's claim. He nodded, said, "I believe

40

you are correct, Lieutenant. I'm going below. You have the bridge." Not even waiting for a response Semmes raced below to Breckenridge's quarters and knocked forcefully on the door. After a moments wait he opened the cabin door in response to the statement, "Enter." A grin on his face, he entered the tiny cabin that was still shaded in the soft light of dawn. He said, "General Breckenridge, Sir. It is with the greatest pleasure that I am able to inform you that we expect to make landfall today."

Breckenridge sat on his cot, disheveled and groggy with sleep, as he took in the enormity of the news. Slumping back against the shuddering ship's bulkhead, he looked at Semmes, and in a voice mingling pleasure and awe said, "My God, Raphael, there were so many pitfalls and dangers, yet here we are almost home and successful." Shaking himself lightly, he arose and reached out to grasp Semmes's hand in his own. "Our success is due in no small amount to the ability and courage of you and your outstanding crew, Captain. I offer you the thanks of a grateful nation."

Abashed, Semmes responded with, "My duty and my pleasure." He turned and made his way back to his post, his stride and posture proclaiming his pride. That evening the *Alabama* returned to the dock she had left so many months ago.

Several days later, Breckenridge arrived in President Jefferson Davis's capitol office, to make his report. The President stood up as Breckenridge entered the office and walked towards him. Breckenridge's sallow complexion and gaunt features offered silent testimony to the tremendous stress his mission had enforced upon him.

Offering his hand to Breckenridge, Davis said, "Welcome home, Sir. Please sit."

"Thank you, Mr. President," responded Breckenridge, as he slowly lowered himself into the indicated chair.

"So," said Davis, walking back to his desk and sitting behind it. "I can see that the mission has tasked you greatly, General. I hope you are well."

"I'm well, sir. Well, but somewhat tired."

"Perhaps if you could give me a summary now and we can go into the details later."

"Of course, sir," said Breckenridge.

He sat for a moment to collect and marshal his thoughts, "Let me begin by saying that all our talks were held in secret and there was no official recognition of our presence. Both the European parties expressed positive views regarding the overall plan. We've had some success but not as much as could be. They will provide us with a substantial amount of circumspect aid. Economic and logistic support such as loans, transportation, arms, supplies and equipment will be forthcoming. As before, any diplomatic recognition will depend entirely on our achieving a successful military and political solution. We must provide a viable and stable government. Otherwise, all our efforts will be in vain. Our allies to the south are implementing our agreements as we speak. I believe that they will remain firm and resolved and can be depended upon."

"Then," replied Davis," we must strike before the situation becomes untenable."

"Sir," said Breckenridge," We must also wait until all parts of the plan are in place."

"You and your team have done an admirable job. Your country is in your debt. I thank you on behalf of our nation." said Davis, his voice tight with emotion.

Breckenridge replied, "Thank you. Captain Semmes and his crew were invaluable."

"I'll see to it that their contribution is recognized. One more thing. My understanding is that a successful military action is a prerequisite."

"Yes."

"Then it lies in Lee's hands."

"Mr. President, there's not a soldier in the world more able then he."

CHAPTER SEVEN

February, 1865

Petersburg Line, Virginia

As the Civil War ground on year after bloody year, the two main armies, the Union Army of the Potomac and the Confederate Army of Northern Virginia, had become locked in a death grip. The two forces faced each other across miles of Virginia countryside, each positioned behind extensive fortifications.

Grant's strategy was twofold. The first part was to keep Lee's Army in constant contact with the Army of the Potomac. The second part was to continually extend the Union lines to the south and west, in an attempt to encircle the cities of Petersburg and Richmond. This would, in effect, isolate both cities, as well as the Army of Northern Virginia, from the rest of the Confederacy.

General Lee, having agreed to the Phoenix Gambit, was required to implement a strategy similar to Grant's, but for very different reasons. He had to maintain the Army of Northern Virginia as an intact fighting force, at the same time providing General Breckenridge with the time he required to pursue his international diplomatic efforts. This mandated he place his command in a defensive posture, allowing him to husband his manpower and supplies.

The convergence of the two strategies resulted in the creation of a defensive line of trenches and earthwork forts in northwestern Virginia that became known as the Petersburg line.

Captain William Borden, 3rd Carolina Infantry, Picket's Division, squinted into the morning sun as he tried to see the distant Federal lines. The Captain was in an observation post on the far right flank of the Confederate position. "Looks like command finally got it right, Lieutenant. They are definitely up to something. I see what appears to be a substantial troop movement behind their line. Order up the ready reserves and inform headquarters that they are trying again."

While Confederate forces assembled themselves in an effort to once again repel the invaders, the Union troops made their move. This time the veteran VI Corps would be the Union assault force, launching yet another attack on the extended Confederate right. The Corps advanced slowly, its movement on winding country paths and across grassy fields difficult. The Union soldiers closed on their target as the day progressed and the sun burned off the last of the morning fog. As foreword units neared their objective, orders to form for attack filtered down the dust-covered ranks. With veteran precision the long columns reformed. Regiments quickly began shaking themselves out from marching columns to assault fronts. After a final halt to dress ranks and allow skirmishers to advance ahead of the main force, the formation resumed its advance.

As the lead elements reached the Richmond Pike Road they began receiving musket and artillery fire, incoming rounds from fortified positions to their front and left flank. The fire increased in intensity and accuracy and the Union troops began taking substantial casualties. The blue formations halted their advance, the units on the left flank pivoting to face their hidden foe. With the front rank kneeling and rear rank standing they began trading rounds with their entrenched adversaries. Enemy fire intensified, canister artillery rounds ripping huge gaps in the exposed Union lines, shredding men and equipment, while rolling volleys of musket fire added to the carnage. Clouds of acrid smelling gunpowder began to obscure formations and positions. The advance ground to a halt as here and there individuals and small groups of soldiers began falling back.

"No, Damn it! Keep them moving! Keep up the pressure! Smash them! Smash them hard!" roared Major General Philip Sheridan as he raced down the blue lines, his staff trailing behind him. "Push them, Damn you! Push them!"

Sheridan reined up his horse, turned to his staff, and staring at the faltering units, ordered his reserve forces to wheel left and hit the newly exposed extreme right flank of the Confederate lines.

A few hundred feet behind the Confederate lines, seventeen year old private Bobby Jacobs, a sniper in the 1st. Mississippi Rifles, sat high in the leafy branches of a poplar tree. Carefully adjusting the scope of his rifle, he scanned the smoke-shrouded battle field before him. Bobby could almost hear his sergeant's voice. "Remember, targets of value only. Any horse's ass can shoot a private." A gust of wind momentarily cleared the area to his immediate front and opportunity knocked. Bobby licked his forefinger, held it up in the air before him, smiled and carefully drew a bead on his target.

The fifty-caliber round caught Sheridan in the upper left arm, driving him off his mount, and slamming him to the ground. Hitting hard, he cursed, and grasping the pommel, stood up only to topple back to the ground. Several of his staff dismounted to aid him while two more galloped off to find medical assistance. Within minutes the General was in a covered ambulance, on his way to the nearest hospital. The attack, bereft of his dynamic leadership, slowly ground to a halt behind him.

A few days later the news of Sheridan's injury reached the attention of General Robert Lee. The dispatch rider galloped up, dismounted and strode towards the shack that housed the headquarters of the Army of Northern Virginia. "I've dispatches for the General, urgent!" he declared.

"What isn't, these days," responded the duty captain. "Okay, let me have them, I'll make sure the general sees them as soon as possible."

A few minutes later Lee was reading General Pickett's note. "The enemy hit us at midday as we had anticipated. We stopped them cold, a small payback. I also have reason to believe that Sheridan was injured."

Lee sat quietly for a few moments thinking, the loss of one of their best generals, a fortuitous event and perhaps another step towards success. He quickly wrote out a message to the Director of Intelligence, and sent it by dispatch rider to Richmond.

Scarcely twenty-four hours later, in the Confederate capitol, the Director of Intelligence studied the note from Lee. Another piece to the puzzle, he thought. Rising from his desk, he walked down the hall to the office of the newly appointed Secretary of War, James Breckenridge. Entering, he gave the message to him and said, "We received this message from Lee. There's been a fortuitous event that we should try to use to our advantage. I think we should contact our Washington team and see if we might move to the next stage. If we do, then we must advise Generals Lee, Johnston and Forrest."

Breckenridge read the note nodded and replied, "Yes, I agree, since they lost Hancock, Sheridan is definitely one of their best. His loss could work to our advantage here."

CHAPTER EIGHT

March, 1865

Washington, D. C.

John Wilkes Booth, born in 1838 to a thespian family of some note, was the darling of the American entertainment industry. He was admired and adored in the United States and abroad as an actor of consummate skill and ability. Booth was currently at the pinnacle of his career, the toast of two continents and the owner of his own production company, "Star Productions," an enterprise which was managed by his elder brother, Edwin. An actor of superior ability, he was also arrogant and amazingly self-centered.

Striding down the cobble-stoned, tree-bordered Washington D. C. Avenue, on a beautiful sun-crowned winter day, he passed the life-size billboard and slowed a bit to admire his likeness. At least these goddamn Yankees can get something right, he thought.

Continuing on his way he arrived at the Surrat home, a boarding house that had seen better days but was perfect for his needs. The building was set back from the street and partially screened from casual view by a row of high hedges that ran parallel to the sidewalk. It offered a number of single rooms for rent by day or week and was situated on a main avenue, which in turn gave quick access to a number of secondary roads leading out of the city.

Booth entered the small foyer, paused a moment to hang up his cloak, then walked into the living room. There he joined another member of the Confederate spy team, Samuel Arnold, who was awaiting him. Arnold was a professional spy who had been a member of the Confederate Intelligence Service since its inception. For the last few months he had served as Booth's number two man. Arnold had a professional's dislike of an amateur, but hid it well. Booth, on the other hand was full of himself, convinced of his native superiority, and expected others to be equally impressed. He was, however, quite intelligent and reasonably competent.

"I've news, very good news," said Booth.

"As have I!"

"Very well then, you first."

"As you wish," answered Arnold. "Parker is an unhappy man. He has liquor and money problems and a failing marriage. He can be bought."

"So," responded Booth, "set up a meeting as soon as you can."

"No problem," answered Arnold. "If we pay him enough he will do the job. It's afterwards that bothers me. The pressure might be too much for him to handle."

"It is your responsibility to handle these issues," responded Booth, with a savage smile. "See to it."

"Done," was Arnold's answer.

"And now my news," said Booth. "Both Grant and Lincoln will view my performance from the same box. Our two most implacable enemies, together," he chortled. "Even the fates conspire for us."

"For this to work we must have Parker," cautioned Arnold.

"Promise him whatever you think he wants," snarled Booth. "We must have his active assistance that night, and remember that he must believe that you command the team. There must be no hint of me, no connection between you and I."

"I understand," responded Arnold. Rising to leave he concluded with, "the biggest problem will be hitting all the targets at nearly the same time so as to prevent any warning."

It took several days of hard work, but eventually Arnold's efforts paid off and John Parker agreed to meet with him. The ramshackle building was situated on Water Street, just one block north of the river-front docks that lined the Potomac. The seldom used warehouse, smelling faintly of fish and mildew, had been rented by Arnold several months ago. It was used as a secure meeting-place for the Washington area Confederate spy team. On this cold, damp March night it had but two occupants. The men sat in the rear office facing each other over a small table. A single shrouded lantern provided meager light and in one corner a small pot-bellied stove strove to beat back the chill.

Arnold began bluntly, "You understand that although you need to be absent for only a few minutes, it is critical that they be the right few minutes."

"I understand what you want, and if I get what I want it can be done," answered presidential bodyguard John Parker, who was about to become a nineteenth-century Judas. Parker was a tall, bearded, heavy-set man, taciturn and morose by nature, with a failing marriage and mounting debt due to drinking and gambling problems. Finding a man in his position and with such exploitable problems had been a major coup on Arnold's part.

Arnold reached across the table, offering Parker his right hand, his left holding a satchel with half the payment. Parker accepted both, gave Arnold an abrupt shake and glanced at the stacks of bills. He nodded, arose and strode from the building, disappearing into the Washington night. As Parker left Arnold was careful to keep the gleam of success from his eyes.

With Parker's active assistance guaranteed, the stage was set and all the pieces in place. Arnold immediately advised Booth of Parker's participation. Booth then ordered him to assemble the entire team. Obeying his superior's directive, Arnold told his men to assemble at their standard rendezvous.

A few nights later a group of men sat in the same office. Arnold regarded each man in turn, and then said, "Each of you has a specific target. Make sure you know where your target will be. Be certain you strike at the assigned time. Coordination and timing are essential; we can't have even one of them warned. All die! Are there any further questions? No? Then remember, follow the plan and have no mercy." As he stood up preparatory to leaving he said, "It will take them months to recover from this blow, and by the time they do, it will be too late."

Booth communicated the newest events by secret messenger to Campbell, who in turn spoke with Breckenridge. "There's a message from agent "Star," marked secret and urgent. He reports that his team is in place and ready to act.

He also gives us the date." The newly appointed Secretary
of War picked up the message and carried it to his desk. He
sat down and smiled, thinking. So! Yet another piece in
place! After a few moments of contemplation, he walked to
the President's office to share the news. That evening, messages went to all conspirators informing them of the date
on which the next phase of the Phoenix Gambit was to be
implemented.

CHAPTER NINE

April. 1865

Confederate lines, Petersburg, Virginia

The briefing for the officers of the brigades tasked as the assault force was being held in an abandoned barn. It was warm and stuffy, with the rich and pungent smell of the prior occupants weighing heavily in the air. The assembled officers were pensive and quiet, the bright spring sun doing little to alleviate their fears or ease the tension. The low rumble of conversation ceased the moment General Longstreet made his appearance. The General dismounted, handed his horse's reins to an aide and strode to the small platform that was set against one wall.

General Longstreet's face was tight with consternation as he began to present the planned offensive. The attack he was about to order was a desperate, high-risk maneuver.

"You are being tasked with conducting an assault in sectors 6 and 7. Your mission will be to attack, seize, and hold the Union position designated as Fort Stedman. Follow-up forces will then expand our bridgehead to the east, north, and south," he said, as he led the assembled officers through their final briefing. "Our goal is to punch a hole in their lines so wide and deep that all of their attention will be on the area of the breakthrough. We want them to be totally focused on this action. We want your commands to break through their line, then to advance to these positions. Using his forefinger, he indicated on the map spread before him locations up to five miles east of the current lines. You are to dig in and hold on as long as you can." I will not ask more of them, thought Longstreet. God help me, I cannot ask more! His inner turmoil increased as he saw the fear and consternation on the faces of the gathered officers.

He rushed to closure. "If there are no further tactical questions? No? Very well then, the attack will begin at 5 A.M. tomorrow. God be with you, gentlemen." he concluded.

Well before the first streaks of light appeared in the eastern sky, Sergeant Jake Randall, B Company, 21st Georgia Light Infantry Regiment, walked down the length of the trench that held the remnant of his platoon. He checked every man, making sure each had his musket with bayonet attached and their cartridge pouch, canteen and knapsack well secured and as full as possible.

"What in hell are we doing attacking them boys," asked private Amos Black.

"Following orders is what and don't you forget it," replied Randall.

"Bullshit," was the succinct response.

Since he had served with Black for better than three years, Randall ignored the comment and walked on until he met with the company commander, Lt. Benjamin Edwards.

"How's it look, sergeant?" asked Edwards.

"About as good as can be, sir, all considered," replied Randall. "I sure would like to know what in hell we're doing attacking those boys," he added, with a glance at Edwards.

"Same thing we've been doing since Manassas," Edwards replied softly, "following orders."

At exactly 5:00 A. M. lead elements of the 4th, 7th and 18th infantry brigades, 3rd Division, I Corps, Army of Northern Virginia, Confederate States of America, initiated its last offensive action. In absolute silence and perfect formation the veteran troops left their entrenchments and advanced toward the Union lines.

In the light of not quite dawn Sergeant Randall, advancing on the extreme right of his platoon, bayonet fixed, rifle at high port, continually checked to his left to keep his front dressed. Banks of rolling mist, some so thick they blotted out the man only two files away, gave an eerie, ghostly feeling to the setting. The assault force closed on the Union position with astonishing speed, the troops moving at double time.

Suddenly, Randall found himself at the first line of entrenchments with not a shot fired. He leaped into the trench and finding its three blue-clad occupants dead or dying, advanced across and up the other side towards the second line of heavier fortifications. These were sandbagged topped trenches with regularly spaced wooden-platform firing positions.

Shots, a few to his left, then a ragged volley followed by a second to his right, signaled the awakening enemy defenses. Turning a corner in the trench, he found himself face to face with a Union soldier. Reacting without thinking he dropped into guard and lunged forward, taking the first enemy soldier high in the chest with his bayonet. Driving off his planted right leg he pinned his man to the rear wall of the trench. The soldier grasped the rifle protruding from his chest with both hands, as if to pluck the offending object from his person, only to slowly sag to the ground, blood pouring from mouth and chest. The need for secrecy gone, the rebel yell sounded as his platoon surged passed him and into the scattered Union troops, hacking, stabbing, and shooting, no quarter asked and none given.

After securing the trench, Randall, followed by his men, ran across the wooden-sheathed front of Fort Stedman and around the corner, then along the northern wall to the rear, through the main sally port and into the fort proper. Dozens of Union soldiers milled about on the ramparts of the fort, confused and uncertain. Several officers in blue conferred on the parapet.

Randall brought his troops to a halt, quickly dressed his line and ordered, "Aim, Fire!" A deadly volley crashed out, sweeping many of the enemy officers from their feet. A second volley, followed by a charge, and the fort was theirs.

He assigned a few of his men to put out fires that had sprung up throughout the fort and others to scavenge what food and ammunition they might find on the corpses strewn about. As his men dispersed, he paused to listen to the sounds of battle, slowly fading to the east and south. Lieutenant Edwards soon appeared with the remainder of the company and informed Randall they had been ordered to hold this position.

A short time later, a grim-faced Major appeared with a force of men, each with the red facing of the artillery on their uniforms. "Lieutenant," he said, "I am leaving these men under your command. I want these cannons positioned to defend from an enemy advance from the east. You are ordered to hold this position. "

Edwards saluted and responded, "Yes, sir, hold this position." He followed that statement with the query, "For how long, sir?" The major responded with a bleak look and repeated, "You are ordered to hold this position as long as possible." He looked around for a moment then left to follow the still advancing Confederate assault columns as they continued driving deeper into Union territory.

As the Confederate assault impacted the defensive line of the Army of the Potomac, Union forces slowly began to respond. Sergeant Ezekiel "Easy," Sinclair, rolled from his bedroll, his subconscious pressuring him to awareness as danger signals pumped adrenaline into his body. Stopping himself in the act of reaching for his weapon, and realizing the danger was not imminent, he reached instead for his clothing. Dressed, he left his tent and stood in the company street, staring up at the blood-red tinted dawn sky.

Easy heard artillery and rifle fire about a mile or two distant, from the north. Rebs acting up again, I guess, he thought. Flashes and growls drifted south, along with the smell of gun powder. Counter attack? He became uneasy as the sounds gained in volume and intensity. That's it, he thought; time to roust the "Boss." Suiting his actions to his thoughts he turned sharply to find himself nose-to-nose with the "Boss," Captain Abel Thomas, CO of D Company, 19th Connecticut Volunteer Infantry Regiment.

Abel Thomas was a twenty-four year army veteran. Enlisting in the army at seventeen, he had received a battle-field commission for bravery while serving under then Captain Robert E. Lee, in the Mexican-American War. When peace broke out he had opted to remain in the Army and had served in several Indian campaigns, collecting a number of medals for bravery in combat along the way. As soon as the massive Union call-ups began he was promoted to captain and given a company level command.

Easy had been assigned to the nineteenth and Captain Thomas had quickly become impressed with the young soldier's all-around competence and dependability, as well as courage and leadership under fire.

"Don't like the sound of that one bit," said Thomas. He turned and shouted, "Lieutenant, Turn them out and form them up. Platoon front facing north."

"North, Sir?" came the querulous response.

"Listen up and you tell me, Lieutenant," responded Thomas.

Easy, seeing that action could be imminent, returned to his tent where he armed and equipped himself then left to form his platoon. He assembled and inspected his men to insure each was combat ready. The moment he deemed his men prepared, he ordered them to fall-in and left to report to Thomas and obtain further orders.

For the next few hours, Easy and his men worked furiously to extend their lines at a right angle from their prior positions. They dug fighting trenches and prepared artillery positions in order to establish a new defensive front in response to the expected attack.

Late morning found the 19th, along with the rest of the Brigade and several other units drawn from any available command, manning a hastily formed defensive line that ran in an east-west direction. Having stabilized the situation, Captain Thomas ordered the company to stand down by platoon and prepare themselves a hurried lunch.

As his platoon left their fortifications to seat themselves near the cooking fires, Easy walked amongst the eating men, taking stock of their mood and thoughts. Stopping frequently to address a remark or respond to a query, he completed rounds then left to return to the trench line.

From his vantage point on the freshly-filled sandbags Sinclair could see small groups of ghostly figures filtering south towards the waiting Union infantry. Turning, he called to his men to return to the lines and form up. Again regarding the enemy advance he thought, too loose, too loose, no punch, no power.

"Hold your fire till you have a clear target," he ordered his men. "Make the first shot count." Following his own advice he waited as the grey ranks closed to a point where he could see the attacker's eyes, and then fired, dropping an enemy soldier in his tracks. The regiment continued to lay down heavy volley fire on the advancing Confederates for several minutes. Return fire was light at first but gradually grew in intensity as the enemy forces formed up into larger units. Shells began exploding on and around the Union lines followed by volleys of Minnie balls.

The rebels regrouped and reformed, ranks of bayonet-tipped muskets aligning themselves next to artillery; then the drum roll of "charge" sent them sweeping towards the Union lines. In some places the violence of the attack swept over and through the defenders, while in other places the attack was stopped cold. Soldiers in blue and soldiers in grey shot, punched, and bayoneted each other ferociously and without mercy until one side or the other died or grudgingly gave ground.

For the next few hours the entire Union line slowly fell back in the face of furious but uncoordinated infantry attacks, taking casualties but finally blunting, then stopping the advance on their front. Throughout the action Easy kept his platoon withdrawing in formation and maintaining fire discipline.

As the day wore on the intensity and frequency of the attacks began to reduce and in late afternoon the 19th's regiment was ordered to prepare to counter-attack. Receiving the order from Captain Thomas, Easy began walking up and down the firing line, talking to his men, checking their equipment and preparing them for their advance. Finding that most of his men were low on ammunition he went to report the situation to the Captain. Thomas directed him to take a squad and find ammunition for the entire company.

Easy and his men moved into the chaos that was the Union rear. Infantry, cavalry and even occasional artillery units were moving back and forth, stopping and starting as they received contradicting assignments. Numerous wounded, some with help but many without either wandered about seeking medical aid or died where they lay.

A colonel, one arm hanging uselessly at his side, uniform tunic soaked with blood, walked up and down growling continually at no one or everyone, "Kill the bastards, hit them, kill them!" As Easy approached the officer toppled over, unconscious from loss of blood. Easy tore the sleeve from the officer's coat, applied it as a tourniquet, then directed two of his men to take the wounded man to the nearest first aid station and continued on his search.

Shortly, he came upon two wagons stopped in the road. All of the horses and the driver had been killed by artillery while miraculously leaving the cargo of gunpowder and Minnie balls untouched. Easy ordered each of his men to take as much as they possible could, then did so himself. As soon as every man was fully laden he led them back to their company position.

As the sun began to cast lengthy shadows, Captain Thomas ordered the company to advance. Easy stood up, signaled the platoon and began walking towards the rebel lines. The Union counterattack was initially slow and in some places either uncoordinated or unsupported by artillery. It gained momentum as more units became involved and properly placed heavy weapons began providing effective fire support.

As the Rebel forces began absorbing increasing casualties, they lost cohesion, with some units attempting to stand and fight, while others began to withdraw. Their defense became ineffective, especially without adequate artillery support. The Union assault continued to drive north, steadily inflicting and absorbing losses.

On several occasions, the advance had to be stopped and some units turned about in order to destroy Rebel positions that were entrenched and refused to surrender. Each of these strong-points had to be taken by bloody frontal assault and ended with hand-to-hand combat.

Eventually, as the setting sun signaled the approaching night, the Union attack was halted and the exhausted troops ceased their advance. Command ordered all units to hold in place overnight and continue their advance at first light. During the night quartermaster units were active, and morning found the Union forces flush with ammunition and preparing to advance again.

Washington, D. C.

As the fighting on the Petersburg line increased in tempo and ferocity, the Union capitol was quiet and serene on this lovely spring day.

"I will return as soon as the meeting is over, my dear," said the President. "Just rest in quiet, my love." Abraham Lincoln closed the door to his wife's room and slowly walked down the stairs to the first floor, where his senior advisors and army commander awaited him.

General Ulysses S. Grant had originally commanded Union forces in campaigns in the western theater of the war. He had beaten several Confederate generals in a number of hard-fought battles. His most notable victory was the conquest of the major southern supply port on the Mississippi River, Vicksburg.

After enduring a series of incompetent general officers in the eastern theatre, Lincoln had called Grant to Washington and given him command of the Union's premiere field force, the Army of the Potomac. Grant's response had been to commence a strategy of constant and continuous combat between his army and Lee's command, the Army of Northern Virginia. Grant's calculated use of the Union's twin advantages of manpower and industrial capacity had resulted in fighting Lee to a stalemate and played to Grant's strengths. Grant's dogged and determined approach had infused the Union Army with a sense of victory.

In addition to military issues there was a deep schism between Lincoln and the majority of his Cabinet. With the exception of the Secretary of the Navy, Gideon Wells, they were very much against Lincoln's plans for the post-war

Confederacy. Lincoln advocated a policy that would, at war's end, reunite all the states within the Union's fold, with a bare minimum of conditions and stipulations. His approach was one of forgiveness. Led by the Secretary of War, Edwin Stanton, the Cabinet wished to implement a policy of retribution and punishment on the secessionist states.

As Lincoln entered the room, Lieutenant General Grant rose, nodded to him and said simply, "Mr. President." Seward and Stanton showed little respect as usual, just looking at him until he began to speak.

"It is only a matter of time before we are victorious. We must begin planning for that eventuality. Don't you agree, General?" queried Lincoln, choosing to ignore the slight from Stanton and Seward.

"Absolutely!" replied Grant. "As soon as Sheridan is fit we'll hit them one good lick and finish Lee's force. Once that's accomplished, Sherman will easily deal with whatever Johnston has left in the field."

"God willing, General," said Lincoln.

"Once the fighting is over we must turn our energies to healing the wounds we have caused each other. We must find a way to become one again," he said, while gazing out the window and perhaps seeing what might be. Turning to his assembled cabinet members, Lincoln asked, "What opinions have you gentlemen regarding my plans for the Southern States when hostilities have ended?"

Stanton rose, and gesturing towards the other seated men, said sharply, "We feel that simply allowing these people to return to the old "*status quo*" is unacceptable. Our economy has been devastated. Thousands of families have lost loved ones. Our very national core has been shattered and you would have them simply say, 'I'm sorry' and be done with it!" His voice rising in anger, Stanton continued, "I think not, Sir! I think not!"

Rising in support of Stanton, another cabinet member said, "They must be made to appreciate the gravity of their actions. They must be made to understand that our Union is sacred in the eyes of God and man. There must be a balancing of accounts, a debt paid."

I don't want this to become an act of national vengeance, thought Lincoln. We must be better than that, we must realize that the most important thing is to restore the Union; to forgive rather then punish, to be greater rather then less.

"I see we are not of one mind in this matter," said Lincoln, his words slow and filled with remorse. "I see there are concerns other then salving the pain and healing the wounds. I see some focus on matters of money and pride. I pray you, don't give in to those baser instincts. Let us rise above ourselves, be great if you can, and let others look to their pockets."

Looking at the faces of most of the men in the room, Lincoln realized his pleas had fallen on deaf ears. These men were set to punish and vent their anger; mercy had no place in their vision of the future.

With a sigh of resignation, Lincoln rose and said, "Gentlemen, we will speak on this again." Gesturing to Grant, he said, "Walk with me a bit, General." Grant stood up immediately and turning to the seated men said brusquely, "Good day," then left to follow Lincoln down the corridor and out into the garden.

"I fear these men may not be up to the job at hand," said Lincoln, as he and Grant walked slowly down the path. "I believe they will seek to line their pockets and opt for revenge."

This is a man of honor, a man of strength and wisdom, a man I can be proud to follow, thought Grant. "Mr. President, I am only a soldier. Give me an order and I will make it so," he said, looking straight into Lincoln's eyes as if to vow the truth of his statements.

"I believe you, General, I have total faith in you and your army," responded Lincoln. "But," he continued, "I hope the time for battle will soon pass and the time for diplomacy will be upon us. At any rate, General, I hope to have the pleasure of the company of you and your wife at the Ford Theatre. I understand the famous Mr. Booth will play the lead role."

Grant, who absolutely loathed the theater, responded, "It would be a great pleasure for both of us, Mr. President, a great pleasure."

Lincoln smiled and said, "Until tonight, then, in the Presidential box, General."

He stood alone for a moment, watching Grant's receding figure. He thought, years of pompous fools, years of horrible blunders, but finally we have the right men in the right place at the right time. With the Lord's assistance I believe we shall prevail.

Union lines, Petersburg, Virginia

In the command tent of General Phillip Sheridan, the ring of senior officers pressed close around the briefing table in order to hear every word. "General Howard's Corps seems to have stopped them, but they have dug in and will be very difficult to dislodge, especially from Fort Stedman," said Sheridan. "First thing tomorrow morning we will bring up Burnside's

Corps from the south and Ord's from the north, fix them in place, and then crush them."

Still recovering from his wound, one arm in a sling, Sheridan paced up and down as he gave his orders. "When Grant returns I intend that the situation will be in hand and those bastards will either be back where they started from, or dead," he snarled. "Now you get it done, and get it done fast!"

A chorus of "Yes, Sir," and, "At once, Sir," greeted his demands, as the individual officers filed out of the room to return to their commands, and implement the orders that would seal off the Confederate incursion. None of them saw him grasp his arm and sink slowly into a chair, a grimace of pain on his face and a thin trickle of blood dripping from his fingertips to stain the dirt floor.

Washington, D. C.

As the moon climbed high into the cloudless night sky the Army of the Potomac started to re-assert control of the battle and events in Washington were fast coming to fruition for the Confederate conspirators. Sam Arnold, wearing the uniform of an usher, stopped just outside the unguarded door of the presidential box. Checking to both left and right, he opened the door and stepped through. Pausing just a moment to verify his targets, he withdrew two revolvers from his coat pockets and advanced towards the four seated figures.

At the sound of gunshots, Booth, who was at that moment brandishing a fake gun on stage, fired his weapon then cried out. He began to windmill his arms then stumbled across the stage, contriving to fall into the orchestra pit. His antics were so loud and disruptive that it took several minutes for the assassination to be discovered.

On the periphery of the city a Confederate agent walked quickly up to the rear door of the darkened Stanton home. He picked the lock, and then quietly stepped through the door into the kitchen. Walking lightly he made his way down the dimly lit hallway to the stair leading to the upstairs bedrooms, where his target lay sleeping. As he slowly ascended the stairs he began looping the garrote tightly around his hands. Gently opening the bedroom door he entered and softly stepped towards the snoring figure in the bed.

In the heart of the Capitol, another agent, wearing the uniform of a hotel waiter, the owner of which lay dead in an adjacent alley, hesitated only a moment before knocking on the door to Secretary of Interior Seward's hotel room. Responding to the shouted "enter," he grasped his revolver in his left hand as he opened the door with his right. Stepping into the room he emptied the six chambers into the body reclining on the bed.

An hour after dawn, Arnold and his entire team were safely behind Confederate lines and well on their way to Richmond. It was several days before John Parker's body was found in a ditch, three miles outside Washington.

Union line, Petersburg, Virginia

The Union Army resumed its advance at dawn, intent on re-establishing its lines as soon as possible. The 19th was in the vanguard. Leaping over a felled tree, Easy came face to face with two Confederate soldiers. Shooting the first, he lunged with his bayonet-tipped rifle at the second man, catching him in the upper right shoulder and driving the man into the ground. The soldier dropped his rifle and clutched at the cold steel protruding from his body, all the while screaming in a high, almost falsetto voice.

Before Easy could disengage, one of a wave of Union troopers advancing with him slammed the butt of his rifle into the side of the screamer's head, to the accompaniment of a squashing sound and spray of blood and grey matter. Withdrawing his bayonet from the supine man, Easy quickly scanned his immediate area. Enemy defenders were slowly falling back while rearguard units, attempting to hold fast, provided cover fire to slow the Union pursuit.

Shouting for his men to rally on him, Easy looked about and saw that his platoon controlled their section of the battlefield. The nearest Rebels units were in full retreat. He ordered his men to halt and dig in and left in search of Captain Thomas. A short distance away he found the captain seated on an overturned and partially burned caisson that was still attached to two dead horses. As Thomas slowly washed grime from his face, he smiled up at Easy and said. "Excellent work! It looks as though they've started to break."

"Looks like it, sir," responded Easy, "but it appears they've punched a good size hole in our lines." Both men paused to listen to the sound of almost continuous musket volleys, punctuated with an occasional artillery blast. The sounds were coming from both east and north of their position.

"We'll hold here until we re-supply and then we'll continue to advance. Our objective is Fort Stedman," ordered

Thomas. "Tell your boys to rest a bit and post sentries." Easy saluted and returned to his men.

After awhile several quartermaster wagons came and shortly thereafter the company received orders to advance. Resistance was initially light, mostly consisting of company and platoon size units holding makeshift strong points. The 19th overran each enemy position it encountered and slowly began to close on Fort Stedman. As Easy's men neared their objective, enemy fire grew in both intensity and effectiveness, causing him to order his men to cover.

As artillery shells ripped overhead and exploded just behind him, Easy dove into a trench already occupied by several bodies. There were also two live, uninjured Union troopers crouched down, well below ground level. "See much to shoot at down there?" he asked, his voice light, but his meaning clear.

"I'm going to move up a bit and I need covering fire," he said, looking straight at the two men. "I'm going on three." Without a backward glance he counted to three out loud then scrambled up the trench wall. Racing forward towards Stedman he discovered he was flanked on either side by the two men that had been in the trench.

In the shattered remains of the fort, squatting behind a battered segment of the fort's wall, along with the remnant of his platoon, Sergeant Randall regarded the approaching Yankees. He drew a bead on one of the blue-clad figures advancing towards his position. One less Yankee, he said to himself, as he aimed and slowly squeezed the trigger. He grunted in satisfaction as he saw his target tumble to the ground.

The man to Easy's left cried out, clutched his leg and fell. Easy, despite heavy fire, handed his weapon to the man on his right, and ordering the soldier to provide covering fire, bent to pick up the wounded man. Lifting his injured comrade to his shoulder, he began making his way back to the safety of the trench they had just vacated.

Randall reloaded and sighted his weapon. War is war, he muttered under his breath, watching the two figures, one wounded and one carrying the wounded man, slowly making their way to the imagined safety of the trenches, before firing a second time.

Easy was at the edge of the trench when he was thrown to the ground by the massive impact of the fifty-caliber bullet. Suddenly he found himself flat on the ground, face mashed into the dirt. First there was pain, a little, then a lot, then a gathering darkness, then nothing.

Several members of Easy's platoon, seeing him fall, rushed to his side. One attempted to bandage his wound as several other soldiers used their bodies to shield his as they provided covering fire. Completing the first aid, they quickly carried Easy to the rear. When they arrived at the aid station, his men insisted that he receive immediate attention, despite the fact that there were a number of casualties with more serious wounds awaiting the attentions of a doctor.

Three days later, Easy's fever broke and he regained consciousness. Looking down to the side of his cot, he discovered one of his platoon members sleeping on the dirt floor. His men had such a high regard for him that they had taken turns providing him with care.

Confederate Lines, Petersburg, Virginia

While combat raged along the Union's Petersburg positions, the Army of Northern Virginia commenced its movement. Colonel Charles Venable, knocked lightly on the door and then entered the room. "General, Fort Stedman has been taken and it appears our forces will at least enjoy some initial success. Generals Longstreet and Hill have successfully disengaged their commands and are on the move to Lynchburg."

"Very well, Colonel," responded Lee.

A few hours later, Lee, accompanied as usual by a small staff and a squadron of Stuart's ever vigilant cavalry, sat his horse beside a narrow country lane as the rear most units of the Army of Northern Virginia passed by.

A cavalry Captain trotted up, and after saluting smartly, conversed quietly with Lee's staff for a few moments. Venable directed the young officer to Lee. The Captain approached the General and reported, "General, I have the honor to report we have lost all contact with enemy forces."

Lee, ever the courteous officer, responded with, "Thank you, Captain. Well done. Please return to your command." Seeing the concern on the young man's features, he offered, "Follow your orders and all will be well."

The Army of Northern Virginia, screened by General Stuart's cavalry, moved quickly westward. First to Lynchburg for resupply, and then to the waiting trains of the Virginia and Tennessee Railroad, then south into the Blue Ridge Mountains, from which point the army appeared to vanish into thin air.

Union General Phillip Sheridan's H.Q.

General Sheridan's staff officer's face grew ashen as he read, then reread the message, its import shaking him almost into insensibility. Discipline winning out, the officer composed himself, then entered the adjoining office.

"Message from Washington, Sir... It's..., Sir, its very bad news." Sheridan, knowing his man, looked up at the captain.

"Out with it, Jack, it won't get better by waiting." Captain Joseph O'Rourke, a brave and decorated soldier, stumbling a bit as tears clouded his eyes, stepped forward and handed the message to the General.

Sheridan remained motionless for a few seconds after he read the message. Looking at O'Rourke he issued orders in a clear and steady voice. "Jack, send a message to President Johnson and tell him the attack here has been contained and we have it all under control. Send a message to Sherman, let him know what has happened, and tell him he must stop whatever he is doing and get to Washington without delay. We have to meet and plan. Go and get it done *now,* Jack!"

Washington, D. C.

It took days of martial law before Washington regained any semblance of normality. The first order of business was to honor and bury the fallen. The city was hushed. Thousands of black ribbons festooned trees, lampposts, and awnings. Throughout the city church bells tolled their dirge. The business and financial districts were closed, every government office empty and silent.

On the day of interment, the crowds, numbering well into the thousands, lined the broad avenue that led to and past the reviewing stand. The multitudes watched in an eerie silence as the muted drums and infantry formations guarding the nation's dead passed them by; each flag-draped, caisson-mounted body slowly making its way down the center of the avenue.

Shock, outrage, and horror were plain to see on the faces in the crowd as the caskets carrying the Lincolns, the Grants, along with most of the cabinet members, and in several cases their wives, wound their way to the burial site.

Two entire Corps had been recalled from the Army of the Potomac to lend their solemn majesty and provide security for this sorry occasion. Each and every man was wearing a black band encircling his right arm. A solemn silence enveloped the three figures standing to the front of the review stand, surrounded by ranks of armed soldiers: Commander of the Union Armies Lt. General William T. Sherman, Commander of the Army of the Potomac Lt. General George Mead, and President of the United States Andrew Johnson. Each man saluted as the convoy of caskets passed by on their way to a final resting place in Arlington cemetery.

The President had ordered that the military, political and business leaders of the Union meet as soon as possible in order to determine their course of action. The meeting was called to order a few days after the completion of the funeral services.

"For all practical purposes, with the retreat and apparent disappearance of the Army of Northern Virginia and Jefferson Davis, conflict between Union and Rebel forces has ceased, except for Johnston's command and a few minor holdouts here and there. These are relatively small, localized pockets of resistance that we can deal with at our leisure," said Sherman.

"The South has been defeated, and we must turn our attention to our future," said Johnson, rising from his chair, "and that is the purpose of our group, to chart the course of action best suited to our needs. Those of us who sacrificed so much must insure that our Union will never again be subjected to such horror. We must reconstruct the southern areas so that one day they too might participate in the fruits of freedom."

"Ah, yes," rejoined another voice from the group of industrialists seated at the foot of the table, "let us by all means reconstruct the South. It is our understanding, General, that the cities, farms, factories, and railroads throughout the southern areas have suffered terrible destruction, not the least from your own forces," said the man. Sherman nodded his reply.

"We also have the issue of freed slaves, armed rebels and a basically hostile population to both govern and protect," said Meade. "With too few troops to do it," he added with a grimace. "Even though these troops will be primarily tasked with civil- occupation duties and need not be front-line quality, I estimate we will require upwards of three hundred thousand men," he concluded.

"Truly an occupying Army," said Patrick O'Reilly, the congressmen representing a heavily Irish district in New York City. O'Reilly had emigrated from Ireland with his father, mother, younger brother and sister in 1832. His father and brother had died on the voyage to America, leaving fourteen year old Patrick as sole support and protector for his remaining family.

When they arrived in New York City he and his family were shocked to find their "promised land" filled with signs saying, "Irish need not apply" or more simply, "No Irish allowed!" After being denied jobs ranging from midnight porter to grave digger, he began to cast about for less mainstream employment opportunities. Eventually he joined an Irish gang, known as the "Dead Rabbits." By virtue of his intelligence, ready wit and even readier fists, he soon rose to a position of importance and leadership.

After a few years apprenticeship in gang warfare and power plays he turned his hand to the rough and ready arena that was mainstream New York City politics. Here his gang connections stood him in good stead. With a support base ranging from the Dead Rabbits to Tammany Hall, he ran for Congress, was elected, then reelected to several terms in the House of Representatives. As time passed he became a political power of note.

"You'll not fill those ranks with impressed sons of Erin," he said, standing to emphasize his point. "We have shed all the blood we will." And he added, "We plan to partake of the spoils of our labors. I am sure that we can find a manpower source sufficient for our needs, just as long as it's not Irish," he concluded.

The council of war lasted for several days and eventual agreement was reached on several points. The Confederate States of America would pay for its infamy. Every senior officer of its Armies was declared traitor, its elected officials' rebels, all to pay for their treason with their property and perhaps even their lives. Under the authority of the "Acts of Reconstruction," the South, her leaders, people, cities and industries would pay penance for decades.

CHAPTER TEN

May, 1865

Richmond, Virginia

Fear and anger hung like a pall over the ravaged city. Months of siege warfare and blockade had reduced the once proud capital of the Confederacy to the point where it had fed on itself in order to survive. The city was pockmarked with burnt-out buildings whose innards had been harvested by the needy. Streets were strewn with the skeletons of dead animals, killed for subsistence for its inhabitants.

When the Army of Northern Virginia had abandoned its lines around Petersburg, there had been panic in the city and its suburbs. Mobs, expecting Union invasion at any moment, had roamed the streets in an orgy of violence and destruction, culminating in the torching of many of the city's grander, more affluent neighborhoods.

In the frenzy following the assassinations of the Union's leadership, General Sherman had ordered the Army of the Potomac to garrison Washington and continue to man the Petersburg lines, while his Army in Georgia was to maintain as much pressure on the remaining Confederate military structure in the south as was possible.

When Union forces did not immediately advance on Richmond, Virginia Governor John Letcher summoned local militia and home guard units and tasked them with regaining and maintaining control of the city and as much of the surrounding area as they could manage. Summary firing squads and group hangings served to enforce martial law and if not stop, then seriously reduce the destruction.

A few days later a delegation representing both civil and military authority, in the persons of Alexander Stephens, Vice President, CSA and General Braxton Bragg, who had been designated as "Commander, CSA forces in Virginia," arrived and attempted to assume control of the situation.

Contact was made with the Union forces in the vicinity in order to begin the process of a formal surrender of both Virginia militia and all regular CSA forces in the state. It took a good deal of time before the appropriate authorities on both sides were able to open a dialogue and an even greater length of time for the actual surrender process to be decided upon.

General Bragg, the military representative of the Confederate States of America, sat his horse at the head of the surrender delegation. "So help me God, if I see but one of those bastards smirk I will shoot him dead and the consequences be damned," he snarled to Colonel William Conrad, Commanding Officer, 8th Virginia State Militia Regiment, who was beside him.

"Might as well be done with it," responded Conrad, with a sigh of resignation, "dragging it out will just make it worse, sir."

"I suppose," was the glum retort, and with that he and his staff dismounted and entered the large tent that had been constructed on the outskirts of the city expressly for this ceremony. The structure was surrounded on all four sides by massed phalanxes of Union infantry.

According to the recently passed "Acts of Reconstruction," as soon as the ceremonies were completed, both Stephens and Bragg were declared traitors in rebellion against the lawful government of the United States of America. They, along with all of the Regular Army officers above the rank of Captain, as well as the senior elected officials of the state government, were imprisoned and sent by rail to the Douglas Prisoner of War Camp in Chicago, there to await trail at the pleasure of the victors. Regular Army and state militia troops were simply disarmed and disbanded.

Mississippi River

After the Army of Northern Virginia left its positions in the Petersburg lines, General Sherman had ordered all available cavalry units to take the field in an effort to locate it.

A brigade, under the command of Union General George A. Custer, made contact with the rearguard of a Confederate cavalry force, commanded by General Bedford Forrest. Custer immediately directed his units to give pursuit.

General George Armstrong Custer was a man of extremes. He had graduated from West Point at the head of his class in horsemanship, small arms and swordsmanship and at the bottom in tactics and strategy. Flamboyant to a fault, he had redesigned his Brigadier General uniform based on the uniform of an Imperial Russian Hussar. A cold, harsh disciplinarian, he was sometimes cruel to the point of sadism. Units under his command killed more enemy, fought in more battles and received more bravery citations then any other unit of similar size; however, they also suffered a much higher casualty rate. Self confidant to the point of arrogance, he would not accept criticism from under officers and often ignored input from seniors. His men hated, feared, and respected him. In combat situations his standing order was, "Follow me."

General Bedford Forrest's Command had been tasked with escorting large numbers of skilled civilian tradesmen, machinery and the governments gold reserves. Bogged down with civilians and heavily-laden wagons, they had been moving as fast as possible. They had reached the mighty Mississippi and halted on the east bank.

Lightning flashes ripped across a coal-black sky as torrents of wind-driven rain slammed into the hundreds of wagons. Escorting cavalry columns stretched for several miles eastward from the river crossing. This ford was one of a number being used as an escape route for those who had been chosen to accompany Forrest's heavy cavalry division.

"By God, Sir!" exclaimed Captain Thomas Brooks, 3rd squadron, 1st South Carolina Light Horse, to General Forrest who, like his men, sat his horse in stoic silence awaiting his turn on one of the many steam-powered ferries busy cruising back and forth across the raging river. "I've never seen it rain so hard."

"It'll make it just that harder for them to track us," replied Forrest, "and God knows we need all the help we can get. Keep them moving as fast as possible and send another squadron to check on our rearguard, Captain. That Union cavalry can't be too far behind us."

Scarcely a week later columns of blue-clad cavalry sat on the exact same bluff, angrily regarding the same river. "General Custer, Sir, there ain't a boat to be had on this side of the river for twenty miles either way," reported Captain Wayne Rogers, 3rd Michigan Cavalry.

"Damn them! Damn those rebels!" stormed Custer. Turning in his saddle, he ordered, "I want patrols out, up and down river. Find us a ferry or a crossing." As his units thundered off to the north and south he sat on the bluff gazing at the mighty Mississippi. He thought, I expected more from Forrest than running away like this. Where can he be going? Texas, Arizona? California's out of the question, so he's got to head south. Perhaps more important a question is why? What is his purpose? He must know that just running will only prolong the agony. He must have some viable goal. It just doesn't make any sense. One thing for damn-sure, whatever he's planning I'm going to be there to stop him, by God!

After a moments more rumination he ordered, "Send a courier to General Sherman, Captain. With my compliments, and inform the General that General Forrest's forces have crossed the Mississippi River and that we will continue the pursuit with all possible haste."

CHAPTER ELEVEN

June, 1865

Confederate Army, Northern Florida

The Army of Northern Virginia had moved as fast as possible, leaving the Petersburg line and pushing hard. As Forrest had moved east Lee had raced south. Using pre-positioned supply caches and alternating between available roads and railways, he had tried desperately to avoid contact with Union forces. Eventually, despite their best efforts, Lee's command was located by Union cavalry. Forces from General Butler's New Orleans Command and General Sherman's Georgian Command began to converge on the Confederates, who were now in the central Florida panhandle.

Colonel Venable entered General Lee's tent, "Sir, General Stuart presents his complements and begs a final word with you."

Lee responded, "Of course, of course," while thinking, he knows there can be no victory for him, that he will become yet another martyr to our cause. Dear Lord, the sacrifice I must ask!

Stuart entered the tent, none of his famed bravado or swagger in evidence. He looked incredibly haggard. The stress he was under was obvious in his countenance. His face was gaunt, his manner focused and intent.

"General, sir," he began, "It has been my honor to serve with you, truly my honor. I will leave and take my command north. I will join General Johnston and continue the fight."

General Joseph Johnston's Army had been ordered to act as a rear guard. Their job was to trade their lives for time. This sacrifice would allow Lee's force to complete the next phase of the Phoenix Gambit. Speed was a major issue, and Lee's Army of Northern Virginia had left all their heavy equipment and artillery behind. Circumstances would now require a similar sacrifice by the cavalry.

"General Stuart," responded Lee, his voice heavy with emotion, "your performance in the Army of Northern Virginia has been superb in every respect. It has been an honor for me to serve with you. The sacrifice that you and your men are making will not go in vain. I will not allow it!" Stuart did not reply, but instead saluted, then hesitantly offered his hand.

Near to tears, Lee reached out to the proffered hand and grasping it said, "Go with God, General. Know that you have my gratitude and the gratitude of our people for the efforts of you and your gallant command."

Almost overcome with emotion, Stuart left Lee's tent, rejoined his cavalry Brigades, and rode north to join General Johnston's force. Due to a combination of exceptionally inclement weather and poor roads the ride north proceeded at a snails pace. It was several days before Stuart and Johnston united their forces.

Johnston's command, the last field force of the Confederacy, was dug in on a series of low hills and held a road juncture which the pursuing Union troops would have to use. His orders were to shield the Army of Northern Virginia, holding the Union forces at bay, while Lee's command completed its escape from the Confederacy. Stuart's arrival gave the Confederates enough troops to launch a series of limited counter-attacks designed to slow, if not stop the pursuit.

The weather had finally turned and two consecutive days of bright, unfiltered sunshine had thoroughly dried the ground. Swirls of dust, driven into the air by the charge and counter-charge of Union and Confederate cavalry made breathing difficult. General Stuart sheathed his saber and reached for his half-empty canteen. He untied his scarf and pulled it from his sweat and dirt-stained face. Taking his canteen, he poured water onto the scarf and proceeded to rearrange the filth covering his features.

With a grin on his face he glanced at his executive officer, said, "Hot work, this. Order the 3rd to swing around their left and try to get into their rear. Have the 1st and 2nd dismount and form a skirmish line. If we can't stop'em we can at least slow'em down." With that Stuart dismounted, handed his horse's reigns to a sergeant and continued organizing his troops.

The outmanned and outgunned defense stubbornly fought on, before finally being crushed by massive Union frontal attacks. General Stuart was killed on the last day of the battle while leading a cavalry counter-attack.

As the battle to the north wound down to its inevitable conclusion the Army of Northern Virginia found itself camped on the Florida Gulf coast. The total combat strength of the Confederate Navy, under the command of Admiral Raphael Semmes, along with a large number of merchantmen flying the flags of a dozen nations, but paid for by England and Germany, were strung out along miles of marshy, insect-infested Florida coast.

"I have a total of four combat ships and thirty seven cargo vessels under my command, sir," reported Semmes, as he faced Davis and Lee on the bridge of the CSA blockade runner *Alabama*. "I don't believe there is another Confederate naval unit afloat," he added apologetically.

"No, no, sir! You have performed a miracle," said Davis. Grasping Semmes' arm he walked briskly to the rail, asking, "Where is Breckenridge?"

"Mr. Breckenridge is on the *Richmond*, Sir," responded Semmes. "He has just arrived from Vera Cruz."

"I want a meeting of the Command Staff to convene as soon as our forces are aboard," said Davis.

It was several hours later and the soft glow of moonlight provided just enough illumination for the men to see each other as they sat on the aft deck of the flagship *Alabama*.

"Gentlemen," said President Davis, "I have been advised that all of our forces will have embarked by dawn. As soon as all our troops are ship borne the fleet will weigh-anchor and proceed to the next stage of the plan. I've ordered the *Alabama* to head south immediately. Admiral Semmes informs me that we can expect a quick passage. I bid you all a good evening and a restful voyage. General Lee, if you would be so good as to attend me for one moment." said Davis, as the group began to disperse and retire to their quarters.

"At your service, Mr. President," answered Lee.

The two men stood for a moment at the stern of the raider as she slipped quietly through the warm, calm waters of the Gulf, a phosphorescent wake trailing from her stern.

"General, as you know the negotiations with our European supporters have been successful in terms of preliminary economic and military support. However, the most vital concern is still recognition, and that is, of course, dependent on military as well as political issues. The situation in Mexico is quite complex, but I believe that between Santa Anna and me we can maintain a political framework that is acceptable and viable. We have agreed that given your stature you will be in overall command of the allied forces. Our success or failure will rest on your ability to create a functioning army and lead it to victory at the earliest possible moment. All political considerations will be subordinate to your needs."

Lee paused to look directly at Davis before replying. "Sir, I am aware of both the gravity and difficulty of the situation. I will be sensitive to all the issues consistent with creating an effective army."

"General," responded Davis, "I am certain of your success and will assist you in every way possible. Good night, Sir."

Davis remained at the rail watching as Lee walked to his cabin, thinking that if there was one single man who could achieve what we need it is that man, and with that thought he turned and entered his cabin.

Lee passed a sentry at the door and entered his small cabin. He removed his coat and sat on the bed. A few moments later there was a knock on his door and Colonel Venable entered. He found Lee still sitting on his bunk.

Concern was plain in his voice as he asked, "Can I get you anything, Sir?"

"No thank you. I find myself unable to sleep. I think a turn around the deck might help." Lee's answer was hollow and drawn.

"Very good, sir," said Venable. After a moments hesitation, still worried, he asked, "Do you wish any company, sir?"

Lee smiled and replied, "No Colonel, I think not. Thank you."

He sat and listened to the footsteps fade then the General left the cabin and made his way back up to the main deck. He walked all the way to the stern of the ship. Lee stood at the rail, watching the turmoil and glow of the *Alabama's* wake continuously unroll beneath him. Crossing his arms over his chest he stared into the dark night. His face was as rigid as a block of granite as his country slowly faded into the distance. His thoughts turned to battles past, victories and losses. Faces, some long dead, some still living, slowly paraded through his mind. He grimaced as he remembered valiant sacrifice and undaunted heroism, mistakes made and opportunities lost. It was almost dawn before he finally returned to his cramped, small cabin. His last thought before sleep claimed him was, *this time, I will not fail, I will not*!

CHAPTER TWELVE

July, 1865

Port of Vera Cruz, Mexico

The city was a sun-baked seaport on the southeast coast of Mexico. It had been founded almost three hundred years earlier as an advance base for Spanish Conquistadors searching for New World riches. Its superior harbor, lack of adequate defenses, and distance from Mexico City, made it ideal from the conspirators' point of view.

As part of the "Phoenix Gambit," Mexican units under the command of Santa Anna's General, Miguel Garcia, had taken the lightly defended city. Numerous scars from musket balls and a few craters from artillery rounds was all that remained to attest to the French Foreign Legion's defense.

The Confederate flotilla, which arrived on station before dawn, lay at anchor in the harbor. Only the smallest of the heavily laden ships were responding gently to the play of the ocean, moving in a slow roll, more soothing than otherwise. The tropical sun provided a warmth that was nicely balanced by a gentle breeze from the Gulf. Hordes of cutters and longboats swarmed around the cargo ships, transferring the Army of Northern Virginia from ships to shore.

One of the largest structures in Vera Cruz was the original Spanish fort. It had recently been the recipient of a substantial physical upgrade, preparatory to hosting this event. Several large tents had been set up on the parade grounds in order to provide additional opportunities for business and social interaction. On this day they were filled to overflow as the introductions began.

"General Lee, President Davis, I present to you Antonio Lopez Santa Anna," said Breckenridge with a flourish, "leader of the Revolutionary Party of Mexico." With a wave he indicated two groups of men standing behind the Mexican. "These men are the party military and civil leadership and representatives of the Council of Five Hundred."

"It is a great pleasure to finally meet Your Excellency," said Davis.

"Yes, my friend, I am equally pleased. There are great plans to be made. We must grasp history and guide it with a firm hand," responded Santa Anna.

"May I suggest that we allow our working teams to commence their labors, while we continue our discussion in a more private setting," offered Davis.

"Absolutely," answered Santa Anna. "You know," he continued, "While I have always felt myself to be a man of great vision and daring, I must say that your aspirations astound me, Jefferson, absolutely astound me. I see a grand and wonderful future before us."

"Your Excellency," responded Davis, "I believe that our two cultures can only have a powerful positive effect on each other. As a united people our ideals will serve to reinforce and support each other." Arm in arm, the two men entered a conference room.

For several years Mexico had been embroiled in a vicious, multi-sided civil war. The first side was the Monarchy of Maximilian and Josephine. Austrian nobility by birth, they were kept in power by Napoleon III of France, in a misguided attempt to resurrect a French Empire in the Americas. The indigenous Mexican people constituted a hostile population and the government was maintained by a French Foreign Legion Army of twenty seven thousand men.

The second side was the Mexican National Revolutionary Party. The Party was divided into two opposing forces led respectively by Santa Anna and Benito Juarez. Santa Anna, having seen the possibilities inherent in Breckenridge's overtures, had immediately redoubled his efforts to assume a leadership position. He had been very successful. His power base was Mexican agri-business, industry and finance along with many middle class professionals.

Benito Juarez, his primary opposition for control of the Revolutionary Party, was a democratic populist, who advocated a democratic, religiously-oriented, government. His support came from the religious, peasant and working classes.

The third party was the "Council of Five Hundred," representing the *Dons* of Spanish nobility. These were men who were primarily interested in protecting their estates and economic interests, many of which dated back to sixteenth century land grants from the King of Spain. Although this group was numerically inferior, it represented a substantial portion of Mexican industry and capital. These men had accepted Santa Anna's leadership in return for economic guarantees.

It was a testimony to Santa Anna's skill as both a politician and diplomat that he had been able to form a cohesive and functioning, if not fraternal organization, from groups whose unifying force was their hatred of Maximilian and desire for wealth and power. The Confederate negotiators, under Breckenridge, had worked successfully with Santa Anna and the Council of Five Hundred to create an alliance, with the goal of uniting Mexico under a single government.

Juarez had refused to ally himself with the expatriate Confederates and had vowed to create a Mexican government free of all foreign interference. Juarez's refusal to join the new coalition had created a situation that forced Davis and Santa Anna to regard both he and Maximilian as enemies.

The working title of the Mexican-Confederate alliance was the Revolutionary Council, with political power shared by Santa Anna and Davis. The council itself, with Breckenridge serving as lead negotiator, had been pursuing a vigorous foreign policy initiative with England and Prussia. In exchange for the promise of allowing substantial foreign involvement in Mexico, Central and South America, essentially gutting the Monroe Doctrine, both countries had agreed to totally rearm and re-supply the Revolutionary Army. They had also agreed to provide substantial loans for infrastructure improvements. Both countries would also provide minimal active military support. This support had been already provided in the form of naval units jointly based in Bermuda and assigned to protect the convoys of supply ships off Vera Cruz.

On the political front, both England and the Prussia had, with stipulation, agreed to recognize the Revolutionary Council as a legitimate government. Recognition was conditional upon the successful solution of both the Emperor

Maximilian and Benito Juarez issues and the creation of a stable Mexican government.

As soon as the Confederate leadership had been off-loaded from the ships, Davis and Santa Anna set the wheels in motion. The meeting of the Revolutionary Military High Command, attended by all officers above regiment level command, was held on the top floor of the old Spanish fortress, with its breathtaking view of the harbor and the ships at anchor. Several tarpaulins, rippling gently in the offshore breeze, provided shade for the assembled generals.

Just before Lee and Venable entered the meeting Lee turned to his aide and said, "Colonel, what I'm about to tell these officers may not sit well with some of them. I want you to watch them. Tell me who responds with anger or fear. It is imperative that I know how they react."

"As you wish, sir," responded Venable.

When Lee entered, followed by his aide carrying a stack of papers, the officers stood as one and saluted. "Gentlemen," said Lee, returning the salute. "I have called for a meeting of general officers, in order to inform you of the decisions that have been made regarding our combined forces. The first step will be to insure that all our troops are fully supplied. Each soldier will receive a complete field kit including a rifle, bayonet, uniform and back-pack. The second step will be to reorganize our forces into three Corps commanded respectively by Generals Longstreet, A. P. Hill, and Garcia. Army of Northern Virginia units will be collapsed into existing regiments and brigades on a state level. All units will be brought to full combat strength. Forces representing the Council of Five Hundred, as well as those under the command of General Santa Anna, will also be completely re-supplied.

All these commands will be integrated at Brigade level, and then reorganized into the three Corps."

At this statement there was a stir among the assembled officers, with several groups of Mexicans and Confederates talking among themselves in hushed tones. As the buzz of conversation grew in volume General Garcia quietly scrutinized Lee. He thought, an ambitious, but quite appropriate plan, General. It is one thing to suggest it, but can you enforce it. Ah, well, my General, time will tell.

Lee resumed speaking, in a louder, gruffer tone and the group responded with silence. "We will also take this opportunity to uniform unit size. Infantry divisions will be composed of three brigades. Each brigade will be three regiments strong, with each regiment having five companies. Company strength will be one hundred men. Finally, each Infantry Corps will have field-artillery batteries and one cavalry brigade incorporated as a permanent part of its table of organization."

He paused for a moment, his eyes surveying the assembled officers, allowing them some time to digest the information, before continuing. "Lastly, we will begin a rigorous training schedule, in order to allow for force integration and coordination. We must also devise tactics that are favorable for the new equipment, specifically our new breech-loading infantry rifle. Distribution of supplies, equipment and training schedules will be handled by Divisional Commanders and will be based on the schedule created by myself."

Lee stopped again and looked slowly around the room, taking stock of the mixed emotions on the faces of his generals. "Gentlemen, I know this is a great deal for you to digest at once. I am aware of the difficulties inherent in these changes. However, we must adapt to our circumstances if we are to be victorious. Our enemies are many and powerful. If we are not successful now I do not see another chance. It is quite simply do or perish. Corps Commanders will remain to assist me in developing strategies for dealing with the French Foreign Legion forces; all other officers are to rejoin your troops. You are dismissed!" As the assembled officers filed out he thought, harsh, but necessary. They need to understand we're in this together, each of us, all of us.

Several days after the arrival of the Army of Northern Virginia a fleet of cargo ships arrived at Vera Cruz. They were part of the agreed upon European support. The vessels carried uniforms and equipment as well as light and heavy ordinance for the army. They flew flags representing a dozen nations, and were escorted by a squadron of frigates flying the English flag.

Several days later found Venable and Lee riding towards one of the bivouac areas. Row upon row of neat lines of tents in company and regiment formations encircled the city. Stopping before a tent, Lee dismounted, causing a small stir as his escort troopers hastened to dismount and maintain their cordon of security.

"Easy, son, easy," he murmured to a cavalryman who had shoved a Mexican soldier back in an effort to clear an area for the two officers. "We all wear the same uniform and every soldier must be treated with due regard."

The two officers walked slowly down the ranks of tents, continuing their inspection on foot, noting that every soldier sported the new uniform of butternut tunic and white pants. Each man had a complete compliment of field equipment including a Snider-Enfield Mark III breech-loading rifle.

This was a state-of-the-art infantry weapon, vastly superior in both range and firepower to the muzzle loading weapons still standard issue to Union soldiers. A bit further on they came upon the artillery park, ten batteries worth, four of them 10 lb. Parrot siege guns, the rest lighter, 3 inch rifles, highly-mobile fieldpieces. All sixty guns, complete with caisson, were fresh from Prussian foundries

"It has been a long time since our men have been so well supplied and fed," said Lee. "God knows they have earned it."

"As you say, sir," answered Venable, "it has been years since all of them have been wearing shoes and eating three meals a day."

Lee's face darkened as he replied, "Let them enjoy their new found wealth, they'll be in the thick of it soon enough." After a short pause he continued, "We must monitor the adjustments we have made to our combat formations. Successful integration will be a keystone to future success." He glanced at Venable as he said, "Some of our officers may be less inclined than others to accept our strategic reality. I need to know who they are."

"As you require, sir," was Venable's response.

General Custer's Command, Central Texas

Far to the north and west a fat, orange-white sun sat high in a cloudless sky. It glared mercilessly down on General Custer's pursuit column, as they made their way across the arid land of east-central Texas. Heat lay like a thick, heavy, blanket as if trying to smother the weary troopers as they walked along leading their equally exhausted mounts. As they drove south, pushing hard, each footfall of man and beast created small explosions of dry-caked dirt. Sand, sandblasted rocks and an occasional dead tree or spiky cactus standing lonely sentry duty beside the trail were the only things to be seen.

"This is about the most godforsaken country I have ever had the misfortune to march through," said Colonel Reno, as he tried in vain to speak without adding to the mouth full of grit already coating his tongue and teeth. "Lots and lots of nothing as far as the eye can see."

"However bad it is for us, it's worse for them. We're pushing them hard," said Custer, with a glance at the discarded military hardware and occasional dead horse or hastily dug grave that marked the Confederate route. "I still can't figure out where that bastard Forrest is taking his command. There is nothing ahead of us but more cactus and then Mexico," he continued.

"If he crosses the border I expect our chase will end with an empty bag," said Reno.

"Unfortunately, I believe you are right, Colonel," rejoined Custer. "The last thing we need now is another enemy."

Several days later they caught up with a portion of the Confederate forces.

"Gather round, Gentleman. I want everyone on the same page before we go into action," instructed Custer, as he addressed his assembled unit commanders. He indicated positions on the outskirts of the town as displayed on the map spread out on the ground before them. "Forrest has left a substantial force as a rear-guard to hold Laredo. The rebels have dug in around the entire perimeter of the city. Their lines are supported by strong points with artillery here, here and here," he continued, using his finger as a pointer.

"I propose to divide our command into three separate forces." Custer paused at the murmur of apprehension his remark had caused. "I am aware of the potential dangers, but time is of the essence. We cannot allow the main force to escape while we bring up reinforcements. Therefore, I consider the risk both necessary and acceptable."

"The command will be divided as follows. Colonel Reno will remain here with the 1st Minnesota. Colonel Benteen will take the 2nd Michigan and move to this position." He indicated a series of dry washes west of town. He looked at Benteen, said, "Your force will dismount and assume blocking positions. I will take the 4th Ohio and attack their lines from this point to the east. Colonel Reno, you will assault from the north at the same time. This gives the enemy two options, stand and die, or continue running south. By leaving them this opening we allow them the opportunity to run."

Custer, reins held tightly in his left fist, right hand holding his saber at the salute, followed closely by his flag, trumpeter and gallopers, cantered across the front rank of cavalry. The Union force waited in formation in a wide gully about a mile from the Confederate defensive positions. The veteran troopers sat their horses, patiently awaiting the assault order.

Reaching the far right of the first rank where the regimental flag flew, he wheeled his horse around and, unable to resist the gesture, raked lightly with his spurs causing his mount to rear, pawing the air with its front hooves. He sat his horse for a brief moment, absorbing it, the men and horses four ranks deep, the fluttering flags, the earth and sky. Magnificent, by God, and terrible in its beauty, he thought! Whirling his saber over his head he shouted, "Follow me!" Without even a glance to the rear he advanced!

As the bugle notes of "Charge" rang out, the dust covered blue ranks moved forward as one, guiding their horses with their knees, each trooper holding a revolver in his left hand and a saber in the right. First at a trot, then a canter and finally a gallop, with flags streaming, they swept down upon the waiting Confederates!

Fountains of dirt erupted in scarlet flashes as the Union horse-artillery found the range and began to pound the enemy fortifications. Defensive fire took its toll of trooper and horse alike as the charge rapidly closed on the Confederate position.

Reaching the dug-in enemy, the charge dissolved into a wild series of deadly group and individual melees as the combatants tried desperately to kill in order not to be killed.

Some troopers raced over and past their foe, then turned their mounts about in order to attack again from the rear, while other troopers dismounted in the enemy lines to fight hand-to-hand.

Custer galloped directly at the dismounted Confederate cavalry to his front, targeting a group of five sheltering behind a fallen tree. As he closed he aimed his pistol and fired three shots, causing one man to clutch himself and fall to the ground. Racing on he used his legs to signal his horse to leap over the obstruction and slashed viciously down with his right hand.

As the horse leaped over the tree trunk, the descending blade opened a kneeling trooper from neck to butt. The stricken soldier screamed, dropped his weapon and desperately tried to clasp his hands over his blood-drenched back. Continuing on for a few strides, Custer wheeled his horse about to continue the fight. One of the remaining grey-clad troopers was kneeling over the slashed soldier, attempting to provide some first aid. Custer aimed his revolver and fired the remaining three rounds, watching for only a second as his target slumped to the ground. Spurring his horse again, he attacked the last enemy soldier who was still facing the other way, firing at the Union troops all around him. In the split second before Custer's saber decapitated him the Confederate began to whirl about, as if sensing his doom.

As the blue waves rolled over and around them the defenders began falling back. Some units retreated in orderly ranks while others simply broke and raced for the imagined safety of Laredo. As the Confederates began to withdraw from their prepared positions, Union troops dismounted, formed ranks and followed their foe into the town.

The combat became fierce, house-to-house. Refusing to retreat, grey-clad soldiers stubbornly held each position as long as possible; sometimes mounting small, fierce counterattacks, sometimes dying where they stood rather than surrendering. On more then one occasion they surrendered a building only when it started to burn down around them.

Slowly, inexorably, the Confederates were forced back by unrelenting pressure from Custer's men. Eventually their lines constricted until they held only the town square and a few adjacent buildings. Custer, who had positioned himself in the thick of the fighting, ordered a cease fire and sent a flag of truce to offer them the opportunity to surrender. When the offer was rejected, he promptly brought up heavy weapons and ordered his artillery to bombard the defender's positions at point-blank range. After some time he followed that with a final assault by his dismounted cavalry.

The smell of gunpowder mingled with the stench of burning wood and flesh as Custer made his way through the dead and dying that littered what had been downtown Laredo's main street. He stopped for a moment as the high-pitched, almost human scream of a horse in agony ripped the air. The shriek ended abruptly with the sound of a colt forty-five discharging a single round. Reaching the center of town he and his escorts dismounted. Custer then climbed a few steps to stand on the town hall porch to await reports from his unit commanders.

A body wearing faded grey hung limply from a second story window of a building across the square. A dark stream of blood had drained from the soldier, staining the parched wood of the store front. Around the town many buildings had been set afire during the battle and as yet there was no attempt to put out the blazes. The unchecked conflagration was slowly consuming what was left of the town; towers of reeking smoke spewing into the air and slowly spreading downwind.

"General, sir," said Colonel Reno, reining up his horse and coughing violently in the acrid, smoke-laced air, "they are broken. Those who aren't dead or wounded have finally surrendered. It appears your gamble has paid off handsomely, sir."

"The secret to a successful gamble, Colonel," came the response, "lies in knowing when. We'll leave a regiment as garrison and continue on at first light," continued Custer. "We must keep the pressure on Forrest."

Mexico City, Mexico

The midsummer sun glared harshly through the tall, arched windows of Emperor Maximilian's office, on the top floor of his palace. The stained-glass tinted light threw a cacophony of colors cascading over the floor and furniture. In the center of the room Emperor Maximilian and his military commander, Foreign Legion General Laurency discussed the situation.

Maximilian, an Austrian noble, had been forced upon an unwilling Mexico by the French Emperor, Napoleon III, due to insolvency by the Mexican government. A Foreign Legion force had been dispatched to keep Maximilian in power. General Laurency, the Legion commander, was a competent, experienced commander, who, because of the unrealistic political ambitions of Napoleon III, had been put in a militarily untenable position.

He had a veteran force of twenty-seven thousand infantry and cavalry. His units were already engaged with two separate hostile forces, those of Santa Anna and those of Juarez. In addition to maintaining two separate field armies he was also required to garrison a number of cities throughout Mexico. Now he needed to create a force capable of dealing with this new, unexpected and massive threat.

"My Lord," said General Laurency, "we have confirmation of reports that large numbers of American Confederate troops have landed at Vera Cruz. They have been met by rebel units under the command of Santa Anna and have received substantial supplies and equipment from a sizable contingent of English and Prussian ships. We estimate their combined force at somewhere between fifty to seventy thousand men. This force includes a heavy weapons component. As our entire complement in Mexico numbers twenty seven thousand we must re-evaluate our military position."

"I will notify my cousin, the Emperor, and press for political action and reinforcements," responded Maximilian.

"General, I task you with providing us with enough time to develop a political response to this incursion. Use all the forces at your disposal."

"As you command," answered Laurency.

General Custer's Command, South Texas

While events continued to unfold in Mexico, to the north General Custer's pursuit column was nearing the Texas-Mexico Border. Lead elements of Custer's exhausted cavalry columns reached a bluff that overlooked the Rio Grande River, the border between Mexico and the United States. Here the trail of debris that marked Forrest's route continued on, first entering then exiting the river, heading south into the trackless mountains and desert that was northern-central Mexico.

"Well, Gentleman, it appears our Confederate friends have abandoned all hope in their cause, packed up their bags and run away," said Custer. "I'd expected something more from Forrest."

Turning, Custer issued his orders. "Colonel Reno, have your command conduct a thorough search of both banks for at least a hundred miles east, I'll send Colonel Benteen west. I want strong security checkpoints at every possible crossing."

"Yes, sir," responded Reno, with a salute. He wheeled his horse about, calling for his banner and trumpeter to follow him as he galloped off to join his command and continue the search.

Custer sat for a moment, gazing at the slow-moving river and asked himself, what in the world was Forrest doing?

Where was he going and, perhaps even more important, why? The blue sky and desert sands offered no answer. He tugged at his horse's reins and led his troops back north.

Once he reached Laredo he sent a communication to General Sherman in Washington that said, "General Forrest's forces crossed the Rio Grande River and entered Mexico on or about July 30th. I have found no evidence of a return north. I have established headquarters at Laredo and will remain on post until receipt of new orders."

CHAPTER THIRTEEN

August, 1865

Washington, D. C.

After two operations and a lengthy, pain-filled convalescence, Easy Sinclair had finally been discharged from the Washington military hospital. Underweight and pale, he sought out the duty officer at the hospital and was happily surprised at the news that he had been issued a thirty-day pass. It was effective upon his discharge from the hospital, courtesy of Captain Thomas's efforts on his behalf.

First he stopped at the paymaster's office. Then he went to the train station to buy tickets to Hartford, Connecticut, the station nearest his home town of Naugatuck. After purchasing his ticket he returned to his quarters to pack his meager belongings. Carrying all his worldly possessions in a sack, he returned to the station, to await his transportation home.

Arriving in Hartford, he proceeded to a local blacksmith shop where, in deference to his wound, he rented a horse and buggy for the final leg of his trip home. Traveling slowly through the rolling Connecticut hills, the neat, tidy family farms gave him a sense of comfort and serenity. Reaching the top of a low hill only a few miles from his home, he stopped and dismounted from the buggy to stretch his legs and enjoy the scenery.

From his vantage point he could see the bounty of the region's summer crops. Acres of neatly tended hay and alfalfa for the livestock competed with corn, cabbage, string beans, and potatoes. Orchids of fruit trees ripened on the slopes of adjacent hills. In the distance, herds of milk cows and goats grazed their respective meadows. The rich soil of the well-tended farms was bursting with growth.

After a brief rest Easy remounted and continued his journey. A short time later he reached a rutted, narrow, pop-lar-tree bordered path that wandered off to his left. Taking the path, he soon came upon a house that was situated just below the crest of a rock-strewn hill.

The barns, equipment sheds and chicken houses, all whitewashed and in excellent repair, formed a rough square immediately behind the residence. They, along with the two-floor, stone-and-wood, porch-fronted cottage, were surround-ed by well tended apple and peach tree orchards that covered most of the hill. A shallow, bubbling brook cut through the hillside and curved around to bisect the path he was on, some hundred feet from the house. A stout, wooden bridge pro-vided a secure crossing.

The Sinclair homestead, thirty acres of prime farm land, was filled to bursting with crops and livestock and gave mute testimony to the hard work and skill of the family. Easy pulled gently on the reins and the horse obediently stopped. He sat and absorbed the feel and smell of home for a few quiet moments, then urged his horse forward.

Nearing the house he stopped as he saw an older version of himself walk out of the barn, hoe in hand. Sensing some presence, the figure turned slightly and upon seeing Easy dropped the hoe and with a cry of delight advanced with arms opened wide. Easy stepped down and moved towards his father, arms akimbo. The two men, father and son, met and held each other tightly for a few precious seconds before separating to hold each other at arms length for a moment more to savor each other. Self-conscious at their teary-eyed condition, both grinned inanely for a few seconds.

"Why didn't you let us know you were coming home, son? Your mom will be very glad to see you right enough, but she'll be mad as a wet hen for not knowing before hand!" rambled James, his father. Stopping, he pulled back, and grasping his son's arm, looked him over again and said, "Perhaps we won't mention the wound for a while, OK?"

"Sounds like a plan to me, Dad," Easy replied.

They continued on to the wide, covered porch fronting the house, where a young woman sat repairing a pair of men's pants.

"Guess who stopped by for a visit, Sarah?" queried James/

Sarah, Easy's younger sister, glanced up, anger at this unwanted intrusion of her labors clear on her face. "Tell our visitor I'll... Oh my God!" her voice rose to a scream as she recognized her brother. She dropped the clothing and threw herself from her chair, actually leaping upon him, laughing and crying in equal measures. "Oh, Ezekiel, Oh, Easy," she repeated as she held him tightly, tears coursing silently down her cheeks, "just wait till Mom sees you!"

Laughing, and putting an arm around his dad and sister, he said, "Then let's let her know the good news." Accompanied by his father and sister, he walked up the steps, opened the kitchen door and with admirable nonchalance said, "Mother I'm home. What's for dinner?"

After a while, when they were all sitting at the family table enjoying a slice of his mother Mary's exquisitely good muffins, Easy, his jaws working industriously, asked, "Where are Joseph and Jacob?" his respectively thirteen and fifteen year old brothers.

"They're plowing the south fields and will be home shortly," responded his father.

"When I left for West Point, neither one could plough worth a darn," said Easy.

"Between the Point and the Army it's been almost three years, son. In that time they've become men. They both do a man's labor," replied James, equal measures of pride and sadness evident in his voice. "All my sons are men, men fully grown."

Easy, sensing his father's thoughts replied, "This war is all but over, the drafts are done with, and soon the Army will be discharging men rather than enlisting them, Dad. About the only important thing left is dealing with Lee and Davis. The boys are safe."

As day became evening, two figures accompanied by a horse-drawn cart appeared. Focused entirely on their task, the two young men entered the barn, removed the horse from the cart, rubbed down, fed, and quartered it, then made their way towards the house. Nearing the porch they stopped, and finally seeing their older brother, whooped with joy and ran to embrace him.

Easy had responded in kind, and the three young men met on the front lawn in a welter of hugs and playful punches.

Eventually, the initial greetings complete, all adjourned to the porch where the entire family sat and shared. After a while mother and daughter went inside to prepare dinner.

The first few days passed in a haze of family and familiar farm chores, keeping him busy from dawn to dusk. On the morning of the fourth day, having just finished breakfast, he said, "I think I'll ride into town today, Dad."

"Sounds like a fine idea, son. As a matter of fact, I wouldn't mind a trip to Delaney's myself," said his father, naming a well known local pub.

Easy glanced at his father just in time to catch the swiftly-disappearing, mischievous smile. He laughed, then sobering instantly, asked, "Have you seen her, Dad?"

"She's a busy, hard-working woman, son, that's really all I can say."

Easy nodded and went into the barn to saddle a horse. He soon arrived in town. He dismounted and tied his horse to the rail in front of Conklin's' Dry Goods. He stepped onto the wooden sidewalk, only to hesitate before entering the building. To his surprise he felt the same flash of fear that he felt just before leading an attack. Taking a deep breath, he pushed through the door to the accompaniment of a tinkling bell. He took several steps to his left and stopped.

She was behind the counter. Her attention was fixed on the customer before her. He stood there for a moment enjoying just the sight of her. Something, some subliminal warning, caused her to suddenly frown, and then glance in his direction. For a single instant they locked eyes. Despite the flush radiating across her features, she coolly consummated the exchange with her customer, then turned to face him.

During his absences they had corresponded occasionally but had made no firm commitment to each other. Each had gone about their lives, with the other a constant presence, deep in the recesses of their minds.

The customer left and she looked at him, her hazel eyes locking onto his blue ones, for what seemed to Easy to be an eternity. She broke the silence with, "Hello, Easy, it's been a long time." There was a short pause as she regarded him, then, "you've been hurt," concern plain in her voice.

"Yes," he replied, "But I'll be fine soon enough." He hesitated only a second, then said, "You look great, Becca."

"Do I, Easy?"

"You always look great to me."

An awkward silence ensued as the two of them sought to mend the damage to their relationship caused by of years of parting.

"I'll be home for almost two weeks and I want to spend time with you, Becca. That is, of course, if you're not spoken for."

"I am not spoken for, Easy." A smile eased across her features and she said, "I would like to spend time with you."

Easy, his heart suddenly beating like a bass drum, palms wet with sweat, stepped closer to the counter, asked, "Can we start with dinner tonight?"

"Yes, Easy, I would like that very much."

In a second they'd closed the distance between them and were wrapped in an embrace. If not for the timely ringing of the door bell they might have found themselves in a most embarrassing position.

For the next few days they fell into an easy routine. He rented a room in town and would arrive at the store each morning so that they could spend their time together, mostly working, sometimes just sitting and talking. After dinner they would sit together on the porch of her family home, savoring the soft summer nights, once again becoming comfortable in each others company.

Sometimes Easy would play his harmonica and she would accompany him on her guitar and sing gospel tunes. On the evening of their last day together they had finished dinner, and were sitting next to each other on the porch swing of the Conklin home. Her mother was in the kitchen with her brother playing with toy soldiers Easy had purchased.

She placed her hand in his callused one and looking him directly in the eyes asked, "What now? Where will we go from here, Easy?" leaving unspoken the fact that he would return to the Army.

After a moments hesitation Easy answered, "Becca, it's not done yet. Lee, Davis and a good deal of the Army of Northern Virginia are still out there. The job's got to be finished."

A soft smile on her face, she said, "And, of course, you must finish it." Anticipating his response, she quickly leaned towards him and placed a finger over his lips while saying, "Oh, Easy, if you didn't need to finish the job you wouldn't be the man I love."

Without thought Easy turned to her and their lips touched, first gently, then more firmly, as if to seal their pact. Their embrace grew more impassioned, each holding tightly to the other. They eventually broke apart. Rebecca grasped Easy's hand, looked deeply into his eyes, then turned and led him towards her bedroom. The next morning, Easy bade her goodbye and returned to his family's farm.

After Easy returned home from his cherished time with Rebecca, the Sinclair family spent the remaining time renewing and strengthening their ties. Every day Easy shared the farm chores with his father and brothers, relishing the opportunity to exercise his still recuperating body. Each evening they would gather together to talk and share plans and dreams. On their last Sunday together the entire family went to service at the Presbyterian Church, where his mother very active in parish affairs.

Easy's Dad was lukewarm towards religion, not an unbeliever, but more undecided. As his children grew he had taken pains to impart to each his three-rule philosophy of life. Rule one was treat everyone the way you want to be treated. Rule two was to be true to your beliefs but listen to the other fellow. Rule three was that two rules were all you needed. He occasionally annoyed his more religious wife by saying, "Sometimes ten rules are just too many."

Rebecca, along with her mother and brother, were at the service. After the service ended Easy left his family to join her. The two strolled along the stream that ran beside the church, hand in hand.

"I'll be leaving tomorrow morning. I don't know how long I'll be gone, but it is my intent to return."

With the shadow of a smile dimpling her face Rebecca turned to face him and asked, "And why would you do that, Easy?"

He looked deeply into her eyes and answered plainly, "For you."

"I'll be here, Easy."

The pact made, they continued their walk in silence, each pursuing private thoughts. At dawn the following day Easy, his family and Rebecca set out for the train station. Arriving early, they sat side-by-side in the cramped railroad station, waiting for the 2:30 to Boston.

"What are your plans now, son? Will you still make a career of the army? Once the war's over will you return to West Point?" asked his father.

"I truly don't know what I'll do. I can continue in the military, or perhaps chance may show me another path. There's a lot of country out west. Might be something for a man to do out there," said Easy.

"What you mean is that there will be danger and action. Don't bother to deny it. I know you as well as I know myself. If I hadn't met your mother when I was furloughed after the Mexican War ..., his voice trailed off as his memory took flight. Shaking himself he continued, "Not that I'm not totally content mind, it's just that sometimes you wonder about what's out there." He looked at his first born and said, "I won't tell you to be careful, but I will tell you to always measure your risk against your need, then make your decision and follow through."

"I will, Dad, I promise," Easy said, as the train pulled into the station.

Standing up Easy bade farewell to his brothers and sister, kissed his mother and went to his father, the two first grasped hands, then hugged each other tightly. Lastly Easy and Rebecca faced each other. Rebecca, arms clasped around Easy, regarded him. "Be safe, my love. I'll be here when you're done. I love you."

Easy grinned down into her soft countenance and replied, "I'll be back as soon as I can. I love you." With no further ado they parted ways. Easy boarded the train, his mind filled with the scent and vision of Rebecca. As the locomotive jerked the cars into motion Rebecca stood on the platform until the last car was lost to sight, remembering the feel of his muscled body and the firmness of his lips.

When he returned to Washington, Easy discovered he had received a battle field promotion to Second Lieutenant. He was then advised he was slated to be an officer in a regiment that was in the process of being formed.

Having nothing but time on his hands he took a room in a boarding house and set about sampling the more restrained and cultured delights the city had to offer. A few days later, returning to his hotel from a days sightseeing, he was advised that a man had left a note for him. Reading it, he discovered it was from his friend, Abel Thomas, now a major.

Major Thomas's unit had been one of those brought into the city for security duties. The entire regiment had been essentially detailed to police activities. These extra precautions were an aftermath from the shock of the brutal and deadly attacks on the leadership of the Federal government.

Following the instructions found in the note, at noon the next day he entered a Washington cafe, walked to a table already occupied and sat down.

"You look well, Easy," said Abel, "very well, indeed."

"I feel good, Sir," responded Sinclair, "as a matter of fact, I'm getting rather bored with this rehabilitation thing."

"Are you, now?" queried Thomas. "You know I've always thought very highly of your abilities as a soldier. I truly believe you've a great future in the military. You have a rare talent and the country needs men like you. There's something in the newspaper that will engage your interest. Have you read today's paper?" he asked, handing a copy of the *Washington Post* to Easy.

About half way down page two an article had been circled. The article was about the assassinations and how the Union had been caught completely unaware. It further stated that the President had created a new command. Recruiting for this "New and Exciting Force" to be composed exclusively of, "Men of courage, tenacity and patriotism who are prepared to defend their country to the utmost," had already begun. The article ended by stating that the new force was to be called the "Office of Strategic Services."

"What has this to do with me?" asked Sinclair, "I'm an infantry soldier."

"You are a natural leader, cool under fire, resourceful and determined. Just the kind of man this... um, this Office is looking for," answered Thomas. "You are wasted where you are now. You still have a few days convalescence left. Give this consideration. I think its right for you." concluded Thomas, rising from the table and grasping Easy's hand. "Duty calls, son," he said. "Whatever you choose, God be with you."

A week later, having been declared fit for duty, and having given much consideration to Thomas' comments, he entered a small Washington office. It was located in the back of a nondescript office building. Easy entered, walked up to the man seated behind a desk and asked, "Is this where I find out about the Strategic Service? "

"That's us," responded the seated man, standing up and offering his hand. "And who might you be?" he asked.

"Ezekiel Sinclair," was the response.

"My name is Andy, Ezekiel. Have a seat and we'll talk."

After a few hours of conversation that focused on his military and strangely, his childhood, Easy was told to return to his hotel. He was told that all the information he had provided Andy would be carefully reviewed and that if accepted into the program he would receive a response.

Washington D.C.

It was a typical Washington, D.C. summer day, hot, humid, and still. The meeting was being held on the top floor of a newly-constructed, four-story, brick, government office building. The windows on both walls were wide open with the shades drawn high in a fruitless attempt to abate the heat.

The men in the room represented the political, industrial and military power of the Union. President Andrew Johnson brought the meeting to order with a single brisk rap of his gavel. "Gentlemen, let us come to order. Each of you has a copy of our agenda. We'll begin by reviewing our current military situation which is, to say the least, unique in the annals of warfare. Would you agree, General Sherman?" he asked.

"Absolutely, Mr. President," replied Sherman. "As near as we can discern, President Davis and several cabinet members, along with a major portion of the Army of Northern Virginia, have left our country and have formed some sort of alliance with a faction of the Mexican-French War. It also appears," continued Sherman, "that a few cavalry brigades and an unknown number of civilians under the command of General Bedford Forrest have crossed the Rio Grande into Mexico. Finally, the last field force of the Confederates, a command under Generals Johnston and Stuart, was engaged by a force under General Warren. The battle was in northern Florida. The result was that General Stuart was killed and General Johnston captured. He has been sent to Camp Douglas and will eventually stand trial along with the others. This constitutes the complete defeat of all organized Confederate military forces in the USA. It seems that a few units will attempt to operate as guerrilla commands, but they are practically without supplies and present little danger."

Turning to Mead he asked, "Do we have numbers on Lee's forces, General?"

"We think he can field a combined army of as much as fifty thousand infantry with an unknown amount of artillery. Our information is that all of his equipment is state-of-art and in several instances superior to ours," was the answer.

Congressman O'Reilly said, "There are two separate problems then. First is to decide what to do with the southern states. Second is what to do about the Confederate activities in Mexico."

"It is our intent to divide the south into Zones of Reconstruction," said President Johnson. "Each Zone will have an appointed governor and general to handle civilian or military affairs, as the case may be. Communication and travel between Zones will be highly restricted. As each zone completes its reconstruction process, the individual state will be re-admitted into the Union. This will make for an orderly and controllable process for eventually reestablishing the United States of America. An additional problem is that we now have several thousand ex-confederate officers as well as the senior elected officials from the rebel states as prisoners. These men are potential trouble-makers and must be incarcerated. It has been decided to keep them all at our detention facility, Camp Douglas. As some of you may know, the camp has been designated as the official prison for all secessionist prisoners. We plan to eventually try them all for treason."

As he spoke, he walked over to a large wall map hanging in a corner of the room, and using a pointer, he directed their view to the area that had constituted the Confederate States of America. The map showed the old Confederacy divided into several areas. Johnson turned back to the table, handed the pointer to Sherman and sat down.

"We will attempt to maintain control by occupying only critical points," said Sherman, as he walked to the map and began pointing. "By placing troops in or near the main population and manufacturing areas that are left we can effectively control just about everything that's worth having. Garrison forces will be infantry units and cavalry." He continued, "We estimate that we are going to need at least three hundred thousand troops for occupation duties."

"There is another issue, one that could become severe. Most of the men currently under arms will have their enlistment expire within the next eight months and it is highly unlikely any useful numbers will remain in service now that the war is won. Our manpower issues will become critical," he concluded.

Patrick O'Reilly stood up, and in a stern voice said, "If you thought the New York riots were bad, just try drafting our boys after the victory has been won. If we don't share in the fruits of victory there will be hell to pay, I guarantee it."

"I understand and appreciate your position." concluded Sherman. "We must find an alternative source for our manpower needs. The free southern slaves could provide a substantial amount of numbers and we have already had success in fielding northern Negro units."

"Gentlemen," said President Johnson, "Our nation is still in mourning, still trying to recover from the horror of that act of infamy. We had no idea what our enemy was planning, no intelligence gathering apparatus to guide us. We were in effect, operating completely in the dark. This country can never allow itself to be in such a position of ignorance again. There must be an agency of government responsible for providing a continuing source of intelligence regarding the activity of our enemies, wherever or whoever they may be, either foreign or domestic. I have therefore decided to create a new government organization. This organization will be responsible for obtaining information relating to the security of the people and government of the United States. It will also report on the activities of foreign governments as well as our enemies, whether at home or abroad. It will report to the Committee on Military Preparedness and Intelligence."

Standing up and gesturing to the man seated at his right, Johnson continued, "Gentlemen, I present to you Mr. Allen Pinkerton, whom I have appointed to the position of Director of the Office of Strategic Services."

Allan Pinkerton had been born in Scotland and immigrated to the United States in 1842. He was a devout Calvinist and devoted family man. Pinkerton had founded the Pinkerton Detective Agency in 1850. His success at undercover and criminal investigations had led to his being recognized as a highly capable sleuth. Lincoln, in order to counter Confederate spying, had charged him with conducting limited counter-espionage activities in the Washington area.

Following a brief discussion it was determined that the Select Committee on Military Preparedness and Intelligence would be composed of representatives from the military, legislative and executive branches of government. Congressman John O'Reilly was appointed Congressional Representative.

Before adjourning the Committee assigned the OSS two tasks. It was to find and bring to justice the individuals who had assassinated Lincoln, Grant and the Cabinet. It was also to determine the state of affairs regarding Mexico.

Revolutionary Army, Mexico

At the top of a gently slopped hill about a mile southwest of Vera Cruz, General Longstreet sat his mount. From his vantage point above the bustling port city he could see for several miles. To his right was the Gulf, its deep blue providing a vivid contrast to the verdant green of the land. To his left the tents, parade grounds, artillery parks and exercise areas of the combined forces, no, he cautioned himself, the Revolutionary Army, spread like a blanket covering almost everything from the sea to his current position.

The last several weeks had been a non-stop, but mostly successful effort to arm, train and reorganize his command. He had been pleasantly surprised at how effective the amalgamation had been and how the political leadership had united behind Lee. Longstreet had thrown himself into the endeavor wholeheartedly, and he had been very successful. He turned slightly to his left and regarded his Commander, who, along with the ever present security team, was accompanying him on a review of his command, I Corps.

"Well, Sir," he said, "seems that refit and resupply has gone amazingly well."

"Yes," was Lee's response, "as have our restructuring efforts."

Colonel Venable had been both diligent and effective in ferreting out a few of the most blatantly bigoted officers, both Confederate and Mexican, and reporting them to Lee. Each officer had received a severe dressing down and in the event the behavior continued, been summarily relieved from command. This prompt action had been totally supported by both Santa Anna and Davis, along with most of the senior officers, and had been very effective in defusing a potentially dangerous situation.

"My Brigade and Division commanders all report an acceptable level of readiness and are ready to take the field, Sir."

"And you, General, what is your council?" came Lee's reply. "What are your thoughts?"

"Sir, from a tactical standpoint we are ready. Our officers and troops have mastered the use of their new weapons. We have developed and implemented new tactics to maximize their effectiveness. The most important thing now is not to give our enemies any more time to gather strength against us. We must strike as soon and as hard as possible. Hit the Legion, take Mexico City, then proceed against the other forces in the north and south while we reinforce and consolidate the center. I grant you it is an ambitious plan. But with all due respect, it's also a plan that gives us the best opportunity

for success." answered Longstreet. When there was no immediate response, Longstreet glanced at Lee, whose features wore
a slight, tight smile.

"There was a day such an attitude might have had a very
powerful effect, General," was Lee's measured response. "Let
us hope for greater success in our current endeavors."

Longstreet stared straight ahead, remembering a day, a
battle, and a country lost. He turned, looked straight at Lee
and answered, "We must do our duty, to the best of our ability, as we see our duty, sir. I can do no more."

The next morning the Command Staff of the Revolutionary
Army, along with the political leadership, sat around a conference table. The room was on the seaward corner of the top
floor of the fort. Windows provided a panoramic view of the
harbor, as well as welcome ventilation.

Jefferson Davis stood and addressed the group. "General
Lee advises me that we have reached a point where the re-
sumption of military operations can be considered a viable
option. I have called this meeting in order that we may
decide upon our next few moves. Has anyone a particular
plan or option for our council to entertain?" In response to
a quick hand motion from his left, Davis recognized Santa
Anna with a nod and sat down.

Santa Anna stood, and gesturing with his left hand, began to speak. "My friends the time has come to strike hard
at the Legion forces supporting the pretender. They know
we are here. Our cavalry has had several sharp confrontations
with Legion Lancers who are patrolling our perimeter. They
are making every effort to centralize their forces. Thankfully,
they are seriously over-extended and have not completed their
redeployment. I therefore propose an immediate advance on

Pueblo, as it is the only major population and military center between us and Mexico City. Taking Pueblo would clear our way to an advance on the capital and at the same time cement our control of all the area from Pueblo to Vera Cruz."

Lee stood and said, "We have been successful in our integration and reorganization efforts. Our troops are proficient in the use of our new weapons and tactics. As of today, we can field seven infantry divisions, three cavalry divisions and ten batteries of artillery. My senior commanders concur with my assessment of our combat readiness. It is my belief that, as of today, our Army is capable of offensive operations."

After some discussion the Council ordered Lee to move on Pueblo. Early the next morning lead elements of the Revolutionary Army, I Corp, broke camp. As Longstreet's force moved westward from Vera Cruz towards Pueblo, it came under the scrutiny of Legion units. Vera Cruz had been surrounded by Foreign Legion cavalry units tasked with providing continuous intelligence updates to General Laurency.

Captain Alan Petain, A Company, 4th Legion Lancers, swept his kepi from his head, ran his dust covered, blue sleeve across his forehead in a vain attempt to remove the sweat from his brow, succeeding only in re-arranging it, cursed and said, "It appears the rebel Army has begun its offensive."

"Apparently so, sir." responded Lieutenant André Jessup, his executive officer. "They also appear well supplied and equipped. I estimate this unit's strength of roughly fifteen thousand infantry and a thousand cavalry, with perhaps fifty field pieces."

"Thank you, Lieutenant," said Petain. "Send a courier to Pueblo Command advising them."

As they marched eastward Revolutionary Army units were covering ground familiar to many Confederate officers who had served with General Winfield Scott in the Mexican-American War. Lee himself had served as an engineer captain on Scott's staff and had surveyed much of this ground during the assault on Mexico City. Because the terrain was familiar the Army moved fast.

The Legion cavalry slowly withdrew westward, maintaining their position ahead of the advancing Revolutionary Army. They eventually found themselves at the gates of the city of Pueblo. Upon arriving Captain Petain reported to the headquarters of the Pueblo garrison commander, Colonel Charles Fontain.

Captain Petain said, "Our forces total four hundred infantry, one hundred lancers and ten canons, for which we have only twenty five rounds of ordnance per gun. I submit to you that our position is untenable."

"So," responded Colonel Fontain, "what do you suggest?"

"I see two choices, my Colonel. A strategic withdrawal or a bayonet attack. Given my love of life I strongly support the former," answered Petain.

"Very well," said the Colonel, with a ghost of a smile, "a strategic withdrawal it is. I will order our troops to prepare to leave."

Two days after the Legion left the city the first of Longstreet's cavalry appeared outside the city gates. When Longstreet advised Lee he had reached Pueblo, Lee ordered him to camp outside it.

The city was situated in the middle of a very wide, shallow valley. Founded in 1588, It had grown from a single Catholic mission until it spread across fully half of the valley floor.

The gleaming whitewashed adobe walls which surrounded Pueblo were ten feet high and five feet thick. While a serious obstacle to Stone Age assault they were totally useless as a defense from four batteries of entrenched 10lb. Parrott siege guns.

Once the mayor formally surrendered the city it lay helpless before them. The Revolutionary Council ordered a celebration and Santa Anna and Davis decided to assume the role of liberators, rather then conquerors. Both men had further decided that they would lead their joint command as a team. They did this in order to motivate their followers, and to enhance the spirit of cooperation between the Mexican and Confederate soldiers. Consistent with that theory, the two men were with the leading Revolutionary Army units to enter the city, riding in the vanguard, side by side. Church bells rang and cheering crowds of peasants and Indians gathered by the eastern gates of the city to await the entrance of the liberating army.

Davis flinched momentarily at an especially vigorous aerial firecracker display that erupted almost directly over the balcony from which the Revolutionary Council observed the celebrations, both in the sky above and the streets below them.

"My countrymen have a great zest for life," said Santa Anna, "and savor any opportunity to show it."

"Yes," agreed Breckenridge, "I can see that they do."

The inhabitants of the city had chafed under the Legion garrison's harsh rule. The French-speaking troops had treated them with disdain and hostility. The celebration of the Legion's defeat lasted long into the warm, starlit Mexican night. Every cantina in the city was filled to overflow with rejoicing citizens, laughing and dancing.

It was scarcely twenty-four hours after the celebrations ended when the work resumed. The Council sat around a heavy mahogany table in what had been the governor's chambers. The chamber's walls were covered by fine tapestries and paintings. The floor was imported marble. The appointments and luxury of the government buildings were in striking contrast to the unadorned adobe construction that composed most of the living quarters in the city.

"Our latest information places Forrest's command south of the Mexican border and completely free of any contact with Union units," said Lee. "He has been instructed to continue at his best possible speed, without making any contact with hostile forces, until our commands are united."

"On the political front I have been advised that pressure will be brought to bear in Washington to minimize interference by the Union regarding our activities here," said Davis. "Circumstances have created a situation where the interests of both Prussia and England are well served by assisting us. Opening trade routes to the Americas and removing French influence are of economic and political value to them."

"This is important news." said Santa Anna. "This will give us more freedom to address the issues of both Maximilian and Juarez with less fear of Union intervention."

"I agree," interjected Breckenridge, who, after a quick glance at John Campbell, continued, "but we must always keep an eye on the Union."

"We can also expect the appearance of units of the English navy in the eastern Gulf of Mexico. Their presence will officially be to preserve complete freedom of international waters to all nations," said Davis, a broad smile on his face. "I also have it on good faith that Bismarck will inform the Union that Prussia will expect them to respect international legalities to the letter."

"Gentlemen," said Santa Anna, raising his glass, "let us toast the continued success of the Revolutionary Council."

CHAPTER FOURTEEN

September, 1865

Washington, D. C.

Easy patiently waited for a response to his application to join the Office of Strategic Services. When it came it was both highly unorthodox and abrupt. Awakened at two in the morning by a loud knock on his door, he was quietly but firmly hustled outside and into a waiting stage by two men who identified themselves as OSS operatives Smith and Jones. The large stage held three other occupants.

Forbidden to talk amongst themselves, they sat in silence while their conveyance sped through the night, windows covered. Arriving some time in mid-afternoon, the same day, the men disembarked to find themselves outside a two-story building.

Standing on the building's porch was a short, bald, middle-aged man. The man introduced himself as Emanuel Short and ordered them into the building. As each person passed through the front door he was given a key with a number on it, reminded to remain silent, and told to ascend the central staircase, find their room and remain in it until called.

Easy found and entered his room, looked about and crossed to the window. Looking down he saw several buildings of varying sizes, all rather nondescript in appearance, all within a few hundred feet of the building he was in. Having completed his reconnaissance, he put the room's only chair next to the window, then sat and awaited events.

Sometime later there was a knock. Opening the door, he discovered Mr. Short, who directed him down the stairs and into a large room occupied by a group of men and, surprisingly, a few women, all seated before a small platform. On the platform was a tall, well-built man of indeterminate age.

"Ladies and Gentlemen," said the man, "allow me to introduce myself. I am William Donovan, Commanding Officer, Office of Strategic Services Training Division, and this is our training facility. For the next eight weeks this will be your home. Those of you who successfully complete the training will be given an opportunity to serve your country as operatives of this organization. You will undergo an intense and grueling training. You will learn hand-to-hand combat, small arms use, demolition and cartography skills as well as escape and evasion techniques. You will become as physically and mentally prepared to successfully complete your mission as we can make you. You will suffer many hardships, and should you complete the training, you will be sent into the field where you will be tasked with identifying and destroying your country's enemies. If there is a man or women here who is having second thoughts about their willingness to sacrifice or even kill for their country, I want you to leave tonight. There will be a stage waiting outside for you at the end of my presentation.

Each of you was given a room number when you entered this building. For as long as you are in training you will be referred to, and will refer to each other, by that number and only that number. No one is to address another trainee by name.

Understand me, ladies and gentlemen; you are in a harsh school. Failure will not be tolerated, and there will be no second chance. If you aren't good enough, you are gone. I wish you every success." Finished, Donavan stood and walked out of the room. As he did so Short stood and directed the men into a large room filled with tables and chairs. Along one wall were several tables filled with food.

"All meals will be served in this room at designated times only," he said, pointing to a schedule tacked to the wall. "If you're not here on time you don't eat."

The training began the next day. Easy, along with a group of nine others, was seated in the hall. General Donovan entered through a side door and strode to a small stage in a corner of the room. There was another door at the back of the stage, next to which Emanuel Short sat.

Donovan walked to an easel which held a large map. Pointing to the map he began to speak. As he did so, the door at the back of the stage opened and a man stepped through it. He walked up behind Donovan, pulled a revolver from his waist-band and fired two shots into his back! The man turned and ran off, exiting by the same door through which he'd entered.

Easy and several others were halfway to the stage door when Short slammed it closed and interposed his body between it and the men running towards him. From the corner of his eye, Easy saw Donovan stand up, apparently having suffered no ill affects from two bullets in his back. Dumbfounded, the running men milled to a stop, confusion rampant.

Easy realized immediately that the entire situation had been a set up and was a test of some sort. He smiled to himself as he tried to determine the exact nature of the test he was certain would come.

Short began walking amongst the trainees handing out pencils and paper. Donovan, seated again on the stage said, "I want a complete description of my assailant, in writing, in less than two minutes."

The training continued. It was designed to give every operative the basic skills they would need in order to function, without detection, in a hostile environment. Physical fitness training consisted mainly of running. Eventually, all successful trainees could cover ten miles without stopping, using a trot-and-walk process.

A makeup artist and an actor spent several days showing the trainees how minimal changes in appearance, gait, and speech could have a substantial effect on how others saw them. The actor walked slowly back and forth in front of the trainee group. He was slightly bent forward at the waist, with a mild limp in his right leg. He held his left arm at an odd angle. His face was the pale grey of an aging invalid.

He began to speak, his voice soft and faltering, almost as if the very act of speaking was too exhausting. "In the trade I am what is referred to as a character actor. One who may be asked to portray people of varied ages and circumstances. Sometimes I may be required to perform several parts in quick succession. It is, therefore, necessary that transformations from one character to another not only be fast and complete but most importantly, believable."

As the man spoke he began to change before their eyes. His arm and spine slowly straightened and the limp became less and less noticeable until it disappeared. He turned his back to the audience for only a moment while his hand, holding a small damp cloth, vigorously wiped his face. When he turned around to face them again he stood tall, a vigorous, healthy, able-bodied man of early middle age!

An engineering officer taught them how to measure distance and height with no other instrumentation except their own body parts, by comparing them to various structures, at different distances. They were taken to view and draw several of Washington's forts and monuments.

Hand-to-hand combat was limited to several lethal or highly disabling moves, practiced until they were second nature. The explanation was that if you had to resort to physical violence then your mission was very likely compromised. Killing, unless it was your intent, might serve no useful purpose. Easy, who enjoyed physical activity, excelled in this arena and was often selected as a sparring partner.

"Sinclair, front and center," ordered the instructor. "Today we're going to learn a few more moves." Looking at Easy, he said, "Attack me!"

Instead of charging in, Easy slowly advanced on the instructor, waiting until their bodies were close before launching himself at his target. The instructor twisted away while grabbing Easy's arm and shoulder and throwing him to the ground. In a flash Easy was up and attacking again, his face set and grim. The ballet of attack and defense continued, with Easy regaining his feet and lunging at the instructor time and time again. More then once the instructor found himself on the receiving end of a punishing blow.

The two men were now breathing heavily, their faces bloodied, eyes grimly focused on each other. The students had formed a circle around the combatants, all eyes now riveted on the spectacle. Finally the instructor became exasperated with Easy's persistence, and having thrown him once again said, "For God's sake Sinclair, will you stay down!"

From his prone position Easy glared his defiance and answered, "No, not till you're down here, too." Easy placed both hands flat on the ground, regained his feet, took a few deep breaths, then advanced yet again. In a carefully calculated move he feinted a lunge to the right, but at the last second before contact twisted left. His body impacted chest to chest with the instructor and both men found themselves on the ground. Easy rolled over, got to his feet and said, "Now it's over."

Operatives were taught there were two cardinal rules of secret operations. Rule one was that the most successful operative was the most invisible operative. Rule two was that if you or your mission was compromised, you should run like hell. However, in tacit acknowledgement that, "even the best laid plans...," trainees learned to kill with their hands, feet and almost anything else that might be available.

Graduation ceremonies were brief and succinct. General Donovan addressed the assembled operatives. "You have proven yourselves to be capable, competent, and willing. You are now Operatives of the Office of Strategic Service. You are the cutting edge of your country's defense."

He paused for a moment and then pointed to a flag on the podium. The flag was a black field with a rendition in silver of the "All Seeing Eye" and the legend "Eternal Vigilance" printed beneath it. Donovan said, "Our flag and our motto, remember them both."

Easy, along with the rest of the group who had successfully completed their training, was immediately posted to one of the OSS regional offices that had been created throughout the occupied southern states.

CHAPTER FIFTEEN

October, 1865

Laredo, Texas Zone of Reconstruction

The sound of hammers and saws reverberated throughout Laredo's downtown area, the smell of fresh-cut wood and saw-dust permeating everything. Reconstruction and expansion continued at a breakneck pace. The city, having been declared the provincial capitol of the "Texas Zone of Reconstruction," an area that included everything from the Mississippi River to the Rocky Mountains, was growing by leaps and bounds. Government buildings for the many departments and offices required by the occupation forces, as well as hotels to house them, were springing up haphazardly on every street and avenue. New roads were being marked out by surveyors as the older ones were repaired and upgraded. Far to the east army engineers were laying railroad track eastward, intending to connect Texas to the eastern states.

"General," said Reno, opening the door to Custer's office, "the delegation from Washington has arrived."

Custer waived an acknowledgment and the Colonel admitted the group of men. "May I present Mr.Garrison of the Office of Strategic Service and Colonel Jeffery from the War Department."

"Welcome to Laredo, such as it is," said Custer, waving his arm to indicate seats around his desk. "Rest easy, gentlemen. Please be seated." After they took chairs he glanced at Garrison, an irritated look appearing briefly on his features, before he continued, "So, what can we do for Washington?"

"Actually, General, it's what Washington can do for you that brings us here," answered Garrison, "but before that Colonel Jeffery has some information for you."

Custer, with a somewhat jaundiced look at the OSS man, interjected, "So. You're from Washington, and you're just here to help me."

Sensing the situation, Jeffrey stood up, said, "It is my pleasure to inform you that you have been promoted to the rank of Major General, US Army. You are appointed to the position of Commander of the Texas Zone of Reconstruction and Commander of the Army of the Rio-Grand. Congratulations, Sir." He offered his hand to Custer.

"A not unexpected turn of events," responded a smiling, rather smug, and somewhat mollified Custer. "All things considered."

"Let me add my congratulations as well," said Garrison, who then continued. "My purpose here is to assume the position of OSS Regional Director for this Zone. My agency was created by direct order of the President. We are primarily a police and intelligence organization. Our task is to insure that our government and military forces will have timely access to intelligence information regarding both internal and external enemies. Our regional headquarters will be here in Laredo. It will be staffed with a variety of OSS personnel, both plainclothes operatives as well as a uniformed force. Our operatives and officers have powers to legally arrest persons and confiscate property of anyone suspected of actions deemed "traitorous" by the Articles of Reconstruction. All non-citizen inhabitants of this Zone will be subject to our jurisdiction in any case involving issues of national security. Some of that new construction you see will be for our offices, barracks, holding cells and interrogation rooms."

"I'm sure there will be no limit to the benefits we will reap from the OSS presence, Mr. Garrison," said Custer, his voice cold. He continued, "My first order of business will be to advise Washington that I require substantial reinforcements. On the order of three infantry corps and at least two cavalry divisions, I should think. Once I have a respectable command I think that, with the able assistance of you and your OSS, I'll have little trouble in controlling the Texas Zone."

"I sincerely hope that will be the case, General," replied Garrison.

Custer responded, "If there's nothing else gentlemen, my duties require my attention. Colonel Reno will see you out."

Reno entered and escorted the two men, Jeffery and Garrison out. He returned a moment later. Custer looked up and said, "Officious bastards, they're the last thing we need. More infantry divisions would be of a great deal more value. OSS indeed, what nonsense!"

The next afternoon Custer received an unannounced visit from Garrison. Garrison entered Custer's office and took the offered seat. He sat quietly for a moment, and then spoke.

"General, I got the distinct impression that you are unhappy regarding me and the OSS."

He paused for a moment and looked Custer straight in the eye before continuing. "I want you to know that I'm totally prepared to place myself and my office under your leadership. Those are my orders, and I will do my level best to carry them out. I have no problem with the chain of command. General, I've lost family to those damn confederates and as far as I'm concerned they're still the enemy."

Custer regarded Garrison with a tight smile and a level gaze. He said, "In that case Mr. Garrison, let me say that *we* should have little trouble in handling the Texas Zone." The two men stood, and as if sealing some unspoken pact, vigorously shook hands, each looking intently at the other.

Garrison was the second of three brothers. His oldest brother, Howard, had lost an arm at the battle of Petersburg. His youngest brother, Arthur, was enshrined for eternity in a small graveyard just outside Vicksburg, killed in the Union's siege. Garrison's hatred of the Confederacy was a constant ache, a never-ending drumbeat resounding deep in his heart. He saw his position and the OSS as tools to be used to punish his nation's enemies, whoever they were, wherever they might be found.

Foreign Legion Command, Mexico City

General Laurency had recalled every possible Legion unit from garrison duties throughout Mexico. This allowed him to maximize his force levels for the forthcoming battle. He reasoned that if his command were beaten then all hope of maintaining Maximilian in power was lost. If victory was theirs, then they could eventually regain the territory that had been lost. When his force had grown to twenty thousand, he moved out of Mexico City and began marching eastward to meet the Revolutionary Army, which had already begun moving westward from Pueblo, towards Mexico City.

General Laurency continued eastward until he arrived at a small, but strategically located village midway between Pueblo and Mexico City. It was called Cameron. Deciding it was a defensible position he set about emplacing his command.

The village sat on a slight rise, in the middle of a plain several miles long and a few miles wide. The plain was bounded by a series of low rugged hills to the north and by sparsely vegetated, sandy ground to the south. Inhabited by a few hundred souls, it was a small collection of one and two-story adobe buildings clustered around two small churches and surrounded by a low rock wall. Cameron existed because it sat squarely on the only major east-west road connecting Pueblo to Mexico City. Most importantly, it was one of a very few water sources between the two major Mexican cities.

As soon as his entire command was encamped the General called a staff meeting. "Gentleman, it is my plan to create a defensive position and force the enemy to come to us. As usual we are outnumbered and outgunned," he said, a frown spreading over his features. He motioned to the dirt mock-up of the immediate area that sat on the table top before them. Using a stick as a pointer he said, "We will create a defensive line from here to here on a north-south line. We will use the existing buildings and walls for our fortifications. Our headquarters will be here in this church. Begin your entrenchment tomorrow, at dawn. If there are no questions I suggest we adjourn for dinner."

Laurency formed his infantry force into four divisions. Three of these divisions, a total of twelve thousand troops, with artillery support, were positioned in two rows of sandbagged trenches. Along the defensive line were a series of strong points, holding artillery and infantry. The fourth division had been broken up into regimental-sized units. These were tasked as ready reserves and posted about a hundred yards behind the main line.

The northern flank was anchored by a strongpoint garrisoned by infantry and artillery. The position was replete with trenches and artillery revetments. The extreme southern flank, however, was lightly held by fifteen hundred Legion Lancers formed in three five-hundred-men regiments. They were positioned at a right angle leading back from the main defensive line.

As the main Legion force occupied Cameron their cavalry patrols kept the advancing Revolutionary Army force under continuous observation and sent daily reports back to Legion command.

"It should be interesting," commented Lieutenant Jessup to Captain Petain, as the two officers watched the slow but continuous approach of their enemy. "For the first time since being sent to this godforsaken country we'll actually be fighting regular troops in a stand-up battle, and not these cowardly hit-and-run types."

"I would recommend caution, Lieutenant," responded Captain Petain. "These southern American troops have done very well in several major engagements in their war of rebellion."

"Done well against northern American troops, not us," shot back Jessup. "Let's see what they can do against real soldiers."

"That opportunity is a certainty. Let's hope we both survive to appreciate the experience."

Cameron, Mexico

While the Legion prepared for battle, the Revolutionary Army was fast approaching. Longstreet advised Lee as soon as his cavalry patrols located the Legion position. Shortly thereafter, Lee and a strong escort arrived and observed Laurency's position. As he rode back Lee thought, it has come, our first battle as a single force. I believe that we will give a good account of ourselves for if we do not then all may be truly lost. This battle *must* be won!

When he returned to headquarters, Lee ordered a council of his Corps Commanders. He opened the meeting by gesturing at the map on the field table in the center of the tent. "Gentlemen, I have drawn out the enemy defenses, and as you can see they are well positioned. Unfortunately, we cannot allow this force to remain in place. We must attack and destroy those people, then continue our advance upon Mexico City. General Longstreet, what are your views?"

"As you say, sir," responded Longstreet. "They are well placed with trenches and fortified positions along the length of their line. The artillery is situated to give their infantry fire support and the guns themselves are as protected as possible. Any attempt to carry their main line by direct frontal assault, while possibly successful, would be at a substantial cost. I believe the attacking force might suffer such casualties as to render them no longer combat effective."

Longstreet looked at Lee, and stepping back from the table concluded with, "A frontal assault is just not feasible. My recommendation is a flanking maneuver designed to get them out of their prepared positions."

Lee quietly regarded the two other generals present and asked, "Have either of you gentlemen anything to offer?"

General Hill cleared his throat, and clearly nervous, glanced at both Lee and Longstreet before offering, "We have quality siege artillery; it might be possible to bombard their lines to a point where a determined assault could carry their position. Casualties in such an attack would be substantial, but it also might give us a quick victory, sir."

Lee regarded Hill quietly for a moment then turned to the third general present and asked, "And you General Garcia, what is your opinion?"

Garcia, who had never commanded a force of the size he now had, was clearly uncertain. However, he was a competent officer and he had personally inspected the Legion positions. He responded, "General, I think that both General Hill's and General Longstreet's suggestions have merit. We must take the battle to the enemy, therefore, we must attack. A substantial artillery preparation followed by a large infantry assault is, I think, required."

"Gentlemen," said Lee, "thank you for your thoughts. I have given this some consideration and to some extent I agree with all of you. I have, however, determined what I believe to be a viable course of action, one that will give us an opportunity to achieve success without devastating losses."

Lee paused for a moment, then continued, "General Longstreet, you will be positioned at the extreme right of our line, and tasked with attacking the enemy's extreme left. You will position your forces so that the maximum blow lands at the point where their lines end in the north. If it appears that you can turn their flank, you are authorized to commit your entire Corps. You are to precede the attack with a substantial artillery barrage. Your attack will commence at sunrise."

He turned to face Hill and continued, "General Hill, you will form the center and left of our line. I want you to keep your forces in movement on your front. You are authorized to conduct only limited attacks. It is critical that the Legion command have their attention focused on your forces. Once you have achieved that goal, you will then advise General Garcia to begin his movement."

Lee turned to his last general and continued, "General Garcia, it will be your task to strike the telling blow. Once General Hill and General Longstreet are engaged you will slide around the extreme right of the Legion position and attack from the south with your entire Corps. It will be your attack that will be the means of victory, General."

Lee stopped speaking for a moment, quietly regarding his three generals. then continued, "Each of you has been entrusted with a part of the coming battle that is critical to our success. I have every respect for your abilities and those of the officers and men of your commands, gentlemen. If your orders are clear, you are dismissed." At this the three men saluted, left the tent and returned to their respective forces.

The following afternoon the Revolutionary Army units under Hill and Garcia joined Longstreet's force and began positioning as the plan required. By late afternoon the entire Army was in place. The Infantry Divisions of I and II Corps were in position in a line parallel to the Legion fortifications, with artillery batteries to their rear. The III Corps was formed in the rear as both a tactical reserve and maneuver force. Lee, having received reports of his force's dispositions, ordered all units to camp for the night with the attack scheduled for dawn the next morning.

The four senior officers had finished dinner and were seated around the dying embers of the campfire. An orderly offered tea, topped off the glasses then withdrew. Lee drained his glass, looked at Garcia, asked, "General, are your troops positioned to your liking?

"Yes sir. My officers have been briefed and their units prepared."

"And your command, General Hill, all is well, I presume?"

"My units are positioned and my officers prepared, sir."

Longstreet, a humorless smile on his features spoke, "I believe, General, that all our forces are ready, sir."

Lee, looking into the last of the flames said, "I must urge you, gentlemen. You must push your forces to the limit, without exception. Our foe is a veteran force and we must be prepared for a vigorous defense." His tone was hard and brooked no argument.

At first light the next day Revolutionary Army units began to implement the plan.

Longstreet had formed his command with a front composed of the 1st and 2nd Infantry Divisions with the 3rd as his reserve force. His intent was to attack the far left end of the Legion line with his assault hitting on an oblique angle. This would allow his troops to hit at a point where the defensive line angled away from the attacking forces thus reducing the amount of fire they would take. The 2nd Division would commence the attack and if there were any sign of success, he would be able to reinforce with the 3rd immediately. The assault would begin with an artillery bombardment from two batteries of siege guns and two batteries of lighter, 3 inch guns.

Corporal Raymond Smith, 4th Mississippi Infantry Regiment, advanced with his platoon. He was already hot, his mouth cottony dry. He could see only a short distance in any direction; his view blocked by moving forms and dust swirls. Smith advanced in bursts, as he had been taught. First running ahead, then kneeling and firing and holding position while others ran through, he closed on the enemy.

Incoming fire was desultory; the occasional shell exploding and sending sheets of shrapnel ripping through air and bodies. Minnie balls zipped by or impacted on flesh with a wet, *thunking* sound.

As they neared the Legion defenses, the troops began to bunch up, units intermingling, men rushing forward in larger groups trying to get out of the killing zones as fast as possible. Volley fire, accurate and fast, slashed the lead units, men falling dead, others dropping to the ground, either returning fire or screaming in agony. As the fire increased and more men fell or took cover, the attack slowed.

An officer next to Smith stood up, pointed his sword at the enemy and yelled, "Charge, Charge!" Suiting his actions to his words he gained his feet and moved towards the enemy. Smith cursed the officer, lunged to his feet and followed him, firing and yelling for all he was worth. Reaching the sandbagged defenses, he joined the other soldiers, laying down a furious barrage at anything that moved.

The Legion defenders counter-attacked and the first line of trenches became a mass of struggling, cursing troops, killing and dying. The officer who had led the assault stood next to the flag, disdaining cover, coolly firing his revolver at the enemy, who were steadily advancing towards him. He was killed while attempting to reload his pistol.

The Legion counter-attack was finally repulsed. Smith, along with the rest of the 4th Mississippi, traded rifle fire with the enemy as they grimly hung on to the ground they had gained. Another unit, composed of Mexicans with a Mexican officer, moved into the position alongside Smith's unit. The young Mexican officer gazed coolly at the Legion position. He drew his saber, held it up and shouted, *"Soldatos, Attack."* He jumped up and ran towards the enemy, screaming at the top of his lungs. Smith grimaced and asked himself why the dumb shit didn't just hunker down and wait for artillery. He grasped his rifle, got to one knee and was shot right between the eyes, dead before he hit the ground.

The Revolutionary Army assault ground to a halt on the right flank when the Legion counter-attacked. Each side assumed a defensive posture and maintained heavy fire. At this point, the superiority of the Revolutionary Army equipment came into play. Legion troops armed with muzzle-loading rifles were facing troops using breech-loading weapons that gave them a major advantage in fire power. General Longstreet, observing the effects of superior fire power on the defenders, ordered two brigades of the 3rd Division to attack to the immediate right of his 2nd Division.

Brigadier General Zenon, commanding the Legion left flank, responding to the increased pressure on his position, ordered his reserves into the line. He also extended his defenses west in order to protect his rear. The General sent a runner with a message to Laurency advising him that all available reserves on the left had been committed. The message from Zenon had barely arrived when heavy artillery fire began impacting on the center of his position.

Believing that the attack on his left was a feint and that the real threat was from the enemy forces opposite his center, he withdrew the infantry units supporting the cavalry on his right flank and used them to reinforce the center of his line.

Sergeant Hans Dietrich, 3rd Legion Regiment of Foot, veteran of eight years in the Hessian Army and ten in the Legion, stepped up to the firing line and looked at the enemy positions to his front. Heat waves caused a shimmering effect, giving the view a surreal aspect. In the distance infantry formations marched and counter-marched, creating rolling waves of dust; occasional flashes of sunlight glancing off fixed bayonets.

He stepped back from his firing position in order to glance up and down the line of waiting Legionaries. His squad was holding part of a strong point in the center of the French defense. "Wait for targets, mark your targets," he ordered. "Keep your heads down when you reload." He flinched as a shell ripped overhead to land some fifty yards behind, deep in officer country.

"Message to headquarters," snickered private Dumas.

"Merde," said Dietrich, "they'll soon fix our position," as a second round impacted a few yards in front of him, the explosion fountaining dirt into the air. After a short wait, he looked over the ramparts again to see butternut-and-white clad infantry advancing towards him in bursts, rifles slanted, bayonets fixed.

In the center of the Revolutionary line General Hill was following his orders. Two Brigades from 4th Division were marching and counter-marching along his front, the movements raising rolling clouds of dust that were pushed westward into the Legion's position by a soft breeze. The dust reduced visibility and made breathing uncomfortable. Revolutionary Army and Legion Artillery traded long-range artilley fire, both sides absorbing losses, and a steady stream of casualties began filling up their respective aid stations.

"I believe their attention is fixed on us, General Garcia," said Hill. "You are to take III Corps and commence your sweep around their right at this point," he said, indicating a spot some mile and a half south and west of the southern most Revolutionary Army position. "Pathfinder units are in place to direct your command. Your assault will be screened and led by your cavalry which will attack the center of the Legion Cavalry force opposing you. The cavalry attack must develop before you begin your infantry maneuver. The entire Legion force holding their far right flank should be thoroughly engaged before you commit your infantry. Remember, get around their flank, then behind them, and then hit them hard from the rear."

"I understand, General." responded General Garcia.

Brigade by brigade, III Corps wheeled left and began its flanking march. The 3rd Cavalry Division, the lead unit, moved into the Legion rear, formed front by regiment, dressed ranks, and charged the Legion Lancers to their front. Charge and counter-charge ensued as each attempted to drive off the other. Legion units armed with twelve-foot lances enjoyed an initial advantage, but the sabers and pistols of the Revolutionary Army cavalry proved superior at close quarters. The troops in blue-and- red were slowly driven back. As the right flank began to crumple from Garcia's remorseless hammer blows, the Legion forces responded as best they could.

Captain Petain jerked to the right as the enemy saber slashed down, missing his head by inches. Stabbing straight ahead was not in the manual, but necessity was the mother of invention, and the tip of his blade passed cleanly through the arm of his adversary. The enemy cavalryman dropped his blade, turned his mount and galloped away. Wheeling his horse, Petain shouted for his bugler to sound recall. When he realized the riders in butternut-and-white were falling back again, he heaved a sigh of relief. A moment later Lieutenant Jessup trotted up, and Petain ordered, "Lieutenant, take a squad and find a water wagon." Squinting at the enemy through the late afternoon light, he said, "Do it quickly, they'll be attacking again shortly!" After several massed assaults the mounted combat had dissolved into a series of small group, fast moving, swirling actions.

The III Corps Infantry Divisions of the Revolutionary Army moved west, around and beyond the Legion right flank. Once General Garcia realized he had reached the Legion rear, he stopped and ordered his units to reform from column into regimental front. As soon as his command had reoriented itself, he attacked the rear of the Legion position.

The assault came at an oblique angle to the Legion defensive line which was already engaged by artillery and cavalry on its front. As Garcia's infantry regiments hit, each Legion unit in turn was overwhelmed and either collapsed or was driven back. The entire right flank began to dissolve into chaos. Pressure from Garcia's assault compressed the defenders and drove them from their prepared positions. Despite fierce resistance that frequently degenerated into hand-to-hand combat, the entire Legion position began to crumble.

Artillery fire on Laurency's headquarters had grown in intensity throughout the battle. Shells were continually impacting in and around the area. Legion counter-battery fire had proven mostly ineffective because it lacked sufficient range.

As the Legion Commander turned to question a staff officer a shell exploded a few feet from his headquarters. The force of the explosion knocked down one wall as well as part of the roof of the building, raining debris on the General and his staff and knocking them all to the ground. Picking himself up with the assistance of his aide he attempted to brush himself off, only to discover his left arm unusable from a shoulder wound. Stepping outside the burning shambles of the church that had served as headquarters, he continued to direct the battle while a medical orderly sought to stem the flow of blood from his wound.

He had hardly left the church when he received a dispatch from General Du Pont, commanding his right flank, advising him of the imminent catastrophe there. In a last attempt to hold the lines, Laurency ordered all remaining reserve units from his center to attempt to reverse their front and attack the Revolutionary Army forces advancing into their rear.

Sergeant Dietrich coughed, his throat raw from the fumes of combat, his canteen long since empty. Slouching down behind the tattered sandbags, he winced as he heard volleys of fire from his rear, behind the outer works of his strong point.

It appears these southern troops know their business only too well and it is a pity we will not be able to have long talks about their admirable tactics he thought; as he stood and ordered the remnants of his platoon to about face and attack in a bayonet charge.

156

Stepping over the bottom half of private Dumas, holding his bayonet-tipped musket at port arms, he led his tiny command toward the sounds of musket and rifle fire, which were now, unfortunately, coming from both his front and rear.

The combat on the Legion rear and right flank continued unabated. Petain had reformed his unit yet again. Having made three charges, the Legion cavalry, both men and horses, was exhausted. Units were completely intermingled, and the officer corps had been decimated. "Lieutenant Jessup," he said, his voice hoarse, "reform the company. I am going to try and find the Colonel."

Riding to where the regimental flag fluttered in the hot breeze, he found the regimental commander. The man was swaying in his saddle, barely upright. His right arm was hanging limp, and his eyes unfocused. Petain found himself shouting, in a vain attempt to gain the officer's attention. Instead of responding, the man slid unconscious from his horse, hitting the ground as limp as a sack of wheat. The Captain ordered the troops around him to follow, and galloped off to rejoin his company.

"They're going to hit us again," observed Lieutenant Jessup.

"So it would appear," was Petain's laconic response.

"It looks like there are several hundred of them."

"Correct again."

"May I say sir, it has been an honor and pleasure to serve under you." said Jessup.

Petain gave his lieutenant a bleak look, and replied, "Thank you Lieutenant, but you're not dead yet."

Jessup was killed in the next attack. He died interposing himself between Petain and several enemy cavalrymen. He killed two of the enemy before succumbing to a pistol shot.

By late afternoon the battle had been decided. The Legion position had been completely overrun. In an effort to save what he could, Laurency ordered a number of units, under the command of General Zenon, to hold as a rear guard. These commands stood their ground and fought, almost to the last man, rather than surrender; buying with their lives the time their fellow soldiers needed to extricate themselves from what was fast becoming a huge trap.

As night fell on the village of Cameron the remnants of the Legion cavalry were still fighting a valiant rearguard action. Infantry units that had successfully disengaged were on the road, marching back to Mexico City. Legion losses numbered almost a third of their force killed, wounded or captured, along with almost all their artillery captured or destroyed.

CHAPTER SIXTEEN

November, 1865

Mexico City

As the remnants of the Legion returned to the capitol General Laurency and the Emperor Maximilian met in the Emperor's Palace.

"So, General, exactly what can we do?" queried Maximilian. "Have we any military options left?"

"The situation is not good, my Lord. Our forces cannot be successful against both the Mexicans and these Southern American forces. We are simply too overextended, outnumbered and outgunned. Since our recent setback at Cameron we have recalled all remaining forces from throughout Mexico. I am in the process of consolidating them here in the capitol."

The Legion officer continued, "As of today we have less then fourteen thousand troops, with only twenty artillery pieces. These figures include wounded who are expected to return to duty. Unfortunately, that still leaves us at a serious numerical disadvantage. We are aware that a column of enemy troops numbering about ten thousand is currently encamped about ten miles east of the city, and another of roughly equal size some where to the northwest. A third column, larger than the other two, appears to be maneuvering to our south and east. It is my appraisal of the situation that we are shortly to be encircled. There is no outside force large enough to relieve us," he concluded.

"So you are telling me my reign can be numbered in weeks, if not days," said Maximilian, staring intently at his military commander.

"That is essentially correct, my lord," answered the General.

When he returned to his office Laurency summoned Captain Petain. "You will take your company and scout to the south and west. Report back to me within five days. We must have as complete a picture as is possible regarding the size and dispositions of the enemy forces facing us."

"As you command, my General," responded Captain Petain, leaving immediately for his lancer company headquarters.

Five days later, Petain returned to Laurency's office. He told him that the city would be completely surrounded within a week, at the most, and that the combined opposing force was roughly fifty thousand infantry with almost one hundred artillery pieces. With luck, Legion forces could keep the southern road from the city open for a few more days.

After receiving this news, Laurency went straight to the Palace to report the unpleasant military situation to the Emperor. On his way there he noticed several crowds congregating in the large squares located throughout the city. Some of the citizens were armed with guns, while other held a variety of implements that could be used as weapons. He continued on his way thinking grimly, enemies without and enemies within, the noose is tightening and our window of opportunity shrinking.

Legion units were being dispatched to confront and disperse these crowds wherever possible. The lack of adequate numbers of soldiers was making itself felt. A few of the marauding groups of citizenry had taken to looting and arson. Several burning buildings were sending thick, black tendrils of smoke wafting into the air.

When he arrived at the palace, he passed through security and entered the grounds. Maximilian met him in the grand hall, empty now save for the Legion guards who were posted at intervals along the walls of the richly-decorated room. "Speak, General," was his opening command. "What news have you?"

As Laurency related the situation, the Emperor's face was blank at first, but as the totality of the disaster became evident, went red with anger. Maximilian had not asked for the throne, had in fact argued against assuming it. He had allowed his cousin Napoleon III to convince him that he would be bringing an enlightened autocracy to a barely-civilized nation. Only after arriving had he discovered the population viewed him as a conquering invader. It was a most unpleasant shock when he found they were right.

When Laurency had finished his report, the Emperor replied," General, I am aware of the difficulties that you and your command have faced. I appreciate the fact that you have been outnumbered and poorly supplied from the beginning. The Legion has maintained its honor on the field of battle. However, it appears that, regardless of their sacrifices, our mission here has not met with success. "

161

"I have prepared an evacuation plan, sir. It calls for a withdrawal south then east to the city of Merida," the General replied. "If Your Majesty will attend me," he continued, as he walked over to a table upon which rested a map of Mexico. He indicated a point on the northern face of the Yucatan Peninsula. "The Legion holds the city. Its port can be used as an evacuation site. We will defend the city while we await ships from home. I think that we have sufficient forces and supplies to make this possible. However, I must stress the fact that our window of opportunity is very small and growing smaller. This maneuver must be carried out as soon as we can if we are to have any hope for success."

For a moment or two Maximilian stood and gazed at the map spread out before him, then, with a slight shrug of his shoulders, he turned to his General and said, "Implement your plan, General. We must save what we can. Honor demands no less."

Mexico City

As soon as the reconnaissance units reported that the capitol was empty of Legion units General Lee ordered the Revolutionary Army to occupy it. It was several days before Lee advised Santa Anna and Davis that the capitol was secure. As they had in Pueblo, Davis and Santa Anna entered the city together and proclaimed a solid week of celebrations to mark the event.

The members of the Revolutionary Council watched from the balcony as the festivities continued for the second straight day, crowds swarming about the city as the church bells tolled almost continually.

"As you have said before, these people love to celebrate," commented Davis to Santa Anna.

"My people are festive by nature and always make the most of any opportunity."

"So far we have been successful, very successful," said Breckenridge. "Let's hope that we can continue to be one step ahead of our enemies."

"We are able, my friend, able and true, and together we shall see this to the end," said Santa Anna, taking Breckenridge's and Davis's arm's in his, and walking to the edge of the balcony to bask together in the cheers of the crowd.

Although the capitol was theirs Lee knew that the Foreign Legion was still a grave danger, a danger to be destroyed.

"You requested my presence, sir," asked Longstreet, as he entered Lee's office.

"Yes General. I've need of your services. The French are still retreating south. They are still a considerable force, quite capable of mischief. I want you to pursue and, if possible engage and destroy them."

"Very good, sir, I'll have my lead units on the road at daybreak tomorrow."

"Excellent. Good hunting."

As General Longstreet's I Corps pursued Maximilian and the Legion, the Revolutionary Council was constantly in session, planning the new economy, a new government and perhaps most important, the new social order of Mexico.

The Council of Five Hundred had demanded that the land grants and titles of nobility originally awarded to their forefathers by the King of Spain be recognized. The concept of a noble class found unexpected allies in both

Davis and Breckenridge. Both felt that southern aristocracy would be more than amenable to acquiring the robes of a newly- created nobility. By simply recognizing the *status quo* and continuing the practice of governmental land grants with appropriate titles, the Council could create a useful social class utterly dependent on the government for its power and existence.

It was decided that the Revolutionary Council would have the authority to grant land and title to individuals who had performed outstanding service to the government. Two titles would be implemented. The first was Squire, which came with a cash pension for the life of the recipient and was not hereditary, and the second was *Don*, which came with both cash and land grant and was hereditary.

CHAPTER SEVENTEEN

December, 1865

Galveston, Texas Zone of Reconstruction

Union command in Washington soon realized that with the arrival of English and Prussian naval units in Vera Cruz, it was imperative to keep track of the Gulf situation. The solution was to have the Navy maintain a Squadron based at the sleepy port of Galveston, Texas. Sun drenched, with a generally mild climate and protected harbor, it was situated slightly north of the Mexican/American border, ideally located for naval surveillance of Gulf waters.

With the official cessation of hostilities between the Union and the Confederacy, the ships which had been engaged in blockade duty became available. Naval units from the Atlantic Squadrons were stationed to maintain a strong Union naval presence in the Gulf and Caribbean waters. The reinforced squadron maintained a loose cordon off the Mexican coast, occasionally dropping off or picking up OSS operatives. Admiral David G. Farragut was given command.

"Enter," responded Admiral Farragut to the knock on his office door.

Staff Lt. Arthur Strong opened the office door, entered and braced to attention. "All Captains present and awaiting your presence, sir." Having delivered his report he stood awaiting further orders.

"Very good, Arthur," responded the Admiral, as he rose to leave the room. "I'm right behind you, son."

"Sir," answered Strong, who then turned about and led the Admiral to his briefing room.

As Farragut entered the room the assembled officers stood and saluted. Returning their salute, he waived them to their seats, then walked to the podium and addressed them. "Gentlemen, we are living in interesting times, a fact that will be reflected by this briefing. As you are probably aware, units of the Army of Northern Virginia have landed in Mexico. Along with Mexican revolutionary forces under Antonio Santa Ana they have joined together to form a Revolutionary Army. This Army is commanded by none other than Robert E. Lee. This force has been re-armed and re-supplied with state-of-the-art ordinance. It has engaged in successful military operations against the government of the Emperor of Mexico, Maximilian, who is maintained in his position by an Army composed of French Foreign Legion troops. "

The Admiral paused for a moment, and then continued, "The resupply was carried out by a combined Prussian-English fleet now operating from naval bases in Jamaica and Bermuda. The European assistance is believed to be in response to a promise that the Monroe Doctrine will not be applied to Mexico or any other territory controlled by this Mexican-Confederate Revolutionary Council. Needless to say, this state of affairs has caused Washington to become very concerned. The political leadership of the Revolutionary Council is a combination of Confederate and Mexican politicians, centered on Jefferson Davis and Santa Anna. Their goal is overthrowing the current Mexican government and replacing it with one of their own creation."

"Our job," continued Farragut, whose features now betrayed a ghost of a smile, "will be to maintain a high profile in these waters, assist with OSS operations upon request, and maintain a constant vigil with regards to our neighbors to the south. We are to be firm but polite to our European friends, offering no undue threat but reminding them they are in our backyard, as it were."

He looked out at his fleet captains, grinned, and then closed the meeting with, "now that you are as confounded as I am, sailing orders and rules of engagement will be issued to all ships within forty-eight hours. Good luck! You are dismissed."

Laredo, Texas Zone of Reconstruction

In Laredo, winter had announced itself. The small potbellied stove in the corner labored mightily to keep the unusually-chilly day at bay. The room held five men: General George Custer, his aide Colonel Marcus Reno, the Mexican Revolutionary Benito Juarez, the Regional Director of the OSS William Garrison, and OSS operative Ezekiel Sinclair.

"Allow me to introduce His Excellency, Benito Juarez," said Custer, gesturing the men into the chairs surrounding the table. "We have, I believe, one thing very much in common."

167

"I agree, General, and the Union stands willing to help you immediately, Your Excellency," said Garrison, with a nod to Juarez.

"I am most pleased to hear this, *senor.* My officers have led me to believe that you will begin shipments of military equipment to our forces within the month," replied Juarez, looking intently at the group of Americans.

"You are correct sir," responded Garrison. "Please allow me to introduce OSS operative Ezekiel Sinclair, who will be responsible for the details of the actual delivery. It is our intent to assist you in your efforts of uniting Mexico under a democratic government. Our official policy will be to maintain strict neutrality; however, the OSS, via Operative Sinclair, will provide your government with all necessary aid short of direct intervention by American armed forces. We will leave you to your planning then. We wish you every success, sir." He, Custer and Reno all stood up to leave the office.

Juarez sat quietly as the room emptied, then turned to regard the young man who stood before him. Young, he thought to himself, then looking more closely at the eyes he thought; young, yes, but experienced, too. So, we shall see what we shall see.

"Mr. Sinclair, our troops have need of better and more equipment if we are to remain in the field against this new Revolutionary Army. If we can obtain the supplies we need, our chances of success will be greatly enhanced," said Juarez, looking intently at the American.

"Well, then," responded Easy, standing up and walking over to a wall-mounted map, "we will begin by building up stockpiles here in Laredo and then moving the supplies into Mexico. We will provide security until each shipment arrives at its staging area in your country. From that point on, your Army will be responsible for distribution to fighting units. At this stage, we intend to make every effort to insure there will be no direct contact between Union and Revolutionary Council forces. Our supplies will include food, clothing, medical supplies, rifles, field artillery and ammunition. I will accompany the first shipment in order to work out any remaining issues. Once I'm satisfied we'll commence regular shipments." With that Easy looked at Juarez for a response.

"Very good, Mister Sinclair," replied Juarez, approval in his voice. "At the earliest possible moment, please! Those supplies are desperately needed by my men."

CHAPTER EIGHTEEN

January, 1866

Southern Mexico

It was the rainy season and the few roads that weren't completely washed out were a quagmire. The constant showers soaked men and equipment and made any kind of large scale movement a nightmare. Despite these hardships, both the Legion and the Revolutionary Army constantly pressed each other, in a series of running battles and sharp ambushes.

Legion forces had fought a brutal and almost continuous rearguard action since retreating from Mexico City. General Laurency kept cavalry units between him and the enemy, to act as both screen and scout force. As his command doggedly moved south and east, he continually established rear-guard strong-points. Wherever the terrain gave him tactical advantage he detailed infantry units to holding actions. When circumstance permitted he executed sharp counter-attacks. He made every effort to slow down Longstreet's advance, as well as making it as expensive to the enemy, in both men and equipment, as possible.

Longstreet's response was to engage and flank each blocking position with infantry and artillery and to use his cavalry to maintain constant contact with the Legion main force. Whenever Legion units formed a defensive posture he would fix them in place, then attempt to flank, surround, and destroy them. The conflict became a series of tactical moves and counter-moves by two master tacticians, each pressing for every possible advantage.

The last man of Legion Captain Petain's light cavalry company galloped past him, lathered horses straining to climb the slight rise, perhaps a hundred yards ahead of their pursuers. He calmly looked to his left and right, noting the hidden infantry occupying the military crest of the boulder and shrub-strewn rise, then raked his spurs to force his mount to a gallop, following his men.

The Legion ambushers held their fire, each man marking his target as the range closed. At the command, each man fired two aimed rounds, sweeping most of the advancing cavalry from their horses, then left his position at a trot. The two infantry companies formed ranks on the trail and double-timed away, leaving behind a thoroughly shattered cavalry platoon; a knot of milling horses and men, in total disarray. A good plan, well executed, thought Petain, as the infantry column trotted past his troopers, who waited in turn to once again become the rear-most Legion unit.

It took almost three weeks of constant combat for the Legion to fight its way to its objective, Merida. Originally a Mayan fishing village, it had grown over more then three hundred years of Spanish, Mexican, and finally French occupation. It had reached the point where it claimed some ten thousand souls as permanent residents and served as the capitol of the isolated state of Yucatan.

Hope had flared briefly when the weary, fought-out remnants of the Legion arrived to see two ships flying the French flag awaiting them in the roadstead. This hope was brutally crushed when, as they began descending from the heights to the west of the city, they observed the arrival of several warships, none of which flew the French colors.

Having no other option left, Laurency ordered the advance guard to proceed into Merida while the remaining Legion units deployed and began digging defensive positions around the town. While the fortifications were being constructed he, Maximilian, and the baggage train in which Carlotta rode, entered Merida, evicting the local government civil servants and taking up residence in the town hall.

A few hours after the arrival of the Legion, the lead elements of Longstreet's I Corps, the 1st Cavalry Division, appeared west of the town. They immediately started to take up positions around the city. Several hours later, the lead units of the 1st Infantry Brigade began encircling the town, throwing up breastworks as they expanded their perimeter. Within forty-eight hours the remainder of Longstreet's I Corps had arrived and the town was completely surrounded.

Longstreet, along with his three Division commanders, sat around the table as orderlies removed the last traces of dinner. "Gentlemen, we have him bottled up by sea and land. This means he has very few choices and none of them good, and *that*," he paused momentarily to emphasize his point, "makes them very dangerous people. So for now we complete the encirclement. Then we dig in and hold in place. A frontal attack is something I want to avoid at all costs."

The conference over, he left the tent and began walking through the soft tropical Yucatan evening towards the defensive line. As he made his way through the artillery and infantry positions, he nodded with approval at the engineering activity still underway. His troops needed no exhortation by their officers. They were all veterans and knew well the value of good fortifications in a fire fight.

Nearing the inner ring of trenches, he continued on until he could see the lights of Merida. He stopped and rested against a tree as he regarded the town below him, ablaze with light and activity. I would have this end with no further bloodshed if I could, he thought. Those men are brave and able, they deserve better than to be discarded. He stood quietly for a few moments more; then, dropping his cigar, he ground it out, turned his back on his enemy, and returned to his tent, still deep in thought.

As soon as the city was in his hands Laurency requisitioned a fishing boat and sent it out to meet with the two ships flying the tri-colors. The boat returned almost immediately with a French officer on board.

"Your Excellency, I am Captain Jacque Armand, of the Imperial Frigate *Tours*. I have brought dispatches from the Emperor for you," said the naval officer, as he advanced to Maximilian, a sealed packet of papers bearing the imperial insignia in his outstretched hand. "I am ordered to place my ships at your command, my Lord."

"Please excuse me. I must review these immediately," said Maximilian, as he took the papers from the naval officer, wheeled about, and strode from the room.

"May I offer you some refreshment while we wait?" inquired Laurency, as he guided Armand towards a side table holding a few bottles of wine and some glasses. The two men helped themselves, then each lighting a cigar, they walked over to a pair of chairs, sat down and waited in silence to hear their fate. After a cigar's-length wait, Maximilian returned. He walked to where the two officers sat. Motioning them to remain seated, he pulled a chair up alongside theirs.

"The Emperor has deigned to send what aid he can in the person of our good captain and his two ships. Two ships!" Maximilian's voice was tight with anger. "For the use of me and my immediate staff only. All others are to be considered expendable. I have been ordered to embark on the ships, regardless of personal consideration or desire."

General Laurency stood and spoke. "As an officer of the Legion there is no choice for me, either. I will remain with my command. I suggest, My Lord, that you begin preparations to embark immediately." He began to walk away, only to feel Maximilian's hand grasp his arm. Turning, he gazed at the Emperor of Mexico who said, in a voice made tight with emotion, "General, each of us is a captive of circumstance and neither is in a position he would voluntarily choose. I, too, have tradition and orders to contend with. I want you to know it has been a privilege to be served by you and the Legion." With that he saluted Laurency and turning to Captain Armand said, "Attend me now, Captain."

Twenty four hours later found Laurency and his senior officers standing on Merida's dock watching the two French ships holding the erstwhile Emperor of Mexico, his wife and their combined staffs disappear into the Gulf of Mexico; leaving him and his men to their fate. As the vessels vanished into the distance, Laurency turned to General Du Pont, and in a level tone said, "All in all, I found the man to be less than optimal for his station in life."

The next morning, at first light, an infantry captain left Longstreet's lines, and under a white flag, began walking towards the Legion position; reaching his goal he was immediately blindfolded and escorted to the Legion's headquarters and then to Laurency's office.

"I have the honor to be the representative of General Longstreet, who wishes to meet with you at noon today in order to discuss possible solutions to the current state-of-affairs, sir," said the flag bearer.

Now that, thought Laurency, was a remarkably diplomatic way to identify a very clear military situation. He laughed, said, "How could I ever say no to such an elegant request? Captain, it shall be as General Longstreet suggests, at the General's convenience."

Noon on the same day found the two men seated in a small tent, situated mid-way between the two forces. Each officer was attended by a single aide. Longstreet began the conversation.

"This has been a long and hard fought campaign. I complement you, sir. From the beginning you have been outgunned and outnumbered and in the final instance, abandoned."

"General," responded Laurency, "we of the Legion do not expect life to be fair. We merely expect an opportunity to fight."

"It's about fighting that I want to speak." said Longstreet. "To be blunt to the point of rudeness I want the Legion to fight for, rather than against us." Holding up his hands Longstreet continued hurriedly, "I have no intention of asking you to break an oath, but it seems to me you have been very badly used, then left high and dry. I would offer you an honorable alliance with the Revolutionary Army, if you can see a way."

"May I have some time to consider this offer?" asked Laurency.

"Twenty-four hours, then I will begin assaulting your positions," Longstreet answered.

A short while later, the Legion Commander sat in the town hall, empty but for him and the senior officers of his command, as they discussed the offer. He made his case to his officers slowly and carefully. He said, "We have not betrayed France! On the contrary, France has turned her back on the Legion. The Emperor has ignored our situation. We have refused no order and in fact it was our adherence to duty and loyalty to a lost cause that caused us to be in this place and situation. There is no dishonor in acknowledging the reality of our situation. I propose that we live to fight another day." After some discussion, it was decided to accept the offer with only one proviso.

"Our parole would, of course, be contingent on the fact that we could not take the field against any French troops," said Laurency, as he and Longstreet resumed their conversation on the following day.

"That would be acceptable terms to me," responded Longstreet.

An awareness that he and his legionnaires might well live to fight another day caused just the ghost of a smile to flash momentarily across his features.

"I think that I will accept your proposal," he responded.

Mexico City

As soon as Longstreet concluded the process of solving the problem presented by the French Foreign Legion he sent gallopers racing north to advise the leadership. In Mexico City the Revolutionary Council was also hard at work.

"Our working groups have performed miracles. We have almost completed a new Constitution and legal system. Our governmental policy task force will present its final report at the next meeting of the council," said Breckenridge.

"Magnificent, absolutely magnificent," replied Santa Anna. "We are far ahead of schedule and still advancing."

A clerk entered the office and, with a glance at Breckenridge, walked to Santa Anna and handed him a message.

"Good news, I trust," said Breckenridge.

"Totally," answered Santa Anna. "We have received a communication from General Longstreet. The General advises us he that has surrounded the last Legion units on the Yucatan Peninsula and successfully completed discussions with the Legion Commanding Officer regarding a cessation of hostilities. He further reports that Maximilian and his bitch Carlotta have boarded a cargo ship that is escorted by a French frigate. The French naval units are being accompanied by two of our ships along with two English warships."

Santa Anna paused, a thoughtful frown on his features, said, "We must use this situation to our advantage. If nothing else we can improve our relations with Napoleon the III by allowing his cousin to return to him unscathed."

Napoleon III had been contacted by the Ambassadors from Prussia and England. The two had independently advised the French Emperor that both counties would consider continued support of the Maximilian government in Mexico to be, "acts not consistent with peaceful co-existence." This was correctly interpreted by the French Monarch as, "hands off Mexico, *now*!"

"I agree, totally," said Breckenridge. "We can permit Maximilian to leave without the loss of dignity that would accompany a formal surrender. We simply allow him to board ship and sail away and in return we may gain some goodwill from the Emperor of France and perhaps another doorway into Europe."

Davis, who had entered just in time to hear Santa Anna and Breckenridge, added, "Anything that allows us to settle that issue with minimal loss is the best path. God knows we already have enough on our plate. I say goodbye and good riddance! We must turn our focus on Juarez and his forces in the north."

Santa Anna said, "You're correct, my friend, Juarez is our primary enemy. His commander, General Zaragoza, is a very capable soldier. Despite his total lack of pedigree. He fights hard and is totally without mercy."

"I suggest we formally authorize the agreement Longstreet's made with the Legion." said Breckenridge.

"Yes, but one thing at a time, my friend," answered Santa Anna. "Let us celebrate this news first," waving forward a servant holding a bottle of chilled wine and several crystal goblets on a solid silver tray.

CHAPTER NINETEEN

February, 1866

Juarista Army, Northern Mexico

"Consider this a down payment from the Union, General Zaragoza," said OSS Operative-in-Charge, Easy Sinclair, "and just the first shipment of many."

Easy, along with the first delivery, had arrived a few days earlier. His purpose was to personally observe the entire supply process and address any problems that might arise.

"The Revolution thanks you, my friend," responded Zaragoza. "I can promise you we will put these weapons to good use."

The Mexican general had met with the young American a few times and had been impressed with his quiet competence and attention to detail. Zaragoza was a short, stocky man, whose Indian ancestry showed plainly. He was a graduate of Mexico's military Academy and a veteran of the Mexican-American conflict. He had served well, rising to the rank of general despite his lack of social standing. When Juarez had begun to consider a military solution to the political situation, Zaragoza had been a perfect answer. He was a hard, honest man, of solid military background with no political aspirations of his own and more importantly, one who shared Juarez's political and social views.

Zaragoza, Juarez and Sinclair sat in a tiny, poorly-appointed *cantina* situated in the middle of a small, mud-brick village in the mountainous region of northeastern Mexico. The town, Ciudad Anahuac, had been originally settled by the Aztecs, and was now serving as the temporary headquarters of Benito Juarez's Revolution. It was located some seventy miles south and west of Laredo and was currently experiencing the bite of the short Mexican winter. The village was the primary staging area for military equipment shipments from the Union. Supplies were stored then reloaded on mules and men and shipped to Juarista units bivouacked throughout the area.

The Juarista Army, some twenty-five thousand strong, occupied a number of villages and a few small cities in the northern third of Mexico. Juarez had declared that as soon as possible, his capitol was to be transferred to the larger, more imposing city of Monterrey.

"Santa Anna has allied himself with the renegades from my country and has beaten Maximilian. We think that their Revolutionary Council will soon consolidate most of central and southern Mexico under their control. We expect them to begin their campaign against your forces sometime in early spring," continued Easy, looking intently at the commander of the Juarista Army sitting next to him. "We will continue to supply you as long as you are willing to fight."

"For as long as the virgin weeps, we will fight," answered Zaragoza, with a grin.

Laredo, Texas Zone of Reconstruction

As the supplies for the Juarista's flowed through Laredo on their way south, General Custer found cause to celebrate.

"I give you success, gentlemen. To the Union and a new year," said Custer, holding up his wine glass.

"To the Union," responded Garrison, as he and Reno stood and drained their glasses.

"It appears our efforts to maintain Juarez as a viable force will meet with some success." said Garrison. "Operative Sinclair tells me our shipments are reaching their destinations in a timely fashion and in quantities that substantially improve the operational capabilities of General Zaragoza's forces."

"I personally can't see that he has any chance whatsoever of victory," judged Custer. "His forces are just not large enough for offensive operations. He will do well to simply garrison some of the northern cities. I doubt his ability to hold them once Lee moves in earnest. For the life of me, I can't envision him undertaking anything more than holding actions. It is my opinion that his only hope of victory is our direct intervention on his behalf."

"I concur, General. However, my actions and yours are dictated by orders from Washington," said Garrison, "and Washington currently wants us to maintain a minimal presence in Mexico. Our orders explicitly forbid any deliberate offensive action by American forces. We are to keep an eye on those southern gentlemen and their Army without any direct contact between their regular forces and ours."

"There is another issue you need to know about, General," continued Garrison. "We have recently become aware that operatives of the Revolutionary Council of Mexico are becoming active in our area. We will be stepping up our undercover activities substantially in order to counter this threat."

"And rightly so," chimed in Reno. "After all, we must remember they are all still our enemy."

"A point well taken, Major," murmured Custer, a thoughtful look in his eyes. "We must remember they are still our declared enemies. I think our regional force levels should be reviewed with an eye towards substantial reinforcements. After all, a mere two Corps to defend thousands of miles of frontier with a potentially hostile neighbor! How can Washington justify that? I will present my case in the strongest possible terms."

Mexico

Far to the south, in the heart of Mexico City, a chill, damp wind caused occasional flare-ups in the well-tended fireplace. Attending the meeting of the Revolutionary Council were: John Campbell, James Breckenridge, Raphael Semmes, Bedford Forrest, Robert E. Lee, Santa Anna, and Jefferson Davis.

Lee sat, idly admiring the solid gold inlay of the conference table. He thought, we've come a long way in a short time and we must take care not to stumble in our haste. Breckenridge, who was chairing the meeting, brought it to order with a single rap of his gavel. "Gentlemen, we will begin with a report from our Director of Intelligence."

Campbell slid his chair back from the table slightly, and grasping several papers in his hand, began reading from the field report summaries in a dry tone. "We know that OSS operatives have been providing military supplies to Juarez's forces by sea and land routes via several of the northern border towns. Their naval units are on continuous patrol along our entire east coast. We have strong evidence that these ships are constantly dropping off and picking up operatives of their OSS. We are in the process of placing a team in Laredo, but it will be some time before we can expect any useful information from that source."

"Thank you, John," said Breckenridge. "And now a naval summary," he continued, glancing at Admiral Semmes.

"We are keeping two ships at sea and two at the port Vera Cruz. Our ships are under orders to take no offensive action at all until such time as they receive specific orders to the contrary," said Semmes.

"General Lee, if you would?" asked Breckenridge.

"Sir," responded Lee, "we are continually receiving the most modern equipment from our English and German allies. I estimate that we will soon be able to field one additional infantry and one additional cavalry division. I am currently completing plans to initiate action against Zaragoza at the earliest possible moment. I have ordered General Hill to advance north with 2nd and 3rd Corps. His objective is the City of Leon. The Legion command of General Laurency is undergoing refit and supply prior to returning to active duty. And lastly, our weapons production facilities at New Tredegar are almost complete. Production will begin as soon as possible, quite probably within the month. Mr. Wilson Agar is the engineer-in-charge."

"Thank you, General." responded Breckenridge, who then turned and gestured to General Bedford Forrest, seated across the table. "General Forrest was entrusted with an especially difficult task as his part of the Phoenix Gambit. He has completed his assignments in a superb fashion and I want him to bring the council up to date."

Forrest had gained his reputation as a bold and daring cavalry commander as well as a fervent believer in the Confederate cause. He had become somewhat notorious as a result of atrocities committed by forces under his command. The action occurred at a Union fort designated Fort Pillow. After being surrounded and fighting until they were out of ammunition, the Union defenders had requested and received surrender terms; however, after it was discovered that the entire garrison of the fort was Negro, things quickly got very ugly.

When Forrest was advised of the situation he allowed his troops to massacre many of the black Union soldiers, even though he had already accepted their surrender. Hailed as something of a hero in the south, he was roundly vilified in the north. When Lee had broached the "Phoenix Gambit" to him, Forrest had eagerly volunteered to play a part, considering it an honor to be part of the plan.

Forrest stood and regarded the seated group of men. "Gentlemen, most of you know that I was ordered to bring as much of our precision industrial tools and the personnel to operate them; as well as a wide variety of specialists in business, industry, and the sciences into Mexico. My command was also tasked with bringing out the remaining gold reserves of the Confederacy. I can now report that these tasks have been successfully completed."

Forrest paused and looked at Breckenridge, who gave a quick assenting nod. Clearing his throat, the General continued, "What only a few of you know is that I was working on another equally essential task, the creation of a secret organization. This organization has two functions. First was to create and operate an underground route that would provide the means whereby more of our brethren from the Confederacy can find their way to us. This project has been code named "Project Home Coming." It allows our people to choose from three options. They can use the land route across the USA-Mexican border, sail from selected ports in the old CSA to Mexico, or sail from Canada to Mexico. As of today, all three options are enabled.

The second project I was ordered to create was a network of spies and covert action groups within the Union. With the most able assistance of Mr. Campbell, I can now announce that the operation is functioning throughout a great deal of what once was the Confederate States of America as well as in several Union States. It has been given the code name of "Klu Klux Klan." Should the need arise, we have access to several thousand armed and organized men emplaced throughout the Union."

"General," said Campbell, "you have done a truly outstanding job. You have both our highest regards and admiration."

"Here, here," said Breckenridge.

"One more item we must deal with," said Davis, "Custer is attempting to create support for a pre-emptive strike against us. If he is successful in convincing Washington that a Union invasion in support of Juarez could be successful, we would be in serious trouble. We think that the Union currently fields approximately four hundred thousand troops and even though almost a quarter are freed slaves, they could simply overwhelm us. An all-out invasion by the Union Army would, in fact, destroy us. Can we take the chance that his views will not prevail or should we consider more direct action?"

"I think direct action is the best course," answered Campbell, "Custer is well known as an agitator. He has created a lot of enemies. A covert operation against him could be managed and our participation could be hidden. Or even better, we could try to place the blame on others."

Breckenridge said, "I think that we must be aggressive in this instance. Custer will not go away of his own accord and the man presents a clear and present danger to us."

Santa Anna interjected, "Gentlemen, if you have a boil, you lance it. If you have an infection, you destroy it. I perceive Custer as a major irritation. Let us remove this irritation."

CHAPTER TWENTY

March, 1866

Laredo, Texas Zone of Reconstruction

The object of Santa Anna's ire, George Armstrong Custer, looked down from his third-story office at the hustle and bustle of his new and expanded headquarters and smiled. "We've come a long, long way, Reno. Washington actually listened to my request for troops. Three additional Infantry Corps, Reno, three! We must make sure the Army of the Rio Grande becomes a force those rebels will have to consider, a force to contend with. I must carefully consider how to employ this command to its best advantage."

Smiling, he walked to his desk and sat. "You know, Reno, it appears everything about Laredo is growing in leaps and bounds! My God, even a new theater," he observed, looking through the window behind him with some distaste at the huge billboard bearing the face of that darling of the arts, John W. Booth. The advertisement hung from the side of the Century Hotel, and obscured his entire view of Third Avenue.

"Well, sir," responded Reno, with a grin, "consider it a sign of civilization."

"I suppose," returned Custer, as he walked back to his desk to continue his never- ending paperwork. As the paperwork and organizational components of directing the Texas Zone of Reconstruction had begun to impact on Custer, he had become less enamored of some aspects of his command.

It was not uncommon for him to make up reasons to leave his office for several days at a time and take the field in order to "investigate or review" outlying units of his command. Reno, loyal to a fault, had frequently been required to double his efforts in order to stay even with the paperwork.

Laredo's mercurial growth had attracted more than just soldiers, businessmen and civil servants. Along with the men came women, children, and of course, the arts. An invitation from the "Laredo Ladies for the Arts" requesting Custer's presence at the opening of Laredo's public theatre had resulted in an explosion of monumental proportions, along with an official edict that any similar requests be directly routed to Reno's office. Ever the loyal and competent subordinate, Reno's able performance of his added duties had served to somewhat reduce Custer's ire.

A gentle breeze jostled the curtain of the fourth-floor room of Laredo's new Century Hotel where John W. Booth and Samuel Arnold were meeting. "Every time I see the Union flag flying in Texas I get angrier," snarled Booth, as he paced back and forth across the hotel room.

"Well," answered Arnold, "why don't you consider it motivation."

The two men, along with the entire production company, had arrived in Laredo as part of a swing through the larger cities of the "Zones of Reconstruction." The tour, ostensibly promoted as a morale booster for Union officers stationed far from home, provided an excellent opportunity for intelligence gathering and coordination of intelligence operations throughout the entire area.

"I'll motivate them all to hell," said Booth, "and that bastard Custer will lead the way."

"As to that, we will need a different approach to get to him, as he is definitely not interested in the theater," responded Arnold, a lopsided grin on his features.

"So, Custer, an unenlightened barbarian, who would have guessed it?" laughed Booth.

"I've got a man in Custer's office, one of the cleaning staff. He lost a brother at Gettysburg. He'll do as much as he can, doesn't even want money."

"Outstanding. Mexico wants Custer taken out, if at all possible."

"If it's possible, we'll get it done."

"I've every faith in your abilities, Arnold, every faith."

Later that evening, as he had been doing for the past few weeks, Arnold began his regular visitations to the bars in the seedier, less affluent parts of town. He went to the neighborhoods where one would find the disenfranchised, the poor and the angry. Arnold was, in effect, trolling for men, the kind who were familiar with and unafraid of violence, and who had proven themselves able under fire. In a matter of weeks, he had assembled a team of what he thought were ex-confederate soldiers and had begun their training.

Several days after Arnold and Booth met, a man stood waiting outside the entrance to a pawn shop in a dingy part of town. He quietly watched the bustling traffic on the busy

Laredo street, slowly and unobtrusively sweeping his gaze up and down. Satisfying himself that he was not being observed, he quickly turned and entered the store. The man walked to the rear of the building, then passed through a doorway into a small office.

"Good to see you, Stan," said OSS Team Leader Harold Evans from his seat behind the desk.

"And you, too, sir," responded Stan Canino, OSS undercover operative.

"So, what's up with the KKK?" asked Evans.

"I think that they're going to be ready soon, so I'm guessing they will commit at the earliest possible moment," answered Stan. "If I can't make direct contact once they give the "go" order, I'll use a dead-drop to advise you as soon as I have anything concrete."

"Excellent," said Evans. "I'll keep our men on standby until we get a confirmation from you, and then we will make our counter-move. Of course, I want as much lead time as possible."

"I'll do the best I can. That Arnold is a cagey bastard. He doesn't let much get by him," answered Stan.

Having completed his contact he turned and left the building, stopping to buy a watch on the way out; just in case, he thought, just in case. Evans remained seated for several moments after Canino had left, then rose and exited by the door in the rear of the office.

Arnold, dedicated and competent as he was, had been very busy. Once he had decided he had enough men and they had been sufficiently trained, he ordered them to remain at a campsite he had chosen, located several miles outside the city. He detailed a few of his men to begin a systematic, twenty-four hours a day surveillance of Custer's daily movements. These teams were relieved every few days. This procedure, along with input from their contact in Custer's office, allowed them to develop a comprehensive picture of Custer's activities.

After careful review a location was chosen and the team began a series of dry runs which continued until Arnold was satisfied that each member was totally familiar with his role. Once the "where" was solved, they began the wait for the right "when." A few days later it happened. Their contact in Custer's office, a civilian clerk, advised them of Custer's schedule for the next day.

The ambush site selected provided maximum protection as well as several escape routes for the eight men of the strike team. Custer and his escort would pass down a relatively narrow street that was bordered on both sides by connected two and three story buildings.

The plan was to wait until Custer and his escort was in the middle of the block. The intersections before and behind would then be blocked by wagons heavily laden with firewood. The drivers would unhitch the horses, and the wagons would be left in place. The shooters, spread out on buildings located on both sides of the street, had been ordered to wait until Arnold fired the first round.

On the appointed day the KKK teams arrived, assumed their positions and were inspected by Arnold, who then left to assume his post. He arrived and sat back, sheltered from sight by the building's façade, waiting to give the signal. Suddenly, he saw one of his team, a man who was supposed to be across the street, creeping across the rooftop towards him!

"What the hell are you doing here? Damn it! You're supposed to be at your post!" He halted in momentary confusion as the man raised his gun and pointed it directly at him. Knowing it was useless, but refusing to simply surrender, he lunged upwards while at the same time reaching in vain for his holstered weapon. His last thought before OSS operative Stan Canino pulled the trigger was that at least one of the other shooters would take out their target. As it turned out, he was wrong.

Operative Harold Evans rode his horse down the narrow street, tensely awaiting the first volley. As team leader, he had the unenviable job of wearing Custer's gaudily-appointed uniform, feather-capped hat pulled down low, riding at the head of the cavalry escort.

At the sound of the shot that ended Sam Arnold's life, he, along with the rest of the troop, threw themselves from their mounts and began returning fire at the snipers. Almost immediately OSS hunter-killer teams, who had pre-positioned themselves before dawn along the route, converged on the sound of firing.

For safety's sake, these operatives were wearing the OSS field uniform, a black hat and tunic with navy-blue trousers, all with silver facings. Each uniform sported a silver shoulder patch of an "All Seeing Eye," along with the OSS motto "Eternal Vigilance."

Evans held his position behind a water trough, rising up to take a shot at his mostly unseen adversaries in order to keep their attention focused on him as his support teams closed the trap. The firing on the adjacent roof tops reached a sudden crescendo and then abruptly stopped. Waiting a moment, then warily rising, ready in an instant to resume cover, he began to walk across the street towards the OSS agents approaching from either end of the road.

"We've cleared the roof tops," reported one of his men. "Only one or two got away."

"Excellent," responded Evans. "Enemy casualties?"

"Two surrendered unhurt, three wounded, two dead," was the response. "A good day's work."

"Yes." answered Evans. "A good days work all around. I'll report to Garrison as soon as we clean up this mess."

A few hours later, Evans completed his report to Garrison, who immediately went to Custer's office to report the good news in person.

"I knew you'd want to know immediately, sir," said Garrison, as he entered Custer's office. "As far as we can tell, we have the entire team!"

Custer stood up, walked over to Garrison, and extending his hand to him, said, "Those traitors are right to hate and fear me. If I ever get the chance I'll make them pay ten-fold. Assassination is a coward's tool and I despise its use as much as I despise those who employ it. By God, someday, some-way, they'll pay!"

CHAPTER TWENTY ONE

April, 1866

City of Leon, Mexico

In obedience to Robert E. Lee's orders, General A. P. Hill began his campaign by sending both II and III Corps northward from Mexico City. Due to road issues the units moved in two parallel columns. His goal was to take the cities of Leon and Monterrey, in that order. Once he'd established control of both cities he would then continue north until reaching the USA-Mexican border.

The Revolutionary Army found transportation a constant problem, The roads in Mexico were often in poor condition, frequently narrow, meandering trails. Bridges were in poor repair and there was a dire shortage of both railroad cars, engines and track. Hill was forced to move at a snail's pace while his troops labored furiously to build or upgrade the required transportation facilities as they marched north from Mexico City. The lack of usable roadway had a severe and negative impact on his campaign timetable from the outset.

It took Hill several weeks of hard marching and back-breaking construction to move his command to a point just south of Leon. On the march he used his Cavalry Divisions to screen his advance and clear out most of the Juarista forces between himself and the city. When he finally reached the outskirts of Leon, General Hill had the Infantry Divisions of both Corps begin the construction of siege works. Despite numerous harassing attacks by the city's garrison, they eventually succeeded in completely surrounding Leon.

His fortifications were composed of two lines of trenches and batteries of both Parrot heavy siege guns as well as lighter 3-inch field artillery. The guns were all positioned on the highest points available. All the artillery was protected by sandbag revetments and connected by communication trenches to their respective infantry support units. Within a few days the walled city of Leon, the southern-most citadel controlled by Juarista units, trembled from the impact of shells arcing in from entrenched artillery batteries.

"We estimate enemy effectives at five to seven thousand troops and perhaps two dozen heavy weapons," said Colonel Gordon, Hill's Chief of Staff and briefing officer. "And," he continued, "It is our intent to take the city by assault as soon as our artillery has silenced their heavy weapons and sufficiently breached the walls. We are subjecting the city to a heavy artillery barrage, which has already severely reduced most of the outer defenses. We have offered them the opportunity to surrender twice. The second time our emissary was returned in several parts."

An angry murmur from the assembled officers greeted this revelation.

"Animals in need of a lesson," grated the III Corps commander, Major General Garcia, "and my men will be happy to provide it."

As the Revolutionary Army tightened its grip on the beleaguered city the encircled Juarstai garrison responded as best it could. High in the bell tower of one of the cities many cathedrals, Colonel Jesus Moreno, Executive Officer of the Zapata Brigade, put his telescope to his eye for his daily appraisal of the Revolutionary Army entrenchments. "Aha," he said to Sergeant Orto Emmanuel, who accompanied him on his intelligence gathering rounds. "Our friends have been busy overnight. They have brought their field guns to within point blank range, and this is decidedly not good."

"Shall I inform General Zapata, Sir?" queried Orto.

"No, my sergeant, allow me to be the bearer of the bad news," answered Moreno. He climbed down and the two men began walking back through the desolation and wreckage that had been the beautiful city of Leon. Moreno and Emmanuel were both veterans, having been soldiers in service to Juarez for several years. Although officer and enlisted man, they had a mutual respect for each other. Moreno, educated, came from a middle class family while Emmanuel, illiterate, was peasant born. Having found a home in the military neither was encumbered by a family or emotional entanglement.

Both men were hard, focused career soldiers.

As the made their way slowly through the destruction, they passed occasional groups of the city's inhabitants. Some were skulking in the ruins of their homes; others wandered aimlessly about in a constant search for anything edible. Although military food stuffs were available, those supplies were not distributed to the general population, whose own stores had been quickly depleted. Starvation had created a situation where the definition of what was edible had become quite debatable, he noted, as he watched a group of small children come to blows over what appeared to be a dog's leg.

"We came to them as saviors but have become instead their executioners," he said to Emmanuel, his voice tight with anger.

"We have God on our side, Captain, do we not?" answered Emmanuel.

"Of course we do. You are right once again, sergeant," answered Moreno, keeping his face completely blank. Reaching the remnant of one of Leon's largest buildings, Moreno climbed until he reached a position from which he could observe a different part of the encircling army. He spent several minutes observing, then returned to the ground. Over the course of several hours he repeated this process at numerous points around the city.

"My General," said Moreno, some time later, as he stood before the seated Zapata, the Juarista garrison commander, "they can be inside our walls within forty-eight hours and there is nothing we can do to stop them."

"Captain," answered Zapata, "you are wrong. There are, in fact, two things that we can do. The first thing we can do is kill as many of them as we can. The second thing we can do is die while we kill more of them."

Zapata paused for a moment as he regarded Moreno. He scribbled a message, then said, "Captain, you have served me well. You are a good soldier. I order you to make sure this dispatch gets to Juarez."

Moreno took the dispatch from Zapata, looked him in the eye, said, "I will send my sergeant with the message."

A few hours before dawn on the following morning sergeant Orto Emmanuel began working his way through the Revolutionary Army lines. Unarmed and wearing civilian dress, moving slowly between piles of rubble and wreckage; he gradually made his way through the battered city until he arrived at the remnants of the city walls, just before dusk. Shortly after sunset, he carefully left the rubble and continued on his way out of the city. Prowling through the dark, he finally found what he was seeking, a large number of cavalry horses picketed in several long lines. Crawling slowly forward, he began to work the last horse on the line loose from its tether. Just as he was about to mount, one of the sentries began walking towards him.

Orto let go of the rope holding the horse, positioned himself on the side of the animal opposite the sentry, and waited until the man had passed him. He stepped quickly and silently from behind the horse and encircled the guard's neck with the only weapon he had allowed himself, a short length of rope called a *garrote*, that became a deadly weapon in his powerful hands. After a few moments of desperate, yet unobtrusive, struggle, he slowly lowered the corpse to the ground and mounted the horse. A moment later he had faded into the dark, leaving the lifeless soldier as sole testament to his trespass. Riding bareback, he left the embattled city behind and traveled north to deliver the last communication from Leon.

After the artillery had punched several huge holes in the Leon's walls, it began pounding the trenches and secondary fortifications, as well as the center of the city, in order to soften up the infantry defenders. When the new targeting became obvious, Sergeant Thomas Brown, A company, 4th Georgia Rifles, left the forward trenches where he had been viewing the artillery strikes and returned to his platoon. The sergeant was a competent, veteran soldier. Single, both parents dead, he had enlisted shortly after Manassas at the age of seventeen. Brown had fought in most of the major battles and campaigns of the Army of Northern Virginia.

As soon as he arrived at his men's position, he began issuing orders. "Ready up, boys! We're gonna be in the thick of it real soon. Check your ammo and canteens and fill'em up if they ain't already." A chorus of acknowledgments greeted his statement and caused a flurry of activity by the men.

A few hours later the Company received an order to prepare to attack. Brown ordered his men into the innermost ring of trenches, and then had them wait for the command. The moment the artillery barrage ended the Lieutenant to Brown's right stood up, waved his sword and shouted, "Follow me, men!" He climbed up the side of the trench, just ahead of Brown. Corporal Biddle, to Brown's left, a four-year veteran, took exactly one step forward, then pitched backward from the lip of the trench, his wound spraying a thin film of blood and brain over the trench floor.

"Charge, charge!" shouted Brown. He and his men ran through the still-smoking breaches in the walls. "Odd number squads over-watch, even number squads advance!" he yelled, rage hardening his voice, as more and more of his men fell victim to the determined resistance of the Juarista defenders.

So valiant was the Juarista defense that as darkness on the first day approached, Revolutionary Army forces had advanced, on average, less than one hundred yards past the walls. The major part of the city still remained in Juarista hands. The few blocks taken by the Revolutionary Army, were in a state of almost total destruction.

Under the cover of darkness Brown strode through the camp of his much-depleted platoon, sending some of the more seriously wounded to the rear and insuring that the remaining men had sufficient food, water and ammunition for what promised to be a deadly day's work. The bloody battle of Leon continued at dawn with a series of attacks and counter- attacks.

Late that afternoon, as the battle for the city still raged, Generals Hill and Garcia met.

"General," reported General Garcia, as he stood before the seated Hill, "they are fighting well, but we are pushing them hard. Soon, I think, most of the city will be ours."

"Perhaps, General, perhaps," responded Hill. "At any rate, it seems that we will pay for this city with more than just a pound of flesh. I am going to commit two additional brigades from 7th Division tomorrow morning. I want to end this as soon as possible without being bled white."

"Whatever it takes," countered Garcia. "Eventually Leon will be ours."

Hill stood and walked to the open tent flap, stepping outside where he could clearly see the depth of destruction his army was causing. Almost the entire wall surrounding Leon had been reduced to piles of rubble. Several raging fires were devouring sections of the city, with a good deal of the rest little more than ruin. The fires dull glow reflected off the low, heavy cloud cover and gave an almost surreal aspect to the scene. Stepping back inside, and turning to Garcia, he said, "They've created their own Hades and it seems that many will choose to die in it."

As dawn's light began to filter through the pall of smoke hanging over the tortured city, Brown's infantry platoon began once again making its way slowly down the wide, tree-lined boulevards that led to the city's center. Advancing in quick bursts, alternating sprinting or providing covering fire, they made their way through constant enemy sniper and mortar rounds. They slowly closed on a grandly ornate but heavily damaged cathedral. It formed one side of a huge square in the central part of the city.

The entrance to the once magnificent church was mostly in ruin. Huge brass front doors were lying flat on the ground, and bits and pieces of statuary were scattered about. Several lifeless bodies were sprawled on the entrance steps. An ornately painted, man-sized reproduction of Jesus, pedestal included, sat squarely in the middle of the avenue completely unharmed. Flames licked hungrily at the surrounding wreckage on the remaining three sides of the square. Columns of smoke drifted slowly into the still air, more than one bearing the unmistakable odor of cooking meat.

A ragged musket volley, fired from positions in and around the partially-destroyed place of worship, dropped two of Brown's men to the ground. One lay motionless, the other shrieking as he held the stump of his now handless left arm with his right hand, bright red arterial blood spurting rhythmically from the wound. The rest of the platoon scattered to find what cover they could.

Cautiously raising himself up from behind the cover of a tumbled pile of masonry, Brown looked over the situation. He ignored the wounded man, whose cries became whimpers, then silence, as the red stain continued to widen. Using hand signals, he ordered his grenadier forward.

Inside the badly-battered cathedral, Captain Moreno reloaded his revolver with quick, practiced hands, as he squinted through the cathedral window towards the enemy positions, carefully marking where the advancing soldiers had taken cover.

"Don't fire till you have a target. Make every shot count, and keep down as you reload," he ordered, in a voice made hoarse from lack of water. "Make them pay for every inch." At that moment a grenade, fuse sizzling, sailed into the cathedral. The captain saw it, and without hesitation, threw his body on top of it. The force of the explosion literally shredded his body, spraying him over several of his men.

For the next few hours the two sides contested for possession of the ruins in a series of deadly, hard-fought assaults by company and platoon-sized units. It was not until after sundown that Brown's men finally took and held the cathedral. The remnants of Moreno's company, outflanked on both sides, fell back yet again from the insistent pressure.

As Garcia's III Corps continued their assault, the casualty list reached alarming proportions, and General Hill ordered General Garcia to report to him again while the advance was temporarily halted. Once again the two officers met in General Hill's headquarters.

"General," said Garcia, "my troops have pushed into the city's central square from the east and south. Although resistance is extreme, we are slowly taking control. In most cases they are dying rather than surrendering. This will prove to be an extremely bloody victory. Even after we flew the red flag they refused to surrender." Here Garcia was alluding to the Spanish military custom of taking no prisoners if the enemy had refused offers of an honorable surrender.

"Surrender or die!" mused Hill. "An interesting concept. At any rate, I leave you to consolidate our victory here. Your orders are to take, secure, and garrison the city and pacify the immediate area. As soon as you have completed those tasks send me the 6th Division with a brigade of cavalry. Tomorrow morning I am going to disengage II Corps and begin my advance on Monterrey."

"As you order, sir," said Garcia who saluted, turned and left the tent.

Remnants of the Zapata Brigade continued to defend the blood-drenched ruins with amazing ferocity, giving ground only in the last extreme and even launching a few minor counter-attacks with some success. Revolutionary Council units continued to press hard and pay dearly for every foot they conquered.

Lt. Brown, recipient of a battlefield commission and so new an officer that he still wore both his sergeant's insignia and Lieutenant's bars, signaled his platoon to halt. Using hand signs, he instructed his men to move to flanking positions, as prelude to rushing the strongpoint. The troops, with an efficiency born of hard-won lessons, silently followed his order, fixing bayonets and gathering themselves for the rush.

Some twenty yards to Brown's left a hand grenade arced over a pile of rubble and exploded, tossing a small cloud of flesh and rock into the air, a fist-size piece of shrapnel ripping past his head. This was followed almost immediately by a second explosion to his right. Almost simultaneously, a group of tattered, filthy men leaped from cover, heading straight for his unit.

Brown whipped up his rifle, took aim and fired several rounds, dropping two attackers, while shouting "Fire, fire!" to his men. The remainder of the platoon opened up with a murderous barrage, killing or wounding almost all the attackers; one of them, his machete falling from his dead hand, tumbled to the ground at Brown's feet. The battle raged on in hand-to-hand combat for a few moments more until all the dying had been done and silence once more settled on this little piece of hell.

Realizing the attack was over, Brown ordered some of his men to secure the perimeter and others to see to the wounded. He made no comment when none of them paid any attention to those enemies who still pumped their blood onto the dirt beneath them. It wasn't until shortly after they had resumed advancing that he realized not one of the Zapata's had tried to give up. All had chosen death to surrender.

When the inevitable surrender of Leon finally came to pass, of the original seven thousand men in the Juarista garrison, there were less than three thousand alive, including the wounded. Fully one quarter of the city's civilian population was either dead or dying, and most of the remainder was homeless. At the battle's conclusion, the city was both liberated and devastated.

CHAPTER TWENTY TWO

May, 1866

Mexico City

General Lee sat in his office, the same once occupied by General Laurency, addressing a mound of paperwork. Colonel Venable entered Lee's office and stopped in front of the desk.

"Dispatch from Garcia's command in Leon. I think you need to see this immediately, sir," he said, his voice cold and distant.

Hearing the tone of Venable's voice, Lee looked up sharply and took the message from the proffered hand. He read it and immediately went white with anger. "My God! What was he thinking? I want to see Santa Anna, Davis, and Breckenridge as soon as can be arranged!"

"Very good, sir," responded Venable, saluting, and then leaving the office.

A few hours later the four men sat around a conference table.

Lee spoke, his voice heavy with emotion. "This is not warfare; this is slaughter, butcher's work! I'll not have any command of mine party to this ever again."

"My General," replied Santa Anna, "please, I see you are most distraught. This situation is unfortunate, but in hindsight almost unavoidable. It is a clash of culture and custom. An honorable conclusion to a battle to the end, conducted according to our military traditions. And, I note, done under the command of General Garcia."

"Yes," said Davis, "A Mexican response to a Mexican situation. We must allow our noble allies the right to their traditions. With all due respect, General, I would ask that you remember the Alamo. General Garcia behaved entirely within his accepted principles of warfare. I hope that you can see that we need not condone it, but merely accept it as a military policy of a valued ally."

"Well, I suppose our institution of slavery may not sit right with our allies," added Breckenridge, "but I have not heard them complain."

"Well said, John," said Santa Anna, who looked straight at Lee and continued, "I would remind you that we in Mexico outlawed slavery many years ago."

"Behavior like this will only make them fight harder," warned Lee. "I tell you, no good can come of it."

As the conversation continued, Lee rose and walked out of the room onto the wide balcony that overlooked the huge central square. He stood at the rail, hands clasped behind him, staring off into space until he heard a slight sound behind him. Without even turning he said, "Colonel Venable, I find myself in disagreement with those people over some of the things we are doing. A massacre of surrendered soldiers does not sit well with me, not at all. We are building a foundation on quicksand and eventually we will pay the price. I have given my word to see this out to the best of my ability and I shall do so, but it does not sit easy with me."

Venable, seeing Lee's pain, responded. "Sir, you have done all that you can. After all, the action was taken by General Garcia. Perhaps we must focus on victory first. After all, Sir, if we are not triumphant, there is no other option."

Lee gazed at Venable for a moment before replying in a soft, ruminative voice, "So the end would justify the means, would it?"

"General, we have so little room to maneuver and the odds are still against us. I think we must accept this in the name of expediency." responded Venable.

Lee turned away and gazing into the distance gave no answer.

Galveston, Texas Zone of Reconstruction

Staff Lieutenant Arthur Strong stood for a moment on the veranda outside Admiral Farragut's top floor office. He paused, enjoying the gentle breeze that brought a slight taste of salt from the dark blue, tranquil waters of the Gulf of Mexico. From his position, he could admire the view of the Gulf Squadron's ships that either lay at anchor in the harbor or were secured to the docks. Sighing, he set his cap square and knocked once before entering with the newest OSS intelligence briefs. He approached the desk, placed the pages in the required box on Farragut's desk, and then quickly turned to leave.

"I think not, Artie," said the Admiral with a smile, as he reached for the just arrived paperwork. "You know I always value your summaries."

"This one is bad, sir, very, very bad," said Strong. "Apparently, culture clash is having a negative impact on our renegade rebels. It seems that the Spanish military has a custom that if the enemy is in the act of armed rebellion then they are guilty of treason. That is a crime punishable by death. Their term for it is "Flying the Red Flag" and if they fly it and you don't surrender right...."

"Good Lord!" exclaimed Farragut, horror clear on his features. "Do you mean to say...?"

"Exactly right, sir," interjected Strong, anger evident in his tone. "They did it to one out of every ten prisoners they took, wounded or not. Some three hundred men were hung along the road from Leon to Mexico City."

"One fine day they might just find themselves on the wrong side of that nasty little military custom," said Farragut, anger clear in his tone, as he stood and walked out onto the veranda, "It would serve them right, though, wouldn't it."

Mexico City

Sunlight streamed through the huge, stained-glass windows of the Revolutionary Palace as Secretary of War John Campbell walked slowly up the grand stairway on the way to Breckenridge's office. The sentries lining the hall presented arms as he walked by. Each Praetorian Guardsman armed with a bayonet-tipped weapon fresh off a transport ship from Prussia and a green and white uniform made of English cotton..

I must check on the weapons production facilities at New Tredegar, thought Campbell. We must not remain so dependent on our allies' good will. Weapons production must be a priority. He continued down the hall, as he pondered the problem, and entered the last office.

Breckenridge rose and said, "More news from agent "Star," I take it."

"Yes," replied Campbell. "We have been dealt a setback. It seems that the OSS was aware of the plans regarding Custer. Our guess is that they infiltrated our operation and Arnold didn't catch on. Almost the entire team was either killed or captured and "Star" doesn't know if he has been compromised. I'm going to relocate "Star" and suspend all operations in that area until further notice."

"Absolutely," replied Breckenridge. "Make sure he distances himself as much as he can. He is much too valuable to lose right now. It could take months if not years to replace him."

"According to him, that would require an act of God," answered Campbell with a grin.

"What is the current status of the rest of our operations in the Zones, John?" asked Breckenridge.

"Better than we dared hope," was the answer. "Our people are responding magnificently. We have begun implementing "Homecoming" in almost every state. We have started the placement procedures throughout central and southern Mexico with great success."

"Excellent," said Breckenridge. "How's Forrest's Klu Klux Klan program progressing?"

"We have been rather successful in that area too, James," replied Campbell. "Most of our personnel are veterans, volunteers from disbanded combat units. We have sufficient numbers to begin fielding KKK forces in most of the old Confederate states as well as several major northern cities. We are limiting our activities to reprisals against selected Union targets. We are also using our "underground highway" to ship arms northward. Forrest has done an excellent job and we are building on his efforts."

"Another outstanding effort by the two of you. My congratulations," concluded Breckenridge.

Georgia Zone of Reconstruction

In the sleepy county seat of Johnsonville, Georgia, the KKK was slowly but tenaciously spreading its tentacles. Jethro Scruggs was unmarried, thirty-two years old, tall and slim with a nervous energy that gave him an inner strength not apparent from his sparse frame. Jethro was a man of strong convictions, one of those being all men were in fact equal, and that slavery was inherently evil. Although seldom expressed, his viewpoints did not make him a popular person.

At an early age he'd discovered that he was captivated more by the elegance and beauty of mathematics then by any member of the opposite sex. Being solitary by nature, his social limitations did not overwhelm him. A graduate of Georgia's State College, Jethro was a civil engineer by training. Given his personal views as well as essential skills, he had spent the war years on the home front, employed as a county engineer. He diligently applied himself to his job, and in doing so became well known for his abilities and competence throughout the state. When his parents died, within months of each other and just before the outset of war, he continued to reside in the same house, comfortable and secure, a sedentary creature of habit.

The original contact had occurred as he was leaving Sunday Service. A man had grasped his hand, shook it, and covertly left a piece of paper in it. Jethro had not reacted right away, but had continued walking back to his home after first carefully depositing the piece of paper in his pocket. When he reached home, Jethro retrieved the missive and read. "Herricks' farm 10 PM tonight."

The small farm was vacant, having been foreclosed by the local bank. It was located about four miles outside of town. Arriving at the appointed time, he was met by a white-robed and hooded man who told him to dismount and tether his horse. He complied and was ushered into the barn by another similarly costumed figure. He was not surprised to see a number of local men present, some of whom he knew.

One of the disguised men stood on a platform that had been set up along one wall of the barn. Behind him, tacked to the wall, was a Confederate flag. The man was flanked on either side by two more gowned men, each holding aloft a burning torch. Jethro, who could on occasion be as cynical as any man, thought to himself, tacky, but at the same time, effective.

The man in the center advanced to the edge of the platform and addressed the group. "I am the regional leader of the KKK. You all know that President Davis and General Lee are building a new land for us. You all know that our struggle for freedom continues in Mexico. We are building a new country and we are inviting selected men to join us. We need men with skills in business, finance and all the sciences. We need brave men who are willing to sacrifice for the greater good. We need men of valor and vision who are willing to use their skills and abilities to assist us in creating our own future!"

As the man spoke, Jethro looked about him at the faces of the men being addressed. On more than one he saw looks of hope as each man began to understand what was being offered them. Despite his natural inclination to avoid change, he began to feel himself drawn towards the idea. Listening to the speech he imagined himself part of a great and glorious mission. He would become part of a crusade, a quest to recreate a new and better Confederacy in a new land.

Since the surrender, things had gone from bad to worse. The economy was in ruins, and the few factories remaining in operation had been taken over by northern industrial magnates with imported Irish management and freed slave labor. Many of the large plantations had been confiscated by the Union and parceled out to political and military people as spoils of war. Many had been broken up into much smaller farms and given to blacks or discharged union soldiers.

Thousands of freed slaves and confederate veterans competed for the few available jobs, most of which offered barely subsistence wages. Gangs of rootless men, both white and black, roamed the country side raping, murdering and looting with impunity. He had not been paid for the last three months as the state, with many elected officials jailed for treason and an almost non-existent tax base, had been forced to declare bankruptcy.

Areas that were under direct Union control fared little better as occupying troops were in the habit of confiscating as contraband any food or other supplies that they might need. In order to make up manpower needs the Union had raised several Corps of Negro troops and had posted them to most of the "Zones of Reconstruction," much to the dismay of the average southerner.

The only hope of protection for most of the population came from a new organization which called itself the

"Knights of the Klu Klux Klan." The KKK was a highly secretive, well-supplied and organized force which had sprung up throughout the South. Despite their rather ridiculous name and apparel, these men often provided the only protection and hope for the oppressed southern people. They would appear and then disappear into the countryside, despite the best efforts of the occupying armies to track them down.

Having completed his presentation, the man on the platform, along with several other similarly dressed men, began to circulate through the crowd, talking to individuals or small groups of men. Jethro stood still until one of the KKK men reached his side and addressed him directly.

"My name is Joe," said the gowned figure, offering a hand which Jethro promptly shook.

"What do you think about the situation here?" asked Joe.

"I think things have gone to hell in a handbasket," responded Jethro, with unusual vigor.

"As do many of us, which is why we're here recruiting men for the cause," said Joe. "Does what I said make sense to you? Do you want to be part of a new beginning? Would you like to build a new country with Lee and Davis?"

Jethro thought about his current state of affairs and how hopeless it all seemed. He also thought about a great adventure. After a moment he said, "I think I would like to hear a great deal more, Joe."

Monterrey, Mexico

Set in the foothills of the Sierra Madre Oriental Mountains, Juarez's capitol, the city of Monterrey sat nestled between two major rivers, its white-washed walls gleaming in the bright Mexican sun. The city had been declared the capitol of the Juarista Republic of Mexico and was currently serving as the primary base for his army. The influx of soldiers, refugees, business men, and other entrepreneurs had swollen the population to twice its normal size and had created an almost carnival air of expectation.

The army was bivouacked in tent cities running parallel to the two rivers that provided water to the city. After his arrival, it had taken Orto almost an entire day to find Zaragoza's headquarters. It had taken almost as long to convince someone to allow him to make his report to the general.

The good sergeant had stubbornly insisted on a face-to-face meeting because Major Moreno had told him to report to the general and that was what he would do. Eventually he had been escorted to Zaragoza who had listened intently, not interrupting even once, until the sergeant completed his tale and stood mute before him.

"Sergeant Emmanuel, you have done a great service for your country," said General Zaragoza. "Go and find yourself something to eat, and then get some sleep. Come back tomorrow and there will be orders for you."

"As you command, my general," responded Emmanuel.

As Emmanuel followed the staff corporal out the door, Zaragoza left his office to find Juarez and inform him of the disaster at Leon.

"So, General, what now?" asked Juarez.

"We currently hold most of the northern third of Mexico. We have access to a substantial quantity of military supplies. The people are with us and willing to support us with food and soldiers," replied Zaragoza. "However, we cannot continue to simply garrison the towns and cities. If we do nothing but maintain a defensive posture, then those bastards will defeat us piecemeal, one city at a time. I must find a place where the terrain is favorable and will serve to offset our enemies' advantages. Their army is a veteran force, better trained and armed, but I believe our forces are capable of winning a defensive battle."

Zaragoza paced back and forth as he spoke, his movement betraying his inner anxiety. He continued, "Once I find the type of terrain we need we will move our entire army there. We will dig in and let them come to us. Our strategy will be simple, bleed them dry, then break them. A victory, or even a stalemate, if destructive enough to our enemy, might be enough for the United States to recognize us and provide direct military support."

"I have faith in you, General," replied Juarez, gazing steadily into Zaragoza's eyes. He thought, this is a hard and capable man, the kind of man we must have if we are to win. He said, "I must know. Is this a plan for victory, or is it our last desperate gamble?"

"My President, in truth it is some of both. I have had some interesting correspondence with the Union General Custer regarding the possibility of joint operations between our two forces. Unfortunately, his enthusiasm for intervention is not shared by his superiors in Washington. Without direct Union assistance, I think that my plan is our only option for success," replied Zaragoza.

CHAPTER TWENTY THREE

June, 1866

Alabama Zone of Reconstruction

The port city of Mobile sweltered as the hot, humid atmosphere of a summer Alabama night smothered sound and coated everything in a layer of slightly salty dampness. Scudding cloud cover sheathed the moon in silvery haze causing land and sea to merge almost imperceptibly. Most of the shoreline was chocked with tall reeds and marsh grass. Man-made sandy beaches were scattered here and there along the shore. Secreted in a few carefully chosen positions, a few dozen ex-Confederate refugees and KKK members waited on one such beach. It sat at the end of a narrow winding trail that led through miles of otherwise trackless bayous. The smell of burning metal emanated from the lantern as it swung back and forth in a short arc. After a few minutes, an answering light appeared on the water.

"Signal seen and received, sir," said the KKK partisan holding the lantern.

"Hold your positions until the boat beaches," was the whispered response.

The white-hooded and gowned men waited in disciplined silence. The sound of muffled oars became audible, quickly followed by the outline of a ship's cutter fast approaching shore. The boat grounded and a group of men raced from cover and began to assist the boat's crew in unloading rifles and cases of ammunition, then reloading them on several small wagons that waited near the water's edge. The first boat had just been emptied when a second, then third, appeared out of the dark and grounded on the shore. The leader of the shore-based men gestured and another group of men burst from cover and ran towards the waiting craft.

The KKK team split into two groups, one helping the men who were boarding the boats while the other continued loading the waiting wagons and driving them away. Within a few minutes the wagons were gone and all the boats, fully loaded with refugees, were making their way back to the deep-sea cargo ship waiting a few hundred yards off shore. The leader, surrounded by several of his team, waited until the wagons and boats were out of sight and sound before mounting their horses and disappearing into the soft, moonless night.

Harry Chester was tall, heavy set, bearded with piercing black eyes. A.taciturn veteran of Bedford Forrest's Cavalry. Born in 1831, some twenty miles north of Mobile, Alabama, he had left his family's sharecropping farm for the city while in his late teens, searching for a life better than that he had been born to.

Arriving in Mobile he soon got a job as a helper for a self-employed teamster, one Robert Anderson. Chester proved to be a valuable and trustworthy employee and after a few years Robert made him a full partner. Chester met and married the love of his life. In short order he became the proud father of a girl and a boy. Successful in business, blessed with a loving wife and healthy children, life was good.

In 1857, Robert was injured on the job and Chester took over the business. By the time secession reared its ugly head the firm was well regarded and growing. He had accumulated three additional wagons, six more employees and expanded throughout Alabama and Mississippi.

He and his family lived in a two story red brick house that sat on the bluffs overlooking the harbor and Mobile bay. A conscientious and god-fearing man, he and his family attended service weekly and donated to the poor. Harry Chester was a happy, contented man, filled with visions of his future.

When war reared its ugly head he heard the call of duty. He left his business, wife and children to offer his services to the Sovereign State of Alabama. Shortly thereafter, he began his military career as a Lieutenant in the 3rd Alabama Light Horse. After a few actions he was promoted to Captain and given command of a company.

On his first and only leave his wife suggested they have a Daguerreotype taken of the family. Chester agreed and one fine day they presented themselves in the Daguerreotyper's office. The two parents carefully explained the forthcoming bright light and noise to the children and were inordinately proud when both held as still as statues.

The horrors of war had become his personal hell the day he received a letter from one of his managers. The letter advised him that during a Union naval assault on Mobile his entire family had been killed. The slaughter had occurred because they had taken shelter in one of the forts defending the harbor. Unfortunately, these forts had been subjected to heavy bombardment and totally destroyed. Ironically, the home they had fled remained intact.

Along with the letter was an oilskin wrapped package. Alone in his tent Chester opened it and saw the Daguerreotype of his family. He sat for hours, holding it in shaking hands, eyes blurry with tears of agony, mind numb. As the days became weeks he grappled with his loss; his grief slowly consuming him, overwhelming him with a deep and unrelenting hatred towards the Union. Rage transformed him into a relentless, merciless foe. He swore eternal hatred for his family's' murderers. Time passed and his hatred became an obsession, retribution his reason for existence. Revenge on the Union was his god and goal.

When word had come that Bedford Forrest was looking for men to serve in a special operations force, he had decided to see what it was all about. His hope was that this new and highly secretive mission could somehow give him a chance to hurt those Yankees a little more, just one more time.

Arriving at the appointed location he found several other cavalry officers already there. A short time later Forrest himself had arrived and explained that he had been tasked with creating a "special operations force" that would eventually be operating as a guerrilla unit.

This stay-behind-force would be tasked with creating as much trouble as possible for the occupying Yankee Army. They were also to be active in providing the local population with as much support as possible, acting as a counter-force to carpetbaggers and overly zealous Reconstructionists alike.

The entire project was to be considered completely secret and only those officers who were willing to sever all connections to their old lives should consider themselves as eligible. After completing his presentation, Forrest told the assembled group they had twenty-four hours to make a decision. Those willing to join should return the following night. Chester was one of five officers who showed up.

The men were told that secrecy and stealth were of paramount importance and therefore all units would, when in action, always wear the uniform of and identify themselves as "Knights of the Klu Klux Klan." Every state of the old Confederacy would have its own statewide KKK organization. Each state-wide division was to be known as a "Klavern." Each would operate under the leadership of a "Grand Wizard." Local groups would be known as "Coven's," each to be led by a "Nighthawk."

As soon as Forrest left for Mexico and the embedded KKK units began operations, Chester's organizational skills and leadership abilities became apparent. Eventually, he was offered the position of Grand Wizard of the Alabama KKK, with his headquarters at the seaport of Mobile.

He was ordered to concentrate on recruiting men to serve as "Nighthawks," men who would in turn recruit membership in local Covens throughout the state. This departmentalization would assist in providing secrecy and security. Once in place, all Covens were to remain inactive and wait for orders before embarking on any major activity. Chester had followed orders and now led an armed force numbering more than two thousand men, grouped in thirty-odd Covens, spread throughout the state.

He was both "Grand Wizard" of the Alabama Klan and the Mobile Coven leader. The Mobile Coven was extremely active because its seaport acted as conduit in "Project Home Coming" operations as well as a major port for clandestine arms shipments due for distribution to Klan forces throughout the South.

Washington, D. C.

Ferns and shrubs about the White House gardens were bursting forth with late spring growth and leaves were heavy on the tree branches. As the southern states continued to churn in turmoil, the Union government embarked on a surreptitious course of action.

President Andrew Johnson sat behind his desk reviewing the latest OSS report. Completing his reading, he rang the bell on his desk to summon his personal secretary. "Make sure this information is included on the agenda for the next Committee on Military Preparedness and Intelligence," he ordered.

"Very good, Sir," was the immediate response.

A few days later the committee met. The men at the laden sideboard helped themselves to coffee, pastry and a casual exchange of information before getting down to the official business at hand. President Johnson, coffee and pastry in hand, strode to the centrally-placed conference table, sat and nodded to Pinkerton to start the meeting.

"As you ordered, sir," said Pinkerton, "I have prepared the intelligence summaries you wanted for each committee member." He promptly handed out the copies to each attendee.

"I must say," commented Committee Chairman, Patrick O'Reilly, "there are many strange rumors circulating about."

"My presence here is to spread the truth and dissipate the rumors," replied Pinkerton, a frown creasing his features. "You will note," he went on, "that the southerners are becoming very active on a number of fronts and we are hard pressed to keep abreast of their efforts. However, at this point I can safely say that we are aware of, and in the process of thwarting, most of their plans. I will deal with their most ambitious project first," he continued.

"The Revolutionary Council has begun importing people from the southern states at an amazing rate. They appear to be focusing on professional and military-age young men, business men and major plantation owners, men with education, skills and abilities. By our count they are being accepted at a rate of several hundred, perhaps even thousands, per month.

We have reason to believe that there is an organization in place that provides the wherewithal refugees require to make the trip. This organization is well-directed and very effective. It has been well thought out. Its members are embedded in the general population. When they are conducting overt operations they wear white robes and hoods. In many areas of the south they are regarded as protectors and saviors. They operate in small groups, rarely more than twenty men, and simply vanish when they have achieved their objective. The organization goes by the somewhat fanciful name of the 'Knights of the Klu Klux Klan,' or more often than not just the 'Klan'."

"What I'd like to know is how much of a threat do they pose?" asked O'Reilly, a look of concern on his face.

"Until we can develop a better understanding of their scope, abilities and purpose we can't answer that," responded Pinkerton.

"Fair enough," said Sherman, who then continued, "What about Custer?"

"Here," answered Pinkerton, "we have met with more success. The assassination attempt on Custer was aborted due to the outstanding efforts of our Texas office, under the command of Regional Director Garrison. Most of the attackers were killed and a few were captured. After extensive interrogation we have reason to believe that the agent commanding their operations in the Texas area was a man named Sam Arnold. We believe he was himself killed in the operation by an OSS operative. As a side note, some evidence connects him with the Washington assassinations. We'll continue working on that. Garrison has done an outstanding job. He and his team are to be commended. General Custer is absolutely furious and has recommended a full scale invasion of Mexico by the Army of the Rio Grand!"

"Led, no doubt, by the General himself," interjected Sherman, a sour expression on his face.

"I think that we need to impress the good General with the need for restraint regarding the Mexican situation," interjected Johnson. He glanced at O'Reilly and continued, "I want you and Director Pinkerton to visit the good General. Make absolutely certain he knows his orders and limitations."

"That'll take some doing," interjected Sherman.

"Absolutely, Mr. President," responded Pinkerton, continuing, "On another front I have grave concerns regarding the activities of certain European countries who are providing substantial amounts of state-of-the-art weaponry to the Confederate/Mexican military. The firepower available to them is far superior to a Union force of similar size. Our experts estimate that their units now enjoy a five-to-two rate-of-fire superiority. In order to respond to this technological issue, I am requesting the creation of an *Office of Weapons Procurement and Development,* dedicated to providing modern arms for both the Army and Navy. I propose that this bureau be headed by Mr. Erskine Allen, a weapons specialist and president of the Springfield Company, a well-known arms manufacturing firm."

"Other than our supply activities for the Juaristas and the reinforcements sent to Custer, it seems to me that we are being reactive rather then pro-active regarding our Southern brethren's activities," said Sherman, a thoughtful look on his features. "I think that short of an all-out invasion, we should consider some additional forms of action," he continued.

"I concur completely," responded Pinkerton, a smile of anticipation on his face, "and to that end I have invited His Excellency Benito Juarez to Washington in order to discuss the current situation in Mexico."

President Johnson said, "Foreign relations are becoming rather strained. We must take care not to totally isolate ourselves from Europe and South America. The Navy is already nose-to-nose with Prussian and English battle squadrons in the Gulf of Mexico. We will increase our diplomatic efforts on the continent with a view to forming economic and military alliances wherever possible. Departments of State and War will interact directly with your office, Alan. I will hold you responsible for it. Communication and information sharing is vital. We were caught flatfooted once and I will not allow such a stain on this country or my administration ever again."

Johnson, his eyes hard and cold, continued. "General Sherman, as soon as possible I would like to review whatever actions you would like to propose. I fully expect this country to be of an offensive mind-set, gentlemen. Do I make myself clear?" Finished, he searched the faces of the men assembled before him and each man nodded individually, responding in the affirmative.

CHAPTER TWENTY FOUR

July, 1866

Washington, D. C.

The capital foliage was in full bloom, majestic oaks and graceful poplar trees providing lots of shade for the carriage as it rolled to a stop on the cobblestone avenue. Alighting from the vehicle, Benito Juarez hurried into the Washington, D.C. State Department Building with hardly a glance aside. Within moments he had been ushered into the top-floor office, where he immediately ensconced himself in a chair directly in front of the empty fireplace. After a short wait, several men filed into the room.

"It is a great pleasure to finally meet you face-to-face, sir. Your reputation has preceded you," said Congressman O'Reilly.

"A pleasure to make your acquaintance," responded Juarez, standing. He looked at the other men present.

"Allow me to make the introductions, Senor Juarez," continued O'Reilly, as he introduced Sherman and Pinkerton. "We are very aware of and concerned about the situation in your country. It is our hope that we can develop a plan that will prove to be to our mutual benefit."

"We are, of course, very thankful for the aid we have received to this point," answered Juarez. "However, the issue of your countrymen's presence in Mexico and their involvement in our War of Revolution is of paramount importance to us. Our current predicament is largely due to their uninvited intervention in Mexican affairs," finished Juarez.

"Senor Juarez, we of course, commiserate with your position. The fact remains that the southerners' presence in Mexico is a result of secret negotiations between the ex-Confederate government and the Revolutionary Council of Mexico, led by Santa Anna. This makes the international legal situation very complicated and when you add the fact that all parties were in open revolt against the internationally recognized government of Maximilian, we really find ourselves in uncharted territory. The Emperor's abdication and return to Austria leaves open to question the legality of any claim to the government of Mexico," responded O'Reilly.

"In matter of fact, it is our expressed desire to formulate a plan of action that is as beneficial to your cause as it is to ours, sir. We have been authorized by the President to create such an agreement and submit it to him. Of course, any such commitment must recognize that the international situation precludes our direct military intervention on your behalf. We have been advised through diplomatic channels that England and Prussia would consider such an action as cause for military response on their part. You must understand that we have just concluded a long and destructive war. This country is not prepared to engage in international hostilities at this time, regardless of how good the reason," said Pinkerton.

Juarez regarded the men around him for a moment, and answered, "The alliance of Confederate and Santa Anna's Revolutionary forces is not a good thing for my country. These men are adventurers who have no thought for the people. They seek personal wealth and gain. They want to create a power structure that will give them control of the people and wealth of Mexico. Santa Anna has wanted to be Dictator since '46 and this is his chance. His advent to power is the death knell of the true revolution of the people. We shall fight to the death, to the death!"

"I think that a substantial increase in the infusion of supplies and equipment would be of great value to your forces," said Sherman. "We are also considering the use of military "Advisors" from the Union Army. Such troops would be deployed outside your command structure, but could provide you with technical and intelligence assistance. OSS Regional Director Garrison from our Texas Zone says that there are many families of Mexican descent who still feel very strongly about you and the Revolution. The OSS is creating a number of volunteer "Special Ranger Battalions." It is our intent to staff these units with Union officers and soldiers volunteers, along with other volunteers as well as selected troops from your forces, which we will arm and train. These units will operate outside regular military channels and report directly to the OSS. We think such a force could be fielded, battle-ready, in short order."

"Such assistance would be of great value to us," responded Juarez. "Since switching to more hit-and-run tactics, we have had more success. Zaragoza informs me that in the current situation we can only keep our army in the field in a defensive posture. If your aid is made available in sufficient quantity we might be able to consider some major offensive operations."

"The President is of firm mind on this matter and has given very clear instructions regarding our joint efforts on your behalf," said Sherman.

"I can speak for all of us when I say that we have every intent on making good on our word, Senor Juarez," said Congressman O'Reilly. "You'll not find us wanting when push comes to shove."

CHAPTER TWENTY FIVE

October, 1866

Texas Zone of Reconstruction

Plans for forming a force of "Ranger Battalions," to be trained and led by OSS operatives, were begun. Troops for this force would be all volunteer and recruited from both the military and civilian population. Each Ranger Battalion would be composed of three hundred Rangers and non-commissioned officers divided into six fifty-man companies. Each company would be composed of five ten-man teams and commanded by a Lieutenant and a Captain. Ranger units operating in clandestine mode would not be uniformed and all equipment purchased from non-military sources..

The initial orders were to recruit, train and field three units to be designated as the Coronado, Cortez and Pissarro Battalions. Training was to be conducted in OSS facilities just outside Laredo, Texas. The first unit to complete training and become operational was the Cortez Battalion.

Each of the six training companies started out with seven ten-man teams, in order to allow for those unable to complete the rigorous training. A group of experts in small arms, artillery, explosives, horsemanship, and armed and unarmed hand-to-hand combat drilled the trainees vigorously.

Men, horses, equipment and supplies had been arriving for weeks. A small city of tents had sprung up, filled with prospective Rangers. A few scraggly mesquite trees and cacti provided scant shade. A small brook provided a questionable source for water and the cooks boiled everything. Training was harsh.

"All together now," said the gravelly voiced non-com, to the ten men lying prone. "Brace your weapon, acquire your target, aim your weapon, *squeeze* the trigger." Ten rounds ripped downrange and seven bulls-eye flags fluttered into the dry, hot Texas air.

"You're supposed to kill'em, you dumb-shit, not scare'em. Everybody up, drop your weapons, five laps at the trot. Sooner or later you'll realize every shot has gotta be a kill shot."

"This is a knife. In the right hands it's deadly at near and close. You can stab, cut, slash, and throw it. When we're done here each of you will be able to kill a man using all those options, and do so without the enemy ever making a sound. Now, I need a volunteer victim. Who wants to die?"

"Gentlemen, I am Major John Blackstone, commanding officer of Cortez Battalion. Welcome."

Easy, along with five other OSS officers saluted. They were the six OSS company commanders assigned to the Cortez battalion. The unit had completed its field training in southern Texas and was taking the field in northern Mexico on its first combat tour of duty.

When the OSS had been ordered to field the Ranger Battalions Pinkerton had first scoured the ranks of his operatives for prospective officers. Given Easy's West Point and combat background he was made a captain and offered command of a company. He'd immediately accepted.

Blackstone continued, "This command is at full strength and fully supplied. The battalion is tasked with a vital mission. We are to enter Mexico secretly. We will assist forces under President Juarez. We'll be operating alongside his units as both raiders and scouts. Our primary focus will be to provide information on enemy movement. We will also attack targets of opportunity as they present themselves We'll destroy enemy supplies and equipment wherever possible."

He gestured to a map of Mexico tacked to the wall. "We'll be operating in the southern and western Sierra Madre Oriental Mountains," he said, indicating by hand their patrol areas. "In order to maximize our efficiency each company will act independently, reporting to headquarters only to provide enemy movement updates or for scheduled re-supply. You'll be provided specific contact locations and dates."

Blackstone paused, folding his arms across his chest. "They're very light on cavalry. They need us to take the field as soon as possible. Acquaint yourselves with your men. If there are no further questions? No? Very well then, dismissed."

Despite his substantial combat experience this would be his first independent combat command and Easy knew a moment's uncertainty. When dismissed by Blackstone he swallowed his doubts, squared his shoulders, left the office and sought out his men's bivouac. The moment he arrived he sought out his executive officer. Easy entered the small, cramped office and introduced himself.

"Morning Lieutenant. Sanchez, right? I'm the company CO."
"Yes sir, Emilio Sanchez. Welcome aboard. I hope you find everything satisfactory."

Emilio Sanchez was one of the many Spanish speaking Rangers recruited by the OSS. An American citizen, his family had lived in Arizona since the mid-seventeenth century. One of his grandfathers had died in the Alamo, sacrificing himself in the cause of Texas independence.

"My name is Ezekiel, Emilio, but everyone calls me Easy."

"Yes s..., I mean Ezekiel."

The two shook hands as they sized up each other.

"We've been waiting for you for several days. I've tried to keep the men busy with training. I've found them to be good men. A lot of veterans from both Union and Juarista's units."

"Excellent. I'm glad you got things moving. I'd like to review the training schedules you've set up."

"Let me introduce you to our first sergeant, Orto Emmanuel. He's a Juarista veteran, a good man."

When Orto arrived Easy looked him over, saw his solid form and quiet demeanor, smiled and said, "Glad you're with us, Orto. I've a couple of ideas I'd like to implement and I want input from both of you."

Emilio looked at Orto and both men broke into a smile. Emilio said, "A pleasure Easy, whenever you're ready."

"Sounds like a plan to me."

The Ranger volunteers were mostly veterans and the training moved onward quickly. By the time deployment orders were received every man in Delta was fully trained and operational. The rangers entered Mexico by crossing the Rio Grande north of the city of Monterrey. Once in-country they advanced south until they made contact with enemy forces.

As Delta Company deployed into Mexico, the first hint of fall had been signaled by the slowly dropping temperatures in the rolling hills and low, rugged mountains of north central Mexico. The sparse foliage was beginning its annual thinning process, which in turn meant less cover for the men who were spread out in a thin skirmish line on the military crest of a hill. At the foot of the hill ran a trail that was frequently used by Revolutionary Army cavalry patrols either leaving or returning to their base camp. The company had taken their positions shortly before dawn in anticipation of ambushing a returning enemy patrol.

Easy, after substantial scouting by himself, Lieutenant Sanchez and Sergeant Emmanuel had chosen the site for several reasons. It provided maximum fields of fire as well as fast egress routes for the attacking force. There was limited protection for the enemy. Finally, it was close to the enemy base which meant the returning cavalrymen would be less alert.

Delta had arrived in position a day early and the men were eager and ready. This would be the company's first combat as a unit and Easy wanted his men to become accustomed to successful operations. Despite thorough preparation Easy had spent an unsettled night, lying sleepless for hours reviewing his first independent battle plan. The knowledge that men would live or die due to his commands was a sobering thought; thankfully, he fell asleep a few hours before dawn.

"Christ, its cold," swore Easy, as he put his telescope to his eyes in order to better view the slowly advancing Revolutionary Council cavalry company. Sunny Mexico, my ass, he thought. His companion on the hill, Lt. Emilio Sanchez, late of San Diego, California, laughed, and said, "Winter campaigns have a charm all their own, my friend."

"By my reckoning they should all be within the kill zone when the first man reaches that point," said Easy, pointing to a group of large cacti along side the trail upon which the enemy was advancing. "Make sure the boys know the plan and stick to it. I don't want any heroes today," he said to Sanchez, who signaled for the team sergeants. As soon as they congregated he relayed the orders to them. The five sergeants promptly began crawling from position to position to insure each team's fire discipline.

The troop was spread out over several dozen yards of dusty trail. The lead Revolutionary Army cavalry trooper rode half asleep in the saddle, exhausted after ten straight twelve-hour days of monotonous patrol. The first volley lifted him from his saddle and dropped him to the ground, dead. A number of his fellow troopers were also knocked from their horses, dead or wounded. The second volley was much less effective, as most of the uninjured enemy troopers were already either throwing themselves to the ground or wheeling their horses about and racing for the nearest cover.

The Rangers began receiving scattered return fire from the troopers who had taken cover along the trail. After dismounting, rallied by their officers, the cavalry reformed and began advancing up the hill in a skirmish line. The charging troopers, taking turns firing their carbines or rushing forward, slowly fought their way towards Delta Company's position. As they advanced the attackers took more casualties, some screaming in pain, some lying still, dead or unconscious. Their losses mounted and the Revolutionary cavalry slowed their advance and began to seek cover.

One of their officers led a group off to one side in what was intended to be a flanking movement. Easy's men held their positions as incoming rounds whistled about them, all the while maintaining a blistering return fire. Each man, being armed with a Winchester rifle and a colt revolver, could fire eighteen rounds without reloading.

Easy gave a signal and the first of his four teams left the firing line and made their way to their horses, which were being held by the fifth team at the base of the reverse slope. At the next signal, Lt. Sanchez, along with a second team, raced to their mounts, followed shortly by the third team, leaving only the ten men of the last team and Easy.

As per plan each man reloaded his rifle and fired several targeted rounds in rapid succession. Almost as one, they turned and trotted towards their horses, mounted and followed their fellows at a gallop. Easy waited until the last man was headed down the slope before he turned and made his way to his waiting horse. He mounted, spurred the animal and raced after the fast-disappearing company.

By the time the Revolutionary Cavalry troopers reached the top of the ridge line, Delta Company was long gone. The Rangers rode on for several hours, intent on distancing themselves from the battle zone. Eventually they found a suitable position and stopped for the night.

"A good day's work, men," said Easy, to the five team leaders grouped around his campfire. He held a map on his lap and pointed at it. "At first light I want us moving west towards this village, La Punta. It's a major supply base and I want to take a good long look at it."

The rest of his force relaxed, the remaining nine men of each team grouped around small, carefully-concealed campfires. After dinner that evening, Easy, along with Emilio, toured the camp, checking on the men. Once satisfied that all was well he retired to his blanket, took out his harmonica and began to play. As the campfires slowly reduced themselves

241

to glowing embers the mournful strains of the instrument wafted over the camp.

For the next few days the Rangers rode hard, driving south to La Punta. When they reached a point several miles from the town Delta Company left the road, which in many places was indistinguishable from the terrain through which it led. The company continued on a parallel course, finally stopping about two miles outside La Punta when they found a suitable place to bivouac.

The next morning Easy left Lt. Sanchez in command and continued on in the company of Sergeant Orto Emmanuel. He and Easy began to ride around the town at a distance. They dismounted their horses occasionally to climb to the top of a vantage point in order to inspect the town from several different locations.

After several hours of riding and observing, they determined that La Punta was not walled, but instead the town surrounded an old Spanish fort. In some places the rear wall of homes and businesses was part of the actual fortification. The town was primarily built of adobe with several brick and stone buildings, these being mostly church or government structures. The city streets were, with the exception of a few central blocks immediately adjacent to the central fort, meandering, narrow and apparently totally unplanned. In several instances, Easy noted that they dead- ended in a *cul du sac*.

On all three recognizable roads entering the town, guard positions had been established. The posts were each manned by about a half dozen soldiers under the command of a sergeant. Security protocols consisted of nothing more than a few cursory questions and little or no searching. After observing several individuals and groups go through the same procedure, Easy decided that they would enter the city to continue their mission. If they were questioned, their cover was that they were two *vaqueros*, or Mexican cowboys, looking for employment.

After successfully negotiating the security roadblocks, the two mounted men made their way slowly through the maze of narrow, refuse-filled streets into the main square. They dismounted, tied their horses to rails, and entered one of the *cantinas*. Easy sat and motioned to Orto to continue on to the bar, which consisted of several crudely cut pine logs resting on two fifty gallon drums. Orto asked for and received two drinks from the bartender. He picked up the glasses, and turned and walked back to the table Easy had chosen.

"Next step will be to scout out their guard positions, egress points, and supply locations" said Easy, as he downed the harsh liquor in a single gulp.

"It will be difficult to get a good look at the warehouses," responded Orto.

"Right," answered Easy. "First things first, let's quarter our horses and find someplace to stay."

Both men downed their drinks, stood and left the cantina. After a short search, they found a blacksmith who boarded horses and left theirs with him. Luck was with them and they found lodgings at a hotel only one block from the fort wall and almost opposite the main gate.

Easy began a slow circumnavigation of the town, carefully noting the best ways to enter and leave as well as all defensive positions. He made sure to walk slowly and when confronted by a squad of soldiers, looked their sergeant squarely in the eye as he responded to questions. Continuing on at a leisurely pace, he scouted the entire town for several hours.

He arrived back at the cantina bordering the main square to find Orto once again seated in front of the *cantina*, a glass of tequila in hand.

"So?" was his question, "is it done?"

"I have all the guard schedules here," whispered Orto, pointing to his head. "Very basic."

"Good work. Now, I'm tired, and I wouldn't mind a hot bath and sleeping in a bed for a change," said Easy.

"Or with an attractive bed mate," countered Orto, who was looking at the three women at the bar who were in turn looking intently at he and Easy.

"Well, you know what they say about all work and no play," said Easy, as he stood up and slowly made his way to his room, alone. With a smile of his own, Orto got up and walked over to one of several women, grouped at one end of the bar.

It was about an hour before dawn when Orto and Easy left their rooms, Orto to verify guard timing and procedures, Easy to find a way into the interior compound. Easy left the *cantina* and keeping close to the walls moved along until he found a place where several multiple-story buildings backed directly onto the fortress wall. He walked down a narrow, garbage-strewn alley, found a door and, after silently forcing it open, found himself in a store room partially filled with dry goods.

After a moment's search, Easy found a stairway leading up to the second floor, which was deserted. There were a few boarded windows on this level and Easy pried the wooden slats from the window nearest the rear wall. Being careful not to allow himself to be seen from the street, he climbed out and onto the roof. He hastened to the rear where the rooftop was only a few feet below the adjoining fortress wall. With a quick motion, he levered himself atop it. He crawled across the walls thickness and in a moment was gazing down into the fort's interior. The sun was well into the sky when Easy, having satisfied himself regarding routines in the fort, slowly retraced his steps to the ground and out of the alley.

It was mid-afternoon when Easy and Orto rejoined each other at the *cantina*. Having each assured the other that each had accomplished their mission, the two men sauntered into the blacksmiths. They paid for and received their mounts, left the city and headed towards their base camp.

That evening the team leaders sat in a circle around the map that Easy had drawn. It clearly identified fall-back positions, access routes to be used, enemy positions to be avoided, entry points into the fort, and the location of the four large warehouses that held the supplies they sought to destroy.

"Two of these hold ammunition. The next two hold rations, supplies and equipment," said Easy, as he notated the buildings on the drawing. "Team A will be tasked with taking out all the warehouses. Team B will be tasked with protecting our withdrawal. Team C will hold the horses at our insertion point. Teams D and E, under Lt. Sanchez will hold in place at the fallback positions in the event they have a reaction force."

Glancing around, he continued, "I want every man to know how to get in, out and what his job is. The garrison strength is about two companies of infantry and at least that many cavalry. The security is pretty lax. I guess they think they're too far from the fighting to be in any danger. I want us out of there before they realize how wrong they were. Team leaders will task their team members. We'll move out at midnight. That way we should hit them around three in the AM. Questions? No? Well then, it sounds like a plan to me." With that each sergeant left to see to the preparation of his team while Easy and Lt. Sanchez reviewed the proposed action one more time.

The moon shed a silvery light almost strong enough to cast a shadow as the assault teams, dressed all in black, black greasepaint covering hands and face, and wearing soft, leather-soled, Indian style moccasins, stealthily entered the sleeping village. Easy, who, as usual, was leading his men, gestured with his hand, ordering A Team to follow.

Moving slowly down one of the narrow, dark, winding streets, they were almost at their destination when they encountered two soldiers at a security checkpoint. A match flared briefly as one man lit a cigarette. In response to another hand signal, A Team froze in place, except for Easy and Orto, who was directly behind him.

At a quick order from Easy, the two men linked arms and, weaving and stumbling as if deep in their cups, made their way towards the two guards. The guards, seeing their demeanor, casually awaited them in the middle of the street. Closing to a point within a few feet of the waiting guards, Easy removed his arm from Orto's shoulder, and making vague waving motions, appeared to trip into the nearest guard. The man involuntarily grabbed Easy in an attempt to keep him upright.

As the guard's arms encircled him, Easy drew his knife, and with a savage thrust, drove it to the hilt through the guards chin and into his brain. Driving the dead guard backward, he shifted to his left. As the second guard turned and started at the sound of his companion's death grunt, Easy jerked the knife from the first man and slashed the second man's throat from ear to ear. Both guards slumped to the ground, the first already dead and the second vainly attempting to staunch the blood flow with hands clasped around his neck. Easy and Orto quickly dragged the bodies into an alley and Easy signaled his men to resume their advance.

A short while later, they reached the building they would use to enter the fort. Entering through the side window, it took only a few moments for the team to access the roof and then the fort wall. Securing ropes to the top of the wall, the team rappelled down into the fort and moved to their assigned objectives.

Two of the team members advanced slowly toward a small guard house set into the wall next to the main gate which had been closed at sunset. Moving with extreme stealth, they gained a point next to the guardhouse door, hesitated a second, then burst in, killing both dozing guards with knives. The remaining eight Rangers formed into four teams of two and each proceeded to their assigned warehouse. Forcing the doors, they quickly entered, each team moving quietly into a building and carefully setting the explosives they carried.

Starting at the back, they lit each fuse, left the buildings, and began making their way to the gate held by their comrades. As the last of his men passed, Easy, who had waited at the main gate, paused for a moment to survey the scene and insure he was, in fact, the last out.

As he and his men moved quickly but quietly down the empty village streets, making for their mounts, the warehouses erupted. The ones containing ammunition and gunpowder literally shredded themselves in massive explosions that roared skyward, the glare momentarily turning night into day. The fiery debris raining down served to add to the destruction and confusion as several windows blew out and secondary fires sprang up throughout the village. Drums, bugles and shouts began to sound as the garrison and population started to react and gather itself.

Easy, acting as rearguard, trotted down the street. He heard shots and the shouts and sounds of gathering pursuit behind him. Rounding a corner he came upon one of his men writhing in pain and lying in a pool of blood, a motionless body next to him. Kneeling next to the prone, moaning ranger Easy removed his bandana and used it to try to staunch the flow of blood. Suddenly Orto was beside him.

Easy said, "you carry him, I'll hold them off." Turning, he trotted back around the corner into the middle of the street. He knelt and began firing at the fast closing enemy. Aiming carefully he dropped two men in rapid succession, the rest taking cover. Satisfied he had slowed them he ran after Orto. Together they carried their comrade to the horses. It wasn't until they began tying him to a horse that Easy realized the man was dead.

The rest of the wounded were put on horses, then the remaining Rangers mounted and all cantered away. As Easy had predicted, despite the surprise of their raid, they were soon followed by a pursuit column of cavalry.

The trail that Easy and his men followed had been carefully chosen. It led into a gradually narrowing valley. After a few hundred yards the valley veered sharply to the left, forming an "L" shape. Halfway up the outside valley wall, on the bottom half of the "L," stood Lieutenant Emilio Sanchez. He was hidden behind a rock outcrop and watched as the assault teams raced by below him.

Sanchez had placed his men on both sides of the shorter, bottom edge of the "L." After situating his men he had moved a few hundred feet further down towards the end of the valley and planted explosive charges under groups of large boulders that were located on or near the ridge top.

A few moments after the last man of Delta Company galloped past him, the first of the enemy cavalrymen appeared around the corner, riding at full gallop. Sanchez waited until the pursuers were less than fifty yards from his position before lighting the quick-burning fuses.

In a few seconds the black-powder charges began exploding. As eruptions rippled along the cliff, huge hunks of rock tumbled down onto the valley floor. The first two squads of cavalrymen disappeared under tons of cascading boulders as the Rangers opened fire from concealed positions.

The pursuers were caught in a deadly fire that turned the valley floor into a churning cauldron of smoke, rearing horses, wounded and dying men. After enduring the hail of bullets for a few moments, the cavalry broke and ran. Sanchez allowed the carnage to continue until the only things on the valley floor were either dead or soon to be, then recalled his men and followed the rest of the Rangers.

Delta Company reformed and headed towards the Battalion rally point. When they arrived Easy found orders awaiting him. He was to leave the Cortez Battalion and report to William Garrison, OSS Regional Director, in the Juarista Capital of Monterrey. Easy advised Emilio that he was now in charge, packed his bags, and left.

The Ranger's destruction of one of the main supply depots had immediate and dire repercussions.

"Dispatch from General Garcia, Sir," said the aide, handing the message to Hill, who sat behind a bullet-scarred oak desk in a *hacienda* his forces had recently liberated. Another supply depot gone! Whoever is in charge seems to really know his business. Someone's thinking strategically, thought the General, as he read Garcia's note.

Hill's march on Monterrey had, for all intent and purpose, ground to a complete halt as a result of poor roads, the constant hit-and-run attacks on his recon patrols and supply convoys. The major raid on his main supply depot was the last straw.

"Colonel," he ordered, 'I want you to cut orders to all our forward elements to fall back to these positions," indicating several points on the map. "We will withdraw all forces that are north of this line, fortify our positions and consolidate our gains until further notice."

"Yes, sir," responded his aide.

Gulf of Mexico

Lt. Commander Jason Patrick, Captain of the USN *Potomac*, a Mohican class, screw-driven Sloop of War, walked up the starboard gangway to the bridge, where he took the salute from First Lt. Chester Darnell, his executive officer. The squall had hit hard and the decks of the USN *Potomac* were coated with a thin layer of salt water.

Patrick was an experienced and decorated naval officer. He'd served with distinction during the Civil War in both blockade and combat duties. As first officer of a gunboat he had been citied for heroism in the battle of Mobile Bay. The *Potomac* was his first independent command.

The two officers stood for a moment, both admiring the beauty of the warship under power, cutting the waves at eight knots, decks gleaming, main sails furled, twin funnels belching smoke. The main armament of twelve 50 lb. Dahlgren's ready at a moment's notice to hurl death and destruction at her nation's enemies..

"Lookouts report a ship bearing south by southwest, range three miles, sir," said Darnell, handing the telescope to his superior.

Union naval units in the Gulf of Mexico had been ordered to make every effort to identify the cargo of any ship they encountered, provided they did nothing to violate international law in the process. Admiral Farragut had made it clear to all his captains that if they were to cause such an incident their next command would be a rowboat in Chesapeake Bay.

"Seems a little low in the water and possibly listing to port, don't you think, Chester?" asked Patrick, with a mischievous gleam in his eye.

"Absolutely," responded Darnell, as he regarded the cargo ship, which was in fact, sailing in perfect trim.

"Then let's take a look, shall we?" said Patrick, turning to the helmsman and ordering his ship to close.

"Very good, sir," came the immediate reply, as the Potomac heeled in response to her rudder, fast gaining on the cumbersome and heavily-laden merchantman.

Reaching the merchantman, the Potomac signaled her to halt and prepare for boarding. At first the signals were ignored, so Patrick ordered a shot across her bows. The signal to stop was again given, which the merchantman promptly did. As the launch closed with the waiting vessel, Patrick, seated in the stern, noted that the ship's name was *Berlin* and that she flew the Prussian flag.

Following his six Marine escorts up to the main deck, Jason was met by the very irate Captain. "I protest, Sir," said the German, his face a mottled red and his hands clenched into fists. "You are stopping my ship on the high seas where you have no jurisdiction! I will lodge an official complaint upon reaching port! You are defying international law!"

"Feel free to pursue any course of action you deem advisable, Captain. I have taken the liberty of stopping your vessel only because of concerns regarding its seaworthiness, and to offer aid if required. As soon as I am certain this ship is in no danger, I will, of course, immediately allow you to resume course," responded Patrick, as he walked past the angry German Captain. He left four of his Marines on deck, and went below with the remaining two, to investigate the passenger area.

Walking up to a man standing in the corridor, Patrick held out his hand and in a conversational tone of voice asked the man his name.

The man shook the offered hand. He replied, "I'm Jethro Scruggs, who are you?"

"I'm Captain Jason Patrick. May I be so bold as to ask what circumstances find you on a Prussian ship bound for Mexico?" asked Patrick.

"Vacation, that and adventure" came the laconic response.

"Yes," replied Patrick, a hint of a smile on his features, "I'm told Vera Cruz is magnificent this time of year." A statement made in an attempt to confirm his suspicions regarding the *Berlins'* next port-of-call.

"I certainly hope so." was the even reply.

October, 1866

Leaving Jethro behind, Patrick continued his inspection below deck, and finding only more passengers, eventually retraced his steps to the main deck, where the impatient German Captain awaited him. Walking up to the highly agitated officer, Patrick, a broad smile on his features, said, "Excellent news, sir, I have ascertained that, despite my initial fears your ship is entirely sea worthy. I wish you godspeed." With that he saluted the flabbergasted German Captain and followed his men over the side and into the waiting launch.

Watching the descending back of the Union officer, Captain Bruno mouthed the words, "Arrogant Yankee bastard," then strode to the railing to insure that the launch had indeed cast off from his ship. Ascertaining that it had, he wheeled around and issued a series of orders. In a few moments the *Berlin* was under power and on her way.

As the warship slowly disappeared astern, Jethro thought to himself that if it was action and adventure he wanted, it seemed that he was going to get it in large portions. What surprised him the most was the feeling of anticipation he felt.

"It's another one,'" said Patrick to his first officer, climbing up the *Potomac's* port side as he returned from his inspection of the *Berlin*, "just like the others. Crammed full of people, and bound for Vera Cruz."

"That makes four ships in less then three weeks, two Canadian, one English, and this one," said Darnell. "Could be as many as a thousand men in less than a month."

CHAPTER TWENTY SIX

November, 1866

Mexico City

In the sumptuous Presidential office suite in the Revolutionary Palace, Santa Anna gestured to the young, attractive, indentured servant to stand and leave. He gave her a leering look and a quick but intimate caress before turning to his companion, Don Diego De Aragon. De Aragon was a senior member of the Council of Five Hundred, from the State of Guerrero, on the Pacific coast.

Santa Anna said, "So, my friend, I am pleased to see you again. How was your journey?"

"I was lucky enough to avail myself of some of our recent civic improvements," answered Aragon, "as I had the good luck to travel on some of our newer roads and railroads."

"Yes," said Santa Anna, "we are proceeding vigorously on many fronts."

"I am here," responded Aragon, "in order to receive another update and also to advise you that we are pleased with the situation so far. Can we look forward to even greater success, my friend?"

"Don Diego, as you know I have been working with these Americans for some time now. I have found them to be determined, reliable and honest. They are, of course, ambitious, but so are we. Each of us has an agenda but I believe the main points are, if you will, on the table in full view. We can, and have, worked well together. It is my opinion that we have established a relationship to our mutual benefit and that our ultimate goals are within our grasp."

Aragon held up his glass of wine and asked, "What is your take on the men themselves?" He drained the glass and stood, awaiting Santa Anna's response.

"Breckenridge and Davis are both highly intelligent and totally focused. Breckenridge is motivated and guided by facts, whereas Davis is committed more to the ideal and can be led by emotion. Lee is a man not given to talking. I find him to be a thinker, much more than just a soldier. He is also a man of deep personal convictions," answered Santa Anna, rising from his chair and leading his guest from the room.

As the Revolutionary Council's Army expanded and consolidated its control of territory in central and southern Mexico, they were faced with several critical needs. Among them were security and order for the territory it controlled, continuing improving existing roads and railroads and building new ones. Breckenridge was also very keen on building and expanding heavy industry, especially the production of war materials. All of these endeavors were high-priority and required major infusion of capital and a substantial labor force, both skilled and unskilled.

A series of agreements with a number of European and South American governments, as well as industrialists from the Council of Five Hundred had served to alleviate most of the monetary concerns. Foreign investment was resulting in substantial growth in the infra-structure. Existing factories, mines and large plantations were expanding and upgrading their facilities. New construction was everywhere.

As the Revolutionary Council solidified its hold, there arose the problem of what to do with the individuals who had supported either the Monarchy or the Juaristas. After much debate the council decided on a unique and rather diabolical solution to this problem.

It had begun appointing Revolutionary Judges who were tasked with the responsibility of hearing all cases regarding issues of state security. These judges had the power to both convict and sentence any individual accused of crimes against the state. Charges of this sort were mostly leveled against the political or business enemies of the Revolutionary Party, oft times with more of an eye to vengeance than truth.

A person convicted of being an enemy of the state then became legally "indentured in service to the state" for some specified length of time, up to and including life. All his property and possessions were confiscated by the government. In extreme instances, the entire family, fathers and mothers, and sons and daughters could be so sentenced.

The individuals classified as indentured servants became, in essence, state property and this, in turn, allowed the government to "rent out" the services of these men and women to any private and public concerns in need of a labor force. As the Revolutionary Council increased its control over more and more of Mexico, the number of indentured servants increased substantially. Indentured servants to the state served to provide a source of cheap labor, but at the same time their numbers caused a security problem.

The Council had also created the *Department of State Security*, the DSS, and placed it under the command of Major General Bedford Forrest, who in turn answered to the Secretary of War, John Campbell. The DSS force was composed of both uniformed and plainclothes men and women, whose duties included both internal police, as well as guard functions for the indentured servants. Security for labor units rented out to others could also be provided by DSS troops, for an additional fee.

Vera Cruz, Mexico

The Prussian passenger ship *Berlin* entered the crowded and newly expanded harbor facilities. The Port of Vera Cruz had undergone a fantastic face lift over the past year and a half. The available dock space, filled with ships from a number of European nations, had tripled. Blocks of large warehouses, filled with imports and exports, lined the roads adjacent to the docks. New construction, both public and private, and in many cases international, sprouted up. Broad, tree-lined boulevards lent a sense of grace, and narrow cobblestone side streets an ambiance that fiercely contrasted with the new fortifications ringing the city. A few miles offshore, an English Battle Squadron accompanied by a small Prussian Flotilla provided additional security.

As the *Berlin* was secured to the dock, Jethro, along with most of the other passengers, lined the railing, anxious for a view of their new home. Everywhere they looked they saw furious activity, cargo ships unloading and loading, new buildings being erected, roads being widened or repaired.

What appeared to be a work gang labored to offload the cargo ship berthed at the next dock. The laborers, both male and female, wore filthy, tattered, white shirts and pants. All were emaciated and stank to high heaven. Several bore marks of recent whippings, as well as other signs of physical abuse.

Standing amongst them were armed men and women wearing khaki uniforms. A few of these individuals were armed with whips, which Jethro observed being applied with what he felt to be unnecessary zeal, to stimulate the work gangs to greater industry. He was shocked when he realized that the work gangs were composed of both men and women and each wore an iron collar around their neck.

A number of large passenger wagons made their appearance on the dock and rolled to a point alongside the *Berlin*. While most of the teamsters remained in their seats, one man got down and walked up the gangway from the dock to the deck of the ship. Walking towards Jethro and the other passengers he smiled, held out his hand and introduced himself as Tom Witherspoon, a "Project Homecoming" Agent.

"This way, folks," he said with a broad smile, "this way to the promised land!" Waving at the refugees who clustered around to follow him, he walked back down the gangway to the waiting wagons. The passengers followed and began boarding the wagons. As soon as all were aboard the wagon train left the dock. After a short ride down the street, they stopped before a building identified by a large overhead sign as the "Department of Homecoming Registration Office."

After dismounting from the wagons, the immigrants entered the building. After some time Jethro finally reached the desk at the head of the line.

"Good day, sir, "said the seated man. "May I have your name and occupation?"

"Certainly, I'm Jethro Scruggs, a civil engineer."

"Excellent. We are in great need of your skills, Mr. Scruggs."

"Well, it's always nice to be needed."

The man gave Jethro a sharp glance and said, "It'll take a few days before you get your official posting. Here are your identity cards. Don't lose them. Please follow the signs to your temporary quarters."

Following the directions, he exited by the back door and walked across the street to a barracks-like building. It was identified as the "Regional Homecoming Relocation Center." Entering through the double doors, he was asked to present his new ID and, upon compliance, was directed to a cot in the men's dormitory. Here he was further informed that, "All meals were served promptly at six in the morning, twelve noon and six in the evening. There will be absolutely no deviations!"

For the next few days, Jethro, along with a group of mostly male refugees who ranged in age from about eighteen to forty, and who were mostly trade's men or professionals, were required to attend a number of daily meetings. During some of these meetings they were quizzed regarding their past lives and occupations. At other meetings they were lectured about their brave new world and the parts they would play.

They were told they were part of a great adventure and tasked with being the founders of a great new society in which they would play a leading role. They were informed that their sacrifices would result in a secure and powerful country dedicated to the principles and beliefs of their forefathers and finally, they were advised to work hard and obey orders.

Having some free time between orientation sessions, Jethro, along with some of the other refuges, wandered about the city. Work gangs, with small units of security troops in attendance, were everywhere. As they passed various work sites, he couldn't help but notice again the pitiful state of the individual workers. Dressed in rags, malnutrition and disease rampant, they worked slowly, prodded on occasion by blows or lashes.

At one point their exploration was interrupted by shouts and pounding feet. A young woman dressed in work-gang rags raced around the corner, desperately trying to outrun three State Security troops. As she came abreast of Jethro and his group on the far side of the avenue, she tripped, striking the ground hard, and was immediately swarmed under by her pursuers.

Two of the DSS guards, each holding a wrist, hauled her roughly to her feet while twisting her arms high up behind her back, eliciting a scream of pain. Grinning, a third guard advanced upon her, slapping her head so hard her head snapped back. He gripped her tattered shirt and tore downward, baring her breasts. Gestured to the two other guards to kick her legs out from under her while releasing her arms, they caused her to fall to the ground, striking her head heavily as she hit.

Grasping the semi-conscious girl's ankles, they proceeded to drag her off the main thoroughfare into a nearby alley. The third guard turned to Jethro and the others and sternly ordered them to go about their business. The guard then turned and followed his brethren into the alleyway. Shaken by what they had seen, the entire group repaired to the quarters that had been assigned them, all the while talking about the incident and what it meant.

Eventually, the refugees completed their indoctrination and were assigned to different groups; each group composed of men from a variety of professions, skills and trades. Each group was then advised it would be assigned a different city as its destination.

On the fifth day after his arrival in Vera Cruz, Jethro, along with several other men, were loaded onto wagons for the journey to their new home. Escorted by a few of the security troops, the trip was both uncomfortable and uneventful.

When they arrived at the city of Oaxaca in southern Mexico, the new citizens of Mexico got off their wagons and entered a small building. The structure was grandly entitled the "Oaxaca Homecoming Relocation Center." Each person was assigned a living residence, some of which had recently become unoccupied as either the unfortunate result of war or harsh legal action by a Revolutionary Council Judge. Some were newly constructed.

At a second desk, they were each assigned a duty based on whatever prior occupation they had listed during their initial questioning. Jethro was assigned as a member of the mayor's staff. He was ordered to report to town hall without delay.

Given directions to the mayor's office, and also to his own living quarters, he proceeded to the latter first. On his way there several things caught his attention. Work gangs and guards were everywhere. Construction of buildings for use as homes, offices and stores as well as the city's exterior walls and fortifications abounded. Parks, roads, water and sewer systems were also receiving substantial attention.

He first verified the existence and quality of his newly-assigned living quarters; two small rooms with a hearth in one of them. Leaving his meager possessions behind, he reported to the Mayor's Chief of Staff, an ex-confederate, one Albert T. Brown. Mr. Brown proved to be both officious and efficient. He escorted Jethro to his new office while at the same time outlining his duties as Chief City Engineer.

After showing Jerthro his office and discussing Jethro's official duties, Albert offered to take him to a neighborhood where many of the other southerners normally congregated in their off hours. Jethro agreed and they both walked through the city until they reached a small building bearing a sign that proclaimed "The Atlanta Inn" and promised the "Best Brew South of the Rio Grand."

The men entered into a small, pine-floored, dimly lit room. A scattering of mismatched tables and chairs, several of which were occupied, were haphazardly placed about the room. One wall was taken up by a long bar at which a few men stood. Another wall boasted a large fireplace. A stairway led upstairs to a number of small rooms that could be let by the day or week. A door next to the bar opened to a kitchen from which a number of delightful smells were emanating.

Realizing he was hungry, Jethro walked to the bar and asked the bartender if food was available. The bartender, a tall skinny man replied, "An honor, sir, one minute while I fetch the waitress." He promptly made good on his offer, returning almost at once with a young lady in tow. "Maria will be pleased to take your order, sir," he said, leaving to attend to his other customers. Jethro found it difficult not to stare at the iron collar locked about the woman's neck.

He ordered his food, walked to one of the vacant tables, and sat down. He had hardly seated himself when one of the men from the bar walked over and introduced himself. Jethro responded by inviting the man, who had given his name as Robert Murphy, to sit.

As the two men began talking, Albert Brown excused himself pleading, "a very heavy workload." The conversation between the two men continued, only interrupted once by the arrival of Jethro's dinner.

"So, how did an engineer from Mississippi get to this sunny paradise," asked Jethro?

"I suspect much the same way as an engineer from Georgia. I went to a meeting, and based on what I heard and how bad things were at home, I decided change was good, "answered his lunch companion.

"You're right, that's pretty much what happened. There's certainly a lot of work for us. But I'm seeing some things I don't like."

"So am I. Some excesses. But I'm not making judgments until I can see the whole picture. After all, you can't make an omelet without breaking a lot of eggs."

"I guess you're right. Time will certainly tell," answered Jethro.

"It's a very ambitious plan. We're surrounded by enemies. We have to be strong and vigilant. It's not that we're cruel, it's what our circumstances dictate," said Murphy.

"Yes, well, on with the great adventure." said Jethro, as he dug in to his lunch with relish.

The conversation continued, focusing on technical issues, until he finished his meal. Jethro made his excuses and walked to his new home where he unpacked his few belongings and prepared to deal with his new world.

Bright and early the next day he reported to the Chief of Staff and began his new life. He applied himself to his work industriously, dutifully submitting both civic and military designs for a plethora of projects. Among his assigned tasks were to review the town's water service, design a new town hall and jail, and survey a number of local roads connecting Oaxaca with several of the surrounding villages, all of which were scheduled for substantial improvements. At his earliest convenience, he was also asked to interact with the local railroad engineer regarding rail and road right-of-way.

Shaking his head ruefully at the magnitude of the job, he turned to one of the men assigned to him and, only half jokingly asked, "Would they like me to design a pyramid in my spare time?"

To his consternation, the clerk replied, "I don't know, should I ask the mayor?"

Over the next several weeks the soothing balm of familiar activity served to calm him and obscure the uneasiness he felt about what he occasionally saw or heard as he moved about the city.

As he and Robert had similar skills, they frequently found themselves working on the same projects and would, when the occasion permitted, dine together. By unspoken agreement they tended not to frequent establishments that used indentured servant labor, as both men found themselves equally disturbed by the practice. Despite the occasional misgiving both felt a keen sense of accomplishment and pride as they watched their designs and creations transformed from lines on paper to buildings, tracks, roads and in some cases, fortifications.

CHAPTER TWENTY SEVEN

December, 1866

Monterrey, Mexico

In his capitol city, Benito Juarez stood on the balcony, shunning the warmth from the fireplace. For the last few months Juarez had begun to despair as he watched the Revolutionary Council slowly expand its control over most of central and southern Mexico. He strode briskly back and forth, awaiting the arrival of General Zaragoza.

The messenger had arrived two days ago. A simple, short statement, "I found it." If the General was right, if he had indeed found the coveted good ground so essential to their success, then their fortunes could take a drastic turn for the better. What had been a bleak outlook, the eventual defeat at the hands of a hated enemy, could now be tempered with some reasonable hope for victory. He turned and walked back into the room where other men waited.

OSS Regional Director Garrison looked up as Juarez entered the room and watched silently as the Mexican continued walking about, hands clasped behind his back, features set in a frown. Turning to the man seated to his left he muttered, "If the good General doesn't arrive soon, I think Juarez may bust a gut, Reno." Colonel Marcus Reno was at the meeting, representing General Custer.

All had agreed that the current Juarista defensive policy was not going to be sustainable in the long run. If something were not done, and done soon, the Juarista forces would eventually be defeated. This meeting was to give all interested parties an opportunity to voice their views and concerns.

The OSS had promoted an increase in Ranger Battalion activity in support of Juarez. Custer representative Colonel Reno had floated an idea from Custer. It called for armed intervention by the Union in the form of a substantial part of the Army of the Rio Grande, led of course, by General Custer.

This intervention would be in answer to a call for assistance from the Juarez government. Garrison and Reno were both aware such an action was in direct contradiction to Union policy and might, in fact, be construed as a treasonable action. Before they left for this conference, Custer had presented his course of action as the only possible one that could lead to victory. The General had convinced both men that once Washington was faced with a *"fait accompli"* their actions would be accepted and all would be considered heroes.

The four conspirators, Juarez, Zaragoza, Garrison and Custer had corresponded secretly, in order to prevent any inkling of their plan reaching Washington. Custer made sure all troop movements in his command appeared to be in accordance with official directives. Since it was expected that the Revolutionary Council military would soon begin their offensive actions, there was some urgency regarding getting a plan agreed upon and in place.

Juarez had requested a meeting to discuss Zaragoza's plan to initiate a full scale battle with Lee and this evening's meeting was the result, No sooner had Garrison made his comment then the clatter of horse's hoofs proclaimed the arrival of a number of men in the *hacienda* courtyard, just below them. The sound of boots on stairs preceded the entrance of General Zaragoza, along with a few of his aides.

Nodding a greeting to the men in the room, Zaragoza motioned to his aides, who promptly walked over to a large table in the room's center and spread out a map on the table top.

"If I might have your attention, Gentlemen," said Zaragoza, as he strode to the table. "I have found what I feel to be good ground. If we use it well it could be our key to victory. I would like you to look carefully at what I propose."

"Gentlemen," said Zaragoza, "Lee will attack us as soon as he is able. It is only a matter of time. If we do nothing, he will defeat us piecemeal." He paused for a moment, than continued. "We are moving from the defense to the offense. Our forces will be concentrated into a single army, here in Monterrey. Once we have our units united, we will move to the ground I have selected. We will use our army to meet and defeat the enemy, in a single, great battle. I have found a position that offers us an excellent chance to engage and defeat Lee. I propose to make a stand, and bleed Lee dry when he attempts to take our position." He stopped talking and allowed a hint of a smile to appear.

He pointed to an area south and slightly west of Monterrey. It was at the end of a long narrow plateau, squarely athwart the only road that Lee could to take when he moved north from Leon. The ground Zaragoza had chosen was slightly closer to Monterrey than Leon, a plateau that protruded southward from the Sierra Madre Oriental Mountains. The plateau's southern terminus was cut by a wide river valley, creating two parallel ridge lines about a mile apart. It was locally referred to as "Two Ridges." Zaragoza intended to fortify the northern ridge and force Lee to attack his entrenched army.

For the next few hours the assembled officers reviewed the plans, making adjustments and marking the placements of artillery and strong points, until they were satisfied they had the best possible tactical positions.

The next morning Garrison and Easy met. Garrison informed Easy that two companies of the Cortez Battalion had been involved in a strike against what they had thought was a major supply train for the CSM. However, it turned out that the wagons contained no supplies, but instead enemy infantry, who had counter-attacked and, after inflicting serious losses, driven the Rangers off. It was at this point that the retreating Rangers encountered the second part of the trap and discovered that rather than being the hunters they were in fact the prey.

The CSM had created dedicated counter-insurgency cavalry units, whose sole charge was to hunt down and destroy the Ranger Battalions. In this case they had first set the bait, and then waited for the Rangers to attack and fully commit themselves. As the Rangers attempted to withdraw from the assault, the CSM units struck. Both companies of Rangers had been decimated.

One of the Companies had been commanded by the major commanding the entire Cortez Battalion. Garrison informed Easy that he was brevetted to major and was to assume overall unit command for the upcoming campaign. All Ranger

Battalions were to be dedicated to recon and strike activity against enemy supply convoys. They were to provide the Juarista Army with as much intelligence as possible, shield them from CSM reconnaissance, and destroy as much supplies and equipment as they could. No one in the Ranger force was part of, or advised of, the Custer plan.

After receiving his new orders Easy left to assume command of the Cortez Battalion. In Monterrey, Garrison, Reno, Zaragoza and Juarez met again to finalize their plan.

CHAPTER TWENTY EIGHT

January, 1867

Mexico City

Uniformed servers were posted at intervals along the walls of the huge room on   the top floor of the Revolutionary Palace in Mexico City.   Ornate, solid-gold chandeliers, suspended from twenty-foot ceilings, spread a soft, golden light evenly around the chamber.   Cloths-of-gold drapes flanked each floor-to-ceiling window.   Lushly carved, granite mantles adorned man-high fireplaces that roared at either end of the huge room, easily driving out the mild chill of the Mexican winter.   The carved oaken table that graced the room's center was surrounded by exquisitely carved chairs and held pads, pens and pure silver water carafes and goblets.

Four silver-helmeted Praetorian guards in ornate green-on-white uniforms stood guard at the massive double doors separating the room from the corridor.   They presented arms as each of the senior members of the Council entered the room.

"Gentlemen," said Santa Anna, "our new constitution has been completed and while we have been forced to delay elections due to military necessity, the population in general has accepted this fact as a necessary evil forced upon us by the aggressors in the north."

"Our planning teams have completed our governmental structure," said Breckenridge, "and our infrastructure, with emphasis on the New Tredegar mines, foundries, and factories, are building ahead of schedule."

"Excellent," said Davis.

"General," he said, turning to Bedford Forrest, who was among the senior staff present, "what have you to report?"

Forrest replied, "Our DSS forces are growing at a satisfactory rate. Of course, we are somewhat below strength, but that is to be expected. The policy of "renting out" work squads of indentured servants has reaped enormous benefits. Their use in the mines, plantations, and other business pursuits are providing us with a net profit, despite substantial costs. We are expanding our presence into the rural areas as fast as possible, consistent with our manpower, equipment and training issues."

"Those plantations and mines will provide the raw materials that both we and our European friends so hunger for," said Davis.

"I am especially pleased with the effectiveness of our Homecoming Program," offered Breckenridge. "While exact numbers are not available, we estimate that more then twenty thousand men have entered this country during the last twelve months. These man are either educated or of military age and we anticipate expanding our program to bring entire families in the near future."

"I would like a review of our military situation, if you please, General," said Davis, addressing himself to General

Lee, who sat somewhat apart from the others at one head of the table.

"At this time our situation is static. We have control of most of the central and southern areas. However, Juarista units have been extremely effective when operating as guerrilla forces and small attack units in the north east areas. These activities, along with the inclement weather and the need to garrison the territory we hold, have placed severe demands on our manpower. Our forces have ceased all offensive activities, but we've used the time to make good our losses in both men and material from the Leon campaign. I have ordered French Foreign Legion units to prepare to move north to Leon. It is my intent to take the field at the earliest possible moment and commence offensive actions."

Lee stopped for a moment to look at the papers on the table in front of him, then continued, "It appears that the Juarista Army, which we estimate to be in the neighborhood of twenty thousand effectives, has changed its tactics and is now converging in force at Monterrey. I think it is possible that they will attempt to meet us in the field. It is my opinion that we would be able to defeat them in a pitched-battle scenario. We will be equipped with our newest weapon, the rapid-fire gun, courtesy of Mr. Agar's New Tredegar plants. This weapon, if properly employed, could prove to be the deciding factor. Once all our units are in place, I will advance north from Leon to Monterrey. My goal will be to locate, engage, and destroy the Juarista Army in a single battle."

"What kind of support has the Union provided the rebels?" asked Davis.

"They are totally dependent on the Union for all their military requirements from field artillery to hand weapons and ammunition. Their weapons are muzzle-loading muskets and light field artillery. Without substantial and continuous assistance, the rebels would be completely unable to field an effective fighting force. As a matter of fact, they would most likely be unable to hold either the cities or territory that they currently occupy," replied Lee.

"We also have become aware, courtesy of our intelligence department directed by Mr. Campbell, that Union citizens of Mexican descent as well as Mexican nationals are being trained as special guerrilla-type forces. They are being commanded by Union officers, and are operating against out regular units."

"It seems those damn Yankees are not satisfied with one victory. They seem to want to hound us forever," snarled Davis. "May they rot in hell!"

"Custer is especially active in supplying aid and assistance to our enemies," commented Breckenridge.

"I agree. Custer is a man to watched, especially since they've given him an army to play with," said Forrest. "He's a hard man, and since our attempt to assassinate him, he's determined to fight us in any way he can."

"I must point out two things," interjected Campbell. "First, that Custer has positioned a unit of his command, the XX Corps, almost on our border. He is in constant communication with that force. Second, our operation against him was deemed necessary at the time and to the best of our knowledge the OSS has not uncovered any proof connecting us to the actual event. But, lack of substantial proof not withstanding, Custer might initiate some rash action against us. I will insert additional agents to watch both Custer and XX Corps."

"Consider that an order, John," said Davis.

"General Lee," asked Forrest," do you think it possible that your taking the field might provoke some rash response on Custer's part?"

"If you are asking me if I think Custer might actually invade Mexico in order to take the field against me in direct opposition to his government's policy, my answer is that even *he* isn't that reckless. Whatever else the man might be, he is foremost a soldier and as such I believe he will obey his orders," responded Lee.

Later that afternoon, Davis and Breckenridge were having a discussion in Davis' office. The issue at hand was the relationship between the ex-confederates and their Mexican allies. "I must say that so far our relationship with Santa Anna and the Council of Five Hundred has surpassed my every expectation, John," said Davis, as he lighted a cigar and sat back in his chair.

"Mr. President," responded Breckenridge, "Santa Anna and his people are more like us than you might imagine. They were on the losing side of a revolution for many of the same reasons as we were. They know how bitter defeat can be. They have been honest with us about both their needs and abilities. I believe that we can work together to our mutual success."

"I have come to the same conclusion, John," answered Davis. "This is a rich land and a good land and I want to create something strong and lasting. Something my children's children can enjoy." His face hardened, and he finished with, "I'll destroy without mercy anything or anyone that stands in my way."

CHAPTER TWENTY NINE

February, 1867

Oaxaca, Mexico

When the news about the invitation from the Revolutionary Council in Mexico City reached Oaxaca and became public knowledge, there was an immediate uproar as to who would have the honor of representing the city. The original Spanish and Mexican groups loudly demanded their place in the sun, while the ex-confederate minority was equally vocal in making their feelings heard.

The mayor, Don Alvarez De Goya, a politically astute and long time member of the Council of Five Hundred, immediately convened a meeting of representatives from all concerned parties. Much discussion produced a solution that was deemed satisfactory by all concerned. The Oaxacan delegation to the festivities in Mexico City would be composed of a group of men representing the Revolutionary party, the Council of Five Hundred and the ex-Confederates. To their great delight, the two friends, Jethro Suggs and Robert

Murphy were chosen as their group's representatives. They were scheduled to leave for the Capital as soon as possible.

Mexico City

Mexico City had been filling with representatives from every town and city in central and southern Mexico for the last week, and was bursting at the seams. The official festivities were set to begin on the newly-created holiday of "National Day." This holiday served to commemorate the victory of the Revolutionary Council over Maximilian and the Legion.

The first "National Day" was to be celebrated by parades and feasts in every major town and city under the control of the Revolutionary Council. During these festivities the first group of recently-ordained nobility, with titles of either Don or Squire, would receive their land grants and stipends in carefully orchestrated, very public, ceremonies.

Thousands of copies of the new Constitution, as well as an outline of the structure of the new government, had been printed, and were being dispersed to the arriving representatives for their advice and consent, as part of the ratification process. The center piece to all this activity was to be Santa Anna's commencement speech.

The crowd that filled the great central plaza of the City swirled and eddied with a life of its own. Thousands of people in various stages of sobriety walked, talked and danced, according to their nature, as they waited for the balcony high above them to fill with their leadership. Small bands of musicians added to the sound level as they played for the crowds. Davis and Santa Anna stood together, preparatory to walking out on the balcony, enjoying a moment of anticipation.

"I believe the time has come, my friend," said Santa Anna. "After much blood and toil, we have written our history. Now we must announce it to the world." With that he placed a hand on Davis's shoulder and in tandem the two men walked out onto the balcony and into their brave new world.

As the figures became visible to the crowd below, a great silence spread itself like a cloud over the assembled masses. The honor guard troops, members of the newly formed Praetorian Guard, were turned out smartly in forest green tunics over white trousers and gilded silver helmets, all piped with silver braid. Posted on the steps below the balcony, they presented arms, their movements timed perfectly to Santa Anna's as he took two steps past Davis. He stood alone, arms raised, high above the silent, waiting crowds.

"My friends and country men," he began. " I come to you with a heart full of joy and wonder. We are here to celebrate our victory and to embark upon a great endeavor. Our mission is to create a strong and stable state, a state that will take its rightful place in the world. We have endured war. We have endured famine. We have endured traitors. We have fought hard and long against enemies from within and without. We have prevailed over those who would destroy us.

We must now create a bold new order in a great new country. A country based on the concepts of nobility and gentility, of service and security. A government based on the idea that it is the duty of the state to provide order and security for its citizens and it is the duty of the citizens to serve and support the state. A government that recognizes such support as it protects the rights, duties and obligations of its citizenry.

I stand before you as the acting President of the Confederated States of Mexico, to present to you our acting Vice President, Jefferson Davis. In recognition of the fact that we are required to deal with enemies from both within and without, all elections will be delayed and until that time, Vice President Davis and I will serve in our posts as caretakers of our great new Nation. My countrymen, with all my heart and soul I give you a new and glorious Mexico!"

The speech, in which Santa Anna outlined the Revolutionary Council's concept of a new and glorious Confederate States of Mexico, was frequently interrupted by roaring ovations from the crowd and continued for some time. Completing his oration, Santa Anna stepped back to a position next to Davis. Both men raised their clasped hands over their heads in unison, turned, and walked back into the room behind them.

As soon as the speech ended, Jethro along with the other members of the official Oaxacan delegation, fought their way out of the main square and headed for the restaurant that occupied the bottom floor of their hotel. When they entered the establishment they quickly saw that pandemonium reigned supreme with servers rushing madly to and fro. Feeling the need for some quiet reflection, they left and began walking slowly down one of the wide, tree-lined avenues that led from the great square.

After a walk of about twenty minutes duration they found themselves in an area of one and two-story adobe buildings that served a variety of mercantile, business and living needs. Twice during the walk they had passed uniformed DSS teams.

Both times they had been stopped and questioned after being required to present their ID. It appears to me, thought Scruggs to himself, that the new regime has serious issues regarding it's faith in its citizenry. It was definitely something to think about.

Coming upon a sign reading *Red Bull Cantina* they entered, found an empty table in a corner of the room and sat down. Shortly thereafter a young waitress wearing a metal collar took their drink and dinner order, reappearing quickly with a round of beers. After a short wait she returned bearing dinner. While savoring their repast they began discussing the speech they had just heard.

"So," asked Jethro, "what about that speech?" "I liked it. It showed spunk, determination. Let 'em know we know what we're doing." responded one of the group.

"Yeah,"offered another, "I thought he told it like it is."

"I agree with things the way they are for a while, at least until we've got everything under control." said another.

"Well, I can understand the attitude, but I'm not so comfortable about the means, especially this indentured servant thing, "said Jethro.

"I'm sure that it's just a temporary thing," said one, "you know, emergency stuff. It'll be over once we've got control."

With a dubious tone Jethro answered, "The end justifies the means."

With an uneasy smile, one of his dinner partner said, "Well, since you put it that way, yes."

As the conversation continued the general consensus was that the new government was taking a firm line to insure that the average citizen was safe and his property secure. One of the group felt that the harshest of the measures would be temporary in nature and would be eventually replaced with more humane, less draconian measures. Scruggs himself offered that once the trouble makers were taken care of, there would be no need for the extremes currently in force.

During the next few days the major boulevards of the Capital were the scene of frantic activity. Residents of the stately mansions, which had at one time housed enemies of the state, and were now home to the new regime's wealthy and elite, strove to outdo each other in lavish displays of solidarity with the new order. Every senior member of the Confederate States of Mexico's military and government had been invited to numerous functions. .

On the eve of the second day of celebration, the main entrance to a mansion occupied by Baron von Steuben, a representative of Prussian business interests, who was also connected to powerful political figures, sparkled with torch light to welcome his honored guest.

As General Lee's coach and its attendant cavalry escort rolled slowly down the grand, tree-lined avenue, Venable turned to Lee and said, "Sir, I must admit to be surprised that you decided to accept an invitation to a grand ball."

Lee turned to face Venable and responded, "In my position I must be both soldier and diplomat. Besides, these people have proven themselves to be our allies and we must be respondent to their needs."

"That's absolutely true, sir," answered Venable. "They've certainly kept their end of the bargain."

"As we will keep ours," answered Lee, his tone grim.

When they reached the mansion, the cavalry escort dismounted and formed a security cordon as Lee stepped from the carriage. Walking up to the entrance he returned the salute of the Prussian Army Officer awaiting him at the door. He walked on, past the honor guard, entering the vestibule. Here a short, pudgy Prussian businessman and his senior staff awaited him.

The Baron offered his hand and welcomed him, in heavily accented, but understandable English. Lee responded with a handshake and smile. With the introductions complete, the two men entered the courtyard which held the main reception line. Lee and von Steuben slowly made their way to the head of the line and von Steuben began introducing Lee to the waiting dignitaries.

The Prussian industrialist said to Lee, "I have been instructed to inform you that certain parties are very pleased with events up to this point. They look forward with anticipation to even closer ties between our countries. However, General, there still is some concern regarding the situation in the north. Until such time as there is only *one* government in Mexico there can be no recognition of any government by my country." He concluded, "It is deemed essential that this problem be, shall we say, clarified."

"First, let me say that we greatly appreciate your country's support and assistance, unofficial though it may be," answered Lee. "And let me further inform you that I am quite certain that both the military and political situation will be resolved successfully within the next few months. It is my intention to take the field against the Juaristas at the earliest possible time."

"And we in turn are grateful for the information as well as the opportunity to establish and expand trade relations in this hemisphere. There are many in my country who have great hopes that the relationship between us will continue to grow. We are pleased that you will reopen your campaign in the north, and I have been instructed to request that we be allowed to attach observers to your forces," said von Steuben.

"I would be a pleased to have an Imperial German officer accompany our Army as an observer, Baron," answered Lee.

"In that case," responded Von Steuben, "please allow me the opportunity to introduce the officer who has been assigned this duty." Turning to his right, he gestured to a tall, lean man, wearing the black uniform of a Prussian infantry officer, who stood waiting nearby. The officer strode across the room and came to a halt in front of Lee.

Heels clicked and steely blue eyes focused directly at him. "Please allow me to introduce myself, General," said the young man. "I am Lieutenant Paul von Hindenburg, of the Imperial Prussian Army General Staff. I look forward with great anticipation to the forthcoming campaign."

Lee regarded the ramrod-straight youth before him with a brief smile and answered, "Lieutenant, I am pleased to meet you. Let us hope for all our sakes that your opportunities to observe are minimal. My aide, Colonel Venable, will make the necessary arrangements and notify your embassy."

Executing another ramrod straight bow, von Hindenburg answered, "I await your orders with the greatest anticipation, sir."

CHAPTER THIRTY

March, 1867

Gulf of Mexico

The USN *Potomac* steamed south over the gentle swells, rolling and corkscrewing slightly as her bow met each wave at a slight angle. The occasional spray soaked Captain Jason Patrick as he stood on the ship's bridge. The *Potomac* was completing her third straight week of patrol. "Deck, ahoy," came a shout from the foremast, "ship to port, heavy smoke." Jason removed the cap from the speaking tube that connected to the engine room and ordered, "All ahead one half," then turned to the helmsman and instructed, "twenty degrees to port."

Turning to his watch officer he asked," What do you think she is, Tom?"

Ensign Tom Watkins, fresh from Annapolis and on his first patrol, glanced at his captain and said, "So much smoke could mean a warship at full throttle or perhaps a merchantman on fire?" Jason gave no reply but leaned against the bridge rail and waited as the two ships rapidly closed on each other.

Within a half hour the ship was visible to both officers and Jason turned to Watkins and said, "Ensign, what you are looking at is the latest and greatest in terms of naval technology. That ugly, smoke-spouting monster is an Armored Cruiser, a direct descendent of the old Monitor, which I am sure you remember from your classes at Annapolis."

The two men watched quietly as the ship in question, fresh from the Brooklyn Navy Yards and on her first patrol, passed a few hundred yards to their port side. The warship boasted a solid sheath of armor from just below the waterline to the top of the bridge. Protruding from the superstructure amidships was the cause of the smoke, two large smokestacks. On the main deck sat two huge round turrets, one in the bow and one in the stern, each holding two 50 lb. breech loading naval rifles, capable of accurate gunnery at a range of three miles. The ship was the first of a new class of armored warship, designed specifically for deep-sea operations.

"Like it or not, your future and mine will be to serve on a ship similar to that one, Tommy." said Patrick.

Alabama Zone of Reconstruction

Following Harry Chester's master plan, KKK insurgent groups were becoming increasingly active. Throughout the old south they were attacking Union facilities wherever and whenever possible. Constant raiding was causing the Union to direct more and more attention as well as military might to activity within its borders.

The late winter night sky was mostly overcast, the moon playing peek-a-boo through the scudding clouds. Chester,

"Grand Dragon and Nighthawk" of the Mobile KKK Coven, along with a half a hundred other hooded and gowned men, waited silently alongside the Birmingham and Southern railroad tracks.

The ambush site he had chosen for the weapon and troop laden train had been prepared along a stretch of line that meandered through a region of rolling hills and streams. The chalky, poor soil supported minimal undergrowth, which in turn created relatively unobstructed movement and visibility along the right of way.

The explosive charges had been set at a point where the rail line paralleled a narrow and fast moving stream for about a hundred yards. Both the tracks and stream were at the bottom of a gentle incline. The KKK strike teams had arrived, prepared the ambush, and then hidden themselves in camouflaged positions.

One of his men turned to Chester and said, "Signal from scout one, sir. Target is three miles out and closing."

The response was an abrupt nod.

A short while later Chester was told, "Signal from scout two, two miles."

Chester moved forward several feet in order to see the place where the last scout was posted, at the base of the incline, close to the railroad. The man held a lantern that would be used to signal when the train was exactly one half mile from their position.

The moment he saw the tiny flare of light, he ordered the fuses lit. The charges had been placed along the stream side of the tracks, and had been perfectly timed to go off in series as the train past over them. The explosions ripped the engine off the tracks and toppled it and several of the cars into the stream.

At this point, the stream had narrowed to a width of about fifty feet, but was more than ten feet deep and fast moving. Sounds of crashing and smashing cars joined with secondary explosions from onboard munitions cooking off. Cries from dying and injured men and animals, along with the hiss of escaping steam, continued to rise in volume as the remaining cars added themselves and their cargo to the havoc. Rifle fire from Chester's hidden men added to the carnage. Panicked troops, desperately seeking shelter from fires, exploding ammunition and rifle fire jumped into the water or tried in vain to find shelter. Many of them thrashed about desperately, but being unable to swim, drowned.

Chester and his men continued to lay down a heavy barrage as the detonations reached a crescendo and the fire raged, consuming more of the train and casting a ruddy glow over the entire area. The heat drove many of the Union troops from cover. The fires and explosions around the tracks clearly silhouetted the uninjured soldiers, many of whom were focused on saving as many of their hurt comrades as they could. The Klansmen, posted in trenches dug along the top of the rise, continued to shoot. They poured a murderous fire into the wreckage, despite the screams and pleas for mercy from the Union troops.

After several minutes of raining death on the hapless Union soldiers, Chester signaled his men to cease fire and retire to their waiting horses. He was the last to leave the ambush site. Reaching the top of the ridge line, he paused to watch the frantic activity below, a savage smile on his face. In short order the raiders had dispersed into the night, leaving in their wake a nightmare of mutilation, death and destruction.

Riding hard for several hours, Chester arrived at his home exhausted. Before going to sleep he enacted what had for him become a terrible ritual of both pain and remembrance. On the nightstand next to his bed was the Daguerreotype of his family. Sitting, he held it in trembling hands, first crying softly then becoming quiet and motionless. He remained in that pose for several minutes lost in a nightmare reverie, hearing over and over the cries of pain from the wounded, seeing the dead, and reveling in grisly satisfaction. Shuddering, he broke the trance and carefully returned the Daguerreotype to its shrine.

Days later found Chester heading north on the same tracks he had so ruthlessly attacked. He was currently in the process of buying two old warehouses, each with their own riverfront dock, along with several new wagons and livestock. Seeking out new business gave him the perfect cover story for his constant and ever expanding travels throughout Alabama and other neighboring states.

CHAPTER THIRTY ONE

April, 1867

CSM Army, Mexico

The primary staging area for the Confederate States of Mexico Army was about ten miles north of Leon, astride the only route usable by a large force moving on Monterrey. Lee had issued his Order of Battle, and for the last few weeks units tasked for the planned assault had been arriving and were being integrated into the main force. The plan was both simple and direct. The Army would advance north until making contact with the main Juarista Army, which he believed intended to fight a pitched battle against his command. As he had told the Revolutionary Council, he would find and destroy the enemy.

The condition of the Mexican roads was continuing to prove to be a major deterrent to the advance. Lee's plan had attempted to take this into account. Prior to commencing his advance, he had tasked several infantry regiments to act as engineering and point-security troops. He had put them to work on improving and rebuilding the roadway a few weeks before his Army took the field.

Lt. Brown strode down the line of sweating, grunting, cursing soldiers as they labored with picks and shovels to transform what was essentially a dirt track into a road usable by an entire army. Brown was concerned about the way his company was strung out along several hundred feet of path that ran through some very rugged country. In some places he could see less than fifty-feet off the road, and the possibility of ambush by those thrice damned Union Rangers was very real. Gazing at the rolling, vegetation-covered hills, he felt a twinge of uneasiness, the mark of a combat veteran in hostile territory.

As he turned to his platoon sergeant to order the pickets moved out another fifty feet, several shots rang out. A shovel-wielding soldier, not more than ten feet from him, dropped in his tracks, the back of his head exploding, spraying brains and blood everywhere. Several more men dropped to the ground, some wounded, most quickly seeking cover, grabbing their weapons and searching for targets.

A sergeant pointed to a spot a few hundred feet up the side of the hill and shouted,

"There, there!" He began running up the steep incline, at the same time firing his rifle at the indicated spot. He had only gone a few yards uphill when more shots rang out, several finding their mark, dropping the man dead in his tracks.

Brown, realizing the futility of a charge, ordered his men to stay down and return fire. After a few moments, he called out to cease shooting and cautiously raised himself up. Not receiving any fire, he stood up and ordered a squad to follow him as he slowly and cautiously climbed to the top of the hill.

Reaching the top, he found it unoccupied. After leading a sweep of the empty, surrounding hills, which caused a delay of several hours, the work began again.

Oaxaca, Mexico

Jethro Scruggs was hard at work when he received a request from the Mayor to report at his earliest convenience to his honor's office. When he arrived, he discovered that he had been ordered to the seaport city of Selina Cruz, on the extreme southern tip of Mexico's Pacific coast. He immediately returned to his home, packed, and with several other specialists and a DSS escort, was on his way.

As the group moved slowly south and west through subtropical southern Mexico, he noted the frequent presence of ragged work crews engaged in repairing and upgrading the main roads and bridges, always in the company of small teams of the khaki-uniformed DSS troopers.

The highway he and his team were traveling on had itself been the recipient of substantial improvement. Pounded gravel surface, runoff gutters, and a border of newly planted trees gave an almost eerie sense of planned beauty. It contrasted harshly with the human misery that was the cost of these civic improvements.

As the trip continued, they occasionally came upon small villages. Some were still occupied and proudly displayed a variety of new civic and military construction; others showed signs of recent habitation but were empty or had been partially burned and vandalized. In one abandoned village, they were horrified to see several unburied, decomposing bodies of men, women, and children lying where they had been shot, except in the case of two females who had been staked out spread-eagled and nude in the dirt, then mutilated and murdered.

Several days on the road found them entering the small city of Hildago, about fifty miles north of their destination. Inhabited by some ten thousand souls, it was a regional center for textiles and clothes production as well as a hub for rail and road transportation. Adobe homes, brick and wooden shops and warehouses fronted on meandering, narrow, dirt lanes. Several large and imposing cathedrals were sprinkled throughout the city. The inner city was graced with a number of palatial private homes and several government buildings; many were set in beautifully landscaped parks next to large open squares, interconnected by wide, cobble-stoned, tree-shaded avenues. Outside the walls the city was almost completely surrounded by fields of corn, barley and wheat, as well as goat and cattle herds.

As Jethro and his companions entered the city they saw fires and plumes of smoke rising from several locations. Continuing on their way, they discovered khaki clad DSS troopers and officers cordoning off entire neighborhoods. They were rounding up groups of people, sometimes what seemed to be entire families, and herding them towards waiting wagons where other guards packed them in like sardines. Speed was achieved by the liberal use of wooden batons and leather whips, applied indiscriminately to body parts. The population of entire neighborhoods were being driven from their homes, into the wagons, and then carted off under heavy guard.

Reaching a small square fronted by a few small adobe structures and a church, Jethro's group stopped. Their way was blocked by a DSS officer and cavalry troop which had dismounted and blocked the road. The officer had walked to the front step of the church and mounted to the top step. He turned to face the civilians who remained standing below him, many crying and cringing in fear. He removed a scroll from a leather pouch he carried, and, in a loud voice began to read.

"Attention please, citizens of Mexico! Our country is in the throes of a great crisis. We are surrounded by enemies. The people who were taken have been accused of crimes against the state. If they are not stopped, they will destroy us. If we are to be saved we must identify and destroy the traitors among us. We of the DSS will be ever vigilant in our defense of our country and its lawful citizens. You are citizens of the Confederate States of Mexico. Be proud, be obedient, be productive, and you will be rewarded. Your legally elected officials will tell you everything you need to know. Follow official directions and all will be well."

Completing his speech, the officer motioned to several priests who, like all the other villagers, were standing in the square. The men were escorted into the church, each by a trooper. Jethro, along with the rest of his group, followed the DSS force into the church.

"It is, as I have already told you, quite simple," said the officer, speaking to the oldest prelate of the group, who had identified himself as the monsignor. "The people must follow the rules. Convincing them to do so is your job. Failure in this will have very, very negative consequences for all of you. Do I make myself clear?"

"We can not. No! We will not be a party to this abomination!" answered the man, his voice tight with anger. "This is evil, and mother church will never condone it!"

"So, do you all share these views?" asked the officer, in a deceptively mild voice.

"I think," responded another, much younger priest, sweating heavily with the stink of fear emanating from him in waves, "that it is our duty to support and enforce the law of the land."

The officer looked at the elderly prelate who had first spoken for a moment, then nodding his head asked, "Padre, would you care to change your mind?"

"My son, it is not within my power to do so. The laws of God must always come before the laws of man," was the Padre's response.

The officer motioned to the two troopers standing just behind the man. One trooper swung his shotgun in a short, vicious arc that ended with a heavy impact on the back of the padre's head. Even as the body slumped to the floor, the second man was binding the prelate's ankles and wrists.

"Inform your people that you are the new monsignor," ordered the officer.

"As you wish, sir," responded the younger priest, "it will be done."

Two of the DSS troopers grasped the unconscious padre's body, carried him from the room to a waiting wagon and tossed him into the back.

"There will be a Revolutionary judge in attendance in the city hall from now on," said the officer to the young priest. "He will be responsible to hear all civil violations and pass sentence on all offenders. We will take a census of the population before we leave. There will be a garrison of Department of State Security troops bivouacked here. Finding food and quarters for them will be part of your responsibilities. In an effort to better serve our citizens a number of families from other, smaller hamlets in the area will be relocated to your town. Building materials and skilled construction workers will be provided for any additional dwellings required. You will be expected to provide the farmers amongst them with the necessary land for cultivation." Eying the priest, he continued, "You personally will do all you can to assist them."

"I understand."

Fixing the man with a cold stare, the officer said, "Your obedience is just as important as your understanding. You and everyone in this place would do well to remember it. The Revolutionary Council will reward those who serve well, but we will also punish traitors without mercy."

As the officer began to leave the building he saw Jethro and his companions watching him. He walked to where Jethro's group stood and said, "Do not allow this to disturb you, gentlemen. Many of these people are either Monarchists, counter-revolutionaries or criminals. This action is essential to the security of the state."

One of the men with Jethro said, "Even if they are criminals you needn't be so brutal!"

The DSS officer looked sharply at the man who had just spoken, and moving to a position directly in front of him, asked in a soft voice, "Who are you and what is your reason for being here, sir?"

Taken aback by the threat implicit in the officer's tone and attitude, the man replied in a subdued voice, "Why, I am a mining engineer and I've been ordered to survey for a new copper mine."

"Well, sir, I'll not tell you how to go about surveying and I'll thank you not to tell me how to maintain the security of my country," responded the officer, who then continued with, "Be on your way, now!"

Realizing that the last was not a request, but an order, the men left the church, mounted and quickly left for their overnight accommodations nearer the center of the town.

As they continued their trek south, their path was crossed twice by large numbers of people in wagons, on horseback and on foot, with DSS personnel in attendance. One night Jethro's group shared a camp with a few of the guards and they discovered that the groups of people had been declared "indentured servants." They were on their way to various job sites located throughout southern Mexico.

Eventually they arrived at their destination, the Pacific Ocean port of Salina Cruz. The city had been founded in the mid-sixteenth century as an outpost for the Spanish navy. It had grown slowly over the years and was now a major port for South American imports as well as Mexican exports to Asia and South America. It featured a magnificent natural harbor. Presenting themselves to the appropriate officials at City Hall they received directions to their accommodations, along with instructions to report back tomorrow at seven in the morning.

Jethro and his companions found their lodgings, and after bathing, set about to take in the sights. As with many of the other mid-size towns in Mexico, Salina Cruz was in the throes of major changes. Streets throughout the city were being repaired and improved. Several areas in the center of the city were being given over to large man-made ponds and tree filled- parks, complete with lush vegetation and gently curving walkways. City Hall was being substantially increased in size, with much of the masonry being supplied by the demolition of several of the town's large churches. A good deal of work was also being focused on upgrading two forts which provided security for the town and port. Almost all of the construction and destruction were being performed by teams of indentured servants with their ever-present DSS wardens.

The group finally reached the southern-most part of the city, which sat on the edge of the water. Pausing to take in the sight of the majestic Pacific Ocean, they stood on the shore and gazed admiringly at the vista before them. Drawn by the soft sounds of the gently-breaking waves, they walked along the shore until they arrived at the outskirts of the docks. Adjoining it was an area given over to small cantinas and boarding houses primarily used by sailors and dock workers.

Since it was almost evening, they decided to find someplace on the waterfront to eat and, after a short search, found a *cantina* situated on a small rise near the docks. The only discordant note was that two of the servers in the dinning room wore the iron collars of servitude. After dinner, the group retraced their steps to their assigned lodgings. Aware that the following day was to begin with a seven o'clock meeting at the mayor's office, they went quickly to bed.

Arriving as ordered at city hall the next morning they were told to see the Regional Director for Public Works, Antonio Gonzales. He proved to be a portly, good-natured man awaiting them in his office. After introductions all around, Jethro learned that he and a fellow engineer had been tasked with determining the feasibility of constructing railroad tracks from the city to a nearby mine. They were also to review the possibility of increasing the size of the mine's foundry.

After a ride of a few hours duration they arrived at the mine. They presented themselves to the foreman who, after reading their orders, assigned them a trooper for a guide and basically left them to their own devices, with orders to report to him when they had completed their tasks.

As they left the main office, the two stopped for a moment on the porch to observe the facility. They saw two, long and narrow, one-story buildings. Each building had a heavily bolted door at each end and steel bars bolted over empty window frames. The buildings were parallel to each other and separated by about twenty yards of sun-baked dirt. At one end of the two parallel buildings was the two story building they had just exited. This building contained the administrative offices and guard's barracks.

While they watched, a group of guards in khaki emerged from the barracks and headed for the nearest of the long buildings. Arriving at the door they unlocked it and entered. Several moments later a group of emaciated men, chained to each other, began to emerge into the sunlight and slowly shuffle towards the mine. The group reached the mine entrance and each prisoner had his shackles removed and was handed a mining tool.

In the area between the two barracks were two sets of two wooden poles set parallel in the ground. Each pair of poles supported a crossbar raised about ten feet above the ground. Dangling from each of the crossbars were two iron cages, each about eighteen inches square. Two of the cages held a nude man, both bodies covered with welts, bruises and burns.

One man was slumped down, either unconscious or dead, while the other held tightly to the bars, his eyes focused on Jethro and his companion, who were in turn regarding him.

The man's body was horribly sunburned, several large blisters had formed and a few were draining a copious amount of thick, evil-smelling fluid. Fixing his eyes on Jethro the imprisoned man croaked, "*Aqua, aqua!*" through bloodied, sun-burnt lips.

"By God, enough is enough!" snarled Jethro, as he turned and walked quickly back into the foreman's office and slammed the door, shouting, "What in the name of God are you doing to those men?" The foreman whirled about, surprise evident on his face, and in a somewhat hushed tone replied, "Whoever you are I see you don't understand how things are done. Those two men are convicted criminals who attempted to start an uprising amongst the inmates. They planned to kill the guards as well as myself and all the other mine employees. They are serving as an example to the others."

"Couldn't you just execute them and be done with it? Wouldn't that be a more civilized approach to punishment? They may be criminals, but they're also human beings. There's a difference between punishment and sadism, and I think you've crossed the line!"

"Listen to me," answered the foreman, urgency clear in his voice. "You don't understand how things are done here. I'm just following orders. I'm not responsible for handing out punishment. That's the job of the security people and I leave that to them." With a stern look, he continued, "I'd strongly suggest that you do the same. Now, leave me alone and go about getting your job done." Knowing there was nothing he could do to lessen the suffering of the prisoners, Jethro made his way back to his companion and followed the foreman's advice.

Laredo, Texas Zone of Reconstruction

General George Custer entered his Laredo office and strode to his desk. Sitting down, he leaned back in his chair and regarded the two men who sat across from him, OSS Director Pinkerton and Congressman O'Reilly. "So," he said. "What can I do for you gentlemen?"

Congressman Patrick O'Reilly replied, "I am here on a fact-finding tour, General. As official representatives of the Committee on Military Preparedness and Intelligence, I felt it was my obligation to get a first hand look at Laredo. I must say, General, I'm quite impressed with what you have accomplished." O'Reilly gestured to the view from Custer's third-story office.

The entire center of the city had been rebuilt. Offices, hotels, and a variety of retail establishments lined the newly-paved roads. Every street and avenue was crowded with pedestrian and horse traffic. The railroad yards, a beehive of activity, held half a dozen passenger and freight trains. Off in the distance, a forest of tents, artillery parks, supply depots, and wooden barracks identified the location of a major part of Custer's Army of the Rio Grand.

Turning back to the General, O'Reilly said, "That's a lot of firepower you have there, General. I need to make clear to you that under no circumstance is there to be any military action taken south of the border without prior consultation and authorization through appropriate channels. General, that's political speak for, "*Hands off Mexico!*" O'Reilly paused for a moment then added, "Just for the record, General."

Custer coolly returned O'Reilly's look, thinking, smug little Irish bastard, who is this man to give me orders on

military matters? How dare he treat me like some lieutenant fresh from the Point! Leaning forward to emphasize his
reply he said, "There are times when immediate action is the
only course available, Congressman. From a purely military standpoint I consider it highly inadvisable to limit our
options."

O'Reilly regarded Custer for a moment, and then
responded in a cold, stern tone, "Due process and authorization, General." He favored Custer with another wintry glance,
and motioned to Garrison to accompany him. Garrison,
Pinkerton and O'Reilly left Custer's office together, walking in silence until they reached the ground floor. Pinkerton
stopped, turned to face Garrison, and said, "Mr. Garrison, I
have some serious concerns regarding the General."

"Director," replied Garrison, "General Custer is a loyal officer in the Union Army. His primary goal is always to serve
and protect his country with every means at his disposal."

Pinkerton looked hard at Garrison then paused for a
moment and said, "I will take you at your word, but should
you see any sign of him acting without authorization you
are ordered to report such activity at once. I repeat, *at once!*"
Garrison responded with a crisp, "Yes sir." Satisfied that he
and O'Reilly had gotten the message across he nodded and
returned to their hotel rooms preparatory to returning to
Washington D. C. The next morning found Custer, Reno,
and Garrison breakfasting together in Custer's office.

"So," asked Custer, scorn evident in his voice, "how did it
go with that nasty little politician, Garrison?"

"About as you expected, Sir," answered Garrison. "They
both suspect something, but there is no evidence. Pinkerton

ordered me to advise him if I discovered you are planning any move on Mexico."

"Excellent," responded Custer. "We'll insure you have no knowledge of the actual plan, then." Turning to Reno, he said, "Have General Terry report to me as soon as possible and dispatch a rider to Zaragoza."

Custer had been in intermittent contact with Zaragoza since he had secretly agreed to send combat forces in support of Zaragoza's actions in seeking out a confrontation with Lee. The Juarista Commander had in turn ordered that the roads leading south from the USA/Mexican border be improved as much as possible in order to facilitate Custer's troop movement. Custer's latest communication advised Zaragoza that Union troops would soon be ready to march and were in the process of being pre-positioned on the border. In acknowledgement of the difficulties, Terry's XX Corps would use horses and mules for transportation, and leave all its artillery, wagons, and support personnel behind.

During several conversations, Custer had carefully sounded out Terry's views and found them to parallel his own regarding the "Mexican Situation," as it was now referred to. Once he had assured himself of Terry's personal loyalty, Custer arranged for Terry's units to be stationed at points along the border that offered immediate access to Mexican trails.

General Terry's command was a force which had been raised after the end of the war. It was composed exclusively of freed Negro slaves and white officers. This unit fielded three Divisions. Each Division had three, two-thousand man Brigades. All the troops were armed with old fashioned, rifled muskets.

Over a delicious dinner, accompanied by fine wines, and served in the private dinning room of one of Laredo's finest restaurants, Custer, Terry, and Garrison met. Their purpose was to complete a plan for a Union invasion of Mexico. This was an action that was in direct contradiction to official policy and standing presidential orders. It was an act which could result not only in war with the Confederate States of Mexico but become international in scope, possibly involving both England and Prussia. At the meeting's conclusion, Custer ordered General Terry to have XX Corp prepared to deploy south whenever Custer should issue the order.

Custer ended the meeting with a toast, "Gentleman, to glory and the final destruction of the Confederacy."

A few days later General Custer called Colonel Reno into his office. "I've received a message from Zaragosa. He's moving the main part of his Army south. He's fortifying the position he found and expects to fight Lee there. I've also been advised that Lee is on the move, headed north." Custer paused, eyed Reno, then continued, "Order Terry to mobilize. We're going after them."

Reno, his face betraying no emotion, but his heart beating like a hammer, replied, "Yes sir. At once, sir."

CHAPTER THIRTY THREE

May, 1867

Alabama Zone of Reconstruction

Harry Chester sat on the top deck of the sternwheeler riverboat, idly watching the shore pass by, as *Star of the South* churned her way up the Alabama River from Mobile to Montgomery. Refusing the stewards offer of a second mint julep, he rose and made his way to his cabin as the ship slowed, veered towards shore, and began docking. He soon found himself waiting on a line that ended at the bottom of the gangplank, where a white union officer, backed up by a Negro infantry platoon, was checking the debarking passengers' identification. Eventually, he reached the end of the line where he showed his papers and was passed through. Chester left the ship and, baggage in hand, made for his hotel.

The city was a mirror of the dichotomy that Reconstruction was creating throughout the defeated Confederacy. Newly constructed factories, stores and apartments sat side-by-side with tents and flimsy, dirt hovels, and abandoned, decaying mansions.

Several times he was forced to jump over rivulets of water that were serving as both a source of drinking water and open sewers. He dodged groups of gaunt and dirty children playing in filth and garbage, watched over by famished, apathetic adults. When he got to his hotel, he confirmed his reservation, got his key. and after refusing the sevices of a bellboy, went up to his third story room to unpack.

Chester spent the remainder of the afternoon in the hotel's bar, successfully negotiating for the purchase of a small, local shipping line. Completing negotiations, he shook hands with the prior owner of his newest acquisition. Passing through the hotel foyer on his way to the dining room, he could not help but notice the larger-than-life cardboard cut outs loudly proclaiming tonight's performance of *Hamlet*. The lead was to be played by that thespian of world renown, John Wilkes Booth.

At precisely 8 PM, he left the bar and walked out onto the hotel front porch. He sat in a chair, a newspaper under his left arm, a cigar in his right hand, and a glass of whiskey on the small table to his right. Chester remained in that position for about half an hour, slowly sipping his drink.

A tall slim man approached him and asked, "Have you a light, sir?"

"I have but three matches," came the countersign.

"Together, they will light the way," was the response.

Without any further ado the tall man ordered Chester to follow him back into the hotel. The two men passed through the crowded dining room and made their way to the rear where more exclusive, private rooms were located. Two large men, obviously guards, barred their entrance to one of the rooms.

Chester's guide signaled to them and they moved aside to allow entry. Several men were seated at the table in the center of the room. The tall man escorted Chester to the man at the head of the table and curtly performed the introductions.

"John Wilkes Booth, meet Harry Chester," he said, then turned and walked away.

"Mr. Chester," said Booth, "I have been informed of the magnificent work you have performed for your country and I deem it a great pleasure to work with you."

Chester, taking Booth's offered hand and sitting in the proffered chair, responded, "We all do what we can for the cause."

Booth smiled, shrugged, then offered a drink which Chester refused, and began to provide Chester with a series of orders for his KKK teams. After delivering the orders, Booth also provided a new set of codes.

OSS Rangers, Mexico

To the west and south of Zaragoza's position at Two Ridges, the Cortez OSS Ranger Battalion was still in the field. Easy, from his hidden position, watched as a cavalry unit made its way across his field of vision. Since their initial action Easy had kept his command in almost constant contact with the enemy, in a series of hit-and-run strikes.

He slid down the sandy slope of the narrow ravine to where the rest of his patrol awaited him. Reaching the bottom he signaled his men to mount their horses and follow him. After several moments riding he gestured to Lt. Sanchez to ride at his side.

"Could be a security force for a supply convoy or just a patrol," he said, eyes alight. "They're moving awfully slow. We'll scout the area and see why." He turned to Emilio and said, "What do you think?"

"I think,'" responded Lt. Emilio Sanchez, "you are right."

"All right, then,'" answered Easy, his face alight with the anticipated combat, "let's see if we can't come up with something special for those boys."

After a careful reconnaissance, they discovered that the CSM cavalry force was, in fact, providing security for a convoy of ten heavily laden wagons. These wagons were following some distance behind the cavalry unit. Easy and Delta Company rode to a point where they were a good distance ahead of both the wagons and cavalry.

While they rode, he and Sanchez worked to create a plan to attack and destroy both CSM units. By evening the two officers had decided on their tactics. That evening they made camp, and after dinner Easy called a council of war for Sanchez, the sergeant team leaders and himself.

"We've scouted this convoy and we know it's for real. Those wagons are filled with supplies, not soldiers," said Easy, his finger pointing out the position of the convoy on the dirt map he had drawn using the meager light from a small oil lamp.

"We draw off the security force then attack the convoy. Then we hit them on their way back to defend the convoy!" finished Lt. Sanchez, a snarl of satisfaction on his lips.

"It's complicated, but it'll work if we can find the right terrain." said Easy. He addressed his sergeants, "All right, now that you're good with the plan, make sure your men are too." The five men rose and went to their teams, leaving Easy and Emilio alone.

"So, are we good, Emilio?"

"I believe so, Easy. I think we've got it covered. We just need the right ground."

"Yeah, I think it sounds like a plan to me, too."

The next day they found it. The road passed through a rugged, hilly section of terrain. One of the hills had a small plateau about half way up its side. From the plateau down to the road was an almost vertical cliff face. The only access to the plateau was a trail best fit for mountain goats. It had been only by a stroke of luck that one of the Rangers had found it.

From the cliff's top several miles of road were visible. From the rear of the plateau to the hills summit everything was covered by heavy undergrowth and dense forest. Several large caves, enough to hold a number of men, had been discovered. The caves, covered by the foliage, were all situated between the hill top and the plateau.

"I'm thinking that this is such an obvious spot, they'll post some people here," said Easy, as he and Lt. Sanchez scrutinized the position.

"I think so, too," agreed Sanchez.

"The caves will easily hold your team," said Easy. "Once your people are secure we'll move on."

"Then let's be at it," responded Sanchez.

With that Sanchez turned to his men and ordered them to dismount, enter the forest and pick some of the empty caves to use as cover. As each man dismounted, he handed the reins of his horse to a trooper from another team. Once all ten team members were on their way to concealment, Easy and Sanchez shook hands. As Sanchez followed his men into the foliage, Easy led his men down the trail where they rejoined the rest of the company.

The remaining four teams made for the second ambush site, which they had discovered earlier in the day. This site was established at a point where the trail narrowed abruptly and wound around the bases of several steep-sided, boulder-strewn, low hills. Easy ordered his men to dismount and take up their positions, about half-way up the hill sides. He placed his men in such a pattern that their fields of fire converged on the trail from both sides.

Each Ranger was armed with a twelve shot Winchester rifle, and a six shot revolver. Many Rangers carried additional personal weapons. The thirty men in hiding were capable of firing almost six hundred aimed rounds in the span of a few minutes. All were well trained marksmen and very accurate. Once his men had taken cover Easy moved along the hill tops, satisfying himself that his men were both concealed and protected. After making a few minor changes the trap was complete. The hapless men riding into the trap would never know what hit them.

Captain Steven Harding brought his CSM cavalry to a halt with an upraised hand. Looking around from his vantage point on the plateau top he remarked to the trooper at his side, First Sergeant Aldo Williams, "You really can see for miles. Hell of a spot for a lookout."

"Nothing to see though, sir," was the laconic response.

"You're right about that, Sergeant. Let's hope it stays that way," answered Harding.

Both men sat their horses for a few moments, each regarding the view from their position. Harding finally broke the silence. "Sergeant, take a squad and man this post until the convoy has passed, give them a couple of miles lead, then mount up and follow them. I'll take the rest of the company and continue on as advance guard."

"Yes, sir," answered Williams.

The brief exchange over, Captain Harding rode back down to the trail, then led the remaining troopers of his command along the road, where they unknowingly followed Easy and the Rangers.

Sometime later Easy and his men watched from their concealment as Harding and his men passed through the Ranger position. Meanwhile, on the cliff, Sergeant Williams detailed his eight men to a variety of duties. He ordered two men to guard positions and others to caring for the unit's horses. In short order, the campsite was as he wished it to be, and all activity, except for the two men walking their posts at either end of the camp, ceased. The rest, including the sergeant, took this opportunity to catch up on much-needed rest.

From his vantage point, above and behind Sergeant William's men, Lt. Sanchez watched as the two CSM soldiers gradually relaxed into the numbing monotony of guard duty. The remainder of the men either fell asleep or lost focus on their surroundings. Knowing that the heavily-laden wagons would take some time to reach this point, he relaxed back into cover.

A while later, Sanchez signaled to his men to take their positions. Seeing his signal, the men of the team left the caves where they had hidden. They slowly made their way through the underbrush until they reached a point where they could observe the enemy, but remain unobserved themselves. Two of his men, armed with bows and arrows, got as close as they could get to the two CSM cavalrymen on guard duty.

The OSS Officer took one last look around, and then gave the call of a mountain thrush. In response to the signal the two expert bowmen fired, the arrows a half-seen blur whose flights abruptly ended in the hearts of their targets. At the same instant the arrows were released, Sanchez and his remaining men were running full speed towards the resting soldiers, each with a ten-inch Bowie knife grasped in his hand.

One of the men, perhaps sensing something amiss, rose up in a vain attempt to locate one of the guards. Failing in that, he did manage to catch sight of his attackers, running towards him and his companions. At the same moment he began to shout a warning, a knife flashed through the air, burying itself in his throat, his cry of alarm becoming a blood-choked gurgle.

In a split second, the area was covered with stabbing, punching and dying men. Sergeant Williams, with the instinct born of experience and competence, awoke and rolled to his feet just as Sanchez, closing fast, launched himself into the air and landed on him. The contact drove Williams into the ground. Bright red arterial blood spurted over Sanchez's face and arms as his knife slammed into William's chest, right up to the hilt. Almost as if in prayer, William's hands clasped the hilt of the knife invading his chest. His face was inches from that of his assailant, who watched without remorse as the gleam of life faded slowly from the soldier's eyes.

Regaining his feet, Sanchez whirled in a crouch. He took two steps, and, in an underhanded throw, launched his knife into the back of an enemy who was straddling one of his men. The attack had been so sudden and ferocious that not a single shot had been fired. Over almost as soon as it started, the

Ranger survivors went about the next step in the plan. Two of their number put on the least damaged or bloodstained enemy uniforms and began to patrol along the edge of the cliff, awaiting the arrival of the wagon train.

A while later, the wagon train made its appearance, and the ersatz guard on the cliff waved the wagons onward with a casual motion. When the middle wagons were at the foot of the cliff each of the Rangers lighted the fuse of a black-powder grenade, and in unison, threw them onto the wagons below.

The initial explosions were quickly followed by numerous additional detonations as the ammunition on board cooked off, shredding drivers, horses and wagons alike. Flame, wagon debris and wet, meaty objects arced high into the air before splattering back to earth. A huge, black cloud mushroomed into the air, fueled by the destruction of the wagon convoy.

At the sounds of the massive explosions to his rear Captain Harding immediately ordered his force to face about and race back towards the trap. Harding was almost out of the shallow valley when the first volley took his horse out from under him. Slamming hard into the ground, he lost consciousness for a few seconds, during which time his now leaderless command was savaged by a deadly crossfire from the rocky heights on both sides of the trail. Coming to his senses, he stood up, just in time to take two rounds to his chest. He crumpled, dead before he hit the ground.

Harding's men responded as best they could. Some dismounted to return fire, others attempting to continue down the trail and ride out of the ambush. Easy had waited until the lead riders were almost out of the trap before firing the first round. His shot was the signal for all of his men to fire at their pre-selected targets.

He and several of his men had deliberately targeted the horses with their first few shots. Shooting the horses first created a mass of fallen, rearing animals that slowed and disrupted the enemy cavalry's movement in the narrow confines of the valley. After dropping the horses they began picking off the men, coolly targeting and hitting a soldier with almost every single shot.

The Rangers continued to pour a blizzard of fire into the trapped men until the remnants of the security force finally broke. The devastated Revolutionary Army cavalry turned back and ran for their lives out of the blood-drenched valley. Easy waited until they had all exited then blew three sharp blasts on his whistle. At his signal the Rangers began moving to their horses. They left behind a carpet of dead, dying and wounded men and animals.

The massacre complete, Easy headed back to Lieutenant Sanchez and his team. Sanchez had left the ambush site and was on his way to join Easy's force. Delta Company, once reunited, continued on, seeking new targets.

Each company had been assigned a rendezvous point. Mounted messengers would wait there and carry reports to and from the battalion commander. Easy planned to arrive at that spot tomorrow so he decided to write his after action report after dinner.

Easy, having had on opportunity to fight side-by-side with both Orto and Emilio, had developed a healthy respect for each man's bravery and competence. After eating he called over both. "Emilio, Orto, I expect to reach our rendezvous point sometime late tomorrow, so I thought I'd write my report tonight. I'd appreciate your input on our actions." Sensing that commenting on a superior's actions could be a cause for concern he said, "If you need you can write up a report yourself. I'll include it with my message."

Emilio smiled, said, "Captain, the only thing I can say is that we've given our enemies some good, hard blows and taken very few casualties. I personally am quite proud of this command and this command's senior officer. As a matter of fact, sir, that's the position of every man in this unit." At this Orto nodded his agreement energetically, saying, "Yes, sir, every one of us feels that way."

Flushing slightly, Easy was mute for a moment or two. "Well, then, if that's the case I'd like both of you to read it after I've written it, just in case I've left something out." Both men readily agreed. That night, after completing his duty, Easy was in such a good mood that he treated the men to his version of both the "Battle Hymn of the Republic" and "My Darling Clementine," *twice.*

CHAPTER THIRTY FOUR

June, 1867

Juarista Army, Two Ridges

Hector Lamas and his friend Ramon Vega labored hard, preparing defensive redoubts on the north ridge. Both men were stripped to the waist and dripping sweat. Hector was wielding a hoe and his friend Ramon a shovel. The two were part of the Juarista force helping to fortify a village that sat at the bottom of the eastern-most part of the ridge.

From the day they had arrived they had toiled ceaselessly. The two had helped to dig trenches, fill sandbags, cut firing holes through the walls of buildings and build strong points for artillery. They had only been in the army for a few weeks, so in their spare time they learned to march, load and fire their weapons.

Hector was a farmer, and Ramon the owner of their village's largest and only cantina. Hector had joined the Juaristas the day after a Legion foraging party had taken his entire crop. They had also taken his wife, a few hours later leaving her mutilated body just outside the village. Ramon had joined because a group of DSS troopers had set fire to his *cantina*. They had forced him and his family to watch until it was reduced to burning embers. The DSS had done this because he had tried to hide a family that had been falsely accused of "Crimes against the State."

The two men, along with hundreds of ex-farmers and workers, spent their days working under the careful direction of their officers. They spent the nights talking softy amongst themselves about the forthcoming battle. The prevailing consensus was that the enemy, seeing the massive fortifications that had been prepared, would simply turn and go back. The opinion of the rank and file was not shared by the officers, who continually urged the men to greater efforts.

General Zaragoza sat atop a large boulder that was situated in the middle of the north ridge. He watched, with growing satisfaction, the activity surrounding him. Along the entire length of the ridge hundreds of figures toiled. All around him soldiers were digging, carrying, and depositing the dirt and rocks necessary to transform this particular piece of land into a killing zone.

The plan called for the building of bastions or strong points at strategic positions all along the northern ridge top. The first such position was on the extreme right flank and was to serve as an anchor and pivot. In addition to several hundred infantry, one of his six precious artillery batteries would be located there. The remaining strong points were to be located along the ridge top. A double line of trenches, about fifty feet apart and paralleling the military crest of the ridge, were being constructed. These trenches would connect all the strong points into a single defensive line. His artillery was also being emplaced. The heavily camouflaged guns were in individual positions along the ridge top. A small village at the base of the ridge on his extreme left flank was being converted into a fortress.

Zaragoza was taking great care to build his fortifications in such a manner as to disguise, as much as possible, both their locations and extent. On several occasions he had moved along the southern ridge, periodically using his binoculars to observe his own installations. He frequently ordered changes in response to what he saw.

At this point, almost two-thirds of his Army was present, and the remainder expected soon. Juarez himself had recently arrived. As the politician in him had come to the fore he had continually walked among the troops, shaking hands and talking about their imminent victory. As Juarez spoke at length and with great passion about the glory and prosperity that their new democracy would bring, Zaragoza, who was withdrawn and taciturn by nature, watched with amusement. Although this slowed down construction efforts, the positive effect on the soldier's morale was deemed to be worth the delays.

Custer's Command

As part of the overall deception, and in part to shield Garrison from official reprisal, Custer had ordered Garrison to conduct a lengthy inspection of the western-most portion of the Texas Zone of Reconstruction. Once issuing marching orders to his command, Custer had immediately joined XX Corps as the unit struggled southward through the Sierra Madre Oriental Mountains. Both men, Custer and Garrison, had been as vague as possible regarding their itinerary and timing.

The issue of the routes XX Corps was to take had proven to be a serious problem. It had soon become apparent that it would be extremely difficult, if not impossible, to improve existing roads to the point where Custer's entire force could use a single trail. After much discussion, it had been decided to split the command into three components.

Each of the three Divisions was to move south separately. The three commands would reunite a few miles north of the Juarista Army, at a point where all three trails descended onto the plateau where Zaragoza was building his fortified position.

Using separate routes allowed his command to move south faster. It also resulted in his forces often being more than twenty miles apart, and so positioned that none could come to the aid of either of the other. They could not easily coordinate their movements or communicate. In the interest of speed, Custer had accepted these limitations, relying on his generalship to allow him to rejoin his command before entering battle.

Custer, as usual, had assumed a position at the head of his column. He marched just behind the advance guard, surrounded by his command and security team. At this altitude the air, although warm, was relatively dry and invigorating, and the troops were moving steadily with a minimum number of soldiers dropping out of formation due to injuries or exhaustion.

Turning in his saddle to regard the long columns of plodding infantry and draft animals stretching for miles behind him, Custer remarked, "I don't expect any of those paper pushers in Washington will understand, let alone appreciate, what we are doing here, Reno. As far as I'm concerned every man in this Army is a hero, willing to sacrifice and perhaps even die for the good of the Union. I feel privileged to lead such men, I truly do."

Reno, riding next to Custer, responded, "General, sometimes it falls to the few who see their duty clearly."

"Those people," said Custer, as he nodded in a generally southern direction, "would usurp an entire country and government for the sole purpose of maintaining themselves in power. They must be brought to task and destroyed without mercy, and that grave duty has fallen to us."

CSM Army

Still far south of Two Ridges, General Lee, having momentarily caught up with paperwork and feeling a need for fresh air, stood and left his tent. He was followed and preceded as always by cavalry troopers. Walking a few paces from his tent he came to a slight rise, which he ascended. From this minor vantage point he could look north and watch his engineer units continue their work on the roadways or turn to the south and see where his lead units were already pitching tents in preparation for the night's bivouac. Returning to his tent, he sent an orderly for Colonel Venable who, after a short wait, appeared, saluted and asked, "You sent for me, sir?"

"Yes, Colonel," responded Lee. "Do you remember that young Prussian officer, the one assigned to us as observer?"

"I do, sir."

"Ask him if he would care to join me and my officers for dinner tonight, if you please."

As always, Venable had ordered Lee's campsite be chosen with an eye to both security and scenery. On this soft, summer evening, the tents had been pitched on the top of a knoll. There was forest to the east but from every other compass point the position offered an uninterrupted view of the thousands of campfires the Army required in order to prepare its collective dinner   The sun having set, the lanterns suspended from the top of the tent were lighted. The smell of hot kerosene mingled with the odor of burning wood, dinner, and dessert. Lee, along with Hill, Longstreet, Garcia, Venable and von Hindenburg, had all finished their meals and were enjoying coffee with brandy and cigars.

"We are honored that the King of Prussia should be interested in our Army," said Hill, a smile of satisfaction on his features as he rolled the goblet of brandy, then brought it to his nose to sample the aroma.

Lee nodded to Hill and said, "It is, of course, our pleasure to have you with us, Lieutenant von Hindenburg. I hope you have found it worth your while so far. Perhaps you might share with us the situation in Europe? My officers and I would be most interested."

Von Hindenburg hesitated a moment, then, in a voice somewhat strained at first, began to speak. "As to that, sir, our relations with most countries, with the exception of France, are quite good. It appears that the Emperor Napoleon the III has aspirations regarding land which the Kaiser considers to be part of the Empire. War is not out of the question. As usual, the situation is in the hands of the politicians. The Army will, in due time, receive its orders."

The German stopped speaking, and glancing at Lee said, "If I may be so bold as to change the subject, sir? It is my understanding that you will shortly engage the enemy and it is, of course, that action which holds my interest."

"Have you seen much action to date, Lieutenant?" asked Longstreet.

The Prussian officer looked straight at his questioner before replying, "As of yet, I have not had the honor of fighting for my country. However, given the political situation I expect to remedy that shortly after I return home."

Looking at the young officer, Longstreet said, "I assure you, Lieutenant, there was no intent to embarrass you. It was simple curiosity on my part."

Von Hindenburg made no reply.

"Do you think there will be war between Germany and France?" asked Hill.

"Our relations with France were somewhat strained when I left home and it would not surprise me should they soon reach the breaking point." responded von Hindenburg.

"It would seem that if it were not for bad luck, Napoleon III would have no luck at all," ventured Hill, his smile growing broader.

"With your permission, might I prevail upon you or one of your officers to provide me with information regarding the current status of the Juarista army." asked von Hindenburg.

Lee glanced at Longstreet before he replied, and said, "Perhaps General Longstreet would be good enough to enlighten you as to the military situation."

"It would be my pleasure," answered Longstreet. "The situation is that we are currently marching north in expectation of meeting an army under the command of General Zaragoza. He commands the forces loyal to Benito Juarez. We now estimate his force to be about twenty-five thousand strong. Although we need to use some units for garrison duties our force here is about forty-five thousand, so we have a definite and substantial numerical advantage. Our best case scenario would be to meet him in the open and defeat him while suffering the least possibly losses. It is also possible, but at this time not considered probable, that we might also encounter a Union force." Longstreet looked at Lee and continued, "Would you concur with my analysis, General?"

Lee smiled and answered, "I find your explanation to be most satisfactory." He then turned to von Hindenburg and asked, "Does that provide you with the information you seek?"

Von Hindenburg stood, saluting Prussian style with his hand and heels said,

"Generals, you have been most kind and helpful and I look forward to conversing with you again. With your permission I shall retire for the evening,"

Lee, watching the young officer leave, said, "A very interesting young man. Now to business. Gentlemen, I would like to review our campaign strategy. We know that Zaragoza has found ground that is favorable to him. He will fortify his position and let us bleed ourselves out attacking him. I think that he believes that a defensive victory might be enough to bring the Union in on his side. We will advance as fast as we possibly can, consistent with maintaining our fighting capabilities. I intend to allow Zaragoza the minimal amount of time to prepare himself. General Hill, as your Corps leads our advance, you will rotate your Brigades from construction to security duties, in such a manner as to insure maximum speed. Our victory will to some degree depend on how fast we can drive north and reach Zaragoza."

As he continued to speak, Lee's eyes took on a hard cast, and his expression became grim. "Our goal will be to destroy his army. Destroy it *completely*!"

One additional outcome of the evening's dinner was that Lee became especially fond of the young Prussian, so much so that they dined together frequently during the march north.

Juarista Army

"General! General!" the cavalryman shouted, as he galloped his mount right up to the front of the flimsy structure that was currently serving as Zaragoza's Juarista Army headquarters. Pulling hard on his horse's reigns, he stopped his horse in a shower of dirt. He leaped from the saddle, ran past the gaping guards and into the tent. "I have dispatches sir," he shouted, waving a piece of paper in the air. "News for the General!"

Zaragoza motioned the excited man to him saying, "Easy son, easy. Let me have that." Taking the message from the rider, he scanned it for a moment, then pursing his lips, said, "Well, the day has come." Turning to his staff he began issuing the orders that would bring his Brigade Commanders to him.

That evening, after dinner, Zaragoza addressed his senior officers. "Gentlemen, our time is nearly upon us. Lead elements of our enemy, cavalry units, have made contact with our picket forces to the south. They will arrive here soon. We have only a short period of time, days, perhaps a little more, to complete our fortifications. You will each return to your commands and urge them to their greatest speed. Each of you has his orders, knows what to do, and when to do it. Our enemy will show no mercy and neither shall we. Follow the plan and we will triumph. Go with God, Gentlemen."

The sky was steel-grey and the morning dew heavy on the ground, hours before dawn, when movement swept like a wave through the camp. A single blanket, still and unmoving, gave silent testimony to an aging man's ultimate sacrifice from his exertions of the last few days.

Soldiers who still ached from the activities of yesterday slowly stirred, stretching and groaning their way to wakefulness. Fires flared, piercing the darkness and guiding the hungry men to their ration of hot, thick porridge and coffee. Well before the sun arose, Zaragoza was leading a group of senior officers and engineers on yet another survey of both the fortifications under construction and those planned.

From the center of his position Zaragoza and his entourage looked south. They stood at the lip of the ridge that was the end of a plateau stretching back several miles to the mountains. In front of them the north ridge sloped down to a valley that was bisected by a wide, shallow river. To their left and right the ridge curved slightly back, forming a broad and shallow "V" shape. To the far right the north ridge ended in a series of steep, rock-strewn, sand-bottomed valleys that ran mostly north-south. To the left the ridge curved around northward, where it became heavily forested, almost impenetrable. A road led from the western flank of the southern ridge, down to and across the valley, through the village at the eastern side of the north ridge and then up onto the plateau. Both ridges were studded about with boulders, trees, and bushes. The sides of the southern ridge were slightly more steep, but the top lower than the northern one.

Custer's Command

Custer and XX Corps were still pushing hard down the central spine of the mountains. A dispatch trooper rode up to the cluster of officers who were sitting their mounts alongside the trail. Saluting smartly he said, "Message from Zaragoza, sir," and handed it to General Custer.

Taking the paper, the General scanned its contents and smiled broadly. "Well, well, good news, very good news! Reno, inform Terry that we must increase speed at all costs. Zaragoza has been in contact with the enemy. Speed is essential."

"I will advise them immediately, sir," responded Reno, as he quickly wrote out a message in triplicate.

Night fell and wrapped in a shroud of darkness, the harsh march finally halted. All along the trail tiny fires flickered as the bone weary troops sought to appease their hunger. Custer was on a promontory near the head of the column. From his position, looking north, he saw the fiery display. Hearing a noise, but without turning his head the general said, "Come on up, Reno, its really quite beautiful."

Reno advanced until he stood next to Custer, said, "Sir, dinner's ready and the surgeon is here to look at your feet."

Custer spoke as if he'd not heard the Colonel.

"You know I believe in destiny. I believe it is my..., I mean *our* destiny to save the Union again. This command will find those villains and destroy them." His voice became stronger, harsher. "We will find them and break them, Reno. Utterly destroy them. I swear it!"

Reno stepped back at Custer's glare, waited in silence for a moment, said, "Please, General, the surgeon and dinner."

Custer grinned a humorless grin replied, "Right you are, Colonel, first the doctor, then dinner, *then* glory."

Before first light the following morning Custer's men were being rousted awake, and the campfires lighted in order to prepare hot water for brewing coffee and soaking hardtack. Each experienced infantrymen took time to inspect each foot carefully, lancing boils, drying and cleaning each foot before donning socks and boots. By dawn, the men were on the move, driving hard, advancing south. Custer, on foot, continually prowled up and down the lines of struggling, sweating men, sometimes cajoling, sometimes commanding them to their greatest efforts from dusk to dawn, day after day. Being the officer he was, he allowed himself even less rest then he gave his men, and they, aware of his heroic efforts, made every effort to increase their speed.

CSM Army

The trooper dismounted from his lathered horse, and after dusting himself off, entered into the headquarters tent of II Corps, General A. P. Hill's Command. He advanced to the officer seated behind a small field desk and, after saluting, handed over an envelope. The trooper accompanied this action with the statement, "Signal from Recon Command, Sir."

"Thank you, Corporal. Dismissed," the officer replied, as he passed the sealed envelope to the runner stationed at his side. The runner turned and walked to the rear of the tent and handed the letter to General Hill. The General glanced at the writing, stopped and read again, his features tightening and a gleam of anticipation appearing in his eyes.

"Send this letter to General Lee," he said turning to a clerk.

When he received the message from Hill, Lee read, "Recon reports contact with large enemy formations approximately ten miles north of my position. They appear to be dug in. I will continue to scout."

Lee was mounted when he received the note. He dismounted and walked a short distance. He thought, so, it is upon us. He turned to Venable and ordered, "Advise Longstreet and Garcia. We have made contact with enemy forces, and tell General Laurency to continue to move the Legion with all haste!"

As the first streaks of red painted the eastern sky the following morning, CSM sergeants began moving among the sleeping men, awakening them and preparing them for the day's activities. Shortly after dawn, breakfast completed, the construction units renewed their road building efforts while the long butternut-and-white columns continued their northward march.

Juarista Army

At the sound of distant gunfire, Zaragoza turned from his conversation with one of his Juarista officers to look south. Turning back, he saw a mixture of fear and uncertainty on the man's face. "Return to your command, Captain," he ordered, while turning to his staff and ordering riders be sent to ride south and find out what caused the shooting.

A while later, a cavalry patrol galloped over the southern ridge, entered the valley, followed the road across it and up the side of the northern ridge, then back along the north ridge until finally arriving at the command tent. The patrol leader dismounted and advanced to Zaragoza.

The General had deliberately not risen from his seat, but had instead focused on the mound of paperwork on the desk before him. He looked up only after the patrol leader, a frighteningly young Lieutenant, had saluted and come to a rigid attention in front of the desk. Zaragoza regarded the young officer with a bland eye and said, "Your report, Lieutenant."

The Lieutenant remained at attention and replied, "General, a group of American Rangers wish to enter our lines. Unfortunately, sir, a few shots were exchanged before they identified themselves. They are waiting at the advance guard post for permission."

"Admit them, and tell their commanding officer I wish to see him."

"Yes sir."

A short while later a group of Juarista cavalry and Rangers arrived at Zaragoza's headquarters. Easy dismounted and, handing the reins to one of the sentries, he entered, walked to Zaragoza, and saluted. Zaragoza stood, first returning the salute, than reaching out and grasping Easy's hand in a firm shake.

"It is good to see that you have remained well, young man," said Zaragoza, as he eyed Easy's drawn, tired face.

"Thank you, General. I am pleased to find you well, also." responded Easy.

"How far behind you is Lee?" queried Zaragoza.

"No more then a few days march, sir. He's pushing his people hard, very hard." answered Easy.

"I would have preferred more time, but one must deal with what one has, not what one wishes. Is that not so, Captain?"

"Actually sir, it's Major. Have you orders for me?"

"Congratulations Major. As you can see, we have been hard at work. It is my intent to fight and defeat Lee here. In a few days we will be in battle. What you may not know is that a Union Army Corps under the Command of General Custer is north of this position, coming south as fast as it can. I want you to take your men, contact Custer with all possible speed, and advise him that Lee is closing on my position. My force is slightly over twenty-two thousand men, and my estimate is that Lee is bringing between thirty and forty thousand troops. As you can see, Custer's prompt arrival is a cause for some concern to me," said Zaragoza, with a tight smile.

At the mention of Custer and his force, Easy's eyes had widened in surprise. He was under the impression that only Ranger units were to be involved in direct conflict south of the border. During his last discussions with Garrison there had been no mention of any change in policy by Washington.

"Is General Custer bringing the entire Army of the Rio Grande? Has Washington declared War?" asked Easy, surprise and disbelief evident in his voice.

Zaragoza paused a moment in thought before answering Easy, then said, "I think it advisable that you have any discussions regarding American military policy with your commanding officer, young man. Fill your bellies, mount your horses, deliver my message to Custer, and then you can discuss the situation with him."

Easy, realizing that he had been dismissed, saluted, turned and left the tent. He found his men at a commissary tent cramming their mouths full of hot food and coffee. Easy joined them and, after eating and drinking his fill, called over Lt. Sanchez and related his conversation with Zaragoza.

Sanchez expressed his surprise and asked Easy the same questions Easy had asked Zaragoza, and received almost the same response. Scarcely a half-hour later, having provided the horses the same relief as the men, they were on their way north. Uneasy about Custer's unexplained actions and the impending battle, Easy drove his men hard.

Custer's Command

General Custer had received news from General Terry's column that although his command was low on supplies and nearing exhaustion, he and his men still expected to arrive at the planned rendezvous in a timely fashion. Custer had also received a similar message from the third column.

The Division that Custer was with, the 68th, commanded by General Walter Scott, was fast wearing itself out, every soldier hungry and exhausted. Bloody feet and aching legs was the norm. Some troops were nearing the end of their strength as well as their supplies. Others had already given their all and small pockets of motionless, worn out troops lay beside the trail.

The Division was stretched out over several miles of road, with stragglers reaching back many miles more. The length of the column itself was greatly increasing the supply difficulties. Custer constantly made his way up and down the lines of exhausted soldiers, exhorting them to greater effort. Despite his own physical situation he still occasionally dismounted and walked, as an example to his men.

The general still expected the entire Corps to rendezvous on the plateau a few miles north of Zaragoza's position. Once reforming his command, Custer planned to join Zaragoza and attack Lee in a massive frontal assault. He was confident that an unexpected attack by three infantry divisions, close to eighteen thousand men, would be enough to turn the tide. The problem would be to insure the timeliness of the maneuver.

Just before sunset that evening, Custer was advised that his advance guard had made contact with an OSS Ranger force and that the unit commander had an urgent message from Zaragoza. Custer ordered the Ranger officer brought to him immediately.

Easy advanced towards the officer who was wearing an ornately embroidered uniform. Saluting, he addressed the General. "I am Major Ezekiel Sinclair, OSS Cortez Ranger Battalion, with an urgent message from General Zaragoza."

Custer returned the salute and eyed the man before him. Although not an advocate of special operations, he took in the steady gaze and calm, certain demeanor of the officer and replied, "And what has General Zaragoza to say, Major? As succinctly as possible, Easy reiterated Zaragoza's message.

"My understanding is that Zaragoza can field twenty-five thousand men," responded Custer. "Would you agree with that assessment?"

Easy replied, "The general puts his numbers at twenty-two thousand, sir. There's no doubt that Lee outnumbers him. I've also received unverified reports of a large force of Foreign Legions troops advancing from the south to join Lee's command."

Custer responded, "Thank you, Major. Have your men see my quartermaster for provisions, and await further orders."

Easy answered, "Yes sir," saluted, and went to find and feed his men.

Eying his executive officer, Custer turned to the other officers gathered around the campfire and said, "That will be all gentlemen, thank you."

As soon as the two men were alone Custer said, "As you know, Reno, I've little use for special operations, spies or anything of that ilk. If that young officer were capable, he'd be wearing the uniform and facing the enemy. No, I don't credit that information. My information is that the Legion was thrashed at a place called Cameron and the remnant surrendered to Longstreet after being chased over half of Mexico. Even if they were present in force, I don't believe they could stand up to us in battle. No, I simply don't credit that intelligence. That will be all. Goodnight, Colonel."

"Goodnight, sir," responded Reno, leaving Custer to his thoughts.

Easy found his men already establishing a camp, lighting cooking fires and beginning to prepare the evening meal. He walked around the camp, briefly addressing some of the men and nodding recognition to others, finally locating the fire at which Lt. Sanchez and Sergeant Emmanuel sat, and joined them.

Easy took the plate, and smiling at Emmanuel while sniffing the plate's contents, asked, "All out of mule, I see?"

Not to be outdone, Sanchez immediately replied, "Yes, Major, but on the other hand, we have lots of horse."

Easy laughed and began to eat. The men sat and consumed their food, culminating the meal with cups of hot, black coffee, lightly laced with whiskey. Draining his cup, Easy caught Sanchez's eye and motioned him to follow.

Walking through the camp, the two men conversed in low tones.

"I think that something is very wrong here. I can't believe Washington would sanction an all-out invasion. Based on all the OSS briefings I've received, it could very well cause an international war," said Easy, his voice hushed but taught with tension.

"You think Custer is doing this on his own?" asked Sanchez, surprise evident in his tone. "Good God, he must be crazy to do something like that!"

"Custer is a gambler, a big time risk-taker, and I think he's taking the biggest gamble of his career! The problem I have," he concluded, a dark scowl contorting his features, "is that he appears willing to gamble the lives of his entire command."

"So what do you want to do," asked his Lieutenant.

"I really need a plan," answered Easy, a rueful smile on his face.

The 68th Division was on the road before the first streaks of pinkish light painted the eastern sky. From his vantage point, Easy could see the long lines of struggling blue- clad infantry snaking their way south towards Zaragoza's position.

Easy, after discussing the situation with both Emmanuel and Sanchez, had decided that only he and Sergeant Orto Emmanuel would remain with Custer's command. He had ordered Lieutenant Sanchez to send riders to the other companies in the battalion, ordering them all north to Monterrey. He further ordered Sanchez to take Delta north, find Garrison and report directly to him regarding Custer's Mexican incursion.

Easy and Orto watched as the last men of Delta Company disappeared from view. Turning south, they made their way after Custer's command. Later that afternoon, Sergeant Emmanuel, riding next to him and watching the struggling infantrymen smiled, lighted a cigar, and inhaling deeply, commented, "It is good to be cavalry, is it not, Major?"

CHAPTER THIRTY FIVE

July, 1867

Juarista Army

The last of the Juarista cavalry cantered over the southern ridge, and into the valley, only a few hundred yards ahead of the pursuing CSM cavalry patrol. When the pursuers neared the top of the southern ridge some left the road to explore the ridge top and some continued to chase their enemy. The running battle continued until the Juarista cavalry forded the stream and entered the fortified town at the northeastern terminus of the valley. Once the CSM cavalry reached the outskirts of the village it contented it-self by firing a few rounds at the walls and shouting a few curses before returning the way they had come.

When Zaragoza received the report that CSM units had entered the valley, he ordered all Brigade Commanders to report to him at once. As soon as he had all his senior officers present, he carefully reviewed his overall battle plan again. He cautioned the officers that no one was to take any offensive action before receiving explicit authorization from him.

He finished by saying, "All you have to do was hold your positions. Remember, they are strongly fortified, well-situated positions with close artillery support. This Army, you and your men, are the sole hope for freedom for our-selves, our families, and our country. I want each of you to carefully review the plan with your junior officers. Now return to your commands." As they filed out he thought, well, one last review and then it's in God's hands.

As soon as the last of his officers left for their units, Zaragoza gathered his staff, mounted and rode to the extreme right flank of his position. The Sonoran brigade, the smallest of his brigades at twenty-five hundred men, held this position.

Formed into five equal sized regiments, their task was to stop any attempt to bypass or outflank the right flank. Three of the regiments were holding forward positions with orders to withdraw only when forced to by enemy pressure. A third regiment was manning what was the actual defensive line, a series of strong points connected by trenches that paralleled a small stream. The wide, shallow stream flowed into the valley, where it joined the river that ran down the center of the valley. The fifth and final regiment held a strongpoint in the rear. This position was also the Brigades headquarters. Six light guns, the brigade's artillery support, were each in individual sandbag emplacements, strung out along the stream. Having satisfied himself regarding the readiness of this unit, Zaragoza proceeded to the next unit in line.

The Chihuahua Brigade, a four-thousand man formation, held the next segment of the line, followed by the Durango Brigade, forty-five hundred strong, responsible for the center of the line. This was followed by the Nuevo Leon Brigade, thirty-five hundred men, and finally the last unit on the far left of the line, the forty-five hundred man Zacateca Brigade.

This last unit's primary duty was to hold the small village at the base of the cliff. In the event the Zacateca was forced out of the village, their fallback position was a double line of trenches running along the top of the ridge. This position was anchored on the far left by thick, heavy forest. Zaragoza had kept one Brigade, the Sinaloa, which was a twenty-nine hundred man formation, as his tactical reserve.

One of his ongoing manpower issues was an overall lack of cavalry. This was due to the fact that his Army recruited primarily from the peasant class, and these men were far too poor to own a horse. The Ranger Battalions had alleviated this problem somewhat, but quantity was still a major issue.

The General rode slowly through each Brigade position, his demeanor calm. He laughed and joked with junior officers occasionally. He spoke briefly to soldiers each time he stopped, insuring that his men got a good look at him. As an experienced leader, he knew that his presence and attitude would have a powerful and positive effect on them.

Once he had completed his tour, he gathered his staff officers and slowly made his way back to the center of his command. Stopping at a point that was slightly higher then the surrounding terrain, he held his telescope to his eye and swept it along the opposite ridge. He focused on a group of horsemen, officers by their dress, who sat their mounts surrounding one man in particular.

The officer in the center of the group was regarding Zaragoza's position and, for one moment, Zaragoza had the unsettling feeling that the man was looking directly at him. Completing his visual review, he and his staff went to his headquarters, which was located on the top of the ridge, in the middle of his position.

CSM Army

General Hill, having finally put troops on the south ridge, ordered a message sent to Lee advising him that his command was in direct contact with the Juarista Army. Lee's standing orders were that once the enemy positions were known, Hill was to advise Lee immediately, hold his position and use his cavalry to recon the enemy. Hill put his lead brigade in a defensive position on the southern ridge and had the rest of his command holding position in the road when Lee arrived.

Reaching General Hill, Lee and his staff, along with Hill, cantered along the ridge top until they reached a point where they had a good view of the enemy positions across the shallow valley. Lee slowly scanned the ridge line before him with his telescope, identifying defensive positions and strong points. Seeing what were, to his trained eye, well prepared and camouflaged strong points and trenches he realized he was facing a capable, competent enemy. Lee thought, now I have him. We must not just beat them, we must *destroy* them! Only one army must leave this field!

As he swept his glass across the ridge, he lingered a moment on a man who was standing on a low hill and looking south. The man appeared to be issuing orders to the group around him. Lee continued his regard for a few seconds more, and then completed his observations. Having satisfied himself as to enemy dispositions, he left the ridge top and signaled for his Corps Commanders to attend him.

Colonel Venable had, as usual, located the command tent with an eye to both security and comfort, and Lee was grateful to dismount in the shade of several large trees. A while later all three of his senior officers arrived and Lee addressed them.

"Gentlemen, we have completed phase one. We have located the enemy. I want patrols out and the entire position mapped by evening. General Hill, you will place one Division on the ridge and one on the extreme left flank. General Garcia, you will deploy both your Divisions on a defensive line along the ridge. General Longstreet, you will deploy one Division on the ridge and the remaining two on the extreme right flank." As Lee spoke, he pointed to the specific areas he was referring to, and looked directly at each officer, awaiting a response to his instructions.

Completing his force dispositions, he continued, "General Hill, tomorrow at dawn you will send the Division on your extreme left to attack the right flank of the enemy position. I want your force to engage the enemy right; maintain continuous pressure and attempt to turn his flank. General Garcia, your command will entrench and hold the center of the ridge; you will have several batteries of field artillery and all of our rapid-fire guns for support. General Longstreet, you will entrench one Division on the ridge and use two Divisions as an assault force on the enemy left flank. Once General Hill has Zaragoza's attention on his right, you will attack the village on your front. After taking that position, you will then attack the ridge position directly behind the village. Once your command has engaged the enemy you will exert continuous pressure on his line. Your assault will be supported by field and siege gun batteries. By tomorrow evening, I expect both of your commands to be totally engaged. To reiterate, I and II Corps are tasked with engaging the enemy and driving back his flanks, while III Corps holds the ridge line. It is my expectation that General Laurency, with ten thousand Legion Infantry, will arrive soon, at which time his command will be committed. Gentlemen, if there are no further questions? Then, I suggest dinner."

At dawn the next morning, leather-lunged Juarista Army sergeants were awakening their men. Company cooks began stoking their fires and the aroma of hot food spurred the awakening men. As the Juarista army ate, Lee's forces began deploying on the opposite ridge. By early afternoon they were in position and the attack began.

General Zaragoza left his command post to walk up to the observation post on the ridge from which he would observe the enemy position. He made sure to walk slowly, talking to any officers he met and smiling at the soldiers. Reaching his goal, he climbed to the top of the low hill and had just begun his sweep when the sound of gunfire came from his right. He called to one of his runners to ride to the Sonora Brigade and return with a situation report.

Custer's Command

As the conflict between the Juarista and Revolutionary Armies began to unfold, General Custer, still miles to the north, redoubled his efforts to speed up his weary columns. Sergeant Ukimbe Washington, B Company, 90th Infantry Regiment, reached out to grab the shoulder of the man beside him for the second time. Holding him up with one hand, he reached over and took the soldier's musket, slinging it over the same shoulder that carried his own.

"Thanks, Sergeant," gasped the man, as they both continued to march.

"No problem, soldier," replied Ukimbe. "Just keep walking."

Ukimbe Washington, born Ukimbe Azwira, a member of the Akira tribe in Central Africa, had been captured by Moorish slavers while on a raid himself. Sold again to a slaver in Tripoli, he survived the grueling ocean voyage to be sold yet again on the Charlestown docks.

Enslaved on the plantation *Blue Bell* at the age of sixteen, he had labored there for fifteen hate-filled years. A hulking, muscular, six foot two inches, he had been first rebellious. Then, as his behavior earned him a series of increasingly painful and dangerous punishments, ranging from reduced food to whippings, he had gradually learned to exist in captivity. What had neither died nor even dimmed was his burning hatred for his oppressors.

Like many other slaves, Ukimbe had been freed by a unit of General Sherman's Army, a by-product of that General's massive invasion of the South. *Blue Bell* had been raided by a Union foraging party. The troops had left the three white overseers disarmed, and the main house, along with most of the other structures, fiery ruins. As soon as the soldiers left, Ukimbe had led the slaves in an orgy of revenge, inflicted upon any white person unfortunate enough to live on, or even near, the plantation.

After their rage had burned itself out, he and a small group had more or less attached themselves to a Union infantry command and served as orderlies for the soldiers. Ukimbe had been astounded when one day he came upon an all negro infantry unit. Discovering that he too could once again be a warrior had led to immediate action. At the first possible opportunity, he had enlisted in the Union Army. Due to his native intelligence, ability, and character, he had soon become a corporal, then a platoon sergeant.

His back and mind irrevocably scarred by the brutality of slavery, he longed for the opportunity for payback, which joining the Union Army could provide. Inordinately proud of both his blue uniform and the three stripes that adorned his sleeve, he worked hard to be a good soldier. He never complained, followed all orders to the letter, and always shared his great strength to assist others.

Giving his mate a comforting pat on his shoulder, the two resumed the march with one man carrying two muskets, bedrolls and backpacks, the other limping along as best as he could.

At the head of his troops as usual, Custer grimaced from the pain in his swollen, battered feet, but continued on. When he had removed his boots last night, both had been filled with blood.

Based on the latest reports, each of his Divisions had lost about thirty percent of their total force. They were closing on Zaragoza's position and were still driving hard. Aware of the situation, Custer had had his command on the move for almost an hour by the time the sun was completely above the horizon.

CSM Army

As ordered by General Lee, at first light General Hill had committed the 10th Brigade of the 4th Division. They were to be the lead element of his attack on the enemy's right flank. Moving into the rugged canyons by regiment, the men struggled to maintain even a minimum of unit cohesion, a task which fell primarily on company and regimental commanders. As each regiment achieved its assigned position, it wheeled right and held in place. Once the entire Brigade was formed, it advanced slowly over the broken terrain. When contact was made with enemy forces the Brigade attacked along the entire line.

The 11th Brigade was already falling into position as the second wave before the 10th began its attack. This assault represented an entirely new concept in warfare, as there were no massed formations with rank-and-file moving forward in lock step, but instead a continuous series of attacks by smaller company-sized units. Half of each unit would advance in a quick burst while the other half provided cover fire.

The temperature was continuing to rise along with the sun, the heat becoming intense. Lieutenant Brown, advancing up a sandy incline, ducked at the unmistakable whine of a Minnie ball passing close by his head. Hunkering down behind a convenient boulder, he signaled one of his squads to advance right and another to advance left, thus flanking the enemy position.

A few minutes later a furious firefight ensued, lasting for several minutes, as both squads attacked the Juarista position simultaneously. The troops around Brown provided covering fire from concealment. Rifle fire rose to a crescendo before tapering off as the defenders fled or died.

He waited a moment, then leaped over the rock in front of him and slid down the steep, but short, side of the *arroyo*. Standing for a moment when he reached the bottom, he turned to watch the squad he was with repeat his performance. Once they had regained their feet they climbed the ridge in front of them to find several dead and one wounded Juarista.

The enemy soldier had been clumsily bandaged and still bleeding, but was sitting up, awake. Brown watched stoically as one of his men fired a round into the man's head. Without comment, he reformed his unit and ordered them to advance. Halfway to the top of the next ridge, Brown and his men were halted yet again by enemy fire.

Foreign Legion Command

After the Legion's surrender to Longstreet, Lee had ordered that it be totally re- equipped and resupplied. General Laurency, the Legion commander, had been authorized to have all the remaining Legion units throughout Mexico unite under his command. With the addition of wounded and stragglers, the total force numbered almost fourteen thousand men.

When General Laurency received Lee's order to join him, he was still a good distance behind the CSM Army. He immediately increased his speed in order catch up as soon as possible.

Corporal Alan Fromage swore silently as his shoulder strap drew blood again. *Merde,* he thought, yet another famous Legion march. I didn't sign up to be a horse, even less a mule. He continued his mind monologue with, the next time I cut a man's throat I'll damn sure do the witnesses, too.

The good corporal had been convicted of murder, despite his tale of traitorous love. When the judge had offered twenty years in the Legion as an alternative to *"Madam Guillotine"* he had of course accepted immediately. He had soon found that the biggest difference between his old and new life was that he now mostly killed the enemies of France, and not just the enemies of Alan Fromage. The killing itself was almost therapeutic for him, as it gave him an outlet for his hatred of a world that constantly connived to thwart and deny him. However, this marching and discomfort had enraged him to the point where even his fellow murderers trod lightly around him.

Alan, along with the rest of the Legion, was maintaining a forced march in an effort to reach the CSM Army in the least possible time. Even the morning sun was brutal and the powers that be showed no sign of reversing the marching orders despite Alan's silent entreaties. The only thing that kept many of the men from falling out in exhaustion was the pride each man had as a member of the Legion.

The men were angry over their recent misfortunes on the battlefield, and the disgruntled veterans were anxious to redeem themselves and regain their honor. It was this chance for redemption in their own eyes that drove them on, despite the fact that insult was piled upon indignity when the squad non-com informed his men that lunch, if any, was to be consumed on the march.

Two Ridges

As the Legion continued its drive north to join the battle, the right flank of the CSM Army struggled to advance in the face of a relentless defense. General Longstreet had ordered his 3rd Division to hold the ridge. To the right of that unit he had had formed his 1st and 2nd Divisions as the strike force. Both these units would form Brigade front behind the ridge then attack. This would allow the envelopment of the village from two sides. At the moment both Divisions were in the process of advancing from their hillside position into and across the valley, using the new method of frontal attack.

Each rank would advance a short distance at a run then kneel and fire at the enemy positions. A second wave would pass through them about twenty yards, then kneel and fire. The first rank would then repeat the procedure.

Artillery fire from hidden gun emplacements in the village was beginning to take its toll on the CSM assault force, as the Juarista gunners found the range and began firing explosive rounds. When the advancing infantry closed they switched to grape shot, shredding the enemy ranks.

Longstreet could see that his troops were pressing the attack despite serious losses. Counter-fire from the CSM batteries, hidden behind the ridge that was his vantage point, continued to impact on the village. Eruptions fountained and pieces of red-hot shrapnel whipped through the air, tearing into soldiers and fortifications alike.

As he watched, infantry in butternut-and-white entered the shallow stream in front of the village at several points. Some were cut down by musket fire while others were either shredded or smashed by artillery rounds. A tremendous explosion, followed by a huge, black, mushroom-shaped cloud marked the destruction of one of Zagaroza's gun emplacements in the village. A moment later, a second explosion, even more violent than the first, marked the demise of the gun-powder filled caisson which, due to the gunner's in-experience, had been located too close to the cannon.

Huge sections of the village wall disappeared under the hammer blows CSM of siege guns. As elements of the 1st Division began to pour through the ruptures, Longstreet received reports that the 4th Brigade, the lead unit of the 2nd Division, had also completed fording the river and was re-forming prior to launching itself at the village's left flank. A rising crescendo of rifle fire gave testimony to the valiant defense that his attacking units were encountering.

CSM units gained access to more village streets, slowly driving towards the center of town. Grenadiers used their weapons to good effect and building after building was cleared. Defenders held their ground as long as possible, sometimes countering with ferocious bayonet counter-attacks, support-ed by well concealed snipers. Juarista cannon fired rounds of grapeshot from concealed artillery positions into charging enemy soldiers at point-blank range. Entire files of attackers were rendered into a fine red mist. Company and platoon-size Juarista units held each position valiantly, fighting fiercely be-fore falling back to the next prepared positions. Once there, they would continue their determined defense.

As the sun passed the midday mark and began its march to darkness, the pressure of attacks on both flanks of the Juarista Army began to tell. Zaragoza was advised that CSM elements had reached the primary defensive line on his right flank. In response he ordered one infantry regiment from the Sinaloa Brigade, his reserve formation, to reinforce his right flank. A few hours later, due to Longstreet's vigorous assault on his left flank, he was forced to send two more regiments from his reserve to reinforce his left flank.

Hector and Ramon, along with a few other men, were holding a position in the village. They were lying side by side behind an adobe wall, firing their muskets through holes they had drilled days before. The sun was high in the sky, and the heat and dust made it hard to breath. The men loaded their muskets, got to their knees, and fired at anything that moved to their front, then repeated the entire process again.

The attackers kept up an even heavier fire and rounds were constantly bouncing off the wall and whizzing past the two men. The enemy troops were relentless, pressing home their attacks despite the defenders best efforts.

A huge explosion rocked Hector, the blast rolling him over, almost deafening him and covering him with a layer of sand and rock. When he looked to his left he saw that a substantial piece of the trench and wall was gone. It had been replaced by a large, jagged-edged hole. The bottom of the hole was filled with broken things, one of them his friend, Ramon.

Hector crawled over and peered into the still smoking hole. Ramon's entire right side looked as through someone had tried to shred it. As he knelt, starring at the butchered remains of his best friend, he caught sight of motion. He turned just as the enemy soldier fired. Hector never heard the shot that pierced his heart.

It was late afternoon when Zaragoza received reports from the commander of the Sonora Brigade that elements of the CSM attacking force were enveloping his far right flank. When he received this information, Zaragoza left for the Sonora Brigade position to see for himself.

Arriving at the command bastion, he ordered the Brigade's General to accompany him to inspect the situation. After getting to the extreme right of his flank, he realized that the entire position was in danger of being overrun. He immediately ordered his last reserve infantry regiment and two regiments from the Chihuahua Brigade, the next formation in line to the left, to move to reinforce the center and right of the right flank. When the additional troops took their positions the entire line began to stabilize, and the CSM advance was slowed, then stopped in its tracks.

Zaragoza remained at the right flank bastion until he was satisfied the situation was under control and then returned to his headquarters. As the setting sun turned the horizon an angry blood-red, Zaragoza left his headquarters and, with a small staff and security detail, once again made his way along the entire line, greeting, talking to, and, in some cases, joking with individual soldiers and officers.

Due to the Juarista reinforcement added to the defenses, the attacks by the CSM Army on both flanks began to waiver. In response to the stiffening resistance, General Hill, on the CSM left flank, ordered 14th Brigade from the 5th Division to be committed, but even with the additional troops the advance was first slowed, then, despite fierce attacks, ground to a halt.

On the CSM right flank, General Longstreet had continued to apply pressure until the sun set, at which point he ordered his units to dig in and hold in place. During the course of the day, the fighting in the village had been particularly brutal, the combat frequently hand-to-hand, quarter neither asked nor given.

Halfway through his journey along the lines Zaragoza was stopped by an officer who informed him that a messenger had been received from Lee requesting an overnight truce to allow both sides to tend to their wounded. He ordered the officer to tell Lee that such a truce would be acceptable to him and then returned to his tour. After completing his inspecting, he went back to his command post and ordered all Brigade commanders to obtain situation reports from their regimental commanders, then report to him.

Leaving his command tent behind the CSM lines, Lee squinted into the red ball of the setting sun, mounted his horse and rode off with his staff and security team to discuss the day with his senior officers. He first met with Longstreet, then Garcia, and finally Hill. He had just completed his conversation with General Hill when a galloper brought word that Zaragoza had indicated his acceptance of the truce.

As nightfall descended on the battlefield the cease-fire began. The darkness between the two armies was sprinkled with the fire-fly dots of stretcher-bearers holding lanterns in order to help them find the wounded.

Lee went to the hospitals in the rear. Accompanied by Venable and his security, he walked up and down the aisles paying silent tribute to the men who had offered up their bodies to the gods of war. After leaving the hospital, he and his entourage returned to his tent.

Dismounting, Lee handed his horse's reins to Venable, who in turn passed them to a trooper. Venable then followed Lee as he walked away from the camp. Coming upon a small moon-bathed clearing, Lee stood quietly, hands clasped behind his back, apparently idly regarding the stars parading their majesty above him.

Sensing his mood, Venable, who had followed behind him, waved off the security men and approached to within a few paces of where Lee stood. Lee spoke, his voice pitched low, vibrant with anguish, "The price of victory, Charles?"

Venable replied in hushed tones, "Victory seems quite possible, sir."

"You saw those brave soldiers, did you not," answered Lee, his voice harsh, almost accusatory.

"I saw them, sir." He hesitated, said, "It's war, sir; nothing can be done; only victory or defeat can stop it, and perhaps only victory can make it right."

"Dear God, Charles! The price! My people!" The pain in his voice tore at Venable, who, of course, could do nothing but stand mute as Lee confronted the ugly truth. Both men stood immobile in the moon-drenched spot for a few moments more, either in silent tribute or grief, then both turned and made their way back.

When he arrived at headquarters, Lee entered the command tent to find his Corps commanders, casualty lists in hand, awaiting his arrival. He called the meeting to order by sitting at the head of the table and glancing at Longstreet with a questioning look. The General responded by reading his casualty list. After all three officers had reported their losses and the concerns of each were addressed, Lee presented his orders for the following day.

He ordered General Hill to reinforce his attacking units with both of the Brigades still holding the ridge, thereby committing all of II Corps to the assault. He also ordered General Longstreet to move his 3rd Division from the ridge top to the extreme right to support the flank attack that would recommence at dawn.

Longstreet waited a moment after Lee finished speaking then said, "Sir, your plan calls for leaving only the two Divisions of III Corps to hold most of the defensive line."

Although his tone was noncommittal, there was an obvious question in his statement.

Lee responded. "General Longstreet, you are entirely correct. However, we have, if you will, two aces in the hole. First are our rapid-fire guns, and second is that General Laurency has advised me that he expects to arrive by midday tomorrow, if not sooner. I believe that the Legion will provide us with more than enough additional forces to carry the day."

Lee sat back, allowing himself to relax, knowing that all that could be done had been done. He glanced briefly at each officer, pausing longest to regard Longstreet, whose presence and proven ability gave him a strong sense of security. He thought, these are proven officers, they know the plan, they know the urgency. They will prevail.

The briefing over, he picked up his coffee and joined the officers for dinner. They were joined by the young German, who had become their constant dinner companion. The Prussian held forth on international European relationships while Longstreet and Hill related tales of Civil War strategies employed. The campfire was reduced to dimly glowing embers by the time the men turned in.

Lee's had now committed most of the Army to attacks on the right and left flank. The entire center of the CSM position was held by only two Divisions under the leadership of the least experienced general officer in Lee's army.

Juarista Army

Since the beginning of the Revolution, General Zaragoza had been hindered by a serious lack of experienced senior officers.

Only three of the men currently commanding his Brigades had ever commanded a unit of even regimental size. Two of his Brigade commanders owed their position to the fact that a substantial portion of the Brigade was personally loyal to them. One Brigade leader had been a bandit, who had endeared himself to the local population by primarily preying on members of the Council of Five Hundred.

Once his officers had assembled and dinner was served Zaragoza watched carefully as they ate, drank and talked among themselves. By watching them surreptitiously he hoped to get some feeling for their state of minds. After listening to the conversations for a few minutes, Zaragoza rapped the table with his knuckles and brought them to attention.

"Gentlemen," he began, his voce stern but positive, "I believe that today the enemy has revealed his battle plan to us. His intention is to encircle and crush us. He will not succeed. What he does not know is that a Union Army, eighteen thousand strong, under the command of General George Armstrong Custer, a great hero of their Civil War and a valiant fighter, will arrive sometime tomorrow. All we need do is continue our strategy of holding our positions until General Custer arrives. Once he is here we will combine our forces and smash and destroy them completely."

As shocked silence reigned, he began giving instructions for the disposition of his Army. He repositioned two additional regiments from the Chihuahua Brigade to his right flank and two regiments from his Nuevo Leon Brigade to his left flank. The effect of these troop movements was to weaken his center and reinforce both flanks. He also ordered all remaining artillery pieces in the village brought out and repositioned on the top of the ridge. Once he had completed his repositioning for the next day he sat back and allowed his subordinates to talk. He watched them, wondering still if each man was capable of the task required of him.

He had committed all or parts of five of his six Brigades, and there remained only a single nine hundred man regiment in his reserve. What was it that noble Roman had said, he questioned himself? Oh, yes. "The die is cast."

CSM Army

On both ridges cooking fires were lit and the men ate their well-earned meals. Some time later lights on both ridges slowly flickered out and for a few blessed hours the battlefield became dark and quiet. Shortly after dawn the siege guns on the right flank began sending the first of many rounds of explosive shot screaming towards the village and the ridge behind and above it.

General Longstreet, had ordered 3rd Division to lead the attack on the ridge behind the village, with the 2nd Division in support. His 1st Division was still embroiled in the struggle for the village itself, and if successful, would be in position to expand or reinforce the breakthrough, if such should occur.

On the left flank, General Hill had moved his command post to a position behind his 4th Division. The two divisions of his II Corps were in line abreast, each with one Brigade in reserve and two Brigades in contact with the enemy. All units were currently completing preparations and awaiting the three red rockets fired into the air that would signal the attack.

Lieutenant Brown, along with the rest of his company, was holding a rock-strewn ridge top about half a mile from a large dirt bastion occupied by Juarista infantry and artillery. The terrain had made it impossible for the use of CSM artillery in close support of the infantry. As he surveyed the enemy positions, he knew it would be a long, hot, bad day.

From the valley behind the ridge a runner from regimental hailed him. Brown turned and watched as the man carefully made his way up to a point just below him. The man stopped and hunkered down, refusing to expose himself more than absolutely necessary.

"B Company commanding officer?" asked the soldier.

"I'm the executive officer, the Captain should be just north," replied Brown, waving his hand in the indicated direction. "What is it?"

"All company commanders to regimental at once, sir." said the soldier from his safe place.

Several moments later the same man appeared and, waving his arms, called out to Brown. "Lieutenant, Lieutenant!"

Brown looked back and, seeing the man, responded, "What is it?"

The messenger replied, "Your captain is dead. That makes you senior officer in this company. Report to regimental HQ."

Before Brown could reply the man turned away, sliding back down the hill and continuing on with his mission. Brown called for his sergeant and advised him he was leaving for regimental HQ. It took him all of thirty minutes, a good deal of it on his belly, before he reached his destination.

The Colonel waited until all his officers were present, and then started the briefing. "Okay, A, B and C Companies, will conduct a frontal assault, D and E will be in support, and for God's sake, don't forget the scaling ladders." He paused a moment then continued. "Everybody on the same page? Good, then. That's it." Colonel Robert J. Braddock, his hard eyes piercing each of the five company commanders in turn, completed his briefing with, "Good luck, Gentlemen."

The moment he got back to his company's positions, Brown sent for his platoon leaders and repeated the orders. He had hardly finished when the signal rockets ripped into the air, three brief, blood-red explosions. The company had barely hit open ground when the first volleys sliced into the charging men. The butternut-and-white clad soldiers returned fire, advancing in quick rushes, then dropping to a kneeling or prone position and firing in support of each follow-on wave. As the attackers closed, the defensive fire grew both ragged and sustained as some troops began to reload more often and their officers ordered individual rapid fire.

Brown threw himself against the bastion's wood-sheathed dirt wall. Crouching down, he looked first to his left and then to his right, then back at the many figures, some still as stone, others writhing in agony, that dotted the terrain he had just crossed. "I want every ladder to hit the wall at once! Grenadiers will throw on my count of three!

He paused for a moment. He gathered himself, took a deep breath and then shouted, "One, two, three! Several grenades, each trailing a thin stream of smoke from its sputtering fuse, arced over the dirt walls. The ladders reared up and slammed into the top of the bastion.

As troops began their ascent, a series of explosions marked the detonations of the grenades, causing a massive slaughter of the defenders. A rain of gore ballooned into the air and descended down onto the attackers as they struggled up the ladders.

Brown was the third man up the ladder. The first man reached the top only to be spitted through the breast bone by a bayonet-tipped musket. The soldier shrieked, grabbed the offending instrument with both hands, and refusing to let go, dragged the weapon out of the hands of the Juarista soldier. He died at the feet of the man who had killed him. The second man on the ladder forced his way over the wall and bayoneted the now unarmed Juarista. As he withdrew his bloody bayonet, he, in turn, had his head crushed by the butt of a rifle swung by another Juarista soldier. Brown leaped over the top of the wall onto the parapet. Firing from a kneeling position, held his ground as more and more of his men made their way to his side.

Foreign Legion Command

As the battle at Two Ridges raged, Alan and his fellow Legionaries had been rudely awakened, fed, and then hustled onto the road well before sunrise. After several hours march in the heat and dust, the men would willingly kill just about anything for the pure joy of watching it die.

Laurency was pushing his men to their limit. The march progressed into early morning, and the sides of the road became littered with exhausted, sometimes unconscious, blue-and-red clad soldiers. The General had just called for the second ten minute break after two hours of forced marching when he observed a squad of lancers trotting towards him.

The cavalry Lieutenant halted his men, advanced to the waiting officer, saluted and reported. "General, our advance guard is in sight of the battle." Laurency immediately mounted his horse, and, trailing staff like a mother duck trails ducklings, raced north to join Lee and his force.

As soon as the Legion officers arrived at the battlefield Laurency and his staff dismounted from their heavily lathered, exhausted mounts and strode towards the observation post. Lee turned from watching the battle and calmly returned the Legion General's salute, saying, "My compliments sir. You and your command have performed to my highest expectations."

"We are most pleased to be of service, General Lee," responded Laurency, his face creased with dirt and exhaustion plain on his features. "I would recommend a short break for my men before engaging the enemy," he concluded.

Lee said nothing for a moment as he regarded the Legion officer, then a ghost of a smile on his face, nodded his head. The two officers, at Lee's direction, entered the tent and sat at a table in the center of the command post. Lee gestured to the map spread out before them.

"We are heavily engaged on both flanks. We are pressing them hard. Our recon units have sent word that a Union force will reinforce Zaragoza soon. This direct intervention is a very serious, but not entirely unexpected turn of events. I believe Custer is in command. I expect him to initiate a frontal attack in the belief that their combined numbers will overwhelm us. Their reinforcements not withstanding, I still believe we can be victorious. The Legion is to be the lynch pin to our success. You will place your command on the reverse of the ridge, behind General Garcia's III Corps, and hold yourself in readiness to counter-attack. The plan is to allow the Union's attack to break itself on III Corps and the thirty Agar rapid-fire guns we have emplaced in his defensive line. Once the attack has been stopped, you will counter-attack. Crush the center, advance across the valley, take and hold the opposing ridge. General Garcia's force will advance with yours. Both Hill and Longstreet will continue to apply pressure to both flanks and extend their lines northward. Our ultimate objective is to encircle and destroy the opposing force in its entirety. Is this clear to you, Sir?" asked Lee.

After a moments hesitation Laurency, responded with, "Eminently clear, General." With that Lee sat back in his canvas field chair for a moment as he regarded the map before him and said, "One great effort and we may yet win this battle. I pray God it may be so."

Lee stood, looked at Laurency, said, "You have your orders, General." He called for Venable to accompany him, and strode out of the tent.

Laurency remained in the tent, looking down at the map, for a moment. Von Hindenburg, who had spent the day at the CSM Army headquarters either watching the battle or observing Lee, stepped forward and saluted. The Prussian introduced himself to the Legion officer.

The Legion General took in the young Lieutenant's Prussian uniform and wryly said, "War makes for strange bedfellows, does it not, Lieutenant?" The question was a reference to the hostile political situation existing between their respective homelands.

"As you say, sir," responded Von Hindenburg. "If I may, sir, a question?"

"Of course, Lieutenant," responded Laurency.

"Your opinion of the battle plan, sir?"

The Legion officer pondered in thought for a moment and answered, "Bonaparte would be envious, Lieutenant." He turned and left the tent to see to the positioning of his forces. It was mid-afternoon before the Legion was in place in the center of the CSM lines, completely invisible from Zaragoza's position.

General Zaragoza had expected what he got, a vigorous offensive action, with simultaneous attacks on both flanks. As the assaults were pressed home, musket and artillery fire became practically continuous. The soft blue haze of expended gunpowder began to obscure his view of the conflict, from his position at the center of his line.

He had ordered each Brigade commander to send hourly reports in an effort to give him the ability to more effectively manage the battle. His officers were following their orders and their reports were beginning to paint an ugly picture.

On his right flank, the command bastion had been overrun, but a heroic counter-attack had retaken it, at least temporarily. The entire right flank of his line was totally engaged with counter-attack following attack and decisions being made by regimental, sometimes company level officers.

On the left his troops were slowly being pushed back despite almost fanatical resistance. The battle in the village had degenerated into a mindless hell of small-unit actions as command broke down and on-site junior grade officers made split-second decisions. Just to the north of the village, on his extreme left flank, CSM units had gained the top of the ridge in two places, but fierce counter-attacks, supported by artillery firing at point-blank range, had halted any further advance and eliminated the incursions.

The heaviest artillery in the Revolutionary Army arsenal, 8 inch Parrot siege guns, had been targeting the Juarista left flank all day. In many areas the double line of trenches had been either totally obliterated or transformed into a moon-like landscape of interlocking craters. Zaragoza began considering ordering additional units from the center of his lines to both flanks.

The wounded being carried to his central and only, aid station were now a continual stream. His medical contingent, understaffed to begin with, was completely overwhelmed. Most of these unfortunates were simply being placed on the ground, as near to the tents as possible, then left to their fate. An entire field was covered with the fly infested, blood-drenched bodies of the dying and the dead.

Custer's Command

Custer had become an unstoppable force. All along the column he cajoled, ordered, and sometimes even threatened his weary men to greater efforts. Most amazing was that he was frequently successful. On foot, limping and hoarse, he drove himself and his men onward.

Ukimbe ignored the pain, concentrating only on next step, holding his friend upright as he carried their equipment. Looking to his right, he saw a man wearing a gaudily-decorated uniform standing on a small rocky outcrop and carefully regarding the soldiers marching past him. When Ukimbe reached a point abreast of the man, the officer looked straight at him, nodded, and with a wave of his hand, urged him on.

As the two black soldiers passed him, Custer turned to Reno and said, "Ten thousand like him and we would be in Mexico City in a week." An exhausted Reno had no answer, but he nodded agreement. A moment later a rider halted and offered a piece of paper to Reno, who read it and gasped out, "By God, we've done it! Lead elements of all three Divisions are on the plateau, sir!"

Custer stared at Reno, his eyes wide, burning with emotion.

"By God Reno, didn't I tell you, we've an appointment with glory! We hold the destiny of our country in our hands." As he spoke his eyes seemed to be focused on something only he could see and Reno felt an icy chill. Custer continued, in a softer voice, "I'm sure my divisional commanders would like to confer with me, Colonel. Follow me!"

It was a few minutes short of midday, when he and a small staff gained the plateau. The lead units of XX Corps were now within miles of the battle. After a while the three Division Commanders arrived to receive their orders from Custer. Custer did not waste a minute. "General Gibbons, you will wait until the lead Brigade from the 68th, 69th and 73rd have united, then lead them forward in column. Generals Scott and Riddly will wait until the rest of all three divisions have completely formed on the plateau then advance under General Terry. It is imperative that the whole of XX Corps advance to Zaragoza's position with all possible speed. I will leave the column and meet with him. Gentlemen, you have your orders."

Zaragoza had watched impassively as the blue-clad cavalry troop reined in their horses, dismounted and made for his headquarters. Custer, as usual, led the way, walking with a decided limp. He advanced to the waiting Mexican officer and both men traded salutes.

The Juarista General opened the conversation with, "Your arrival is timely and welcome, General."

Custer, a tight smile on his face, replied, "From the sound of things, it appears you have started without us, General."

Zaragoza returned the smile and entered his headquarters. Pointing to a sand reproduction of the battlefield resting on a table in the middle of the room, he proceeded to update Custer, who listened silently, then sat quietly for a moment or two, in thought.

"General," said Custer, "I believe I see what Lee is up to. I think that he intends to use these flank attacks as a feint to occupy as much of your command as possible. I believe that the real assault will be from his center. That he will attempt to destroy your command by a *"coup de grace"* attack on the center of your position. My strategy will be to strike first. As soon as XX Corps is in place in the center of your line, we will attack with our combined forces. Breaking the center of his line might very well destroy his entire command, as he has committed so much of his Army to flank attacks. It may be that he will not have sufficient reserves to contain our attack. If I am right, we can use his own tactics to destroy him. How large a force can you provide to support my attack?" With that question Custer stopped talking and looked at Zaragoza.

"General, what you propose is a bold move. Would it not be more prudent to place your forces in such a manner as to reinforce my line? Your command would be more than enough to stop Lee in his tracks," responded Zaragoza, in a slow, heavy voice.

"My point exactly. I did not involve my Army in this endeavor in order to just defeat Lee. We have spoken on this subject before and I've made my views clear. My goal is to destroy his command, utterly and totally. I intend to defeat this Confederate States of Mexico, and end forever this threat to my country. What of your command, General?" Custer waited for Zaragoza's reply.

The Mexican General was silent, regarding Custer, thinking, this man is willing to put his soldiers, his life, and perhaps even more important, his career and reputation, on the line. He believes he can save my country and will risk everything in order to achieve that goal. Can I possibly do less?

He squared his shoulders, offered his hand to Custer and said, "Nine thousand men, General, every available soldier, at your disposal." It was mid-afternoon before the entire Union force had crossed the plateau and all three divisions had positioned themselves in the center of the Juarista line.

CSM Army

General Longstreet had ordered his artillery to retarget on the Juarista rear areas. Some of his lead units had advanced to the point where they were sometimes less than fifty yards from the defenders on the top of the ridge. He had also ordered elements of the 2nd Division to attempt to extend their attack in a northerly direction. Up to this point however, there had been little success despite substantial casualties.

Below the ridge, what remained of the small village was being slowly destroyed as his 1st Division pushed the stubborn defenders from their positions inch by bloody inch. An hour ago he had ordered the Division Commander to cede tactical command to each regimental commander in an effort to allow more fluid and timely response to changing situations. As the battle on the Revolutionary Army right slowly disintegrated into a brawling mass, the conflict on the left began to resolve itself.

Lieutenant Brown cautiously crawled along the rear of the fortification of what had been the main bastion of the Juarista right flank. Occasionally he would lay flat in response to the almost constant musket fire ripping overhead.

His company had attacked three times, before finally driving out the defenders. The remaining Juarista troops were now occupying the last of their prepared positions, a trench line roughly fifty yards from him.

In two days of continuous fighting, the company had lost forty percent of its effectives. The remnants, along with the entire regiment, were currently holding a line opposite the equally-battered units of their opponents and preparing for one more push.

Rolling into a depression that offered some additional cover, Brown signaled for his platoon commanders. In short order both men joined him. "Regiment thinks they're just about played out, that one more push will end it," he said, eying the two men before him.

Both sergeants, one who had one arm in a sling and the other who sported a blood-stained bandage on his right thigh, were quiet, simply awaiting his order with set, hard expressions on their faces. "Orders are to wait until all our people are in place, and then hit them with everything," said Brown, his voice flat and determined.

Foreign Legion Command

While the CSM Army prosecuted its assaults on both flanks, the Legion took position in the center of the south ridge, behind Garcia's III Corps. They were invisible to anyone looking south from the north ridge.

Alan Fromage's company had been ushered into line on the reverse slope of the ridge, behind a row of emplaced artillery. They had been allowed to sit or lay down as they wished, and rations had been distributed as well. Officers walked among them, checking their condition and equipment and ordering them to hydrate and try to rest. Alan removed his sweat soaked "*kepi*" scratched his head and looked casually about him.

"So, Marcel, what do you think?" he queried his mate.

"I think that very soon we will be up to our eyeballs," was Marcel's laconic reply.

Listening to the almost constant roar of outgoing artillery rounds, as well as the occasional impact of enemy return fire, Alan was, unfortunately, forced to agree. The sun was now just beginning its daily slide to oblivion, but the heat had not abated even one degree.

After a short wait, the men were ordered to advance in close formation to a point about twenty yards behind the crest of the ridge. Alan and his fellow Legionnaires fell to, each man automatically finding his proper place in line, a skill born of countless repetitions. Arriving at their new position they were ordered to dig trenches, enter them, fix bayonets and then hold fast.

Custer's Command

General Terry had brought up the remainder of XX Corp to the north ridge. Custer had formed his entire force behind the Juarista line. He had given the men a short opportunity to eat, drink and rest. A quick head-count showed his force at just short of fourteen thousand men. Zaragoza added an additional nine thousand as a second wave.

The remaining guns of the Juarista artillery had all been repositioned to target the CSM defensive line. The guns were firing the last of their explosive rounds in slow, regular, aimed volleys.

Ukimbe sat with the rest of his platoon. The exhausted, hungry men were sprawled in a rough circle, sharing water and the very last of their rations. Chewing his hardtack, he watched his men, noting those who spoke or ate, and noting one or two who simply sat, blank stares on their faces.

Completing his meal, such as it was, he began to move about the soldiers, checking their equipment, making sure every man had his bayonet and rounds for his musket. He had just completed his inspection and reported to his lieutenant when he and his platoon were ordered into line, bayonets fixed and a round in the barrel. After only a few moments wait, the troops were ordered to begin to move towards the ridge top just ahead of them.

Custer and Zaragoza had agreed that the Union infantry would be the first wave and that the three Juarista Brigades, the Neuva Leon, Durango and Chihuahua would form the second wave. This disposition would create an assault force of almost twenty-four thousand troops, advancing on a front almost two miles wide and eight ranks deep. Unfortunately, it would also leave the entire center of Zaragoza's defensive line almost completely unmanned.

The plan called for the remaining artillery to lay down as heavy a barrage as possible while the infantry advanced across the valley floor at a double-time pace; stop at the base of the opposite ridge to dress ranks, fire one aimed volley, then rush the fortifications.

Custer intended to take the crest of the ridge, then consolidate his position. He would then send two Divisions to attack in opposite directions along the ridge top, leaving one Division to hold the center of his position.

The two Divisions would advance, rolling up the CSM line as they went. Zaragoza's forces would be used to reinforce the Union attack. Custer would, of course, lead the charge of the combined forces across the valley, while Zaragoza would remain behind to insure the flanks held.

Before leaving to assume his position just behind the center of the first wave, Custer called Reno to his side and said, "Colonel, you will remain behind with the headquarters staff. I will take my flag, bugler, and half the security team. Once I've taken the ridge I will fire two rockets. That will be your signal to come up with the staff horses and any stragglers. See you on the ridge!" Custer was speaking in an unnaturally soft, almost gentle tone so out of character that Reno almost recoiled. He straightened, returned Custer's gaze, saluted and responded, "As always, sir, at your command."

Custer moved to the center of the line as Reno gathered his part of the headquarters unit around him. Across the valley, in his command post, General Lee, with Laurency beside him, watched through their telescopes as the first wave of dust-covered blue infantry appeared on the top of the opposing ridge. Lee maintained his vigil for a moment, admiring the dressed lines, weapons at port, sunlight flashing off bayonets, the discipline and spirit of the attackers evident.

Laurency stirred as the Union troops reached the bottom of their ridge and the lines of the Jusrista second wave made their appearance, their formations and dress less impressive, but their resolve just as firm.

CSM field artillery batteries were targeting the advancing lines of soldiers and subjecting them to heavy fire. Counter-battery fire from Juarista guns was less effective. Here and there, throughout the attacking formations, fountains of dirt and things unmentionable erupted high into the air as CSM artillery acquired their new target. However, the gaps in the advancing infantry formations were closed almost as soon as they appeared. The units themselves were shrinking but maintaining position and cohesion as they continued to cross the valley, battle flags proudly leading the way.

"A formidable sight, General, is it not?" Laurency said, not removing the telescope from his eye.

Lee sighed, responded, "Brave men," in a soft, reflective voice.

"General, report to your command!"

Laurency turned to face Lee, saluted and left for the center of the Legion line.

On the north ridge, Captain Brown wolfed down the last of his rations and tilting the canteen, emptied its contents down his parched throat. Finished with lunch, he watched as a line of men brought up cases of ammunition and began to distribute it along the firing line. The ground ahead and behind was carpeted with bodies in the uniforms of both armies. Rifle and musket fire was extremely heavy, making it difficult to remove the wounded. Their cries for succor and screams of agony added a falsetto counterpoint to the deeper, more guttural sounds of weapons fire.

Brown called over the wounded sergeant, and asked him if he knew the whereabouts of his other platoon leader. The sergeant's reply was to point wordlessly at a body torn nearly in two and sprawled on top of a destroyed Juarista cannon. Following the direction of the finger, Brown responded with a terse, "Right!" then leaned in close to the soldier and began to give orders for his troop's dispositions for the next attack.

As the Juarista defenses were slowly pushed back on each flank, in the center Custer and XX Corp, along with Juarista Army units, prepared to advance. From his position in the second rank, Ukimbe could see the opposite ridge clearly. The fortified trench line, occasional flashes of sunlight off metal, battle flags stirring in the light breeze, and impacts from artillery wreaking havoc were all visible. A few dozen yards to the left of him, Custer and his dismounted security detail marched.

The lead rank reached the middle of the valley and began taking heavy rifle fire. Soldiers fell, some regaining their feet to march on, some screaming their agony or defiance, some as still as the ground they lay on.

Ukimbe noticed a sudden flurry of activity from a number of positions in the enemy trench line. What appeared to be multiple-barreled small canons poked their snouts above the trench wall. As the guns opened fire in unison, a ripping sound filled the air and a hurricane of lead began to shred the advancing Union lines. Rank upon rank, file upon file, the attackers fell in quick succession, victims to the incredible volume of remorseless fire.

General Garcia watched as Custer's units slowly closed the distance. He had ordered his special artillery, the Agar rapid-fire guns, to hold their fire until the enemy formations were at a range of fifteen hundred yards.

The Agar guns were new, multiple-barrel weapons able to fire at a rate of slightly more than two rounds per second per barrel. Each gun fired a total of three hundred rounds per minute and had almost as much firepower as an entire regiment, with a much greater concentration. For technical reasons they fired in thirty to forty second bursts, with a one minute interval between bursts. This pause allowed the barrels to cool and be reloaded.

These weapons were the late Confederacy's answer to the Union's Gatlin gun. Their presence at the battle was directly attributable to James Breckenridge's foresight. It was he who had decided that the blueprints for the gun were to be brought south and he who had ordered that production facilities for the weapon be built at New Tredegar as soon as possible. The rapid-fire guns on the line today were from the initial production run.

As the Union lines absorbed the first horrendous blows from the Agar guns, the advancing formations, subjected to an unprecedented volume of fire, first faltered, then stopped, their ranks decimated and their officers stunned by the carnage.

Custer stared, eyes wide, at the effects of the new weapon. Soldiers being killed and wounded at a horrific rate, squads, platoons even companies dissolving before his unbelieving eye, from the overwhelming fire power of this new enemy weapon. He stood erect , sword and pistol in hand, frozen in place for a split second, then training and personal heroism reasserting itself, did the only thing he could. He screamed, "Follow me!" and raced full speed towards the enemy. After a brief hesitation, he was followed by his command entourage, battle flags streaming, buglers blowing. All of them charging straight into hell, and knowing it.

Ukimbe felt the whirlwind of death closing in on him as he dropped to the ground, firing his weapon. A sudden movement to his left caught his attention. The General, saber pointing at the enemy, was attacking, leading the way as a good leader should. Ukimbe felt a great pride that he and the General wore the same uniform and were brother warriors. Filled with a sudden rage at his enemies, he leapt to his feet, and dragging his friend upright with him, yelled his defiance and followed his General.

Despite horrific losses, the Union troops continued to close on the CSM trenches. Without stopping to reload, the blue ranks raced towards the enemy, desperate to get out of the field of fire of this new weapon.

Custer was the first to gain the trench line, miraculously still unwounded. Reaching the defensive position he thrust over the trench top with his saber at a CSM infantryman. He buried his sword to the hilt, then drew back the bloody blade and jumped into the trench, firing his Colt revolver, one aimed round after another.

A sudden sharp pain in his left shoulder caused the weapon to drop from numbed fingers and drove him back and against the trench wall. Looking down, he saw his shoulder was covered with blood as he felt himself sliding to the bottom of the trench. Something blocked his vision to his right, one blue-clad leg followed by another.

Suddenly there were men in the trench, backs to him, firing at the slowly retreating enemy who, as they withdrew, took care to remove most of the rapid-fire guns, and disable the ones left behind. The defenders sought and found cover in a second trench line some twenty yards past the one Custer was in.

As he looked about, he observed a huge Negro, the one who had been assisting others during the march, making his way down the firing line, ordering men to appropriate positions and directing their fire. The man made his way to Custer, knelt and helped the General to a standing position. The soldier picked up the fallen revolver and offered it to him. Custer sheathed his bloody sword and accepted the gun with a curt, but heartfelt, "Thank you, sergeant." Without a word Ukimbe turned and went back to his duties.

Custer stood and looked back over the valley. There was a carpet of Union soldiers, some moving, many still, covering most of the ground from his position to a point about halfway across the valley. The Juarista forces of the second wave were just now making their way up the incline, and would soon be able to add their numbers to the next attack. Custer looked around for his staff. He ordered his bugler to sound officers' call and for his battle pendant to be displayed.

General Garcia had watched as the Union force crossed the valley, absorbed the defensive fire, and took the first trench. He noted that most of the rapid-fire guns visible to him had been taken by his retreating troops and repositioned in the second trench line. As soon as Garcia saw that his Corps had completed the retrograde movement and that his position in the second trench was secure, he sent runners to so advise Lee and Laurency.

On the Juarista right flank the CSM Army pressed home its assault. Enemy fire slackened slightly, and Brown looked to his left and his right, hesitated a second, then leaped to his feet, screaming, "Charge!" Accompanied by his men, he ran towards the Jusrista line.

The soldier to his left staggered then slumped to the ground. The man to his right, screaming his rage at the top of his lungs, fired, moved forward and fired again. As Brown reached his objective he jumped into the trench, but he landed on a corpse and tripped. He found himself face down on the bottom of the trench, lying atop a collection of body parts. Brown gagged, threw up, rolled over and leaped to his feet. The soldier standing next to him was taking aim when the man suddenly arched backwards, the back of his head exploding outwards in a gray/red fountain of gore.

The sound of firing began to reduce in volume, and when he looked about Brown realized that they had just taken the last prepared defensive position. The enemy soldiers who continued resisting were doing so completely exposed. He and his men continued to return fire. For several minutes the Jusrista soldiers held their ground, but as their losses mounted, first individual soldiers, then small groups, began to drop their weapons and run.

For the first time today, Brown felt, rather than heard, the roar of battle slowly begin to diminish. Glancing upward he saw the sun was well on its way towards the horizon. He was suddenly filled with hope.

From his position, in the center of the south ridge, Custer ordered that as soon as the Union and Juarista forces joined together, the unified command should attack. He still fully believed that a single massive blow, against what appeared to be an inferior force, would carry the day. As his surviving generals made their way back to their commands, he stood quietly regarding what he believed to be the enemy's last line of defense and the final obstacle to his victory.

He stood, adjusted the sling that now supported his left arm, took a deep breath, and climbing out of the trench, ordered the charge. For a second time today those infernal machines ground out their spew of death and again his soldiers answered his call with heroism almost beyond belief.

Exhausted and bloodied, they fought their way up to and into the enemy trench, men dying by dozens every step of the way. Shooting, stabbing, and hacking they closed on and gained the enemy position. For the second time today they drove the occupiers back, the Negro giant and the General leading the way.

Ukimbe jumped into the trench, driving his bayonet into the first enemy soldier. He reversed his weapon, smashing the butt of his rifle into the head of a second man. Releasing his grip on the shattered weapon, he grabbed a third man by his neck and crotch and, first lifting the screaming man high into the air, brought him down with bone- crushing force on his raised knee. He cast the man aside, dropping the lifeless body to the dirt.

At his position behind General Garcia's defensive lines General Laurency watched as the line of battle engulfed the second trench. When he judged it had reached its crescendo, he ordered the Legion to attack. Rising up as one, bayoneted rifles at port arms, the perfectly aligned ranks of blue and red charged over the ridge's crest and smashed headlong into the mass of fighting men.

Legion corporal Alan Fromage, standing in the second rank, was consumed with battle rage. Almost immediately the front rank was engaged with the enemy. The man directly in front of him appeared to fly into the air. Astounded, Alan stopped dead in his tracks, only to realize that the

Legionnaire had been lifted up into the air and then thrown to the ground by a black giant who was suddenly directly in Alan's path.

Ukimbe had just picked up another weapon and was thrusting with the bayonet when the first ranks of Legionaries charged over the ridge top. Not understanding the meaning of the sudden appearance of soldiers who wore partially blue uniforms, he turned to Custer for guidance.

One look at Custer's' glare of hate gave him all the answer he needed. Together, the two warriors once again waded into the enemy. As his troops tried to absorb the impact of the surprise Legion attack, General Custer and Sergeant Ukimbe found them-selves fighting side by side, each alternately protecting the other or attacking. Custer fired the last round in his revolver, dropped the empty gun and drew his saber.

Ukimbe had just smashed a soldier to the ground when he realized the next enemy soldier was aiming his rifle at his chest. Knowing there was nothing else to do, he began to lunge at the enemy when he saw Custer's sword descend upon the rifle, knocking the barrel away from him.

As Alan Fromage brought up his bayonet-tipped rifle to fire, the barrel of his gun was deflected by a saber. Glancing to his right, he saw that the saber was held by a gaudily dressed officer with one arm in a bloody sling.

In a move he had performed a hundred times in practice and dozens more in combat, Fromage thrust his rifle up and to the right, forcing the saber away from his body. He dropped the barrel of his weapon down, and in one smooth motion, aimed at the officers' chest and fired.

The next few seconds played themselves out as if in slow motion. Ukimbe watched, horrified, as the soldier moved with a practiced ease, first blocking Custer's weapon, then aiming and firing almost instantaneously. For a split second nothing happened, and then Custer's legs started to give way. The saber slipped from his nerveless fingers and his body sagged to the ground.

By the time Ukimbe reached Custer's side, the unknown killer had moved on. The tide of battle washed over them as the force of the Legion attack first halted, then crushed, the advance. The formations of Union/Juarista troops began to give ground, grudgingly at first, as individuals, then small groups, broke from the battle line and headed down the ridge and back across the valley.

General Terry, who had seen Custer fall, sent runners to advise all units that he had assumed command. The General, considering the present position untenable, quickly ordered a withdrawal. At first, the tattered regiments began an orderly retreat, each rank firing, and then falling back in good order. As the troops reached a point about halfway down the ridge slope, the rapid-fire guns opened up, subjecting the soldiers once again to a withering fire that no command ever fielded could hope to withstand. Within minutes, the retreat became a rout and then a slaughter. Ukimbe, though suffering minor wounds in both right leg and left arm, still had the strength to carry one of his wounded comrades down the hill and into the valley.

The Union-Juarista force was halfway across the valley floor before the last of the rapid-fire guns ceased fire, being either out of ammunition or range. Once free of the deadly hailstorm of fire, the troops, exhausted beyond measure, simply stopped running. They either sat or lay wherever their flight had taken them. General Terry immediately began to reestablish lines of communications throughout his command, and shortly he and his officers began the task of attempting to reform their units into a cohesive battle line.

Easy and Orto had followed the rear guard of Custer's column as it joined the battle line prior to the initial attack. When the two men neared the Juarista trenches they left the Union formation and made their way to Zaragoza's headquarters just behind the ridge top. The atmosphere in the headquarters was thick with tension and fear. Shortly after the attack began, Zaragoza entered the command post. Easy advanced towards the General, saluted and said, "Major Sinclair reporting, sir." Zaragoza responded with a terse smile and waived him up to the parapet. For several moments the two men watched the Union's valiant charge advance across the valley.

Easy became aware that the firing from his right was growing in intensity and getting closer. He swept his telescope across the right flank, then repeated the procedure to his left. He quickly determined that both flanks of the Juarista position were in danger of being overrun.

Easy returned to Zaragoza, who was still watching the advance of the combined forces. He heard Zaragoza inhale sharply. At the same time he heard a loud, ripping sound emanating from the opposite ridge. Both men, telescope to eye, stood frozen in place as the battle played itself out before them. From his position in the command bunker, Zaragoza watched his Army, his ally, and his Revolution ripped apart.

As Custer's attacking units, showing unbelievable courage and determination, reformed and continued the attack, Easy and Zaragoza watched avidly. Combat swirled about the southern ridge top and victory actually seemed to be within grasp. The sudden appearance of rank upon rank of French

Foreign Legion troops stunned both men. They continued to watch as broken remnants of the proud Union and Juarista units fled back down into the valley.

Zaragoza lowered the telescope, knowing defeat and disaster was imminent. Calling for riders he scribbled the same message several times and ordered the riders off. He strode over to Easy, and, in a voice tight with emotion said, "Major, I am giving you a dispatch. I order you to deliver it to the Military command in Laredo. I order you to leave on this mission immediately." Zaragoza handed the note to the young Ranger officer and looked at him expectantly.

When Easy took the message but made no move to leave, Zaragoza stepped closer. Speaking in a low voice only Easy could hear, said, "Young man, we have no need of more heroes or martyrs. The valley below is covered with the bodies of such men. *Go! Now!"*

Easy left the bunker and gathered up a waiting Orto. They mounted their horses. Together they began to make their way out of what was fast becoming a death trap. Moving at a canter, they passed through the field of injured men. Pushing on, the two passed the last of the medical tents. As he rode, Easy saw men in butternut and white appearing to his right. He motioned to Orto, drew his revolver and spurred his horse into a gallop. At his side, Orto duplicated his maneuver.

The enemy infantry were closing together from both flanks, attempting to encircle the entire position. Easy saw that with a little luck he would just be able to break through and make his escape. Unfortunately, several enemy soldiers were already between them and safety. The two riders spurred their horses, increasing their speed. Both mounts were galloping at full tilt and they fairly flew over the ground.

As several of the attacking soldiers knelt and fired, Easy saw Orto stagger and drop his revolver, a bright red stain blossoming on his right shoulder. He and Orto pressed themselves flat against their mounts necks, raking their horse's flanks with spurs. Easy emptied his revolver at their attackers. The two galloped through the encircling infantry. Soon a curve in the road soon hid them and they slowed to a trot. A few moments later they stopped and Easy bandaged Orto's shoulder. The first aid complete, the two mounted and started their long trek north.

In the corpse strewn center of the valley General Terry had gone a long way towards restoring order to his battered units. He had begun to issue orders for an orderly withdrawal, when to his absolute horror, he saw Juarista troops leaving their trench lines on the north ridge, and heading down into the valley, many turning to fire to their rear. They were quickly followed by waves of CSM Army troops, who began filling the just-vacated fortifications on the ridge top.

He and his staff stared in stunned silence, as the last of the Juarista troops were pushed from their positions, and forced down into the valley. The Juarista soldiers then joined Terry's now completely encircled force. The General, looking about, quickly assessed the situation and realized his position was hopeless. He ordered white flags to be flown and all firing by his units cease.

Lee, along with Generals Garcia, and Laurency, was in his command post when messengers arrived from both General Longstreet and General Hill. The messages advised him that both had succeeded in enveloping the enemies flank, and were in the process of completing the encircling maneuver. As Lee began to read the communications from his field commanders, he heard a slow but steady reduction in the volume of firing throughout the battlefield.

He sent riders with orders to both Generals. They were to complete the maneuver, drive the enemy from their positions into the valley, then cease fire and hold in place. He dispatched a second group of riders to the Union/Juarista forces in the valley. Under a flag of truce, the surrounded units were advised of the situation and asked to surrender. As he left the command post, Lee realized the sun was just about to set, and his longest day was finally over.

The answer from the Union commander was a request for surrender terms. Lee responded to the Union commander that hostilities would cease immediately. All wounded would be cared for, and formal discussions regarding surrender begin at dawn on the following day. General Terry accepted the terms. As soon as he received Terry's surrender Lee penned a short letter for Mexico.

Mexico City

Several days later, James Breckenridge knocked and then entered Vice President's Davis' office. "Jefferson," he asked, "is it true, has Lee done it?" Receiving no immediate reply, he strode forward, urgency in his voice saying, "My God, man, out with it!"

Davis, a huge smile spread across his features, answered, "I've received a message from Lee. He has engaged the enemy and has been victorious! An incredible victory! Our enemies smashed in a glorious battle! I will inform Santa Anna and the Cabinet and request an emergency meeting, John."

Breckenridge gestured to an empty chair and when Davis nodded, sat down. "We must respond quickly. This should be just the leverage we need for foreign recognition," he said, staring at Davis. That afternoon the Acting President, Vice President, and Cabinet of the Confederate States of Mexico met to discuss Lee's triumph, consider their options and make choices.

Dawn the following morning found dispatch riders leaving Mexico City, on their way to the battle site. They were followed shortly thereafter by Revolutionary Court Judges escorted by Department of State Security troopers. Additional DSS units, with wagons filled with chains and steel collars, trailed behind them.

When Lee received the return communication from Mexico City he read it, then sat quietly for awhile thinking, *so it has come to this. I cannot, no I will not* condone this dishonorable course. *No army under my command will ever perpetrate such an atrocity. My honor forbids it. All the sacrifice, all the deaths, have they been for naught?*

After much agonizing and soul searching he made his decision, then summoned Venable. When the Colonel entered the tent, Lee handed him the letter he had just received and waited while Venable read it. When he finished, Venable, his face rigid, asked, "What can you do, Sir? These are orders from our civilian government. To disobey is treason."

The instructions, signed by both Santa Anna and Davis, ordered all the surviving enemy combatants to be tried by special judges, and if found guilty, to be remanded to the Department of State Security as "Indentured Servants to the State." To complete their dismay, the order included all officers.

"I fear I have come to the same conclusion, Colonel. I have been a soldier most of my life and I consider it a profession of honor. These people, however," continued Lee, his voice hardening in anger, "would choose to sully the honor of this Army with this act. I have made my decision. This order in contrary to everything I believe. Effective immediately, I will resign my commission and turn over command to General Longstreet. Tomorrow I will go and see those people in person and state my case."

A few hours later the sounds of voices raised in anger sounded from the command tent as Lee made his wishes known to Longstreet, Hill, Garcia and Laurency. By night fall, almost every soldier in the Army had heard at least one of the several versions of the tale.

Rising at dawn the next morning, Lee donned a uniform from which all signs of rank had been carefully removed, as per his orders. Entering the front part of the tent that usually served as his field office, he found Venable awaiting him, standing at attention. Looking Venable in the eye, Lee hesitated a split second, then almost shyly offered his hand to Venable while saying, "Charles, I believe we are finished with that."

"As you say, sir," replied Venable, coming to parade rest, "your escort is ready, General, and the command would like to say farewell."

Lee raised an eyebrow in an unspoken question and Venable replied by holding open the tent flap. When Lee exited, he found every officer and soldier who was not on duty or too seriously wounded, standing at attention. Officers were congregated nearest the tent. Soldiers, four to five ranks deep, lined the road as far as he could see. Mounting his horse, Lee, followed closely by Venable and a security team, slowly made their way down the road. Lee held a salute until they had left his Army behind.

He arrived in Mexico City late at night and, of course, first saw to the quartering of his troops. After seeing to his men he followed a gaudily dressed servant to his quarters. As the sun rose the next morning, so did he, luxuriating in a hot bath and frowning at the metal collars on the servants who served him.

Venable arrived, and when breakfast was delivered, Lee had to order Venable to sit with him. Lee poured coffee for both of them, saying, "Charles, I am finished. I have done what I can. I will tell these people what I think then go my way. I cannot in good conscience ask you to follow me, so I think it is time for goodbyes."

At that moment their was a knock on the door and an officer of the Praetorian Guard, resplendent in full-dress uniform, entered the room. The officer saluted, then informed Lee that he was to escort him to a meeting at the President *"Pro Temps'"* office at his earliest convenience. Lee rose, and with Venable one step behind, followed the staff officer to the meeting.

Davis and Santa Ana were seated and Breckenridge was standing next to them when Lee and his escort entered the room. Breckenridge immediately advanced towards Lee, grasped his hand and guided him towards a vacant chair. Davis stood up and said, "General Lee, your victory was magnificent. It is an honor to be in your presence. Your success is the foundation upon which our country will rest. In short, sir, you are, in a very real sense, the father of our country." With that he paused and looked at Lee expectantly.

Lee had refused the offered seat and stood quietly for a moment, letting his gaze rest momentarily on each man. Then he looked directly at Davis and said, "Gentlemen, I am a soldier. I have been one almost my entire adult life. I wear this uniform and defend my country with honor and pride. The orders I received from you violate every military principle that I believe in. I will not, can not, condone or support such a course of action."

He reached into a breast pocket and withdrew an envelope. He continued, "This is my resignation, effective now. I have assigned Lieutenant General Longstreet to temporary command. I urge you to support his appointment. Gentlemen, I bid you good day and goodbye."

Lee turned and marched from the room. He strode down the hallway and out of the building, followed by Venable, who was, of course, trailed by the entire security detail. He left behind a stunned CSM leadership, sitting quietly, staring at each other in shocked silence. Santa Anna and Davis had been caught completely by surprise and were aghast, each man sitting in a chair rigid with shock. .

All three men wore expressions of confusion and concern as they sought a solution to the potential catastrophe caused by Lee's abrupt resignation. Both Santa Anna and Davis turned to face Breckenridge, who said, "I can't say that I am totally surprised. Our policies are, in fact, open to interpretation. His reaction was based on his military code, and in hindsight, completely understandable. Lee is as much an institution as a man. We must minimize the impact of his response. We must manage the situation to create an appearance of normalcy." Breckenridge had been the least surprised. He knew Lee's feelings regarding military protocol, as well as his views on what amounted to political slavery. He had, however, underestimated the vigor of Lee's response."

"How can this be accomplished?" asked Davis. "What can we say to change the situation, to make it appear as though he is with us?"

"He's already given us half the answer," responded Breckenridge. "He's retired, taken himself out of the loop. The next part is to get him somewhere out of the spotlight, somewhere where he would be out of sight and out of mind. Remember, we control the press."

Santa Anna offered, "An excellent idea. I think I can help. We will find a vacant *hacienda*. I know of several. We will reward and honor him. Present him with a retirement present from a grateful nation. Get him out of the limelight. Yes, a wonderful idea."

For the next few days Lee remained in Mexico City. Santa Anna and his friends from the Council of Five Hundred made their plans. A large *"hacienda,"* perfect for their needs, was secured. It was located near the city of Tampico, on the Gulf coast, dozens of miles from the nearest town. Its prior owners were now serving the state as indentured servants. Aside from a few scorch marks, blood stains, bullet holes and a smashed-in front door, it suffered only from a recent lack of maintenance.

A delegation of leading citizens, including Davis and Longstreet, visited Lee, in order to plead their case. Eventually, after prolonged talks, he accepted their offer. A few days later, he and his entourage left the capitol, to take up residence in his new home.

CHAPTER THIRTY SIX

September, 1867

Washington, D. C.

The Committee on Military Preparedness and Intelligence was in session, the capitol's glaring summer sun raising the room temperature to uncomfortable levels, despite the half-closed blinds and opened windows. General Sherman gaveled the meeting to order, and nodded to Pinkerton to open the session.

"Gentlemen," he began, "we have had an opportunity to review the reports and question several eyewitnesses. We've officially concluded our investigation into what has become known as the "Custer Affair." As you are aware, there have been investigations by this committee as well as military tribunals and the OSS. Our efforts to minimize the story in the press have met with mixed success. It appears that Custer is to become a hero of sorts. Regional Director Garrison has been thoroughly questioned. He will be disciplined and reassigned. We can't prove actual duplicity, so in essence he'll be convicted of stupidity. Colonel Reno has been court marshaled. His testimony was that he was following orders. He will maintain his commission but be reassigned. The consensus of opinion is that both men were guilty of, at a minimum, gross incompetence and negligence. Treason, given public sentiment and lack of proof, was not a charge. OSS Operative Ezekiel Sinclair gave supportive testimony."

Pinkerton paused for a moment, cleared his throat, took a small sip of water from a pitcher, then continued. "To summarize, General Custer is dead; General Terry and an unknown number of other General officers are either prisoners or dead, along with the remnants of XX Corps. Our total losses are, including officers, non-commissioned officers, and enlisted men, over eighteen thousand dead, wounded and captured. Zaragoza is either captured or dead and his army, for all intents, has been destroyed. Juaurez is still leading what's left as a guerilla movement in northeastern Mexico. He is, in fact, more the hunted then the hunter.

The new government of the Confederated States of Mexico has been recognized as the legitimate successor to Emperor Maximilian by a number of European and South American nations. Our response is being debated in Congress as we speak. The ambassadors from Prussia and England have informed us that their countries have signed economic treaties, duly recognized and traded ambassadors with the Confederate States of Mexico."

The OSS Director stopped his narrative, and glanced up at the committee members before saying, "Now comes the interesting part. All of the prisoners taken by the Revolutionary Army at the battle, Juarista and Union, officers and enlisted men, have been sentenced for life as "Indentured Servants to the State." Our State Department is protesting, but as

Custer was in direct violation of a standing residential order we don't think we have much of a case. .Lee received orders from Mexico City, left his command the next day and travelled to Mexico City. He received honors and has retired."

"I can't believe that Lee could be part of something so totally against Military Custom and Law," interjected Sherman.

Pinkerton replied, "Lee's personal feelings on this subject are unknown to us. However, based on his past performance, we are working on the assumption that he found those actions onerous.

What we do know is that we have a new neighbor to our south, one that possesses a capable, well-led and equipped army. This country has powerful international friends, and a great dislike for us. My Office of Strategic Service will, of course, begin planning covert operations at the earliest possible moment. I'm quite sure our neighbors to the south are similarly engaged."

Mexico

In the battered city of Leon, Ukimbe hefted the sledgehammer, then once again brought it down with violence. He spent his days turning large rocks into small rocks with a mind-numbing regularity, as he and his fellow servants rebuilt the shattered city.

After the surrender they had taken away his weapon and uniform. They had left him with nothing but his determination. Many of his fellow soldiers and not a few officers had died. Some from wounds, some at the hands of the sadistic DSS guards, some at their own hands, others from overwork and lack of food, and some had just given up and gone to sleep. Ukimbe, however, kept a low profile, following orders. He worked diligently, always watching, always alert, biding his time.

Connecticut

The moment he got off the train at the Hartford train station Easy was enveloped by his family. Mom, Dad, sister and brothers thronged about, a sea of smiling, happy faces. After a few moments, his father, seeing his son glance about, said, "She's not here, son. She has business to deal with. You can stop at the store on our way home."

Easy smiled his thanks as he continued to embrace his siblings. It was a long time before the hugging and kissing stopped. Eventually, greetings over, the family boarded the waiting wagon and made for Naugatuck.

The very next morning found him standing on the sidewalk outside the Conklin's store. He had thought long and hard about his life and his feelings for Rebecca. He had eventually made his decision. He knew what he felt and what he wanted, and was here to make his desire plain. Easy squared his shoulders, took a deep breath, and more frightened then he had ever been in combat, turned the doorknob and pushed the door open.

The bell tinkled softly, announcing his presence. Busy with her books, it took her a moment to look up. Since their last time together she had thought long and hard about Ezekiel, and about their relationship. She knew what she wanted and had decided to make her decision known to him at the first opportunity. When she saw him step into the store, her response was instantaneous.

He smiled as he walked towards her, his eyes agleam with a mixture of fear and anticipation. She was already coming from behind the counter. She met him halfway across the room, leaping into his outstretched arms, laughing and crying, all at the same time. They held each other tightly for a moment, then a moment more, kissing deeply. Breaking their kiss, they held their heads apart, each looking deeply into the other's eyes.

"I love you, Becca."

"I love you, Easy."

"Becca, will you marry me?"

"Oh yes, Easy, I will. I will."

Washington, D. C.

In OSS Headquarters, Washington D. C., Assistant Deputy for Requisitions and Supply, John Garrison, labored. He had been reassigned after giving his testimony in Washington. Garrison's activities and relationship with General Custer had been thoroughly scrutinized by the Committee on Military Preparedness and Intelligence. He had had been found wanting in several instances. No specific charge against him could be proven. There was, however, a preponderance of rather damning circumstantial evidence, and the hearings did not go well for him.

Garrison signed another form and transferred it from his in-tray to his out-tray. As his office had no window he would occasionally consult his pocket watch in order to determine how many more mind-numbing minutes still remained in each relentlessly tedious day.

Texas/CSM Border

In a small cramped office in the lonely fort, deep in the desolate Texas panhandle, Colonel Reno labored. The journey from the defeat at Two Ridges to his current posting had been a nightmare. Following the disaster at Two Ridges, Reno had taken the few remaining Union soldiers with him and returned to Laredo. Recalled to Washington, he had testified before military tribunals, congressional committees, and, of course, the Committee on Military Preparedness and Intelligence.

He still didn't quite understand what had happened. It had begun shortly after his return to the capitol. The looks, the side-long glances, a refusal to meet his eyes, the whispered comments behind his back; it was as if his survival branded him as a traitor to Custer's memory. It had gotten so bad he became accustomed to spending most of his time alone, in his room, even eating his meals in solitary.

Tainted by his participation in Custer's defeat, his career was ruined. He had been given command of an infantry regiment and assigned to building part of the fortifications continually sprouting up along the Union/Mexican border. Sitting there, alone in his tiny office, he had finally realized that he would spend his remaining career in a military purgatory, dead-ended, going nowhere, a pariah.

In his mind he'd replayed those last few moments on that ridge a hundred times. He vividly remembered the long, silent ranks, the waving flags, the bright sun, and of course General Custer. Custer had stood on the crest, sword in one hand and pistol in the other, looking at him. He'd ordered him to remain behind, then to follow up with the headquarters unit. Why had Custer done that? What had he been thinking? Had the vainglorious General some inkling of disaster? Had it been an honest attempt to save him, or just the vagaries of fate? His not knowing why he found himself in such circumstance only served to compound his disgrace and discomfort.

Reno slid his chair back from his paper-filled desk. He stood up, stretched, slowly working out the kinks in his back that had accumulated from hours of office work. In need of a break, he left his office and walked across the small fort's hard-packed, dirt parade ground. Reaching the wooden wall, he climbed up the rickety ladder until he was on the parapet.

From this vantage point a vista of empty desert, interrupted by an occasional tall cactus or lonely mesquite tree, stretched away into the distance, much further than his eye could see. As he idly watched, a dust devil kicked up, swirling around for an instant before collapsing back into nothingness. After a few moments he sighed, then descended.

As he crossed the parade grounds on his way back to his office, he found himself face-to-face with one of the engineering officers that were supervising the construction of the Union's ever expanding southern border defenses.

"Colonel, I need your authorization for the revised supply requirements for the ninth battery emplacements and the updated lumber requisitions for Fort number eighteen." With a weary nod he signaled the officer to accompany him back to his office. He went to his desk and searched through a few stacks of papers before finding the requested forms. Without a word he handed them to the engineering officer, who accepted them with equal taciturnity.

A few hours later there was a knock at the door. He coughed, said, "Enter." A private with a tray of food entered. Without a word the man placed the tray on his desk, then saluted, turned and left. Reno sat quietly for several moments, his gaze moving from the tray of food to the closed door, then finally to his service revolver in its holster hanging from a peg on the wall. His entire body shuddered, as though in the grip of a severe fever. His vision blurred as his eyes filled with tears. Ignoring the tracks of wetness lining his face he stood up, walked over to his weapon, withdrew it from the hostler and began to raise the weapon towards his head.

Boston

In the plush lobby of the swank Parker House Hotel in downtown Boston, Harry Chester sipped the last of his wine, then reached into his pocket and removed two cigars. Offering one to the man sitting opposite him, he lighted his and drew deeply.

"Thanks for dinner," he said.

"My pleasure," responded John W. Booth. "This will probably be the last time we'll have the pleasure of each other's company. I'm changing contact protocols. From now on my brother, Edwin, will handle all face-to-face contacts. Since those fools screwed up in Laredo, the OSS has been asking lots of questions, so I need to distance myself from field operatives. Edwin has my total confidence."

Chester, who had friends among the dead KKK men lost in the Custer assassination attempt, responded with a non-committal grunt. "Fine with me. Just make sure he knows what he's doing, Booth. As you've discovered, screw ups can be costly, and I've no intention of spending my life in a Yankee jail."

CHAPTER THIRTY SEVEN

December, 1867

Confederate States of Mexico

In his sea-side *hacienda* just east of the city of Tampico, Robert E. Lee had been bombarded with requests to attend the "National Week" ceremonies. .He had listened to eloquent arguments from Santa Anna, Davis and Breckenridge, even Longstreet, with equally deaf ears. However, a brief conversation with Venable had changed his mind.

He had been standing solitary watch on his veranda overlooking the Gulf. Venable had approached him and asked permission to speak. Torn from his reverie he had replied, "Yes, of course, Colonel."

"General, may I speak freely?"

"Yes, Colonel."

"Sir, I know it's not my place, but I understand you will not go to Mexico City for the ceremonies. It's about the honors and awards. If you accept them then you validate every death, the ones at Petersburg, Cameron and the Two Ridges. Sir, it's as if you are accepting for all those who cannot. If you don't accept, then it's as if those men died in vain, for nothing. I apologize if you feel I've overstepped my bounds, but I thought you should know a lot of us feel that way, sir."

Lee had said nothing, merely nodded. A few days later he told Venable that he would attend the ceremonies and ordered him to make the required arrangements.

CHAPTER THIRTY EIGHT

March, 1868

Confederate States of Mexico

The first nationwide general elections in the Confederate States of Mexico were history. Santa Anna had been elected President and Jefferson Davis Vice-President, each for a single, non-repeatable, ten year term. Grand Senators, two from each Mexican state, had been elected to renewable four year terms in the Grand Senate. The vote had been taken during the first week of March, 1868. The collection and tabulation had taken a while, but it was done.

The week immediately preceding the national inauguration ceremonies had been designated as "National Week." Inauguration of all Federal officials was to occur on the first day in April, in the national capitol, Mexico City. Swearing in ceremonies for state level officials would be held in the individual state capitols, at the same time. The activities honoring those who had performed outstanding or exceptional services to the nation would also happen in Mexico City. The recipients, both men and women, would receive either one of two titles, "Don," or "Squire."

405

CHAPTER THIRTY NINE

April, 1868

Mexico City

In the Grand Plaza, in the center of Mexico City, huge crowds filled the grand plaza, consuming vast quantities of food and drink that had been supplied by the stalls ringing the enclosure. Small groups of musicians, sprinkled throughout the throngs, played for thrown coins. The music blended with the crowd noise into one huge sound. A number of celebrants, having indulged too freely in wine and food, slept peacefully in odd corners.

The swearing-in ceremonies for the leadership had been completed. Dignitaries and heroes of the Republic had gathered from all over Mexico to participate. Stands had been set up at one end of the square. Splendidly uniformed units of the Praetorian Guard, with gleaming bayonets attached to highly polished rifles, insured that the crowds kept their distance from the assembled dignitaries.

Jethro Scruggs was to be one of the award recipients. When he had been advised of his forthcoming recognition for his engineering work he had been pleased, but restrained. The Mayor and City Council of Oxaca, knowing his feelings, had made it clear that his attendance at the National ceremonies on behalf of their city was mandatory. It had taken a good deal of argument before he had agreed to participate.

He had traveled by train to Mexico City, frequently on tracks and over bridges he had designed. Jethro had not joined in the general merry-making. He had, instead, enjoyed some quiet meals and a few sightseeing tours of the capitol.

A tremendous amount of construction and renovation had been completed. The city lived up to its reputation, and was truly a national show-piece. His tours had taken him past lush parks and gardens, imposing new office buildings, and even grander edifices, dedicated to numerous government concerns.

After dinner he had enjoyed a cigar and a short walk. Returning to his hotel room, he found a scantily-clad young lady, kneeling on the floor in the middle of his room. Stunned, he reacted harshly.

"What the hell are you doing?"

"Please, sir. This is for you." With a hand trembling with fear the girl held out a scrape of paper.

Taking the paper he read, "Our gift to you. A reward for your service to Mexico." The note was signed, "In gratitude, from the Hotel Management."

Jethro stood for a moment, silently regarding the indentured servant. He was angry. How could anyone offer a human being as a gift? How could anyone accept another person as a gift? He thought about complaining but quickly reconsidered. It would be the servant who would be punished, regardless of her innocence.

Realizing the girl was still kneeling, he asked her to stand, offering her his hand. She took it and stood up, a smooth, almost sinuous motion. He was so close her perfume enveloped him in a fog of sweet essence. Her costume displayed a great deal of her body, both exposing and accentuating her lush curves.

She looked up at him, and he realized that her features were those of a teen-age child, rigid with fear. He stepped back, dropping her hand and clearing his throat. He put as much distance as possible between the two of them. Her eyes widened again in fear, and he gestured to calm her.

"I won't hurt you," he said. "What's your name?"

"Serena," was the whispered answer.

"Serena, nothing will happen to you. I swear it.'

"I was told I would be punished if I failed to please you."

Anger, at the person who had told her that, surged through him, and he answered,

"There will be no punishment." He thought for a moment, and then asked, "Are you hungry, have you eaten?" A shake of her head was her answer. "I'm going to leave for a few moments. I want you to sit in this chair and wait for me. Everything is fine, so please don't worry. I'll be back soon." When he returned he carried a tray in his hands. He placed the tray on a small table next to her chair. He removed the top, exposing several plates of food.

"I wasn't sure what you would like, so I got a few things."

The girl looked at him with tear-filled eyes, asking, "This is for me?"

"And more, if you wish."

Jethro sat near her as she wolfed down the food. Finishing the last morsel, she stopped eating and folded her hands in her lap. He saw her hesitation, and guessing her thoughts, said, "Now that you're finished eating I suppose you're quite tired. You'll sleep in the bedroom, alone. I'll use the couch when I return later. Goodnight, Serena."

He stood up, turned and left the room, locking the door behind him. When he returned, late in the morning, Serena was gone.

It was mid-afternoon on the following day, when Jethro, along with a few dozen others, were escorted to their seats on the reviewing stand. He listened while Santa Anna, Davis, and then other notables praised the award recipients effusively. He caught himself nodding off, and had to bite his lip to remain awake.

Eventually, it was his turn to step up to the podium. He received the medal and handshakes from the line of politicians, nodding and smiling, as was expected. As soon as he stepped down from the platform, he removed the ornate medal from his neck and placed it in his jacket pocket.

Two days after the carefully orchestrated public ceremonies, the President of the Confederate States of Mexico, Santa Anna, stood before the floor-to-ceiling mirror, smiling as he admired his resplendent reflection. He had come a long way he thought, from disgraced and defeated Dictator to President. His climb back to a position of power had been long and hard-fought, but he and his allies had scratched, clawed, and kicked their way to the top, and that is where they intended to stay.

He preened a moment more, and then turned to leave. One of the two young, female, indentured servants, who were standing behind him, jerked slightly at his abrupt move. Santa Anna paused, and reaching out to cup the young girls chin, smiled a mirthless smile and said, "Have no fear, my sweet; you shall have your chance to please me tonight."

He left the room and passed through his sitting room, entering his private office. Vice President Jefferson Davis and Minister of State John Breckenridge were seated at a small table, sharing a brandy. At Santa Anna's entrance both men stood up.

Gathering the two men in his arms, Santa Anna led them from the room. They walked down the hall, past the Praetorian Guards, to the top of the Grand Stairway, which overlooked the ballroom.

The Presidential Grand Ball was the culminating event of National Week. An "invitation only" occasion, the invitee's gathered below represented the cream of the social, business, political, and military spectrum of the Confederate States of Mexico.

Above the dance floor a dozen crystal and gold chandeliers held hundreds of candles that cast a bright glow over the well- dressed crowd. The seventy–five man Praetorian Guard Orchestra played and the party goers swirled, bowed and curtsied to the tempo. Suitably attired, but collared none-the-less, dozens of indentured servants carried trays holding fine wines and rare treats, select offerings for the pleasure of the elite.

Longstreet and Laurency, along with Lieutenant von Hindenburg, stood together, their respective full dress uniforms contrasting vividly. The three men were on the ballroom floor, slightly apart from the other guests, as they spoke.

"Congratulations on your appointment, sir," said Laurency, gesturing to the insignia of the newly-created CSM Army rank of Field Marshall, which adorned Longstreet's collar.

"Thank you, General."

"Are we to have the pleasure of *his* company tonight, Field Marshall?" asked Laurency.

"I'm afraid not," replied Longstreet, concern plain in his voice. "General Lee has declined to participate in any further festivities. He plans to leave at dawn tomorrow and return to his *hacienda* in Tampico.

"How unfortunate," said von Hindenburg. "I looked forward to paying my respects to the General. I wanted him to know I have been ordered back to Berlin."

"I will make certain that he is advised, Lieutenant." responded Longstreet.

"Thank you, sir."

Across the room, Major General Forrest reached out and took a glass of champagne from a tray. Turning to his right he asked, "Would you care for a glass of wine, Baron?"

"Absolutely," answered Baron von Steuben.

Sipping his wine, he continued his conversation with Forrest. "We'll be in the market for labor, both skilled and unskilled, and in substantial numbers. Can we expect your office to fill our needs?"

"Unskilled is no problem, but trained technical workers are scarce," responded Forrest. "We hope to upgrade our workforce skill levels and have technical training available in the near future. Why don't you send me a list of your needs and we'll begin work on addressing them." Just as the German was about to answer, there was a stirring at the top of the stairway, and both men turned in that direction.

At the sight of movement at the top of the Grand Stairway the crowd below began to turn and face the stairs. Dignitaries, ambassadors, politicians, and power brokers from dozens of nations stopped their conversations to look upward at the three men standing silently on the top step.

From their vantage point, Santa Anna, Davis, and Breckenridge looked down at the room below. Bathed in the light from solid-gold chandeliers, and the warmth from fires in two polished-granite fireplaces, the Grand Ballroom beckoned. A half step ahead of his compatriots, Santa Anna led the way into their throngs of admirers.

As the dignitaries danced the night away at the grand ball, Jethro returned to Oxaca by train. He was now "Don Jethro Scruggs," a certified hero of the revolution. He was a man of means and position. When he returned home he put his medal in a draw and returned to his work as soon as he could, burying himself in a dozen major projects. Every once in a while his thoughts would turn dark, and he would lay awake for a while, thinking about Serena.

A few miles northeast of Mexico City a column of mounted men moved northward at a walk. They still had a long trip ahead of them so they were sparing their mounts. All wore a uniform of sorts, a dust covered butternut. Not one man boasted a unit insignia. Robert E. Lee, with Colonel Charles Venable at his side, led. In Venable's saddle were the medals, the official recognition of Lee's title, along with the land grant and pension documents.

The bright midday sun beat down, warming man and beast. Lee took off his hat and rubbed his sweat-soaked features and thinning grey hair with his handkerchief. Venable, noting Lee's action, guided his horse next to Lee's.

"Should we stop and rest, sir?"

"I think so. I've something to say to you and the men."

"Yes sir."

Venable ordered the troop to halt and form up in a half circle before Lee.

"As you all know, I've resigned my commission. You are no longer required to follow me. You are all officially relieved of duty. I am no longer your commanding officer." The men around him regarded him silently. With some asperity in his voice, he continued, "Do you understand?"

Answering for himself, as well as all of the men who rode with him, Venable responded, "Yes sir, General. We all understand."

Lee was silent for a while, the only sounds interrupting the quiet were from the warm breeze and a horse's stomping hoof, and then, in a voice just loud enough for every one of his soldiers to hear, said, "Thank you."

Look for

A MANIFEST DESTINY

AN ALTERNATIVE HISTORY OF

THE CONFEDERACY